One Promise Too Late

A novel by

Peggy Poe Stern

Moody Valley
Boone, North Carolina

Published by
Moody Valley
475 Church Hollow Road
Boone, N C 28607
moodyvalley@skybest.com

Cover painting by Peggy Poe Stern
Cover design by David K. Stern
First published 10/31/2022

ISBN: 978-1-59513-073-0

Dedicated to Bill Brooks

Who once wrote:

There is a new voice of the Appalachian Mountains readers will want to become aware of if they haven't already. Author Peggy Poe Stern. Her tales and stories are forged from the real lives of the region's people. Her novels deal with love and death, sorrow and tragedy, the sweetness of a first kiss and the strike of a copperhead. To read one of her books is to live in the house of her characters, to share a meal at their table, to split a cord of wood, to fight and bleed, and to surrender to passions and folly. She is as original and compelling as many of the finest Southern Gothic writers who proceeded her. Flannery O'Conner, Carson McCullers, and Harry Crews. Her plain-spoken style and natural storytelling abilities make her a writer to be reckoned with for some time to come. – Author Bill Brooks

Chapter 1

~~~~

I love life. Especially in springtime. There's something about new life starting all over again that makes me want to laugh out loud and dance about.

Today the April sun was shining down warm on my bare arms. The robins and peewees were flitting about and calling to each other from the treetops as they chased each other from limb to limb. I was thrilled at hearing their songs on such a wonderful spring morning. It made me wish I had a song to sing, but God didn't grant me the ability to sing. My singing voice sounded more like a chicken squawking.

The smell of fresh turned earth filled the air with the tangy aroma of rich, black garden dirt as Dad tilled Mom's garden with the new rototiller he'd just bought for his tractor. Dad was a poor-land mountain farmer, just as his father and grandfather before him. The land was worn out and lacking in fertility, but Dad refused to give up and seek a cash-paying job. Only the garden patch was still rich with the horse and cow manure Mom insisted Dad put on it each winter.

Mom, Grant, and I were watching the job the tiller was doing with amazement. It did a better job of pulverizing the earth than a plow and disk had ever done. The long, eight-inch knife-sharp tines were chewing up the plowed clods of dirt like a chainsaw eating into a tree – casting out fine bits of dirt until the ground was nice and smooth, ready for planting. I watched Mom bend over to stick her hand in the dirt. Her fingers sunk less than four inches.

"It's not tilling deep enough," Mom hollered at Dad, but the sound of the tractor's diesel engine and the clanging of the tiller keep him from hearing her. Mom always claimed good growing roots needed at least eight inches of soft dirt.

"Needs more weight on the tiller," Grant told her.

Grant had always been Mom's look a-like as well as her pride and joy. He had flashing blue eyes and jet-black hair that shinned in the sun light. He was tall and muscled like Dad with broad shoulders and a strong back. He was the boy that all the girls chased, and none was able to catch.

"You know nothing about farm work, Mom," Grant continued in his usual sassy way when he was wanting to aggravate Mom for the fun of it.

He dearly loved to pick on Mom. It was always a give and take with them. There were times when he tried to tell her how she should cook and clean house the same way she was always telling me. Mom would end up insisting he should show her how it was done, to which he refused claiming he didn't want to show her up. Their playful bickering never ended.

It was clear that they worshiped each other. Grant was her boy, her much adored male child she'd always dreamed about being a mother to. In Mom's eyes he was perfect. Dad felt the same way about his only son. Dad treated him as an adult as they discussed farming and other man-things.

Dad never paid any attention to Mom and Grant during what he called *their carrying on*. I have to admit *their carrying on* kind of hurt my feelings. She never did it with me. She was always strict and to the point with me.

Dad and Grant spent time hunting and fishing and walking over the farm discussing what should and shouldn't be done in order to earn a better living. Dad told Grant the farm and everything that went with it would someday belong to him.

Grant had the freedom of driving to town, courting, and going to the movies or roller skating.

Mom claimed God intended for boys and girls to be different. Boys and men were given freedom. Girls were destined to walk the straight and narrow in order to protect their virtue.

Mom was afraid of other people's opinion of her. She made sure I didn't end up like Dad's sister's girl. She got in the family way before she was married. She had a shotgun wedding, but she was ruined just the same.

Mom's sister, Aunt Ellie, only allowed her daughter, Martha, to date one young man, and then only with supervision. They got married when Martha was in the tenth grade. She quit school and started working in a factory. Mom approved.

"Don't give me none of your smart mouth," Mom told Grant. "I know more about farming than you ever will. The Good Lord knows my dad had me in the fields the minute I was big enough to hold a hoe handle in my hands."

"That was way back in the olden days. You don't know a thing about modern farming," Grant told her as he gave Mom a hug.

She gave him a playful shove. It was obvious how much they adored each other

"Don't be trying to feed me foolishness. All mouth and no do is what you are," Mom told him with the grin on her face.

"I'll prove to you that I'm right," he said with a bragging laugh and took off at a run to catch up with Dad and the tiller.

Much to my amazement Grant jumped on top of the tiller to add extra weight to make the sharp, digging tines go deeper. Dad was looking straight ahead, not knowing what Grant had done as the tractor drove over a hidden root and bounced the tiller hard.

"No! No!" Mom screamed as she saw Grant losing his balance. "Stop the tractor, Ben. Stop it! Stop!"

I thought Grant would surely jump off, but he didn't. Instead, I watched his feet fly out from under him. He fell into the space beneath the tractor's PTO shaft and the tiller. The tines caught him, pulled him under the machine with its knife-sharp tines digging out chunks of flesh and bone.

Grant's screams of pain and Mom's screams of terror mixed together until they filled the hollow and bounced off the mountains in an echo that raised the hair on my head. It took seconds for Grant's screams to go silent. Mom's screams sounded as though they would go on forever.

Dad didn't hear their screams over the sound of the racing diesel engine and kept on going. When the tines hit bone, it chugged down until it caused the tractor's engine to die. Dad looked over his shoulder to see what had stopped the tractor. The tangle of blood, bones, and Grants clothes were a horror Dad had not expected to see. He leaped off the tractor and rushed to the tiller.

Mom had already beat him to Grant.

Dad's screams joined Mom's.

It was Boyd Lewis's boy, Drake, who heard the screaming and came running to see what was going on.

"My God!" were the first words that came out of Drake's mouth as he stared at the tiller. "There's blood and guts tangled in the tines," Drake added as though what he saw couldn't possibly be real.

Momma was still screaming, but Dad had gone silent. I heard pitiful whimpering. It was coming from me.

"Gotta get Dad," Drake mumbled and took off running back the way he came. He met his dad running in the plowed ground toward the tractor.

"What happened?" Boyd Lewis asked his son.

"Somebody - - it's bad. Mighty bad. There's . . ." Drake stopped talking and stood there're as though he couldn't get more words to come out of his mouth.

Boyd came around to the back of the tractor and saw Dad trying to lift the tiller off what was left of Grant's body.

"Go to the house and call for an ambulance. I'll wait here with them," Boyd told Drake in a voice that was filled with a desperate calmness. "Tell your mother not to come anywhere near here. No need for her to get tore up seeing this. Don't expect I'll be able to sleep good for a long while to come."

Drake took off running again. I watched his long legs leaping over rocks and limbs as he cut through the woods. I didn't want to look back at the horrible scene, but I couldn't stop myself.

Boyd put his hand on Mom's shoulder. Her screams had turned into a hurt-animal kind of keening. "Katie, go to my house and stay with Mary. Tell her to give you a double shot of my good whiskey."

Mom knocked his hand off her shoulder. "Help Ben get him outta that thing We've got to put his guts back in. We can't let him die!" her voice rose from keening to shrieking.

"Go on now, Katie. Stay with Mary," Boyd said again, but Mom paid him no mind. "Ben, get up from there and take Katie to my house. She ought not to be seeing this," Boyd told Dad in a voice that had started to tremble. Dad didn't appear to hear him. He had dug Grant's head out of the soft ground with his hands and was holding it as his fingers tried to rake dirt out of his mouth and nose.

Mom started screaming again. "My boy! My boy! You've killed my boy. You didn't stop the tractor. You ran over him! You killed him, Ben. You killed him!"

Dad didn't move or say a word. He kept staring at Grant's dirty face like he'd never seen it before.

I'd never imagined I'd see such a horror as was before us. Minutes ago, Grant had been laughing and picking at Mom. This couldn't be real. It couldn't have happened. I had to be having a horrible nightmare. I closed my eyes, and everything started turning black.

"Grab hold of her," I heard Boyd Lewis say from a long distance off. "Run fast, Drake. Grab hold of her."

I felt arms go around me, holding me upright. I was shaken hard.

"Don't you pass out," Drake told me in a rough sounding voice. "We've got enough to deal with right now without you adding to it."

Slowly, the darkness faded to a kind of gray before I was able to see again. It was difficult for me to realize I had almost passed out. I'd never done something like that before. I was embarrassed by doing it while Drake was right there watching me.

"That a girl. You're okay," he said. "Turn your back and don't look."

He turned me loose, but I didn't look away, I couldn't turn my back on what just happened. Mom was still moaning like a wounded animal, but she was no longer screaming accusations at Dad.

Boyd had started quoting the Lord's prayer as though it might help get through this horror. I thought it odd that a man who made and drank as much whiskey as he did would know the Lord's prayer much less be able to repeat it.

Mom claimed Boyd was a sinner for brewing and drinking sinful liquor, and so was Drake. In Mom's opinion they were part of the unsaved sinners who were surely standing at the entry of the devil's door. Odd I would think of such as that at a time like this.

The sun was no longer shining. The birds had stopped their singing. I no longer loved life. Drake had hold of my arm and practically dragging me to a tree that had just started putting out green leaves. He sat me down beneath it and then rushed back to where Grant was still tangled up in the tiller. I got the idea that he didn't want to miss any of the action, including the unbelievable misery Mom and Dad were suffering. Me, I just wanted to sit there and let everything go black again. Blackness would be a blessing right now.

I don't know how word about Grant spread so fast. Folks started showing up like hornets returning to their nest. In what seemed like minutes, half the hollow's residents had shown up. Every one of them rushed to where Grant's body was still tangled in the tiller to get a firsthand look at the horrible scene. Some of the women were trying to hug Mom up and drag her away, but she was having none of it. Nothing or no one was going to take her away from her boy. Men were putting their hands on Dad's back and shoulders as they spoke softly to him, but he wasn't responding at all. He still squatted in the freshly tilled dirt clutching Grant's head between his hands.

A few of the women rushed past me, bent over to puke in the edge of the woods, then wiped their mouths on their dress tails. Some grabbed their children and rushed back to their vehicles after seeing more than they had expected. Other women gathered in a group and whispered to each other.

"That tiller cut his liver out," one woman said. "I saw it laying there in the dirt."

"Did you see how his guts were entwined in the tines?" another asked.

"A lot of us will be having nightmares for a long time to come. It's nothing short of morbid what happened to that poor boy."

"I've got to get away from here. I never expected the awful smell. His guts are ripped open."

"It's the smell of death," another said as though the smell was to be expected.

"How did it happen? Katie's accusing Ben of running over him."

One of the women spotted me, and several of them rushed over.

"What happened, Ellie? How did your dad run over him?"

I didn't want to talk, didn't want to tell what happened, but they needed to know Dad was not responsible for running over Grant. He had nothing to do with what happened. He was tilling Momma's garden.

"Grant thought his weight would make the tiller dig deeper. He jumped on the tiller, lost his balance and fell backward between the tiller and tractor. Dad didn't know

Grant had shown up, much less that he'd jumped on the tiller." I didn't mention the tractor bogging down.

"Why didn't he stop the tractor in time to save Grant?"

"It happened too fast," I managed to say as I felt a cold trembling begin in the pit of my stomach.

"Katie saw it happen?"

I nodded my head.

"Did you see it happen?"

I nodded again.

Thank goodness the sound of an ambulance's siren sounded in the distance. The women wandered away to be near the ambulance when it arrived. I listened to it as it sped up the long, narrow dirt road that led to our place. I was glad it was finally arriving, but it was far too late to do any good for Grant. At least they would be able to get him out from under the tiller and put his guts and liver back inside his body where the folks couldn't gawk at them. I wondered if they could make Dad let go of Grant's head.

The sheriff's car and the ambulance showed up at the same time. I stood up, felt my shaky legs move as I made my way back to the silence of an empty house.

Chapter 2

I don't know how Mom managed to hold herself together enough to arrange Grant's viewing and funeral, but she did. She insisted I go to the funeral home with her to see all the caskets along with the different services the funeral home offered. I felt as though she wanted me to experience the pain, she was going through, caused by every earthshattering decision she had to make.

She picked out the most expensive casket available for Grant, although I couldn't tell much difference in what they were offering other than the cost. Our house wasn't good enough for Grant to lay in state. Mom decided it was best for him to be in the funeral home surrounded by blue velvet drapes, mournful organ music, and a room full of the heady aroma of thousands of white lilies.

Mom specified white lilies because she loved white lilies and claimed Grant did too. I never knew Grant to even look at a white lily or any other flower. He was interested in the crops he and Dad grew on the farm.

He was studying agriculture in school and planned on attending N. C. State University in the fall. Momma was skimping and saving every dime she could get hold of to make her son's education possible.

Mom was furious at Dad because he refused to go to the funeral home to make Grant's burial arrangements.

"I can't," was all Dad was able to tell her before he headed away from the house to the barn.

There wasn't any way he could get out of attending the viewing and the funeral service, although I knew he wanted to - as did I. There was such a thing as pain that went too deep to share with good wishers.

~~~~

The funeral director finally convinced Mom there was no way they could make Grant suitable for viewing, although they washed the dirt away and tried to put him back together as much as possible. Once Mom had a look at his once handsome face, she agreed.

Dad refused going to the funeral home to have a last look at his beloved son before the viewing. He shook his head and refused to budge even when Mom insisted. I agreed with Dad not wanting to see what my brother now looked like, but it did me no good. Mom wasn't going to face the ordeal alone.

"You've got to fix him better. I can't bear him going to his grave looking like that," she told the mortician as though the way Grant looked was his fault.

"We've done the best we can," he assured her in his trained condolence voice he used with the bereaved.

"No. No, you've not. You'll have to make him look more like himself. He is such a handsome boy."

The mortician's head bowed, and his voice filled with sympathy I thought might be real. Attempting to console those with earth shattering loss every single day had to be the worst job in existence.

"We will continue doing our best, but you have to understand we can't create miracles."

That evening Mom made me go with her again to see the results of what the morticians had done with Grant. They had tried to glue hair over Grant's broken skull and filled in the gashes on his face with some kind of putty and makeup. Some sort of filler along with his body parts had been stuffed together in a suit of clothes that concealed his injuries, which made his upper body look almost normal. Nothing they did had made Grant look the way he had only days before.

Mom let out a gasp that could be heard all over the building when she saw their efforts. She turned beseeching eyes on the mortician and make-up artist. "Please . . ." she whimpered. I can't let my boy go to his grave looking like that. You've got to do better for him."

The mortician gave her a pitting look as though he was the only person who could possibly understand her grief. "We'll keep trying, but I suggest you go with a closed casket. Our makeup artists are the best, but they can't perform the impossible," he repeated what he told her earlier.

He made Mom as mad as fire when he said that. Her fists clenched and her body trembled, but she finally gave in and agreed to a closed casket. She wouldn't allow anyone to see Grand looking less than perfect.

I dreaded Grant's viewing. I knew it was a final tribute – a final good-by and a show of respect, but I resented it. I felt my loss, my pain, was personal and not to be shared with the public. There was such a thing as pain that went so deep it had to be endured alone. I knew Dad felt the same way.

Mom insisted that her and dad's brothers and sisters had to stand in the reception line with us. Grand deserved no less.

When it was time for the viewing, we all took our places near the closed coffin to receive condolences.

I don't know how many hundred viewers hugged Mom and sympathized with her loss. They shook Dad's limp hand and moved on as soon as they looked at Dad's face.

"Is your dad still in shock?" some of the women whispered to me.

"He's in mourning," I told them through thinned lips. Need they ask? Wasn't it obvious we were all in a state of shock? How could we be elsewise? Not only was our loss tragic, but what we had witnessed was far more than a mother, father, and sister should ever have to go through.

We stood there for hours aching in body and soul as all the people said their condolences. The room was stifling hot with body heat, sweat and the overwhelming smell of the women's perfume along with the suffocating odor of white lilies.

The next day Grant's funeral service was no less devastating. Dozens of friends and several preachers had to stand up and go over their memories of what a wonderful person Grant was.

I understood their need but listening to them made the loss of my brother hurt even worse. Mom held a wet handkerchief to her eyes as her body shook with her sobs. Dad sat there, head hung, transfixed on something the rest of us could not see. Finally, all the eulogies were over, and the pallbearers came for the casket.

Mom, crying and broken by her grief, was ushered out first with a silent Dad and me following behind her.

Dozens of people followed us to the graveyard on the hill. We were guided into front row plastic seats covered with maroon velvet cloths to watch Grant's casket being lowered into a grave that the neighbors had dug. Several preachers droned on about God calling Grant home. After the preachers hushed, other men stood up to talk about the good things they had seen Grant doing. Finally, everyone prayed, and Mom's mournful cries reverberated in my head.

Dad didn't make a single sound as he dragged Mom away from the graveyard so she wouldn't see them shovel dirt over the top of Grant.

About a third of the people at the viewing brought food to our house. I refrigerated and froze as much food as I could. There was no way it would all be eaten even by the huge number of well-wishers that came to our house after the funeral and burial.

Finally, all the sympathizers were gone and there was little left other than the silence of an empty house.

~~~~

Days, weeks, and months of silence passed– except for the sound of Mom's crying.

Mom cried every day, most all day long as well as all
night long. I wondered if she ever slept. Dad became even
more silent and withdrawn. He walked over the farm while
Mom cried. I often heard him going out the door as darkness
came on and not returning until dawn.

At least going to school was kind of normal for me. That
was until school closed for summer vacation. Then there was
no way I could escape from all the misery that now filled what
was once a happy home.

One warm summer night I had cooked supper and Mom
insisted we set down together and eat. My parents made a
feeble, silent effort, but ate little. Mom finally got up from
the table and went to the window as though something had
suddenly beckoned her to it.

"Ben," she said. "Come here a minute."

Dad went to her side and looked out the window into the
gloaming of late evening.

"What do you see?" Mom asked him.

"Grant," Dad whispered.

"You can see him too. He's standing underneath the apple
tree," Mom said. "He's looking through the window
watching us."

Dad nodded and much to my amazement all those unshed
tears were now running down his cheeks. "My Lord," Dad
moaned as though he was in mortal pain at seeing Grant.
"He's come back because ..."

Dad didn't finish the sentence, but I knew he thought
Grant had returned to haunt him for his death. Dad was
blaming himself for what happened. Mom certainly blamed
Dad. She told him Grant would be alive today if he hadn't
bought the deadly tiller. Dad never said a word.

I went to where they stood, looked around them until I
could see out the window. There was no one under the apple
tree. I didn't even see a shadow that could be mistaken for
Grant. I wasn't sure if I was disappointed or relieved. I

wanted to be able to see my brother again, but I didn't want a ghost haunting my parents or me.

What I couldn't understand was how both Mom and Dad claimed they saw Grant if I couldn't. A shiver ran over my body, and I rushed into my bedroom and closed the door. Tears filled my eyes and ran down my cheeks. Since Grant's death everything had changed for the worst. At times I wished it had been me instead of Grant. I knew it would have been easier on both Mom and Dad if I was the one under the dirt on the hill.

Every few days Mom and Dad both claim they saw Grant, but I never did. I was convinced that their imagining seeing Grant was wearing heavily on them. They had both lost weight and clung to their grief as though it was the only thing holding them together. Dad's head hung lower; his back bent more. I never saw more tears come from Dad, but it didn't mean there weren't any.

"You're not seeing Grant," I made the mistake of telling them. "You're only imagining him."

I hadn't expected the way Mom turned on me in fury. "How dare you say something such as that to us. You don't want us to see him. You're jealous of Grant, always have been. He's still here because he's my beloved son. He has no intention of leaving me to suffer."

In a way it was true what she had accused me of. I had been jealous of their obvious love and pride in Grant, but I wasn't jealous of Grant. I had loved him too. I simply didn't want them thinking they saw Grant's ghost when he wasn't there. They would never heal if they clung to their imaginary Grant. I feared their sorrow was affecting their minds.

I thought Mom would forget my words of denying they saw Grant, but she didn't. I saw the anger in her eyes as she looked at me. I could almost hear her saying she wished I was the one who had died instead of her beloved boy. No matter what I did, or how hard I tried to please her, that anger at me had replaced a tiny part of her grief.

~~~~

Every Sunday Mom insisted we go to church where she would break down as she prayed and cried for Grant. Folks prayed with her and sympathized with her grief, but they soon realized there were no words or prayers that could possibly ease her hurting. It was something that time and Mom had to do for herself. Afterwards, Mom would insist we go to Grant's grave where she would pray and cry until Dad led her away.

One Sunday a young man attended the services. He was introduced to the congregation as a visitor and a man who was an upcoming young minister. His name was Calvin West. He appeared to be an easy-going young man, if not on the shy side. He was kind of short as far as most men go, with blond hair and pale skin. He might have weighed thirty pounds more than I did. I wasn't sure what color his eyes were because he wore odd looking glasses, and I didn't want him to catch me staring at him.

I don't know why Mom appeared to perk up when she looked at him, but she did. Maybe it was because he appeared to be a harmless as a baby duck. No way would anyone think Calvin West was a bad boy.

He didn't resemble Drake Lewis in any way what-so-ever.

Drake knew Mom refused to allow me to date, but it didn't stop the way he looked at me when no one was around, or the excuses he used to be close me. He kind of took my breath away when he was near. I couldn't stop myself from remembering the feel of his arms around me as he took me to the tree the day Grant died. His arms were strong, protective and surprisingly gentle. I liked the feel of them touching me, and wished he'd do it again. If for no other reason other than for me to see if his arms would feel good a second time.

After the service was over, Mom surprised me even more when she asked Calvin West if he would go home with us and share our dinner instead of her usual visit to Grant's grave.

He accepted her invitation.

"You ride with him, Ellie, to show him where we live."

"He can follow us easy enough," I told her. Our house was at the end of the road. All he had to do was go up the road instead of down the road.

"He's parked near the road. We're blocked in. Go on. Stop your infernal aggravation. I'm tired of listening to your insistent arguing with me all the time."

Her words hurt. I didn't think I argued, nor did I think I was aggravation to Mom or anybody else, but I might have been wrong where Mom was concerned. I turned my back on her and marched to the young man's rusty, dented car and opened the passenger door with a loud squeaking of rusty hinges.

"Mom said for me to ride with you to show you where we live," I told him.

"Sounds good," he smiled.

I noticed that he did have good Ipana toothpaste white teeth along with a nice smile that lit up his face and eyes. Both made up for the odd-looking glasses he wore.

"Are you a scholar?" I found myself asking him right out of the blue.

"You could say that; I suppose. I am a believer in higher education."

"You have to go to college to become a preacher?"

"You do if you want to become a Presbyterian minister, but not a Baptist. All that is required of a Baptist is to claim you've been called by God to preach his word and you'll most likely be ordained."

I thought I heard a slight edge to his words. I wasn't sure if it was resentment, ridicule or my imagination.

"I've attended college for several years. I like stimulating my brain powers. It's the most powerful organ the body contains. It controls everything you do, everything you think. Are you in college?" he asked.

"Mom says girls don't need college. All they need is a high school education and a good husband."

He grinned. "She might have a point," he said kindly. "You don't by chance have a husband picked out, do you?"

I thought of Drake. "No, not yet."

"I'll wager there are a lot of young men waiting in line for your attention if not your hand in marriage."

"Mom doesn't allow me to date," I told him, and then wished I hadn't been so honest. It made me sound like a child with a domineering mother – which wasn't far from the truth.

"When a girl is as pretty as you, I can understand why her mother is strict."

I frowned, not liking his words even when they were a compliment. I didn't consider myself pretty, but I wasn't ugly either. Mom oversaw the clothes I wore as well as the way my hair was fixed. She cut my hair herself, keeping it short. For some reason, Mom hated long hair. I dreamed of having long, silky locks that hung down my back in waves like most of the girls on Lawrence Welk show. Mom and Dad were one of the few people in our hollow who had a television. Up until recently, the preachers claimed a television was pure sinful. Mom hadn't wanted it, but Grant bought it with his own money he earned hiring out to farmers.

"Do you believe televisions are sinful?" I asked suddenly.

His bushy eyebrows shot up over his glasses. "What kind of question is that?"

"Preachers used to claim people who watched television were evil."

"Do you believe such as that?"

"No," I told him. "Do you?"

"Hardly. Inanimate objects are not evil. Only a few bad people are evil. Most people fall in the category of good and not so good."

"I agree."

"How far up this pitiful road do you live?" he asked with the slightest hint of irritation.

"It's not much farther."

"Doesn't the state keep up this road? There're holes deep enough to bury a bus in."

"Not often. Dad says there's not enough people with the right politics living on the road for the state to work on it."

He rolled his eyes but said no more as Blake Lewis's rattle trap truck showed up going in the opposite direction to us. He'd salvaged parts and pieces then wired and welded them together until he got the truck in running condition. Drake backed the truck up until he came to Oran Well's driveway on the right side of the road and pulled into it. As we passed, Drake looked me right in the eyes. His expression made me feel odd causing me to quickly look away as though I was doing something wrong.

"Incredible," Calvin said.

"What is?" I questioned.

"That rust heap actually runs."

I didn't think he had room to be critical considering what he was driving, but he seemed to think his rust heap was an exception to Blake's rust heap. He must have realized what I was thinking for he responded.

"I've got my engine purring like a kitten. Next week, when I have a little free time, I'll have the outside bonded, sanded and painted."

"That's good," I told him. "Do you live with your parents'?" I found myself asking right out of the blue. I hadn't planned on asking that question. It just slipped out of my mouth.

"No."

"Oh, I forgot. You go to college. That means you live in a dorm."

He didn't answer as his car came to a stop.

"I assume you live here since I've come to the end of the road and there's a barbwire fence blocking the – uh - road. I can't drive any further."

"This is it," I told him, and wondered what he thought of our house. It was a small farmhouse that had been recently painted with a fresh coat of white. Mom had a lot of pride and did her best to make Dad maintain things to her satisfaction. When Dad claimed he didn't have time to paint or mow the grass, Grant would hop to it, which made Mom love him even more.

Grant had painted the house only days before he was killed. Dad had recently mowed the grass, but it wasn't the pristine job Grant would have done. I thought our place looked good compared to some of the other places in our hollow. I had watched Calvin West's facial expressions as he drove up the dirt road. The houses were nothing fancy, but they were home to people who lived there. They lived, loved, and survived the best way they could. There was no shame in that, I assured myself.

"Where do you live?" I asked him again once we had gotten out of the car and stood in the yard waiting for Mom and Dad to arrive.

"Near the college," he answered slightly evasive.

"Where do your parents live?"

"In Oaksboro. Do you know where that is?"

I wasn't sure if that was a put-down or a genuine question.

"I know where it is, but I've never been there," I told him.

"Your parents don't travel much, do they?"

"They have no reason to. Home is here. They spend their time working instead of traveling." The same as all the people I knew.

"My parents travel a lot. They take a vacation ever summer to visit my grandparents."

"You go with them?"

"I did when I was younger."

"Do you have brothers or sisters?"

"No. I'm an only child."

"Where do your grandparents live?" I was curious and not just asking questions to pass the awkwardness of waiting.

"One set live in Florida and the other set live in Pennsylvania. My parents take summer about visiting them for several weeks. They also visit other relatives rather often."

I thought his parents had to be well off if they could take vacations during the summers and travel hundreds of miles. Dad was always complaining about the price of gas. I hated to admit it, but I had only traveled a short distance from home.

"Dad used to travel to Florida with his brother," I told him. "His brother rented farmland down there when it was winter here. Dad said it was the most miserable place he'd ever been. Dad said he was always being bit, stung, poked by thorns, or burnt to a crisp by the sun. When his brother died, he never went back again – never wanted to."

"He doesn't ever go back to Florida anymore?" he asked even though I had just said that.

"Not since his brother died."

"I was told your brother recently died in a horrible accident."

"He did, but don't mention it to Mom and Dad. They're still grieving. Talking about it makes it worse and brings all the horror back to them."

"Doesn't talking about it bring it all back to you?"

"Of course, it does. He was my big brother, my protector. Life has been tough since he died. Mom cries all the time and Dad grieves in silence. I don't know which is worse." It was as though life had left Dad when it left Grant. The difference between Dad and Grant was that dad was still walking on the top side of the ground while Grant was lying under it.

"You're an only child, now?"

I nodded. Thankfully, the sound of Dad's old truck was rumbling up the road. I didn't want to talk about Grant. I still had nightmares of seeing the tines ripping Grants flesh from his bones, and there wasn't a thing I could do to stop what happened then – or stop the nightmares I was still having.

Dad didn't go in the house to make small talk with Calvin. He headed to the barn while still wearing his Sunday best. Mom would let him know about his carelessness with his clothes and shoes as soon as the young preacher left. I knew Dad needed the swallow his daily dose of whiskey he kept hidden from Mom – as though she didn't know what he was doing. Dad was now drinking whiskey in hopes of numbing his suffering enough to continue living. I knew what kept him alive no longer existed – his son. Regardless of how much I wanted it, I would never be a substitute for Grant.

Calvin went into the kitchen with Mom and me to cook Sunday dinner. Thankfully, Mom had already made a meatloaf that morning. She had a pot of pinto beans soaked overnight and was cooking while she fixed breakfast. All we had to do was peel and cook potatoes, open a canning jar of corn, bake the cornbread, and make a pie.

On cue, Dad came inside as I was setting the table. We all sat down, and Mom asked Calvin to say grace. He did a fair job, but I was surprised he didn't do better since he was a preacher, or in the process of becoming one. His words were dry, utilitarian without any emotion.

Mom seemed to be really pleased with his saying grace. Dad bowed his head while Calvin said grace, but Dad's face was blank. I bowed my head, but I was busy peeking at everyone's faces. I put more truth on what their faces told me than what they said.

Chapter 3

It was obvious Mom had something in mind where Calvin West was concerned, and I wasn't sure if I was going to like it or not. On one hand I kind of wanted a friend, if not a boyfriend to make me feel special. On the other hand, he wasn't anything like the boyfriend I pictured in my mind.

"I'll clean up. You sit with the preacher," she whispered to me when I picked up plates from the table. I came in a hair of telling her that she should entertain him since she was the one who invited him to Sunday dinner. I held my tongue because I didn't want to listen to her ranting at my insolence for days on end, so I took Calvin West to the seldom used living room and sat beside him on the couch.

He rambled on about the Bible and the words of God for a while. After he realized, I wasn't equipped to carry on a conversation about the pros and cons of the written Word, he changed the subject to the people living along our rutted road. I put on a smile and did the best I could at a conversation that was uncomfortable for me. Finally, he seemed to wind down with all his questions.

"Now that I've given that delicious dinner time to digest, I best be on my way," he told me. "You are a lucky girl to have a beautiful mother who can cook the way she does. I don't know why you aren't fat," he said loud enough for Mom to hear him in the kitchen if she was listening. I knew she was.

"I'm not a big eater," I responded.

Mom hurried into the front room. "You're not leaving already, are you?" she asked with what appeared to be genuine regret of his pending departure.

"Best get started back to my place. It's a long drive," he said. "I need to do some studying before class in the morning."

"Too bad you don't have your books with you. You could study here and eat supper with us."

I almost strangled on the gasp I had to swallow to keep it from escaping. This behavior Mom was exhibiting wasn't like her in the least. She was always courteous to people, but never this openly welcoming to a stranger. Something was up with mother, and I wasn't sure if I liked it.

"Thank you for the invitation, Mrs. Goins. Maybe I can take a raincheck on your offer."

"That you can. Anytime you attend church, you're welcome to share a meal with us," Mom said with what sounded like a genuine invitation.

Mom shook his hand as he left. I stayed in the background as much as possible as he left. I wasn't sure what I thought about this young man. I wasn't sure what I thought about Mom either. I opened my mouth to ask her questions, and then snapped it shut deciding it would be best for me to remain silent.

That evening I jumped at the chance to go bring the milk cows in. The sound of bird songs, the sweet aroma of earth and blooms surrounded me. On these days when they were getting some grass, the cows didn't want to come in to be milked. Normally, I would be enjoying the beautiful evening, but I couldn't keep Grant's accident from haunting me. Mom and Dad were still seeing Grant at times on the farm, but not as often as they once did. To me, that was a blessing. Seeing Grant, or believing they did, was nothing short of being haunted. I knew both Mom and Dad blamed themselves for Grant's death.

Mom knew if she hadn't wanted the tiller to dig deeper, Grant wouldn't have challenged her. Dad knew if he hadn't wanted to do a better job of preparing the ground for planting, Grant would still be alive.

Me, I felt guilty at being alive when Grant wasn't. The way Mom looked at me, and the way Dad tried not to look at me at all, made me feel even more guilty for being the one alive.

For some strange reason, tears suddenly filled my eyes and ran down my cheeks. By the time I'd reached the top of the hill, I was consumed by grief. I found the cows laying in the shade of the woods instead of eating the grass. Their tails were swishing at flies as they chewed their cuds.

"You took long enough climbing that hill. I've been sitting here for an hour," a voice surprised me. I jumped about a foot, and then was instantly embarrassed because Drake would be sure to see me crying.

"What are you doing here?" I demanded as I tried to wipe my face with my hand without him noticing.

"I've been trying to get a shot at the groundhog that's eating up Mom's garden. It has a hole under that stump over there. It's ruined a good half of her beans." He made a point of laying his rifle down on a log and turned toward me.

"Ah, Ellie," Drake said as he stood up and came toward me.

He reached out his arms and surprised me by wrapping them around me and pulling me against his chest in a most gentle sort of way.

"Ah, Ellie," he repeated. "I might as well admit that I've waited years for this," he said as his soft lips found mine. I pulled away, shocked, but only for a few moments. Part of me wanted to know what it was like to be kissed by Drake, while another part of me wanted to be irate by his actions.

Mom's warnings had sunk into me more than I realized. At the same time, her warnings had served to challenge me. She had always claimed Drake was one of the bad boys that good girls needed to stay away from.

"Take things easy with that sissy, want-a-be preacher, sweetheart," he whispered in his most gentle voice. "Your mom may be shoving you at that wimp, but I'll be damn if

I'll let him be the first one to kiss you. That honor belongs to me."

Don't know why his words affected me the way they did. Somehow, I was mad at him for saying Mom was shoving me at the wimp. I resented being told I was shoved at someone.

Another part of me really did want Blake to be the first one to kiss me. I didn't like being sixteen and never been kissed. I wanted to have experience similar to some of the girls I went to school with. I knew a lot of their talk was just talk, but surely some of it was true. The fire, the passion, the burning desire was something I longed to experience. More than that, I dreamed of a forever-after kind of love. The kind that was in fairy tales – *lived happily ever after* kind of love.

Drake's face moved toward me in what seemed like slow motion. His lips touched mine, and I found it was exciting, something I wanted, needed. Yet, at the same time there was a lacking inside of me that I wanted Blake to fill.

I certainly hadn't planned on my arms being around Drake's neck, but they were. I was holding onto him and kissing him back as though my life depended on it.

"Easy," he whispered after he moved his lips away from mine and let them rest in my hair near my ear. "Don't want to do anything you'll regret, my sweet Ellie."

Instead of kissing me again, his hand cupped the back of my head and pressed my face against his chest.

"Go ahead. Cry it out, sweetheart. I can only imagine the nightmare you've been going through. I've been having nightmares of my own in more ways than one. It's time someone looks after you for a change instead of catering to your mother's trauma."

His words made everything worse. I didn't want anyone looking after me, and at the same time, I did. Folks were always giving Mom and Dad compassion and understanding for what they were going through. I was treated like I was an outsider, someone too young to be affected by death as deeply as my parents were.

I was surprised when his thumbs wiped away my tears. I hadn't even realized I was still crying.

"Appears your mom has decided you've finally come of age. Think you ought to know that I am first in line where you're concerned. Hear me, Ellie? I staked my claim on you when you were twelve years old. I won't stand for anyone else jumping my claim."

What was he talking about? I'd never heard such talk coming from the bad-boy Drake before. He'd always treated me like an irritating kid, that was, until recently when he'd taken to looking me over. His words sent a cold chill over me. Where was the gentle person who was consoling me only minutes before? Why had he changed so quickly?

"I gotta go. Dad will be wondering what's taking me so long." I knew that wasn't true, but Drake didn't. Dad would be doing up the work without one thought about what was taking me so long.

Drake held onto me with a firm grip for a few moments longer. "You're mine. Tell that to that wimpy preacher or I will," he said before he turned loose of me.

I took off running down the hill as fast as I dared. I needed time and distance from Drake. He scared me a little. Always had. Bad boys were only safe when observed from a distance.

Mom had supper ready by the time I got through milking. It consisted of the usual pinto beans, boiled potatoes, cornbread, chopped onions, sliced tomatoes, and sliced cucumbers. I hurriedly washed my hands and made Dad a cup of instant coffee. He claimed Mom didn't made it as good as I did. Since Grant was killed, he never commented on the coffee or what he ate or how it tasted. I don't think he cared about food any longer or much of anything else.

Mom was the same way. She was losing weight and always seemed pale and kind of sickly.

There was no longer happiness, no playful bickering about anything. Our house had become a place of silence and brooding. There were times when Mom hardly ate anything.

Once or twice, I caught her slipping out behind the house to throw up the food she had eaten. There would be tears streaming down her face as she looked toward the hill where the family graveyard was located. I feared that Mom and Dad would be in their graves before they ever stopped grieving over Grant. I'd heard people say you should honor a person's life instead of grieving their death. I could understand their point of view, but also understood that it seldom happened.

I no longer asked either of my parents much of anything. I'd learned not to question them about believing they saw Grant, or about giving up all hopes of happiness in order to continue their grief and loss. We all three seemed to exist in our own kind of misery.

~~~~

Much to my amazement Calvin West showed up the next Sunday for church. He was sitting in the front row on the men's side but turned his head to smile at me where Mom and I sat on the women's side of the church. Several of the women noticed. I saw Mamie James poke Sue Blake in the ribs with her elbow as though she was pointing out some kind of transgression. Several of the girls my age or younger looked Calvin West over with interest, but not the same kind of interest they had always given toward Grant.

Of course, Mom invited him to eat with us.

"Ride with him, Ellie," Mom told me.

"Why?" I said with a hint of stubbornness. "He knows the way."

Ellie Lynn Goins. I'm sick and tired of the way you've been acting lately. You won't let me get a bit of peace and quiet," she said warningly. When she said my full name, I knew she was about to come down hard on me.

"Fine. I'll ride with him," I said as I marched straight to his rusty car and got in without saying anything further to Mom. His car was slightly cleaner and more organized than it had been last Sunday. It even smelled better, like he had sprayed some kind of sweet air freshener in it. I had to smile at his effort. It showed he had some pride in what was his.

"I was beginning to wonder if you were coming with me," he said as I settled in the passenger seat.

"I didn't want to seem too eager," I said, although I wasn't eager at all. There was something about Calvin West that didn't feel quite right to me. Preachers had a way of thinking they were the chosen ones. I suspected the seemingly shy Calvin West was no different. The rest of us were only the congregation – the ordinary sinners.

"Too eager wouldn't be the words I'd use to describe you," he said with a slight grin. "Young, beautiful, innocent would be a better description."

I knew he was trying to butter me up because I wasn't beautiful. I wasn't ugly either. I didn't plaster my face with makeup or stuff my bra with cotton like some girls did. I thought I had good enough self-esteem regardless my many faults.

A lot of older boys looked me over, whistled, or made comments that came close to being insulting. I didn't like their comments, but they didn't hurt my ego. Most boys my own age had not gained enough testosterone to be as forward. They were far too young to get my interest. I found the idea of a boy practicing his fumbling, slobber kisses on me as being repulsive. I was attracted to those who happened to be known as older bad boys – like Drake.

Calvin West was older. I found myself looking at his mouth and remembering his nice teeth. I wondered if he would be a good kisser. I wondered how it would compare to Drake's. I wasn't sure a preacher knew how to kiss or if they were allowed to kiss. According to most of the preachers who gave sermons at out church, anything that led to sex was a sin, and it would definitely include kissing. This puzzled me. Preachers were married and had children.

"Do you believe in kissing?" I surprised myself by suddenly voicing the question that was in my mind.

His eyebrows raised in surprise, and he grinned. "Yes, I do," he said with a touch of humor.

"The preachers at our church claim kissing leads to sinning." I tried to explain my question. "And yet they have children."

"Maybe they had help." His grin deepened.

"Had help?" Was he making fun of my question? I felt my face redden when I realized what he meant.

"Never mind, my own kind of humor. No, I don't think sharing a kiss would amount to a sin. However, on their thinking, I assume they are referring to unmarried people who don't stop at kissing. God only gave married people the right to become one flesh."

So that was what becoming one flesh meant.

He drove his car to a spot in front of our house and stopped. He turned to look at me. "Would you like to indulge in a tiny bit of sinning?"

"What?" I questioned, puzzled at the look he was giving me.

"Would you like for me to kiss you before your parents arrive? I assure you, we won't have time to do any sinning afterwards."

At first, I was shocked and then amused at such a suggestion coming from a preacher. If he could ask me such a direct question, then I had the right to give a direct answer.

"Yes. I think I would."

He turned more toward me, put his hand behind my head, and pulled me toward him. His lips met mine in a gentle kiss that wasn't anything like Drakes. Calvin's kiss was more like coming from a friend, where Drakes came from passion. Drake's kiss scared me. Calvin's didn't.

"Sweet sixteen and never been kissed, no longer applies," he said. "That's enough for now," he told me. "I hear your parents coming." He let his hand squeeze my shoulder. "There's plenty of time for more later, sweet, innocent Ellie.

He opened the door and got out. I did too. I was disappointed along with being kind of embarrassed. What was worse, I found him terribly lacking, but then, what had I expected from a preacher.

As usual, Dad busied himself outside while Mom hustled about in the kitchen preparing food for dinner. She made a point of not having me help her.

"Keep the preacher company," she told me as though it was my duty.

The term 'pick a date fit for a mate' entered my mind. Was the preacher dating me or was he simply after a free meal? I uncharitably thought if Mom served fried chicken, we'd never get rid of him. Instantly, I felt guilty for my thoughts. It stood to reason he wouldn't travel this far away from his home to get a meal Mom and I had cooked. He had to be after something more. Could it possibly be that I was the more? Was Mom trying to get rid of me? She had lost one child. Would she want to get rid of another by marrying me off?

How silly I was being. Mom had invited a preacher to dinner twice and here I was having crazy thoughts about her wanting to be rid of me. Why would she want to be rid of me? It was true I had never been her favorite child, but I was now her only child. She was always pointing out my failings, which were many. Still yet, I told myself I did my share of work in the house. I even helped Dad on the farm. Not only that, but what would a preacher, a man, several years older than me want with a girl as young as I was? He would want a full-grown woman. Most likely one with a job who could support him while he finished his college education.

I kind of settled back and watched as Mom and Calvin talked to each other while Dad and I busied ourselves eating dinner. Dad never had much to say at his most talkie times. I usually talked a lot, but the preacher caused me to become tongue tied. I didn't know what to say to a preacher. Mom had the opinion that preachers were the right hand of God. They could do no wrong. I wasn't so sure about that.

Dad didn't show an opinion one way or another. He was becoming more silent with each day that passed. Grant died a horrible, sudden death, but, in my opinion, Dad was dying a little at a time. I wasn't sure which death was the worst.

As soon as Dad finished eating, he stood up and left the table without saying a word. Mom gave his back a disapproving look as he crossed the kitchen floor and walked out the door.

"He doesn't mean to be rude," Momma told Calvin. Since Grant's death, he can't sit still for long."

"I understand," Calvin to her. "Losing someone you love isn't an easy thing to get over. It haunts you for the rest of your life."

"Have you lost someone you love?" Mom asked.

"Who hasn't," he returned with compassion.

"Who was it?" Mom boldly asked.

"A friend," he said. "We grew up together."

"What happened?" Mom asked Calvin as though she longed to know she wasn't the only person who lost a loved one. "Was he in an accident?"

"No. He had some type of uncurable disease. It was something they couldn't diagnose. Something I don't like to talk about," he told her gently as though he wanted to change the subject. "Would it be okay if Ellie showed me about the farm? Perhaps climbing that high hill in front of the house will help our digestion. I couldn't stop eating your wonderful food. I've looked forward to it all week."

"Of course," Mom said, her eyes bright with unshed tears. "You're welcome to eat with us every Sunday if you want."

Those words coming from Mom got my full attention. Was she thinking Calvin West was a suitable husband for me? Surely, she didn't want to get rid of me now that I was her only child.

Once we had left the house and was far away enough where neither Mom nor Dad could overhear us. "Tell me about your brother's accident," Calvin said.

"I rather not. It hurts too much to think about it," I told him.

"Then take me to the place where it happened."

"Why?" I asked, thinking he was one of those people who liked to witness the morbid.

"Because you need to face your demons and get it out of your system. Your parents have fallen so deep into their grieving they have just about stopped living. I don't want you to be in the same type of grieving."

Chapter 4

Spring turned into summer. Dad kept busy in his fields from the break of day until it was too dark to see. I found myself working beside him, but I would never be a replacement for his beloved son. Dad didn't even come inside for the noon-day meal. I went to the house and made biscuits and jelly from leftovers Mom had made for breakfast and took them, along with a quart jar of ice water, to the field for Dad. He sat under the shade of a tree and ate, while I sat beside him. He didn't thank me or comment. Dad remained the silent man, and seldom answered any of the questions I asked. I got to the point where I stopped asking questions and accepted silence between us. His entire focus seemed to be on growing his crops. Most of the time he ignored me as though he didn't care if I was there helping him or not. Sometimes I would work all day long and other times I would take off after a few hours.

Mom insisted I help her in the house and seemed to resent the time I spent with Dad. I noticed that Mom was acting odd, or should I say odder than normal. She ate little food and seemed to be exhausted all the time. Often, I came inside the house, I found her on the couch asleep. She always denied that she was sleeping. She claimed she was only resting her eyes. I noticed there were blue semi-circles beneath her eyes, and her face was paler than usual.

When her stomach started to increase, I feared she had some kind of horrible disease that was slowly killing her.

"Mom, are you sick?" I asked her.

"No, I'm not sick," she snapped at me. "I wish you'd stop aggravating me all the time. A body can't get a minute's piece when you're around."

Her words shocked me as well as hurting me to my core. I turned and went outside. Dad caught me before I got far. I didn't realize he had overheard her.

"She didn't mean that the way it sounded. As you well know, Katie's not been herself lately. You'll have to overlook her right now."

I sure knew that all right. Seemed nobody had been their selves lately, including me. I wanted to talk to Dad, ask questions, but he turned away and rushed toward the barn as though he couldn't stand to talk to me any longer.

~~~~

The next Sunday, Calvin West showed up again. This time he didn't sit up front with the preachers and deacons. He made a point of worming his way past the people who sat in the same pew as me until he was next to me.

"Excuse me," he kept saying politely to the women he squeezed in front of, trying not to step on their feet. They nodded and grinned knowingly as they watched him sit down beside me.

I didn't know what to do or say. His public display was telling everyone in the church that he was courting me. Such gossip would be spreading to everyone in the hollow before their Sunday dinner was over. I sat there feeling as jumpy as a jar full of fleas. I feared Mom would be furious since she said I was too young to court. I didn't think she would give me credit for having nothing to do with Calvin's public display.

As soon as the meeting was over and we were out of ear shot of others, Calvin asked Mom if it would be all right if he took me to town to eat.

"I suppose so," she told him. "But don't be gone long." She made sure she gave me one of her warning looks that told me I was in trouble when Calvin had his back turned. Surely, she knew I had nothing to do with this. I wasn't the one who agreed to go with Calvin. Mother had given him her permission.

"Your mother is an interesting woman," Calvin said as we drove away. "I can't decide if she likes me or not."

I didn't tell him I knew that feeling only too well. "She hasn't gotten over Grant's death," was all I could think to say to describe the way Mom was. It seemed the only person who ever got past her hard shell was Grant. Now that he was gone her shell had grown thick enough to enclose her forever.

"I'm sure she never will. No mother ever gets over losing her child. Is she somehow blaming you for his accident?"

I didn't know how to answer that question. I didn't see how she could blame me, but that didn't mean she didn't. "She's the one who is partly to blame. Truth is Grant did it to himself. He should never have jumped on the back of that tiller just to prove to Mom he was right. He lost his balance and fell."

"Then why does she seem angry with you?"

I looked out the window and shrugged my shoulders. I didn't want to admit what I thought, but I did. "Sometimes I think she wishes it had been me instead of Grant."

Calvin slowly nodded his head as though he understood far more than I was telling him. "Appears every time she looks at you, she's reminded of the child she lost. You know, anger at those who survived."

"I think so. She cries when she sees something that reminds her of Grant, and everything she sees reminds her of him, including me."

"Do you think she would be happier if you weren't around?"

"Perhaps," I admitted, but I didn't know how to accomplish such as that until I was older. I was still too young to be on my own, although I felt like an old woman, a desperate one. I was living in misery the same as Mom and

Dad were, and it wasn't all about no longer having my older brother. There were times when I would do almost anything, including running away if it were only possible to hide from Mom's anger, and the misery we were all forced to endure.

He nodded as though he was in deep thought and was silent for a few minutes. "I understand your position. You and I both need to pray on it. I'm sure there is a solution if we ask God for guidance."

I looked at Calvin's expression and was unable to read his expression. He did seem to be seriously in thought.

~~~~

I hadn't expected Calvin to take me out to eat at a fancy restaurant, but I did expect a local drive-in. He surprised me when he stopped at a roadside table and got out.

"Come on. We'll sit at that picnic bench over there," he said as he took out a brown paper bag from the backseat that looked like it had been there for a while.

I was taken speechless when he produced two cans of beanie weenies, a jar of water, two cups and two spoons. If this was my first date, I would have liked for it to be kind of special. I tried to convince myself this was kind of romantic, but I failed. I wasn't very hungry but going by a drive-in to see if any of my school friends were there would have been nice. Plus, I would have liked my classmates to see me on a date. I then considered he might not have enough money to buy a burger. Besides, Mom had prepared a large Sunday dinner figuring Calvin would show up. We'd get to eat it for supper. I did my best not to be disappointed, but I was.

The sound of a loud muffler came barreling down the highway. It was Drake Lewis. He slowed down as though he was going to stop, but he didn't. He only gave us a death glare, before he gunned the engine and sped off.

"Your neighbor," he said in his soft, gentle tone of voice.

"It appears so."

"Could he be following us?" Calvin asked.

I thought it possible, but I wasn't about to admit such to Calvin or myself. Drake had ignored me for many years. I saw no reason for his attitude to change regardless of what he'd done when I went after the cows.

"Don't see why," I said.

"Maybe he's interested in you?"

"That's unlikely."

"Why do you think it unlikely?"

"He picked on me as far back as I can remember. He called me a bratty girl. He obviously didn't want me around. Mom said he was one of those bad boys she made sure Grant and I were to stay away from."

Calvin nodded slowly. "I see," he said, as though he was seeing things I didn't.

We didn't stay long at the roadside table. Calvin seemed to get bored and impatient fast. The sound of traffic appeared to bother him, especially when the sound of a loud muffler came again and Drake ground gears as he zoomed past us.

"Ready?" he said. "He's pathetic. Let's go before he turns around and comes back."

I stood up. Calvin made a point of cleaning up everything, including tiny bits of trash other people had left behind. I admired his determination to leave things in pristine condition, but he seemed overly irritated at other people's trashiness.

"Some people have no respect for the environment, or respect for others," he said as his eyes looked down the highway where Drake's truck had disappeared. It crossed my mind that Calvin was from off and knew nothing about the people in this area or the way they were raised. I bet his parents didn't have a trash pile out behind the barn. I bet they never used cow, horse, and hog manure as fertilizer.

"Were you raised in the city or on a farm?" I asked.

"I'm familiar with both. My parents own land in a farming community as well as a house in the outskirts of a city. They don't believe in littering. I can't believe how people around here throw trash out the car windows to litter the sides of the road."

I wasn't sure if he was bragging or simply stating a fact. It sounded like bragging to me even though he'd said it in a humble sort of way. Mom was always throwing trash out the car window, or down the steep bank where rain could wash it down into the river and disappear. I wasn't about to admit that to him. I wasn't sure what to think about Mom doing such as that. It was dumping trash on land that didn't belong to her.

~~~~

The next Sunday Calvin didn't show up. Oddly enough, I was surprised. Perhaps even disappointed. I liked the idea of having someone paying attention to me. Mom had prepared another Sunday meal expecting Calvin to be there.

She'd asked me last Sunday what kind of meal Calvin had bought me. When I told her, she laughed right out loud, which was something she didn't do lately.

"Poor boy. He obviously doesn't have money to waste being he's going to college. Looks to me like his parents should help him out more than they obviously do. It's a parent's job to help their son get ahead in life."

"Isn't it their job to help their daughter as well?" I couldn't resist speaking what crossed my mind.

"Girls are different. They don't need more education than graduating from high school, if that. Don't know why businesses wants high school graduates, but they do. Going to college is nothing but a waste of time and money. Only doctor's kids and teachers kids go to college."

"Calvin is going to college," I pointed out.

"Foolishness," Mom said with conviction. "God knows when to call men to preach. A man don't need to go to college to learn how to preach. God always tells a real preacher what to say. If you ask me, it's blasphemy to be taught how to preach."

I was surprised to hear Mom admit what she thought. She'd been acting like she approved of Calvin and his going to college.

"What that boy ought to do is get a job and get married. If God wants him to preach, He'll see to it without all that fancy college stuff," Mom added for good measure.

I hardly had time or the energy to think about Calvin or anything else. The bigger farmers in our area had beans ready to pick. Pole beans as well as bunch beans. Picking pole beans was a pleasure compared to the back-breaking bending over of picking bunch beans. But folks did what they had to do in order to earn money. Farmers paid men with trucks to drive by folk's houses every morning to pick up those who wanted to work and return them in the evening. Truckers were paid fifty cents for every picker they hauled. Pickers were paid fifty cents for every bushel of beans they picked. Some of the women were able to make as much as six dollars a day, which was mighty good money.

Kids were lucky if they made two or three dollars. I made about three dollars a day in bunch beans and five dollars in pole beans. Mothers and children piled in the back of large trucks to pick enough beans to buy school clothes and supplies. It was just about the only way for some folks and children to earn money.

Few men were willing to do the work women and children did. A lot of men grew their own small patch of beans and expected their wife and children to pick them after the hauler brought them home in the evening. It was a good thing summer days were long.

Most farmers also grew a small patch of burley tobacco that brought in a little money near Christmas time. Beans and tobacco helped folks survive, as did the gardens the women and children grew and canned.

Mom wasn't doing much gardening or working in the beans as she usually did. Instead, she stayed in the house more moving about slowly and accomplishing very little. The work fell on me after I got home in the evenings. It finally dawned on me why? I felt like an idiot for not seeing it sooner. Mom's belly was growing. She was either bloating up with some kind or disease or having a baby. Could such a thing be possible? Was Mom and Dad not too old for such as that? I wondered if she was trying for a replacement for the son she had lost. Somehow, my mind had trouble envisioning what Mom and dad did when no one was watching.

I made a point of cornering Dad at the barn. "Dad, is Mom going to have a baby?" I came straight out and asked.

Dad turned his back to me and tried to act like he hadn't heard me.

"Is she?" I persisted. It was obvious that Dad was embarrassed and didn't want to talk about such a thing, especially with me. I had no intention of going away without an answer from him and he knew it.

"I reckon so," he finally said with his back still turned to me. "Don't mention it to her. She'll get mad." He hung his head, hunched his shoulders and hurried out of the barn as though he had to get away from me fast.

"When?" I called after him, but he didn't answer. At least I now knew why Mom seemed to be sick a lot. I expected Mom and Dad to be happy at the idea of a baby, but I feared Mom was too old to safely give birth. I would make sure I helped her more than I was already doing.

When I went inside, Mom noticed me staring at her stomach and realized I knew about her condition. My observation of her growing stomach appeared to make her mad as fire. Her face flushed red. Her eyes shot darts of anger.

"Go outside and help Ben. You're under my feet and in my way. I don't know what's gotten into you," she told me angrily. It seemed being pregnant made Mom have a lot of things that aggravated her. A thought came to me. If that was true, Mom had surely been pregnant since the day I was born. I couldn't help thinking as I went outside.

"Go fetch the milk cows," Dad said when he saw me. "Don't know what's wrong with them lately. Don't come in for milking the way they used to."

Going after the cow would be a blessed relief to me. I needed time to recoup what little sanity I had left. Sometimes climbing the hill to bring the cows in was the balm I needed to endure my horrible existence for a while longer. I could only hope that Mom would change back to her more tolerable self after the baby was born. I had an idea she would want me to help care for it, but it was impossible to tell about Mom these days.

The air was brisk and turning cooler the higher I climbed. The warm summer days were long over, and the timber was already changing colors. Animals and fowls were growing thick coats of fur and feathers. Yellow jacket bees were buzzing about with a temperament as ill as hornets. Birds were starting to flock together in the treetops as they readied themselves for flying south. I wished I could fly south, or in any direction to get away from the unhappiness that was gathering in me. I felt hopeless and without a solution to the devastation I was feeling. If anything, it was worse than the helplessness I felt after Grant's death.

"It took you long enough to get here," Drake said as I reached the top of the mountain where he was slowly feeding the cows handfuls of corn. "I've used dang near fifty pounds of corn this week alone."

"You've been waiting on me?"

"For a long time, my Ellie. A very long time."

I ignored his double meaning, if that was what he intended.

At least he didn't find me in tears this time, but my sorrow was probably greater now than it had been when I cried my heart out while he held me. I was now consumed with hopelessness that would never end. It would be two more years before I would be able to get a job and seek some kind of life of my own. That was if Mom didn't turn me into her permanent babysitter along with everything else.

"Okay. What is it you want from me?"

"Everything," he told me in his joking sort of way. "I want all of you."

"Too late," I told him deliberately ignoring his double meaning again. "Life has already claimed all of me."

He laughed. Drake actually laughed at my words.

"I'm not being funny," I told him. It took great effort to hold in my tears, but I managed.

"You're being dramatic, but I have a solution for that. I'm perfect willing and able to love all your unhappiness away."

"Really?" I said as sarcastically as I could manage.

"I'm magic that way," he said as he reached for me.

I let him take me into his arms and didn't pull away. I hoped he had magic. I hoped it worked on me. His hands rubbed up and down my back until they came to rest on the sides of my face. His lips met mine with a passion I hadn't expected but should have. The Drake I was most familiar with was all fire and fury with no slow and easy, no built up. I didn't think slow and easy were in his makeup and that had always scared me and intrigued me at the same time. Oddly enough, I felt none of the fire or the fury that he was so obviously feeling. Instead, I felt a kind of repulsion. His mouth tasted like cigarettes and whiskey. It was disappointment that made me want to cry. I found Drake disgusting. The secret dreams I had always had about being with Drake was slowly fading away as reality took its place. My fantasies about Drake were just that - fantasies.

"What will it take to make you come alive?" he whispered as his mouth eased far enough from mine until he could speak words.

"I don't know," I answered truthfully.

"I want to make you mine," he whispered near my mouth. I smelled his stinking breath as I remembered the things Mom said about Drake. I knew Dad didn't approve of him either.

Panic came over me. I pushed him away, lunged at the cows to make them get a move on and followed them down the hill as fast as I could get them to go. Drake made no attempt to leave the shelter of the woods where he could remain hidden. I knew he didn't want to take a chance on Dad seeing him.

I imagined what it would be like married to Drake. He would always be coming home drunk with the smell of some woman's cheap perfume on him. Drake never would be able to hold down a job or provide his wife and children with a respectable life. His wife would always have to work her fingers to the bone just to provide enough food for them to eat. The same as his mother did. Most likely Drake's future would be bootlegging cheap whiskey much the way of his father. That wasn't the kind of life I wanted for myself or my children.

I imagined the kind of life I would have married to a preacher. A man of God would be gentle and loving and kind. He would never drink liquor, beat his wife, or commit adultery with bad women. A preacher might never make a lot of money, but he would certainly provide a good, clean life for his family. His children would never go hungry or unloved.

Chapter 5

It was on a cold winter day in late January when Calvin came to church after missing the services for several weeks. I didn't know what had happened that kept him away. Oddly enough his absence left me with a mixture of disappointment and relief. My feelings would have been more to the relief side if Mom wasn't growing in belly as well as ill temperament. She demanded I do everything and nothing at the same time. She wanted me to become a ghost person, one that got everything done without her having to see me doing it. If a dish wasn't washed, it was my fault. If the cold wind blew too hard and caused soot to puff out of the wood stove, it was my fault. If the floors needed sweeping or dust had gathered on a light fixture, it was my fault. If she had a headache or her back hurt, it was because I had neglected to do something, and she'd had to do it. I felt as though my own mother hated me more with each day that passed.

Dad was lucky. He was able to hide in the barn except for mealtime and sleeping.

"Why does Mom hate me so much?" I managed to corner Dad long enough to ask.

"Expecting women are like that," Dad answered as he shoved the pitchfork into the pile of hay and hurriedly climbed down from the barn loft and made a beeline away from me. "Especially if the woman is as old as your mother."

I knew Mom had married Dad at sixteen and given birth to Grant exactly one year later. I'd heard Mom say her baby son was the God given treasure of her life. She told everyone she never knew the meaning of true love until she held her son in her arms. He encompassed all the pure innocence and beauty in existence, and she had given birth to this perfect son. She said he was her treasure – all hers.

~~~~

Seeing Calvin's rusty vehicle in the church parking lot stirred a feeling of relief in me. If he chose to eat Sunday dinner with us, Mom would be nice to me while he was there. She would be a little more like her old self before Grant was killed.

"Look at that," Mom said as she nodded her head toward Calvin's vehicle. "Appears he's not deserted you this Sunday."

"Why would he desert me?" I managed to ask.

"Humph," she grunted as though I should know and was deliberately taunting her. "Get out and go find him since you're in such an all-fired hurry to get to him."

I wasn't taunting her neither was I in a hurry to get to Calvin. I didn't know why Calvin had stayed away so long. To be honest with myself, his absence hurt in a way similar to mother's treatment of me. It was obvious neither of them cared about me, not really cared in the good way I wanted them to care.

Calvin was in the church house yard talking to some older women when he saw me. He grinned.

"Excuse me," he said to the women and hurried toward me. "Good to see you," he said with a big grin. "Let's go inside and get a seat."

I was surprised when he didn't go to the front to set with the preachers. Instead, once again, he took his place on the left hand of the church where the women sat. Only the men who were seriously courting a girl sat on the left with her. And now he had done it twice. Did this mean Calvin was publicly announcing that he was doing more than courting? Was he declaring in God's church house that he intended to officially court me? If so, shouldn't he at least ask me if it was okay with it first? After all, marriage was between two people, not just one.

~~~~

I was taken by surprise when Calvin asked Mom if she was agreeable for me to marry him. Mom said yes without either one asking if I was agreeable. I'm not sure how I would have answered if either had done so. On one hand I wanted to graduate high school and go away to college. I dreamed of a chance to be on my own where I could find a good job and earn my own money. In reality, I knew such as that would never happen. Mom would never allow me to attend college even if I got a full scholarship. I'd end up living with Mom and working in a factory, while Mom controlled every aspect of my life, the same way she was doing now.

Maybe, just maybe I would have a chance to fulfil some of my dreams if I married Calvin.

"It's most likely for the best," Dad told me when I cornered him in the barn. "You're old enough to live your own life."

"But . . ." I tried to tell Dad how I was feeling. I needed to talk to somebody about my dreams and my fears. I'd always thought I would fall head over heels in love, get married and live happily ever-after. I liked Calvin good enough, but was what I felt for him true love? Did the way Calvin treated me show his love for me?

"Won't Mom need me to help take care of the baby?" I tried to reason with Dad.

"Most likely Katie won't let me touch it the same as she did when Grant was first born. She thought he was hers alone and that I had nothing to do with him, but she came around, somewhat," he added as though saying the truth was an afterthought. "She's obsessed with the idea this baby will be a reincarnation of Grant. She thinks it's Grant's way of coming back to her. She doesn't want anything or anyone to stand between her and her reincarnated baby Grant."

"Mom needs . . ."

"Don't say another thing," Dad told me firmly. "Might as well marry and get it over with. You could do a lot worse than marrying a preacher. At least he ought to be good to you."

I watched Dad turn his back and stalk out of the barn. I stood there feeling helpless and totally confused. I wasn't ready for marriage, but then I hadn't been ready for Grant's death or what Mom and Dad were going through. Maybe it would be best for all of us if I married Calvin. I could make it work out for the best.

~~~~

I had always dreamed of having a beautiful wedding. A white, flowing dress, flowers, love, happiness all for me. I had dreamed of walking down the aisle on Dad's arm to the sound of *here comes the bride* playing until I stood by the side of a smiling groom waiting just for me.

It wasn't going to happen.

"You've committed to this," Mom warned me when she saw how nervous and undecided I was about marrying Calvin. "You back out now and your life won't be worth living from now on."

Mom would see that was true.

I hadn't said a thing to Mom as she drove me into town to get our marriage license. She had to sign because I was underage. How could I possibly explain to her how afraid I was? My whole life was going to change, and I wasn't so sure it would be changing for my benefit.

~~~~

Calvin seemed willing to get married and mighty pleased about it when he showed up on Saturday morning. His confidence and smiling face eased a little of the apprehension in me, but not all of it. Another fear was how were we going to live? I didn't have a cent to my name. As for Calvin, he was a man going to college, one without a job, and obviously had no money. Calvin had told me he did have a rental place he had shared with a roommate, but the roommate had moved out a short time before our wedding day approached.

Mom had a preacher come to the house. I stood beside Calvin in what Mom considered my most appropriate dress. There was nothing white or flowing about it. It wasn't even pretty since Mom was the one who chose and bought all my clothes. The preacher said a few words that made me feel as cold as the temperature outside. Snow was on the ground, but it was no longer snowing. The wind was blowing hard. The sound of it sending an icy chill through me. I hoped it was not the harbor of bad omens for my married life.

The preacher read a quote from the Bible without one word penetrating my brain. I think he then read something similar to wedding vows I had heard before on television, but those words didn't sound promising. Instead, they sounded as though they were a warning that a woman was forever deemed by God to serve her husband and do exactly what he demanded. I didn't even get to say the dreamed about words *I do*. The preacher had me and Calvin say I will instead.

And then, as though nothing at all had changed, the preacher announced that Calvin and I were now man and wife.

Where were the words *'you may kiss your bride'*?

It seemed the preacher didn't believe in the public display of affection. Hadn't he once stood before the pulpit and once claimed what was between a man and his wife should only be condoned in the privacy of their own home. Okay, so be it.

After the papers that made me legally married were signed, Mom handed me a brown paper bag containing a few of my clothes. "I know you want to be on your way before the weather gets any worse," she said to Calvin. I'll go by the courthouse and put your marriage certificate on file for you."

Calvin nodded without offering to pay the preacher. I doubted he had the money. I'd once heard him talk about stopping at closed gas stations and draining what little gas remained in the lines into his tank. I didn't think that was what a preacher ought to do, but he didn't think it was stealing. To him, it was the act of a man in need of gas when the gas stations were closed.

We were at the door getting ready to leave when Dad did something I hadn't expected. He crossed the room, took me in his arms and gave me a hug. What he did next was even more of a surprise. He slipped a handful of money in my hand.

"This is for you alone in case you need it. Don't let him know you have it," he whispered near my ear.

Dad turned around as though his display of affection embarrassed him and disappeared into the kitchen. I stuck the money in my skirt pocket as discretely as I could. I heard the back door open and knew Dad was headed to the barn. The place he went when he wanted to escape whatever was going on.

~~~~

I sat in the passenger seat of Calvin's beat up rust bucket that had never been Bondoed, sanded, or painted as we drove down the road with him dodging the potholes that had never been filled. I had expected him to say something encouraging to me if not something loving, but he was silent. The expression on his face told me he was in deep thought.

"How much money did he give you?" Were the first words he said to me.

I knew exactly what he was talking about. Calvin had seen Dad give me money even when Dad and I both were being careful. Oh, well. Calvin was my husband now. What was mine was his and what was his was mine. That was how a marriage should work. With a sinking feeling, I reached in my pocket and pulled out the small roll of twenty-dollar bills.

There were five of them. More money than I had ever seen together at one time. I would feel more secure with that amount of money hidden away in case I needed it. Calvin reached out and almost jerked the money out of my hand. It was all I could do not to grab them back. That money was meant for me. Dad made it clear that it was not for Calvin.

Before I could blink twice, Calvin had the money stuck in his far pants pocket where I couldn't reach it if I tried.

"Thank the lord," he said. "I didn't know how I would afford to buy enough gas to get back home. All the gas stations are open this time of day. I was afraid I'd be stopped beside the road until after closing time. I'll be able to buy gas, pay rent I'm behind on, and have the electricity cut back on."

"But it's my money," I objected. I could see using my money to buy gas, but I didn't think he should take my money to pay for what he owned before we were married. Such as that should have been paid by him and his roommate.

"You need to get something straight up front, Ellie. I'm in control of all the money in my household. A husband is the head of the family not the wife. God took a rib from the man to create a helpmate for him. The Bible says a man is the woman's master, and it's time you know that."

I didn't know what to say to his remark. Dad certainly wasn't Mom's master, and I didn't intend for Calvin to be mine. However, I did intend to be the best wife a man ever had. I had always dreamed of having a happily married life and I wasn't going to start out by letting a few words, or a lot of money, ruin that dream for me.

When Calvin stopped for gas, he made me feel a little better by bringing me a five-cent candy bar. I dropped it into my purse.

"Aren't you going to share it with you husband?" Calvin asked as though I was being selfish.

I took it out of my purse and handed it to him. He opened it, took bites so large there was only a small bit left before he handed it back to me. I ate the last bite.

~~~~

A short time later, Calvin started talking.

"A man and a woman had just gotten married. They were riding in a wagon pulled by two horses. One of the horses balked and refused to move. He did it best to get it moving, but it refused. *'That's one warning,'* he said and tried again with no luck. *'That's two warnings,'* he said and tried again. The horse didn't move. *'That's three warnings'* he said, pulled out a gun and shot the horse dead. 'What have you done?' demanded the wife. You've killed a perfectly good horse that you needed.' The husband turned to her and said, *'That's one warning.'*

"That's a horrible story," I told him.

"It's one every wife needs to hear."

I gritted my teeth and said no more. I didn't want to argue with Calvin. Wedding days were supposed to be special.

Hours later Calvin pulled in beside a building and stopped his rust bucket.

I had no idea what kind of place Calvin and his roommate had been sharing. Admittedly, I was surprised along with being disappointed. It was a two-room shack with gritty tarpaper siding. It was getting close to five o'clock when we arrived, but it was still daylight enough for me to see how rundown the place was.

I got out of the car and walked the short distance to the only door. I stopped, expecting Calvin to pick me up in his arm to carry me over the threshold.

"It's not locked," he said. "Open the door and go inside."

So much for my romantic expectations. I opened the door and went inside.

In one room was a gas range, a chipped and rusted sink that was once white, and a broken-down couch pushed against one wall. The bedroom had an uncomfortable looking bed and a dresser with drawers that didn't close properly. At least there was a bathroom of sorts with a bucket sitting beside the commode.

"You have to catch water in the bucket to flush it," he told me when he saw me looking at the bucket. "Don't turn your nose up like you're doing. We'll rent a better place after you go to work and can help me pay for it."

The way he said that sounded like he thought I was a snob. To be honest, he might be right. Mom always tried to live as good and anybody else, if not a little better, and I had come to think anyone who lived in a place like this was a no-account who was too lazy to work and do better.

"Where can I get a job?" I said more to myself than to him.

"There's a restaurant near where I go to college. They're always looking for dishwashers. I checked with her a few days ago. The woman who owns it will hire you and pay you under the table. I'll take you by tomorrow. Lots of people eat there after church on Sunday. They leave fairly good tips."

Just what I wanted to hear on my wedding day. My husband had already lined up a job for me. "What does pay under the table mean?" I asked.

"They won't be taking anything out for the government. I heard that dishwashers there don't last long enough to go through all the paperwork. I expect you to be an exception. Washing dishes is something even you can do."

I didn't argue or ask another question. I was expecting Calvin to take me in his arms, carry me to the broken-down bed and make wild passionate love to me the way newly-weds did on television.

He didn't.

"There's a broom and mop behind the bathroom door. You ought to clean up this place a little. Make it look more like a home while I go to the store and buy something for you to cook for dinner. I'm hungry."

I felt like crying as Calvin got in the car and left me behind. Nothing was the way I had expected it to be. I sank on the broke-down couch and cried until I was ashamed of how disappointed I was in the day I had dreamed about since I was a little girl. I tried to tell myself life was different than fairy tales young girls fantasized about, but it didn't ease the hurt I was feeling.

It seemed bad was headed toward worse when the sun set, and the shack got dark. Calvin had been gone a long time. I reached for the light switch so I could see how to clean the place up better. There was no electricity.

By the time Calvin returned, it was pitch black inside the house and dark outside.

"Why haven't you lit the candle?"

"I didn't know there was one," I told him.

"It's in the drawer along with the matches."

How was I to know what was in the drawer? I hadn't gone through the drawers. He sat a brown paper bag on the rickety table and opened the only cabinet drawer. He sat the candle that was stuck in a cup on the table and struck a match to it. It gave off enough light for me to see the bag contained a box of cereal and a quart of milk.

"This is all you bought?" I found myself saying.

"We don't have electricity. The refrigerator doesn't work. Besides, you'll be able to bring home leftovers from the restaurant Monday.

After we finished eating bowls of cereal by candlelight, Calvin picked up the cup with the candle in it and went into the bedroom.

"Bedtime," he said. "You want to use the bathroom first, or do I?"

"Go ahead I told him. I'll turn down the bed."

There was a sheet on the bed, a threadbare quilt and two pillows. I wondered if he and his roommate slept in the same bed being there was only one. When he came out of the bathroom wearing only his boxer shorts, I tried not to look directly at him – not that the candle gave off enough light to see more than his shadow.

"Did you and your roommate share the same bed?" I found myself asking.

"No," he was quick to say.

"There's only one bed," I pointed out.

"We had bunk beds for a while. The landlord asked if I wanted to exchange them for this bed since I would be the only one staying here. Your turn for the bathroom."

If I was disappointed in the shack of a place, I was even more disappointed in my wedding night. He kissed me a few times, took off the petticoat I was wearing as a nightgown along with his underwear, and rolled on top of me. A moment later I felt his man part poking at my inner thigh. He reached down, felt around a little, and then guided himself into me with his hand. I expected him to give one good hunch like a bull did to a cow, but he hunched in and out a half dozen times before he let out a groan, lay still for a minute, and then rolled off me. A few moments later he was snoring.

I lay there not knowing what to do or think. Much to my surprise, I felt tears slide down my cheek to soak into the worn-out pillow.

~~~~

I was surprised to discover I didn't mind washing dishes even when I realized the staff were doing their best to make me do all the clean-up work, especially the breakfast to lunch staff. The two worst slackers were Marie and Judith. They didn't appear to take their jobs serious, although it was evident, they needed the job the same as I did. The work wasn't a whole lot different than what I did at home. At least I was being paid even if it was only minimum wages for a lowly dishwasher. Calvin was wrong. I got no tips.

I listened to the waitresses talk even when I found a lot of what they said embarrassing. It was evident they had lived through a lot more experiences than I had.

The way they talked about men surprised me. I had been raised by a religious mother who pounded into my head that what went on between a man and a woman was never talked about. No decent woman would ever utter the word sex much less talk about the act.

Not so in this restaurant.

The size, shape and performance of a man was discussed with vivid descriptions along with obvious delight at my embarrassment.

"I got a look at that would-be preacher when he came in to ask Iva Lee about hiring you. Let us in on what kind of junk that preacher husband of yours has," Marie, the mouthy waitress with flaming red hair that came out of a bottle, said to me.

"Junk?" I questioned. One thing was for sure, his car was filled with a lot of junk.

"Don't play dumb, Ellie. You know I'm asking if he's well hung. Some men's junk is so big it hurts too much to enjoy, while other's junk is so small you don't hardly know when he's got it inside you."

I was taken back, not as much by the question, but by what she was saying. It never occurred to me that men's junk came in different sizes.

"You do know the four words men hate to hear, don't you?" Marie, the red-haired loudmouth, asked me.

I shook my head.

"Is it in yet?" she chuckled out her amusement at her own joke.

"Don't pay any attention to Marie," Judith, the dark-haired loudmouth said. "She's well known for being an expert at holding her liquor."

I didn't have a comment.

"You want to know how Marie holds her liquor?"

I still didn't comment.

"She holds him by the ears," Judith roared with laughter.

"Ah, Judith, you and Marie leave her alone. It's obvious she's not been around the block and down in the gutters the way you two have. You're corrupting the innocent," Iva Lee, the cook and owner who happened to be listening to the waitresses, told them.

"Yea, yea, it's obvious she's a young thing who hasn't even stepped on the block yet much less been around it. It's our duty as her co-workers to help educate her. Evidently, her preacher of a husband hasn't been doing his job right or she wouldn't be so naïve about the fun side of marriage."

"Ask me, he's trying to keep her that way," Judith said.

"He's wise in that," Marie had to put in. "What she doesn't know about, won't be missed."

Iva Lee gave them a look that silenced them momentarily.

"I heard he's going to college to become a minister. Is that right?" Iva Lee asked me.

"That's right. He'll be through with the seminar this fall."

"Will you leave here then? We'll miss having someone as naïve as you to keep us entertained," Judith, the know-it-all with dyed black hair, got her two-cents worth in.

I could only shrug. I had no idea where Calvin would find a church. He never shared his plans with me. It was almost as though he didn't consider me as being a part of his life. He acted as though my role in this marriage was to serve and obey.

"Are you on the pill?" Marie wanted to know. "Some preachers don't believe in taking the pill, but I sure do. I don't intent to go forth and populate the earth with a bunch of snotty nosed brats."

I didn't approve of the way Marie talked about children. Didn't she realize babies were a gift from God? I was on the pill all right. Calvin saw to that. The trip to the health department came before the job and the electric company. It was obvious he didn't want a baby at this time.

"Calvin doesn't want children until we have a place of our own and can afford for me to quit working."

Both Marie and Judith laughed as though what I said was funny.

"Dream on, honey, Judith told me. "If you think you're tied down to a husband, just wait until you have children. Your life won't be your own again until old age has set in and crippled you up so bad you can't even enjoy a good screw."

"Even if you might be able to spread 'em when you get old," Marie added. "He won't be able to do anything about it."

"You've heard about a man being too old to cut the mustard, haven't you?" Judith asked.

I didn't know how to answer that, but she continued.

"If you're lucky, he'll still be willing to lick the jar," she added with a roaring laugh.

"You two shut those filthy mouths and get back to work. There're customers out front," Iva Lee told them. "You can further educate Ellie about the doldrums of your boring lives on your own time."

The two waitresses didn't pay much attention to Iva Lee, even though she was their boss. Iva Lee was a lot older than those two, plus a lot easier going and without the foul mouth both Marie and Judith had. Still, they slowly went back to work, but I knew they would continue picking on me every chance they got. At least it appeared they were doing it for their own amusement instead of malice. I simply had to buck up and learn to tease them back if it were possible?

"Don't let them upset you," Iva Lee told me after they were out of ear shot. Those two good-ole-gals actually have hearts of gold – if you can dig deep enough through all their crap to find their hearts."

"Their picking doesn't bother me," I told her what I hoped was true even when it did bother me somewhat. I'd never come into contact with such talk before, even on the school bus.

As time passed on, I learned not to respond shockingly to what they came up with. Actually, I found their vulgar rantings rather educational about the side of life I knew nothing about. They came up with things I didn't know existed. Like Judith's description of oral sex, and Marie describing what she called butt-fucking. Judith also talked about gays and lesbians. Something else I didn't know existed until I was cleaning a table when a clean-cut blond man came in. His hair was so blond I didn't think it could possibly be the real color, but surely a man had too much pride to his bleach his hair. Folks back home would never stop laughing at a man doing such as that. His clothes were pressed to perfection, and I couldn't help but notice that his hands were softer looking than Calvin's. But then, I was used to the stained, callused hands of Dad and the men back home. I found myself often comparing Calvin to Dad as well as other men. It seemed to me the men back home were much tougher and worked a lot harder than Calvin. Even Boyd and Drake Lewis were willing to get their hands dirtied up with work.

Marie was his waitress and made sure she flirted with him more than she usually did with men. He took her teasing in stride, ordered a salad with avocado and stuffed olives. Afterwards, leaving her the exact amount of tip. Tipping was something else I didn't know existed until Calvin mentioned it, and I started working here.

"How did you like the looks of Teddy Green?" Marie asked me when I sunk his dirty dishes into the wash water. "You might want to pour some bleach in there just in case he has aids."

"What's aids?" I asked.

"Good grief. You really are a naïve babe-in-the-woods, aren't you? Aids is what men get from butt-fucking each other."

I think my mouth must have dropped open, but I certainly wasn't going to ask her any more questions. I made a point of turning my back on her quickly.

"I don't know for certain he's gay, but I'd say he'd hold a dick in his mouth until the swelling went down." I heard her say as she walked away chuckling at her own brand of humor.

I could feel Iva Lee looking at me. She let out a tired sigh. "Marie has a way of calling things the way she sees them. She's had a hard life and copes by pretending to be a hard woman. She makes a point of talking vulgar to hide the fact that life has hurt her far too many times. We have to ignore and forgive unhappy women like her."

I suppose Iva Lee was right, but it didn't alter the fact that Marie's vulgar talk was way over the limit. I thought, as the boss, Iva Lee should put her foot down on Marie's and Judith's vulgarity, and yet she didn't.

"Is what she said true? About aids and men?" I couldn't keep myself from asking.

"I'm afraid it is. Men who lay with other men are known as gays. Women who lay with other women are called lesbians," she told me as though she was informing a child of something unpleasant because she thought that child should know the truth.

"I don't like listening to Marie's and Judith's vulgar talk," I managed to say.

"I don't either, honey, but you'll find there are a lot of things in this life you won't like listening to but is a real fact. Both Judith and Marie like the shock-effect of vulgarity. All the advice I can give you on such things is to get used to it. Such knowledge might come in handy at some time or other. Let what they say flow over you like water poured on a duck's back without ever taking offense. It's about their life, not yours."

I chose not to tell Calvin about the way those two waitresses talked. I didn't think a preacher would approve of me working with such people. One thing was for certain, without what little I earned the rent wouldn't be paid, the lights wouldn't be on, and the car wouldn't have enough gas to get us back and forth from college and work, not to mention the expenses of Calvin's education. Thank goodness I got to take leftovers home for us to eat. I wasn't earning enough money to buy food.

"You need to work extra hours on Sunday as a waitress," Calvin told me one night when he picked me up. "You're not bringing in enough money."

"When do you think you'll be able to find your own church?"

"Soon, I hope. It's not as easy as you think."

With Calvin, nothing came easy, the thought came to me, but I sure didn't say anything. He had a way of blaming his every failure on me.

"In the morning ask if you can waitress a few hours on Sundays," he told me firmly. You need to earn your keep around here.

~~~~

Iva Lee agreed to give me two hours of waitressing on Sundays and another two hours on Friday nights as long as I managed to keep up with the dishwashing at the same time. I wasn't much good at being a waitress at first, but I learned to be good enough to get by.

Calvin was right about church goers coming to eat after church. Thing he wasn't right about was the tips. Church goers were notoriously stingy. They seldom left more than a dollar tip for a table of four. Those with small children almost never left a tip.

The Friday night dinners were a little better. The best tippers were men who were eating after some sort of meetings or outing. Home ball games were great income makers. Women were the worse tippers. Not only were they stingy with a dime, but they were also critical and demanding their food be just so so. They expected a waitress to be right there the moment they needed something, but absent when they were gossiping about someone.

One man came in every Friday night and made sure he sat at my table. He always left a whooping two-dollar tip, which was almost as much as his meal cost. He was nice and friendly, while being slightly reserved. His name was Don. He was about fifteen or twenty years older than me. A nice, clean-cut kind of man.

"You're new here, aren't you?" he asked the first night I waited on him.

"I've been here a while. I've always been the dishwasher."

"Working your way up?" he asked with a slight grin. I didn't know if it was friendly talk or if it was slightly insulting toward being a waitress.

"Dishwashing doesn't pay much. I'm hoping waitressing will pay a little more."

I saw and felt his eyes look from my face all the way down to my shoes. He pretended to be looking at the menu. I knew he saw how runover and worn my clothes were under the restaurant jacket Iva Lee provided for me until the uniforms she had finally ordered for me arrived. She wasn't going to waste money on buying uniforms until she saw that I was going to be working for a long time. There was no way he could not see how poor I really was.

"Working your way through high school?" he asked.

"No, I'm married. May I take your order? I was here to wait on him, not tell him my life story.

"I'll take the hamburger steak with mushrooms and onion gravy. A baked potato with sour cream and carrots."

The carrots surprised me.

"Coffee with cream and a glass of water," he added.

When I returned with his order he asked: "What's your husband's name, Ellie?"

I was surprised he knew my name until I realized I was wearing a name tag Iva Lee had written my name on.

"Calvin," I told him.

"Calvin what?"

"West. Is there anything else I can get you?"

I thought I saw a slight frown on his face. "Not at this time. You can refill my coffee cup when you get the time. No hurry though."

I took an order from another table and then went in the back for a fresh pot of coffee.

"Seems Don has taken and interest in you," Iva Lee said as I filled the coffee carafe. There're not many people he takes a shine to."

"He asked a lot of personal questions."

"He likes to flirt with the pretty girls. Be nice, but not too friendly and you'll get better tips," she advised.

I thought I was always nice, but I didn't point that out.

"He's not entirely harmless. No man is. Not even the gay ones."

"Is he one of those kind?" I asked.

"No, I don't think him being such as that has ever occurred to him," she said with a little chuckle.

I wasn't sure what she meant by that, so I didn't respond.

"Some men know the right way of setting a young girl up to trust them. It goes back to the cave man days when there were hunters and gathers. The hunter would stalk a woman when she went out to gather. When her guard was down, he pounced."

I wasn't sure what she meant by that, either. "Are you trying to tell me something?"

"I'm just saying when a girl is as pretty and naïve as you are, don't take anything a man says seriously. Men are always interested in sex. It's in their nature."

"It's not in my nature," I assured her.

She grinned as though I didn't know what I was talking about. One thing was for sure, I was a married woman who believed in the sanctity of marriage. There would be no way I'd ever commit adultery, and neither would Calvin. Even if he wasn't a minister. He'd told me often how important it was to be a virgin before marriage. He admitted he wouldn't have married me if I hadn't been. He claimed a man should divorce his wife immediately if she ever committed adultery.

Chapter 6

I can't describe how happy I was when Calvin was through with the seminar and ready to find his very own church to preside over. Finally, he could be the one bringing in money. Soon, we might even be able to have the baby I dreamed about having. I hadn't been able to go back home to see the little boy Mom had given birth to. When I knew it was past time for Mom to give birth, I had made a point of calling to make sure she and the baby were okay. After all, Mom wasn't a young woman. She was in her thirties.

Dad surprised me when he was the one who answered the phone. At the sound of his voice, tears came to my eyes. Not because I feared something bad had happened to Mom or the baby, but because of the sudden bout of homesickness that took hold of me. Until that moment I hadn't realized my very being was longing to return to the only place I had known as home.

"Is Mom okay?" I had asked.

"She had the baby yesterday," he told me. "She and the baby are doing good."

"Is she there?" I asked, although I didn't particularly want to talk to her.

"Oh, no. She didn't have this baby at home the way she did with Grant and you. We didn't want to take a chance considering how much this baby meant to her."

Again, a stab of pain hit me. Maybe it was caused by jealousy from knowing Mom didn't consider me as important as this baby, but then Grant had been born at home the same as I was. I know how much Grant meant to Mom and Dad both.

"I would love to see the baby," I heard myself saying as though there might be a possibility of me going home.

"He's a fine, fine-looking boy. Weighed in at eight and a half pounds. Katie is so protective over that baby she hasn't let him out of her arms since he was born. The doctor has to fight to check him. She gets mad when a nurse steps into the hospital room. She hasn't allowed me to do more than look at him."

I knew he was telling me Mom wouldn't want me to see the baby even if there was a way I could go back home, which there wasn't. I doubt Calvin would be willing to go from gas station to gas station to drain the gas from the pumps now that he considered himself a minister of God.

"What did she name him?" I asked.

"Grant," he said. "She named him Grant. It was good talkin' to you," he added as though his words were a dismissal. "No need to worry or call back for a while. Phone calls are expensive."

"Okay," I said. "Bye." I held the receiver for a few moments before I eased the pay phone back in its cradle. I wondered how old my new baby brother would be before I would ever get to see him. I missed having a family to belong to more than I ever thought possible. I didn't like feeling all alone in a place where I didn't belong. The only people I knew were the people I worked with. Of course, there was Calvin, but I saw less of him than I did my co-workers. After his classes, he had to study at the college library during the time I was working. He and I both were exhausted by the time he picked me up at night. Considering the hours I worked, I was allowed two meals per day. I ate lunch and saved the supper meal to take home at night for Calvin. He ate hardily and then fell right to sleep. I found that I had lost weight, plus I was always exhausted, especially when I had to wash our clothes in the sink and hope they might dry by morning.

~~~~

That phone call home had been several months ago, and I hadn't called back. I knew Dad, Mom and the new baby Grant were getting along just fine without me. That thought hurt. I still wanted to be a part of my parents' lives. I wanted them to still be my family.

As for Calvin, he was finally one happy man. He had been notified the availability of having his own church and his own congregation. He agreed to take it on with unbridled happiness. He was taking the job to heart by telling me how responsible he felt for each and every church member.

"I'm not being paid much, but they are people in need of me. They are the poorest of the poor. God chose me to lift them up and make their lives better. You don't have time to gawk at the church," he told me when I asked to see the church he had taken on. Not only that, but the housing they provided for their minister was a dilapidated mobile home.

"Don't turn your nose up like that," he told me as I looked at the old trailer he referred to as a mobile home. "You're not too good to live in a mobile home. Besides, it comes free of rent."

It was obvious why it was free of rent.

I wasn't too good to live in such a place. I simply wasn't a good enough miracle worker to make it presentable, especially when I had no money. All I could manage was a gallon of bleach and a rag to tackle all the mold that covered every inch of the place. Even the commode lid was molded. The inside of the commode was worse. It appeared to have been clogged up for years."

"How long has it been since this place was lived in?" I asked Calvin.

"Don't know. The last minister had his own place."

I could understand the reason for that.

"At least this place is free," he repeated.

I had once thought I would stop being a dishwasher once Calvin got a church, but Calvin certainly didn't want me to stop working. He said we needed the extra money if we were to ever get ahead. I had considered not having to live in the sorry little rental he and his roommate once shared as getting ahead. I recalled the time I stayed awake one night after work scrubbing the little rental and packing the few items that belonged to Calvin. Oddly enough I found a delicate looking, not so clean, handkerchief on the floor behind the bed when I moved it to clean. I asked Calvin about it.

He shrugged as though the question was useless, but he answered. "Probably belong to the owner's wife or someone who rented the place before me. This place never got cleaned often. You aren't the best housekeeper, you know."

I figured he was probably right, but there was still the smell of perfume lingering on the handkerchief. The owner's wife or whoever had some mighty strong perfume to linger this long on a dirty handkerchief.

He changed the subject by saying, "You'll be able to ride the bus from the mobile home to the restaurant. The bus picks up and drops off not that far from there," he told me. "Most likely you'll never be able to get a different job anywhere else. You're not qualified for high paying jobs. After I get a better church and start earning more money, you can quit work and start being the kind of minister's wife I should have," he added as though I'd been failing him as a wife. "Actually, instead of being ashamed of your lack of education, it would be a benefit to us both if you went to night school. Should be easy enough being you work next to the college. They have special programs for people who lack a good education.

Most of the congregation who attend my new church are well educated even though they are poverty stricken. It would be a bad reflection on me to have the congregation find out I have a wife who didn't finish high school. They would think I couldn't do better. It's obvious not one person of higher intelligence ever came out of that mountain hollow. Your parents didn't even know how to speak correct English, nor did anyone else in that area. Thankfully, you can learn how to use correct language while getting your GED."

If his words could kill, I would have been a goner. I hadn't realized that he was ashamed of me, and it hit hard. I had worked all three meals a day at the restaurant. From six o'clock in the morning until eleven o'clock each night seven day a week to support him while he got his college education. Now he said he was ashamed of me, and that I wasn't fit to be the wife of a minister of a rundown church.

The next day after lunch was over, I asked Iva Lee if it would be okay for me to take a little time off to go by the college to check on the GED program."

"What's that husband of yours got you into this time?" she asked.

Her comment puzzled me, but I decided it was just the way she talked. "Calvin thinks I need to get my GED now that he's minister of his own church. I don't have to work as many hours now that he's earning a salary," I added to let her know we weren't as desperate for money as we once were, which wasn't exactly true. Calvin had told me he now had to start paying back the student loans he'd borrowed for his education.

Iva Lee gave me one of her knowing looks. "Sounds like a good idea to me. Take as much time as you need. I'm one who believes in being educated – regardless of what kind of education it is that one might get."

I discovered I could go to night classes three times a week from seven o'clock to nine o'clock or I could go two times a week from seven until eleven. I wasn't sure Iva Lee would agree to three nights a week. I was right.

"Three nights a week doesn't seem good to me. Not when you can go two nights and get the same education for staying a little longer. It will save you travel time, plus you get to earn more money washing dishes."

I kept enough money out of my pay for classes before giving all the rest to Calvin and signed up for two nights a week. The instructor's name was Bret Grason.

When Calvin counted the money I gave him, his teeth clenched for a few moments before he spoke. "Where's the rest of the money?"

"I had to pay for GED classes," I told him.

"Then you'll have to cut down on what you spend to make up for it. I still have bills to pay, while you'll be working fewer hours."

How would I be able to cut down on spending? All I was spending anything on was bus fare now that classes were paid for. I couldn't walk that far to work and to class. Bus fare cost less than it had for gas needed to drive Calvin to and from college. I didn't know why he was complaining. He was the one who suggested I get a better education.

"You're making money now. Surely, you'll be able to make enough income for the time I take off for classes," I told him.

"This church pays their minister less than any other church. As I told you earlier, most of the members are poverty stricken. It'll be a while before I find another church where I'm paid enough to live on. Besides, I'll need decent clothes fitting for a minister, plus a vehicle that's not an embarrassment to drive."

Most of the church members were poverty stricken and yet he needed clothes along with a vehicle that wasn't an embarrassment. What happened to all those well-educated members who would look down on me because I wasn't well educated?

Chapter 7

I was both excited and a bundle of nerves when I headed to classes Tuesday after work. I clamped my teeth together and tried to pretend I not only knew what I was doing, but that I knew where I was going. Calvin had made a point of telling me I would find learning difficult since I had spent my entire childhood lacking the proper stimuli for advanced learning. He said children needed an educational base to build on, which I didn't have.

"A child needs to be subjected to the process of being educated early on when the brain is capable of learning. Unfortunately, where you were raised, had the poorest educational system in existence. But then, it's well documented it is a waste of time and effort to attempt to educate those who don't have the capacity to learn."

"Are you saying I can't learn?" I asked, both puzzled and hurt by what he'd said.

"I'm sure you can learn enough to get your GED if you put your mind to it and study really hard. I'll even be willing to help you with your lessons if I can find the time. You do realize how busy I am. I have an entire congregation to consider. From now on, I'll owe my time to the church congregation."

I was recalling what Cavin had said as I walked down a long hall looking at the numbers on doors when I heard a man's voice say, "Are you lost?"

I jumped and looked behind me to see a man coming out of an open door. He was slightly above normal height with wavy brown hair and a good tan on his face and hands. He was wearing a dress shirt, blue jeans and fancy cowboy boots, which seemed to me at odds with his dress shirt. He wasn't exactly knock-dead gorgeous, but he was better looking than average in a rugged sort of way. There was something about his eyes that drew me in and held me for a moment. It wasn't exactly a sadness but more of an understanding of what life could deny a person.

"Actually, I'm looking for the room where the GED classes are held," I told him.

"I see," he said. "Do you realize you are a good twenty minutes early before any classes start?"

"Blame it on the transportation," I told him. "I can arrive early, or I can arrive late depending on which bus I take."

"Where are you catching a bus from?"

"Good Eats," I told him the name of the restaurant. "I work there. Iva Lee is letting me take time off to get my GED." I told him.

"Good for your parents," he said right out of the blue.

"What?" I questioned.

"I commend parents who encourage their children to work their way through school," he said as he took in my shabby, well-worn clothes and runover shoes with both big toes sticking through. It was obvious I needed to work.

"I'm married," I informed him once I figured out what he meant.

He nodded in surprise, and then grinned slightly. "Sorry about that. I'm married too. Come with me and I'll show you where the classroom is. I usually get here early. That way I get the best parking place."

I followed him making a point of looking him over the way I thought he had done to me. It was obvious he was well-off enough to afford almost new clothes and those fancy boots. It was also obvious that his wife kept his clothes spotless and ironed to perfection. Even his cowboy boots were polished to a shine. I reminded myself that I needed to make sure I paid extra attention to Calvin's clothes. I wanted to be the best wife in existence. It was plain to see his wife did a better job than I did. Thinking of clothes and wifely duties helped ease my anxiety a little.

But not for long.

Even the room he took me to, had a way of overwhelming me. It was cold and pristine. Nothing at all like the small, comfortable classrooms where I attended school. This was a place for those Calvin referred to as the privileged.

I knew I would be the poorest and least intelligent person there, and I was proved right as other students came into the room. Their clothes looked new and expensive. Their big toes were not sticking through their shoes. There ended up being four boys and five girls, not including me. They appeared to be so young and innocent they made me think of a song some of the women back home were fond of singing about the difference between a single girl and a married girl. I sat in a back seat and looked at the five other girls who were giggling and talking together as though they were the best of friends. I ran the songs' lyrics through my mind as I thought of the difference between them and me.

Single girl, single girl
She's going dressed so fine
Oh, she's going dressed so fine
Married girl, married girl
She wears just any kind
Oh, she wears just any kind
Single girl, single girl
She goes to the store and buys
Oh, she goes to store and buys
Married girl, married girl
She rocks the cradle and cries
Oh, she rocks the cradle and cries
Single girl, single girl
She's going just where she please
Oh, she's going where she please
Married girl, married girl

Baby on her knees
Oh, baby on her knees

Suddenly it hit me. I hadn't had my period in a long while.

I almost forgot that I should have periods when the man who had shown me to the classroom came through the door and took a seat at the metal and leather teacher's desk. I stared at him, but he paid no more attention to me than he did the other students.

"I assume everyone is here that is taking this class, so we'll get started. My name is Bret Grason." He took a piece of paper out of his briefcase. "When I read off your name, say present."

He called names in alphabetical order. One boy, John Grieves, didn't answer. Bret called his name again. When he didn't answer he went on down the list. West came last. "Here," I said barely loud enough for him to hear me. I didn't want anyone to look at me if I could help it.

Five minutes later, while Bret Grason was going over the syllabus, a young man walked in, glanced about the room, gave Bret Grason a half-handed solute, and came to sit next to me. Mr. Grason paid no attention to him.

"Hello, pretty girl. I'm John," he said.

At the sound of his voice Mr. Grason did look up. "If there is anyone who has trouble remaining silent in my class, you're welcome to leave now," he said in a voice so low and gentle that it put a chill up my spine.

John rolled his eyes, and shrugged his skinny shoulders, but surprisingly, he was silent the rest of the class.

"I'll walk you to your car. I could use a ride," John said as he got up from his seat after class was over. Before I could answer, Mr. Grason spoke to me.

"Mrs. West, I need to speak to you for a few minutes."

John shrugged his shoulders again and headed out the door. I went to the front of the room.

"I realize I have given everyone a long list of books to buy in order to get their GED. As being the only student who is not being financed by their parents, I thought I would give you first choice at the secondhand books I happen to have."

He couldn't imagine how glad I was to hear what he'd just said. I had no idea how I would be able to afford to buy the books I needed from the college bookstore. The price of each book was staggering. For some reason, it hadn't occurred to me that I would need to buy books until he gave us the list, which was stupid of me. Calvin had used part of my earnings to pay for his books. They cost more than the rent. I wondered what he had done with all those books. He must have packed them in boxes when we moved.

"Okay. How much are they?"

"Ten dollars to rent them. You'll have to give them back when the classes are over so another student can use them."

"I don't have the cash with me right now," I told him.

"That's okay. You can pay it all at one time or a little at each class."

"Thank you," I told him.

"You're welcome. Where do you live? I can drop you off and save you bus fare if it's on my way home."

I wasn't sure how Calvin would take me having a man drop me off, but if it was to save the bus fare, I thought he would agree. I had to catch a bus from here to the restaurant, and then a different one from the restaurant home. I didn't like the idea of waiting on the bus if the restaurant was closed, which it might be if there were no late customers. Plus, I would save two bus fares. I told him the spot where the bus dropped me off not too far from the trailer.

"No problem. It's on my way home."

"Thank you," I told him, but I couldn't help feeling self-conscious. It hurt my pride for anyone to know I couldn't afford the things I needed even when I was working seven days and five nights a week.

He picked up his briefcase, held the door for me to go out, clicked off the light to the room and closed the door. We walked down the hall together, our feet making slight sounds on the tile. I felt as out of place as a June bug in a duck lot.

"I've had John Grieves in two other classes. He's a difficult student, hardheaded and determined to go against the rules. He takes advantage of anyone he can. I warn students to steer clear of him. To never let him get them in a compromising position, especially the girls."

His statement didn't surprise me in the least. I'd known boys who were like John Grieves. I tried my best to ignore them back then, and I supposed I could ignore John Grieves too. What I didn't know how to do was comment on what Mr. Grason said.

"He seems rather arrogant. I think he was late intentionally to see what you would do," I finally told him.

"You've already pin-pointed him. Might want to let him know you have a very jealous husband," he said with a grin.

"My husband is a minister," I told him. "I don't think the word jealous is even in his vocabulary, at least not where I'm concerned."

"Minister? What is his name?"

"Calvin West."

He seemed puzzled for a few moments as he gave me a closer look.

"I had a young man by that name in one of my classes some time ago, but I don't think it could be the same person. He didn't seem like the minister type."

I followed Mr. Grason down the halls and out of the building. There were only a few cars left in the parking lot. The bus I was supposed to catch had arrived a few minutes before and had its door open. John Grieves got on the bus.

"Is that the bus you're supposed to catch?" he asked me.

"Yes."

"Umm," he kind of grunted. "I'm glad you're riding with me."

The way he said that made me leery of John Grieves.

Fifteen minutes later, Mr. Grason stopped at the bus stop near the mobile home. It was almost forty-five minutes earlier than I would have gotten home if I'd rode the bus back to the restaurant and then caught another bus home.

"Thank you," I told him as I reached for the door. "See you Thursday," I said.

"You're getting off here?" he questioned. "Where is your house?"

"Around the corner."

"Close the door. I'll drop you off up there. This is the rough side of town. It's not safe for a girl to be walking around here after dark."

"I walk by myself all the time since Calvin became the minister of the church. I catch the bus to the restaurant from here and then back from the restaurant every night about this time. It's a lot better place than where we lived before."

"Where was that?"

I told him to see his eyebrows raise slightly.

"Were you raised in that neighborhood?"

"No." I told him where I was from and went on to explain. "Calvin lived there with a roommate before we were married. His roommate moved out, but Calvin stayed there until he got to be minister of this church."

"From now on, I'll drop you off when you're in my class. I feel responsible for the safety of my students. I might even be able to give you a ride from the restaurant on the nights I teach college classes."

I didn't argue. I did think about the nine other students. Did he feel responsible for them as well?

I used my key to unlock the trailer door and go inside. All the lights were out, and I could hear Calvin's snoring coming from the bedroom. I was careful not to wake him up as I took off my clothes and got in bed. I didn't want him to know how early I was, or why.

~~~~

Most everyone I met were different than the people I had grown up with. Even Judith and Marie were different in their own vulgar way. People in this town appeared to be in such a rush to get somewhere. Others seemed to want to get hold of something that was out of their reach, be it money, prestige, or happiness. No one appeared to be thankful for what they had. Folks back home were thankful for every single thing God granted them – at least for the good things.

Neither Marie nor Judith seemed to have one single smidgin of thankfulness for the job they had or the nice cars they drove to work. Part of me wanted to know more about them, while the other part wanted to stay as far from them as possible. They picked on me even harder after finding out that Iva Lee was letting me off two nights a week to take classes at the college to get my GED.

"Trying to get above your raising in life, I see," Judith said to me.

"Before you know it, she'll get too uppity to wash dishes," Marie added.

"I don't know how you two were raised, but I see that being waitresses isn't above your raisings," I told them sweetly.

"Atta girl," Iva Lee hollered and then roared with laughter coming from in the kitchen. I was beginning to think she had ears that could hear a whisper from out on the street.

"Smart mouth," Marie said to me. Judith acted insulted. I thought it good enough for both of them to get a taste of their own medicine. They could sure dish it out where I was concerned. It was time I fed them some of the same back.

~~~~

I studied hard, determined not to be the stupidest person in the class, but I couldn't shake feeling that I was, and so did Calvin.

"Don't feel so bad about lacking intelligence. No one expects you to know much considering where you came from," he told me in his gentle tone of voice he used when he didn't want to hurt my feelings.

"No one knows where I come from," I said in self-defense.

"Sure, they do. Have you ever listened to the way you talk? Not everyone loves your Hicksville accent the way I do." He put his arms around me and hugged me close a moment before he took his glasses off. Removing his glasses spoke louder than words as to what he had in mind. One thing was for sure, Calvin loved having sex. He could enjoy it two or three times a day. It didn't take up much time, he was on an off like the proverbial rabbit. Most of the time he was snoring a minute after he rolled off me. It didn't matter if we were in bed, or if the mood struck him when I was coming in the door from work, or in his rattle trap driving home for his classes. I always gave in to him like a good wife was supposed to do. I didn't argue even when I was very uncomfortable with the situation.

I think it was one of those times when neither of us had the money to buy the protection we needed.

Calvin showed no emotion whatsoever when I told him. Instead, he said, "It shouldn't stop you from working at the restaurant until it's born, then you'll have to stay home. You don't earn enough money to pay for childcare. So, you'll have to earn a lot of money before then. You can still take classes since you had to pay for them in advance. You best not let anyone know about your condition. Pregnant women are looked down on as a liability and an embarrassment."

I didn't understand what he was telling me. How could a pregnant woman be looked down on? How could she be a liability or an embarrassment? No one would exist if there weren't pregnant women?

The first chance I got, I took some of my tip money and went to the pay phone outside the restaurant. I dialed Mom's number needing desperately to tell her that I was expecting. I was both excited and afraid. I didn't know what I expected from Mom, but I needed a kind word, and perhaps a little encouragement.

"Hello," she answered, sounding tired and irritated at having to answer the phone. I could hear a baby crying in the background.

"Hello, Mom," I said."

"Why are you calling?" Mom demanded. "What do you want?"

Those words were exactly what I didn't want to hear. Somehow, I couldn't tell her about my baby or much of anything else.

"No reason. I don't want a thing. I was just thinking about you and Dad and decided to call to see how everyone is doing. How is the baby?"

"I'd be doing a lot better if I didn't have to answer the phone when my baby is hungry. You interrupted his feeding time."

"Oh, I'm sorry. I didn't mean to interrupt anything. Are you all doing okay?" I said, hoping she would ask me the same thing.

"We're fine," she said. "Are you're wanting something from us?" She sounded angry at such a possibility.

How did I tell her I had become so lonely and afraid that I wanted to hear a comforting voice, but it was obvious I wasn't going to get it from Mom.

"I want nothing. How's Dad."

"At the barn like usual. I'm glad you're doing good. I have to take care of my baby if you're through talking."

"Okay," I mumbled. "Tell Dad I called."

"I will. Bye."

I held the phone in my hand for a few more moments as though the disconnected buzzing could give me some sort of comfort, but it didn't. I regretted spending my tips on the phone call. Talking to Mom had made me feel worse. That's what I got for expecting more than I deserved. It was time for me to accept the fact that I was no longer a part of Mom and

Dad's family. I had my own family now. I had a husband and would have a baby of my own in seven or so months. I needed to realize I was no longer a part of my parents' lives. Hadn't I learned that lesson the other time I called and talked to Dad?"

"Who were you calling?" Marie asked as she came up behind me.

"My Mom."

"You've got a mom? I thought you were hatched from a turkey egg that was fertilized by an old rooster."

"Only you and Judith hold that honor," I shot back at her. "Too bad those two eggs hadn't rotted. It would have made this restaurant a more pleasant place to work," I told her as we entered the restaurant.

Iva Lee could be heard cackling at my comment. "You best watch out, Marie. She'll be able to put you and Judith in your places one of these days."

"No way. We've not educated her enough for that yet. She's still a wet-behind-the-ears baby."

"Stop flapping your jaws and take these plates to your table before the food gets cold," Iva Lee told her.

Marie snorted, grabbed the warm plates, and headed into the other room.

"How are your classes going?" Iva Lee asked as though she was actually interested.

"Okay," I told her. "I kind of feel out of place."

"Why would you do that?"

"I never had a very good education to provide me with a background for learning. Calvin says the school I went to was the worst school in the state."

"How would he know?"

"I guess he checked. He loves to quote statistics on things."

"Sounds like he's become a well-educated man on the subject of higher learning."

"He is," I assured her. I was glad I married a highly intelligent man instead of one of the red-neck boys I grew up with. Someone like Drake Lewis. I wanted my children to have one intelligent parent along with a chance of being far better educated than I had been. I wanted the very best for my children.

That night when I got home, Calvin was waiting up for me. "How was work?" he asked.

"A little slow. Not as many customers as usual."

"That's not good."

"It is when it means I don't have as many dishes to wash."

"I've been meaning to talk to you about that."

"About dish washing?" I questioned.

"Waitresses make a lot more money than you do, right?"

"They get less pay an hour, but they usually get enough tips to make more than a dishwasher."

"Then why aren't you making more at being a waitress?"

"Because I only waitress a couple of hours on Sundays, and the after-church crowd doesn't tip good. Plus, I have to wash dishes at the same time. Why do you need more money?" I asked him.

"Because we've got bills to pay plus student loans to pay off. I don't want to get behind. It wouldn't look good on a minister. Besides, you've not got a limited time to work before you have that baby. You need to contribute more to our living expenses before that time comes. The restaurant won't be giving a lowly dishwasher paid maternity leave."

"I thought I had been contributing to our living expenses."

"Not enough. You're not earning as much since you're going to classes twice a week."

That was true, but Calvin was no longer in college. He should be able to make it on his salary without me earning as much as usual. Plus, he was saving a little on gas money since I was riding the bus. I started to point this out but decided it would be best not to.

"You make sure you ask if you can waitress more than you already are. No need for those other women to take home all that money instead of you."

"I'll ask Iva Lee if there's an opening for me to waitress more often than only on Sundays."

"Make sure you do, and don't make excuses and chicken out."

"Why would I chicken out?"

"Just because you can't talk proper to customers doesn't mean you can't carry a plate of food the same as those other women."

I had no response to that, but it did make me feel inferior to those upper-class people who could afford to eat out.

Chapter 8

As soon as I entered the back door of the restaurant, I smelled the bacon Iva Lee was frying and had to make a run for the bathroom. When I came out of the restroom Iva Lee had her back turned to me.

"You're a mite pale. Anything you want to tell me?" she asked without even looking at me.

"No." I remembered what Calvin had said about not letting anyone know the condition I was in.

"Good. You're early. I'm prepping for breakfast. Won't open up for another thirty minutes. Why did you come in early this morning?"

"I wanted to talk to you?"

"Then talk."

"I'm not making as much money since I'm working fewer hours because of school. Could I possible do a little more waitressing to earn more?"

"What do you need more money for?" Iva Lee asked.

"To pay bills with."

"Doesn't that husband of yours make enough to pay bills since he's no longer going to college?"

"He has student loans to pay off."

"So, he's counting on you to pay off the loans he got before you were married?"

"College and seminar were expensive," was all I could think of saying.

"It certainly seems that way," Iva Lee said. "Never been to college myself. Had to work ever since I knee high to a duck."

"Me too," I said.

"What did you work at?"

"In beans. It was the only way most folks had to make money where we lived. We twined pole beans in the spring and picked beans in the fall. Sometimes we hoed weeds out of the rows."

"How did you meet your husband?"

"He came to our church."

"And you fell head-over-heels for him?"

"Not exactly," I mumbled. To be honest, I didn't know what head-over-heels in love would feel like. Once upon a time I had fairytale images of falling in love with my knight in shining armor who came ridding in on a white stallion, but not any longer. Reality had a way of stepping up and taking away fairytales. Calvin was not only my husband. He was my reality, and I was still determined to be the best wife ever.

"Not exactly?" she repeated what I said. "Then why did you marry him when you are still so young? Why not wait until you graduated high school? Chances are you wouldn't be working in a restaurant and going to night classes to get your GED if you'd waited a little while longer."

"Calvin asked Mom if it was okay to marry me and she said yes."

Iva Lee turned to give me a look before she went back to frying bacon she used to crumble in scrambled eggs.

"He didn't get down on bended knee and propose to you?"

"No," I said with a slight chuckle at the thought of Calvin doing something like that.

"Then why did you marry him?"

I didn't want to go into detail about what happened to my brother and the despair that overcame my parents and me. Talking about it brought the horror back. I said the only thing I could think of.

"It seemed like a good idea at the time. I always dreamed of having a husband and a life of my own."

"I see," she said. "*It seemed like a good idea* at time are eight words that leads to most of the problems people have. I've heard them many said times before," she let out a long drawn-out sigh. "Oh, well. I suppose you can pitch in as a waitress on Mondays. Marie and Judith both bitch about having to work on Mondays and Sundays. Monday nights are a slow time. But you'll have time to wash dishes as well. I can get waitresses. I can't get good reliable dishwashers. If you come in an hour early each morning, you can help me prep. Pays the same as dishwashing."

"I have no problem with that," I assured her. Actually, I was doing a lot more dishwashing than I was doing waitressing. The man named Don was the only customer who always asked for me to be his waitress. I was always thankful for his two-dollar tip along with his kind words. It was Don's two-dollar tip that I saved for bus fare to classes and money to pay on books.

The fact that I was working from daylight to midnight seven days a week, except for the two nights I went to class, meant I never got to attend church with Calvin, but he didn't seem to mind, and I didn't either.

"I'm the kind of minister that church needs," he told me. "Once you have the baby, you'll be able to administer to the needy the way a minister's wife should. Until then, you need to concentrate on earning enough to pay off as many of our bills as possible."

I had wanted to scream that I was already earning as much money as I could possibly earn. At least he wasn't insisting I stop taking classes, which surprised me. Here lately he'd seemed more interested in me bringing home money than getting an education.

~~~~

I'd managed to hide three dollars of tips in my shoe from Monday night. It was all the tips I had gotten that night. I got to class early as usual. Instead of going to the classroom, I knocked on Mr. Grason's office door.

"Come in," he called out.

I opened the door and went in, closing the door behind me.

"What can I do for you, Ellie?"

I walked over to where he sat behind his desk and handed him the three dollars. "Payment on the books," I told him.

"Thank you," he said as he took the money. It was all I could do not to jerk my hand away when his fingers touched mine. I didn't seem right for another man to touch my hand, even accidentally. I knew I was being silly, but that was the way I felt.

"How do you like classes so far?" he asked.

"I like them. I'm learning a lot."

"How are you managing with the homework being you work all hours both day and night?"

"Working seven days and five nights a week doesn't give me much time to study. I read when I ride the bus and do the paperwork when I take breaks at the restaurant."

"Does that mean your husband helps out with the cooking, house cleaning, and laundry?"

"Oh, goodness no. Calvin would never do women's work. I do it when I get home at night. I did do some homework early of a morning, but I've started going in to help Iva Lee prep an hour early each morning."

"Who did the women's work for him before he married you?" Mr. Grason asked.

That stumped me. He surely did some women's work back then. Or did he have roommate who did it?

"He had a roommate," I said.

"Male or female?"

"Male of course," I said feeling irritated at the question. How dare he suggest Calvin would have a woman roommate. Calvin would never do something like that. He was a man of God.

"My wife allows me to do my share of women's work around the house. I often do my own laundry, and I can cook enough to survive if the need should ever present itself."

"What does your wife work at?" I assumed she would have a job if he did some of her housework.

"She doesn't have a job per say. She's stays at home. As her husband, I feel it's my job to take care of her needs."

I almost told him I was going to stay at home after my baby was born, but I couldn't tell a strange man something such as that. Folks back home claimed it was sinful to tell a man about a woman's bodily functions and that included pregnancies.

"Come on," he said as he stood up. "I'll walk you to class and check on your homework. I can help you on anything you need help on before class starts. I can also help you after class if you need it," he assured me.

"I don't want to impose."

"You won't be imposing. It's my job to help those who seek to learn, especially when they are as intelligent and worthy as you."

"I'm not intelligent," I said before I caught myself. As for worthy, I wouldn't even comment on that.

"You're the most intelligent student I've had in a long time. I don't see how you manage to keep up while working seven days and five nights a week. Doesn't your husband object to you being away from home that amount of time?"

"Oh, no. It was his idea. He thinks I should work longer hours at the restaurant to make up for the time I'm in school. That's why I started going in an hour early each morning."

He was silent for a few moments, before he stood up, put his hand on my back and guided me to the door. I squirmed a little at his touch. It was all I could do not to jerk away when he was just being a gentleman. Mr. Grason was the most courteous man I'd ever met. I'd never met a man who treated a woman with such respect.

Once class was over, I stayed thirty minutes after class to let him help me with math.

"I'm terrible with math," I told him.

"Don't feel bad. Most women are terrible in math, while most men are terrible in English."

"I like English and Literature."

"I've noticed," he said.

Mr. Grason dropped me off at the trailer and waited to see that I'd gotten safely inside before he drove away. I had tried to get him to let me off at the bus drop off, but he wouldn't hear of it. My pride suffered for him to see where we were living. My only consolation was that it was too dark for him to see its real condition. The trailer was old, rusty, and covered in green mold. If I ever got some time off and extra money, I was going to clean it with bleach. I had mentioned to Calvin that he might consider cleaning it himself. He didn't hesitate to tell me taking care of our living quarters were my responsibilities not his. He informed me again that his responsibility was for the members of his church instead of doing what was my work.

"What about your responsibility to your family?" I asked.

"You're not my family. You're only my wife," he informed me. "Family is relatives. You and I are not related. That makes my parents my family, not you."

That Calvin didn't consider me his family hurt my feelings to the core, but what could I say? I wondered if he would consider our baby as being a part of his family or would it only remain a part of me?

I wanted to know more about his parents since I had never met them. Calvin never talked about them, not that we were together long enough to talk about anything. My few hours at the trailer were spent doing laundry and such before I spent a few hours in bed beside a sleeping Calvin.

I walked in the trailer thankful Calvin was in bed snoring as usual. I wasn't sure what he'd to say about me continuing to ride home with Mr. Grason. Most likely he would think it was still a good idea as it saved bus fare. It was also possible he would change his mind about my teacher giving me a ride after class. I found it difficult to know how Calvin would react to the things. So far it seemed as long as I was bringing home money, he didn't pay much attention to what I did. I could also feel the disapproval in Calvin where Mr. Grason was concerned.

I considered taking a quick shower, but I was too tired. Plus, I didn't want to take a chance on waking Calvin. I never knew when he would want his husbandly rights with me – be it early morning, when I got home, or in the middle of the night. I never objected, although I was usually tired to the bone, I mostly slept through it. Someday, I promised myself, I would be able to go to sleep early and wake up late. Like I sometimes did on a Saturday when I was a young girl back home.

The only time Calvin wasn't asleep when I got home was on Fridays. Friday was payday. On Mondays and Sundays, he woke up early enough to collect my tips before I went back to work. I always tried to save the two-dollar tip Don gave me to pay for my books and bus fare. Calvin never asked me about the books even though I carried them to and from work each day. He seemed to have forgotten that I was taking classes.

The next morning when I arrived at the restaurant, I had to make a fast run to the bathroom. I hadn't eaten much the day before, so it was mostly dry heaves. When I finally came out of the bathroom to help Iva Lee prep, she looked me over with a critical eye.

"Have you seen a doctor yet?"

I kind of laughed. "When would I have a chance to see a doctor? I live here except when I go to class and sleep at night."

"That's what I thought. You're losing weight and look pale all the time. I wonder if you're working too much."

"Washing dishes isn't hard work. If I was at home, I'm sure Calvin would have me doing more than I'm doing here."

"Does he do the housework and such being you're gone from five o'clock in the morning to twelve o'clock at night seven days a week," she asked me almost the same thing Mr. Grason had asked.

I had to grin at that. "Calvin draws a line at doing what he considers women's work. He said he married me to do that kind of stuff."

"Appears to me he married you because he wanted a slave. He ought to be doing all the housework considering the hours you're away from home. All the preachers I know only work on Wednesdays and Sundays. Actually, most of them hold down jobs the rest of the week."

"Calvin says he has a lot of elderly and poor people he has a responsibility to visit and care for. He mentioned that he sometimes has to drive them to their doctor's appointment."

"Looks to me like he ought to take care of his wife a little more than he obviously does. A wife is a man's first responsibility instead of his church members."

I didn't know what to say to her remark, so I remained silent. I didn't want to admit it, but I had started wondering the same thing. It didn't seem to matter to Calvin in the least that I was gone most all the time, exhausted, throwing-up, or pregnant with his baby. I was beginning to think the only reason he married me was so I could work to help pay for the debts he had incurred before we were married. I wished I had parents I could talk to about what I thought, but I didn't. It seemed Iva Lee was the only person who might care the least bit about me.

"I'm going to give you time off one morning to go see a doctor. In my opinion you're puking too often and dropping too much weight."

"I'll go to a doctor as soon as classes are over. It'll take me that long to save up enough money to pay for a visit."

"I'll be glad when those classes are over. I'm tired of trying to cook and wash dishes at the same time. Don't know if it's a blessing or a curse that we haven't been that busy on Tuesday and Thursday nights lately," Iva Lea said.

I assured myself that I didn't need to see a doctor. It was only the smell of all the greasy food that made me throw-up so much. I'd heard there was nothing that could be done about that. Most likely my morning sickness would go away on its own.

Marie came bounding in the back door with an extra surge of energy. It was obviously she was feeling extremely good. Her makeup was applied thick, and her red hair had a recent dye job. She said good morning to Iva Lee and turned to me.

"Have you heard about the preacher over at the Presbyterian church?"

"I've got an idea you're going to tell us," Iva Lee said without much enthusiasm.

"I certainly am. If Ellie was married to a preacher like him, I'd go to his church," she told us.

Iva Lee rolled her eyes.

"Anyway, Sunday morning the Presbyterian preacher decided the meetings were getting too boring. So, he decided to change his usual Sunday sermon in hopes of involving the congregation more, or at least waking some of them up. He closed his Bible, folded his hands, and leaned forward over the pulpit.

"This morning we're going to try something different," he told them. "I'm going to say a word and I want everyone to start singing the hymn it brings to mind.

The pastor shouted out "CROSS." Immediately the congregation started singing in unison, "THE OLD RUGGED CROSS."

The preacher said "POWER." The congregation sang "THERE IS POWER IN THE BLOOD" wonder working power in the blood of the lamb.

The pastor hollered out "GRACE." The congregation began to sing "AMAZING GRACE, how sweet the sound.

The Pastor said "SEX" The congregation fell into total silence. Everyone was in shock. They all nervously began to look around at each other, afraid to say anything.

Then all of a sudden, way in the back of the church, a little old 87-year-old grandpa stood up and began to sing "PRECIOUS MEMORIES" how they linger."

Iva Lee let out a chuckle. "Yep, that's your kind of preacher, all right," she told Marie. "HIND END," she called out. "Get yours in the dining room. A customer has just come in."

Chapter 9

Wednesday was the worst rush we'd ever had at the restaurant. There had been some kind of special ado at the college and tons of people attended. We were packed for breakfast, lunch, and dinner. Plus, all the between hours. I bused tables and washed dishes that piled up faster than I could scrub them and pack them in the Hobart dishwasher. Iva Lee was cooking top speed. Neither she nor I had time to prep anything. It was grab and run every minute of the day and night. We didn't get breaks, just fast runs to the bathroom when we couldn't hold it any longer.

"Since Ellie is having to buss your tables, you have to give her ten percent of your tips," Iva Lee told the waitresses. Of course, Marie and Judith were the two that complained the loudest.

"We've never had to do that before," Judith whined.

"That's because you bussed your own tables. Stop arguing with me and get back to work before I hire someone to replace you. I have pretty college girls applying for waitress jobs every single day."

Judith and Marie went back to work. I couldn't help wondering why Iva Lee didn't replace them, considering how much they did complain about everything.

"They need their jobs," Iva Lee told me when I dared to ask. "Both of them have children to support. Marie divorced her husband, and Judith's husband is dead. Both of them are living hand to mouth."

Interesting. Both of the women acted like they didn't have a care in the world. "Children?" I questioned. "They're old."

"Old compared to you. Their children are teenagers. The age where they demand more money from their parents than a gold mine could bring in."

"Oh," I said, wondering why neither of them ever talked about their children or their home lives. Maybe their lives weren't as easy as they pretended. "What about the other waitresses?"

"Everybody has their own hard-luck story. We all do the best we can," she said and then rushed to the freezer to take out what steaks were left.

I wished I was out there waitressing. People who ordered steaks could afford to leave good tips, not that all of them did. At least I might get enough from the waitresses to finish paying Mr. Grason for my books, since Calvin wouldn't be expecting the extra money. I cashed out what I'd gotten from the waitresses for a five-dollar bill and hid it in under the sole of my only pair of shoes. I could pay Mr. Grason and have a little left to buy a few necessities.

Tired didn't apply by the time I was to go home that night. I'd had to stay late cleaning up and missed the last bus. Iva Lee had agreed to drive me home if I would stay and help her with the cleanup and closing. Interesting enough, Iva Lee had become the closest to a friend I had.

I hadn't expected the look on her face when she stopped in front of the trailer. I still had enough pride to be embarrassed by the rusty piece of tin, but something in me was giving in to not being able to do any better than the trailer at this time.

"You live there?" she questioned as her headlights shined on the trailer. It really did look bad.

"It's what the church provides for their minister," I told her, suddenly humiliated beyond belief. I recalled how Mom looked down on people who lived in similar conditions. She called them 'useless never do wells.' I would be mortified if Mom saw where we lived.

"You've got to be joking? What kind of church provides such as that?"

"Calvin said the preacher before him had a house of his own and the church didn't provide anything."

"Looks to me like the church members could do better than that for their minister."

"At least it's rent free," I tried to come up with something that might ease my devastation at Iva Lee's reaction.

"Can't your husband fix it up a little? He could at least wash the green mold off the tin. I can guarantee he doesn't work the hours you work."

"He says he has to work every hour he's not sleeping. He tells me he stays too busy working for the church to do any improvement to the old trailer. He also claims the trailer isn't worth his time working on it," I said as I got out of the car and closed the door. I was so embarrassed I was actually hurting inside. Two people now knew what horrible conditions I lived in. I simply couldn't take it any longer. Instead of going to bed beside a snoring Calvin, I got a bucket of water and a rag and started scrubbing the green mold off the outside of the trailer. I had no detergent and no bleach, making cleaning more difficult. I had one bar of Ivory soap I used for washing myself and clothes. I didn't want to use that.

It was after two o'clock when I could clean no longer. I needed to rest a few hours before I caught the bus in the morning. I was asleep the minute I hit the bed. It didn't matter how uncomfortable the bed was or how loud Calvin was snoring.

I woke up to Calvin shaking me. "Get up. You're going to be late for work. Here drink this. I made some coffee."

I came straight up out of bed as Calvin shoved the cup of coffee in my hand. This wasn't a first for Calvin. Surprising enough, he had started getting up early enough to make me a cup of coffee before I went to work. I gulped the bitter stuff down. I had never liked the taste of the coffee Calvin made.

Calvin sipped on his own cup of coffee like he had just given me diamonds. He appeared pleased with himself.

I jerked on the same clothes I wore yesterday. I grabbed my purse, put on my shoes, and didn't even take time to comb my hair as I ran to catch the bus. The door to the bus was closing as I got there. I was dizzy from running. I made a jump for the door, but it caught me half in and half out. I fell face forward on the metal steps hitting my head on the stop step. I saw stars. I tried to stand as the driver opened the door to release me. Everything was spinning around so fast I couldn't catch myself as I fell backward onto the pavement.

"Oh, my goodness!" one of the male passengers said as he got up from his seat and rushed to my aid. He got me on my feet and helped me get back in the bus. "Are you hurt?"

"I'm all right. Just shaken," I managed to say.

"Are you sure?"

"Yes," I said. I was a little disoriented, but that must have come from the fall I had just taken.

He walked me to a vacant seat and sat me down. I was hurting all over, but too embarrassed to admit it. By the time the bus reached the restaurant I was feeling better. I was no longer seeing stars, but I was walking carefully because I was still dizzy. Every time I stepped hard made my head hurt both inside and out.

"What happened to you?" Iva asked as she looked me over.

"I tripped on the bus steps and fell."

She came closer to me and pushed hair up from my forehead. "My goodness. You've got a huge goose egg on your forehead. It's turning purple. "Let me see your eyes." She turned me toward the light. "Your pupils are even. You don't have a concussion."

"I'm okay," I told her. "Just feeling stupid for jumping too slow and missing a step."

"Okay, but if you get to feeling funny, let me know."

"I will. Really, I'm okay." I didn't tell her I was already feeling funny.

"I hope so. I'm thinking we're going to have another busy day."

I wasn't sure if I wanted a busy day or not. Busy made the time past faster, but it was also exhausting without allowing for proper breaks.

By the time for me to leave work and go to class, I could barely get one foot in front of the other. It took all my determination to drag myself onto the bus and take a seat. I found myself wanting to sink down into the hard cushion and not ever move again. Regrettably, the bus stopped at the college building, and I had to get off.

Mr. Grason was coming out of his office as I walked down the hall. He glanced at me and then did a double take.

"What's wrong?" he asked

I didn't know how to answer him. "Nothing. I'm just tired. It's been a hard day at work."

He frowned and came to my side. "Your forehead is swollen and bruised. Even your eyes are turning black."

"Oh. It's nothing. I tripped and fell as I got on the bus this morning."

He reached out his hand and very gently lifted my hair from my forehead. His frown deepened.

"Did you have a doctor check you out. That's some pump knot you've got there."

I tried to make light of it regardless of how bad I was feeling. "Got one almost as big on the back of my head," I said, and tried to smile at my own stupidity for oversleeping and having to make a run for the bus.

His hand reached out and touched the back of my head. I jumped at the pain it caused me.

"I'm taking you to the college nursing department and have you checked out. They'll be open for the next thirty minutes."

"Oh, no," I told him firmly. "I don't need to see a nurse. It's been twelve hours since I fell, and I've worked all day. Besides, I can't afford a doctor bill."

"The college provides free medical treatment to students."

"I'm not a student here," I told him.

"You're my student. You get the same services as any other student."

"Oh. I didn't know that."

"Don't argue with me. Come on right now. We only have thirty minutes before class starts."

He grabbed my arm and all but dragged an unwilling me to his car. Five minutes later he went with me in to see the nurse. I didn't know what to think of that. I had only been to a doctor once when I was growing up, and only my mother went in with me. I had a raging high fever caused by scarlet fever at the time. A painful shot in the rump, plus several days of sleeping cured me.

"What brings you this evening?" the nurse asked.

"I fell this morning and bumped my head, but I'm okay."

The nurse felt of my pump knots and shined a light in my eyes. She asked me several questions to check my coherency. I thought I answered them brilliantly.

"I don't think you have a concussion, but you've got to have pressure from the swelling along with a lot of pain. "I'll give you a prescription for pain medication. It will make you sleepy so don't drive or run dangerous equipment while taking it."

I didn't say anything as she wrote out the prescription. I took it even though I knew I wouldn't fill it. I couldn't afford a bottle of aspirin.

"See," I told him as we got back in his car. "I told you I'm okay."

"It's better to be safe than sorry," he told me as he reached out and patted my leg.

Most of the students should already be in the classroom by the time we arrived. Mr. Grason told me to go on to class. He needed to stop at his office for a moment. John Grieves made a point of looking me over with a *know-it-all* grin on his face. I took a seat in the front row. I had rather the students looked at the back of my head rather than at my face and my black eyes. John left the back row to move into the seat behind me.

"I saw you leave with Teach," he said. "Did you two share a quickie?"

I wasn't exactly sure what a quickie was, but I had a good idea and it made me mad as fire. It was all I could do to hold in my temper. John would have enjoyed it too much if his words caused me to flare up. "Not that's it's any of your business, but I fell getting on the bus. Mr. Grason drove me to see the college nurse."

John stuck his head in front of my face. "Well, shit," he said. "Looks like you really did fall, or somebody beat the hell outta you one. What did you say your main man's name is?"

"Are you referring to my husband?"

"If that's what you want to call him."

"His name is Calvin. He's a minister."

"I know a fellow by that name. He's no minister. At least not of a church," John chuckled with his own kind of humor.

I was thankful when Mr. Grason came into the room. He gave John a look that shut him up and made him sit back in the seat.

"I think I should warn everyone in class to be careful when getting on and off the bus. It is easy to trip on those metal steps and take a painful fall. Mrs. West can testify to that. Now, that everyone has an answer to Mrs. West's black eyes, let's get back to our studies and getting a GED."

I didn't know if I was thankful for what Mr. Grason said or not. At least the other students wouldn't be speculating about what happened to me.

After class, Mr. Grason waited until all the students left to drive me home. "Are you okay?" he asked once we were in the car.

"I'm fine. Just not anxious to wash my face or brush my hair," I said, trying for humor.

"I don't know if a pharmacy will be open this late at night, but we can drive by a couple to check."

"No," I told him quickly. "There's no need for that. I'm not in the least bit of pain."

"Are you sure?"

"Positive."

Was I ever good at lying. I saw no need in telling him I was aching all over. There was hardly a place on my body that didn't hurt. Plus, my insides felt odd as well. It wasn't only in my face where evidence of my fall showed itself. I did my best to act normal and ask questions about the topic he covered in class tonight like I always did.

Again, I was embarrassed for Mr. Grason to see where I lived. All the scrubbing I had done on the trailer didn't improve its appearance enough to warrant the time and effort I had spent. I hadn't been able to reach high enough to get all the green mold off and it showed in his headlights.

"Thank you for the ride and the trip to see the school nurse," I said politely.

"You're most welcome. See you Tuesday night."

"Right. I'll try to have the rest of your money for the books by then. Fridays and Saturdays are good tip days."

"How many days of the week are you working now?"

"All of them," I told him the same thing I'd told him before as I got out of the car and closed the door as noiselessly as I could.

As usual, Calvin was in bed snoring away. Part of me wanted to wake him up and tell him how bad I was hurting, but I knew he would either be mad at me for waking him or want to indulge in his husbandly rights, which I certainly didn't want. I took my clothes off and silently slipped into bed. I was more aware of the uncomfortable mattress than usual. The bed springs were shot, and the mattress sagged in the middle where Calvin always slept leaving me hanging on the very edge of the bed. I did my best to fall asleep. I didn't want to wake up late again in the morning.

An hour later I was wishing I'd had enough money to get the pain medication or at least a bottle of aspirin. Miserable didn't describe how I was feeling. Finally, I eased out of bed and went to the bathroom to relieve my bladder. The bathroom was a little better than a chamber pot and a lot easier than going outside. The commode still didn't flush. We had to catch water out of the faucet in a bucket and pour it in the commode the same as we did at the rental shack.

I hoped emptying my bladder would relieve some of the pain in my belly, but it didn't. Actually, it caused my belly to cramp worse. I bent forward as a cramp gripped my insides causing more to come out. It made me feel kind of lightheaded.

When I stood up to flush the commode with the bucket of water, I was shocked to see how much blood was in the water along with what appeared to be bloody strips of mucus. I made my way to the bedroom to wake Calvin. I wasn't sure what was happening, but I knew it wasn't good.

"Calvin, wake up. I'm bleeding," I turned on the single light bulb hanging from the ceiling. I grabbed him by the shoulder and shook him.

He grunted and jerked away from me.

"Did you hear me. I'm bleeding and I don't know what to do. Wake up. Please wake up," I said as I shook him by the shoulder again.

"Why are you waking me up?" he grumbled and pulled the worn quilt over his head to block out the light along with my voice.

"I'm bleeding," I said again as I pulled the quilt down.

He opened his eyes to slits to look at me. "How did you black your eyes?" he asked lightly.

"I fell and I'm bleeding. I don't know what to do."

"Put a band aide on it and turn out the light. I need my sleep. I have to work tomorrow."

"You're not listening to me. "I think I'm miscarrying."

"I doubt that. Most likely your period has just started. Tear a rag and get back in bed."

"Calvin!" I said with near hysteria. "Get up. I need to go to the hospital. I think I'm losing my baby."

That seemed to wake him up a little. "If I were to take you to the hospital, where do plan on getting the money to pay a hospital with? Tell me that?"

"I can pay them a little each week," I said as tears came to my eyes.

"No, you can't. They want paid at the time of service. It's taking every cent I can scrape up to pay the bills we already owe. Not to mention you're blowing time and money going to those stupid GED classes."

"You wanted me to go," I reminded him.

"Not if you're going to bankrupt me. You need to get a better paying job. Besides, I knew a girl who miscarried. She bled a lot until all the stuff came out, and then she spotted for several days just like she was having her period. She didn't go to the hospital, and you don't need to go either."

"I'm scared," I told him again.

"Don't be. I know what I'm talking about. Go sit on the commode until the bleeding stops. Turn off the bedroom light on your way out."

I was stunned beyond belief. What kind of man refused to take his wife to the hospital when she was miscarrying? Didn't he care anything about his baby? Didn't he care anything about his wife? I was shaking all over by the time I got to the bathroom. I sank down on the commode as a tremendous pain hit me. It felt like my insides were ripping from the inside out. I wasn't sure if the tiny room started to spin or if I was spinning.

When I opened my eyes again, I was lying on the floor with the bathroom light still on. I managed to sit up. My clothes were a bloody mess. It reminded me of what had happened to Grant. The room smelled similar. I pulled my clothes off and looked at my legs. They were covered in blood. There was what appeared to be blood clots between my legs. I rubbed my finger through it to uncover what reminded me of a baby chicken I'd seen as a child when I broke open an egg before it was near time to hatch.

"My baby," I whispered. I was holding what was the beginning of my baby in my hands.

It was then that Calvin came into the room. He looked at the mess in the floor and what I held in my hands.

"My baby," I sobbed as tears ran down my cheeks.

"It's not a baby. It's just a bunch of cells."

"It's dead," I managed to get out through my sobs.

"Stop it," he said as he reached down an took what remained of my baby from my hands and tossed it in the commode. He grabbed up the full bucket of water and flushed the commode with it.

I just sat there not knowing what to do or what to think. Calvin had flushed my baby down the commode. I wanted to bury it in a little grave where I could visit and put flowers on its grave. It had been alive. Might still be alive if Calvin had taken me to the hospital.

He reached down, took me by the arm, lifted me to my feet. "Get in the tub and wash yourself. You're a bloody mess."

I let him help my shaking legs step over the side of the tub and sank down. He put the stopper in the drain and turned on the tepid water and tossed the only wash rag at me. "Don't just sit there. Wash up. It's about time for the bus."

"I can't go to work," I said.

"Of course, you can. It will be better for you than moping around here all day."

I washed myself as Calvin took two pieces of a cardboard box and scooped up the mess in the bathroom floor. I couldn't believe how much time had passed from the time I'd woke Calvin until now if it was time for me to go to work. I must have passed out because I didn't think I'd gone to sleep, not with all the pain I had felt and was still feeling. Pain, I thought, it was there and yet I wasn't exactly feeling it. I had a numb, unreal feeling all over. I was moving without intending to move. I washed myself including my hair using the small bar of soap to lather the wash rag. When I had finished, I got the towel and dried myself off. I stepped out of the tub by holding onto the wall. I was surprised that Calvin had actually mopped the floor. It was something I had never seen him do before.

"Here," he said as he came into the bathroom carrying one of his ragged undershirts. "Tear rags out of this. Like I already said, you'll bleed a little for a few days. It shouldn't keep you from doing what you usually do."

I just stared at him as I took the undershirt from his hands. I felt that I should be thankful for the undershirt and him cleaning the floor, but I wasn't.

I found myself sitting in the bus seat on my way to work. I didn't remember walking from the trailer to the bus stop, but I must have. I did remember the wind blowing on my wet hair. It made me cold. I was still cold.

I got off the bus at the restaurant and walked in like I always did. Iva Lee turned to glance at me and then took a second look. "You sure have black eyes this morning in a mighty pale face. What's wrong with you?"

"I miscarried last night," I told her.

"Dang," she said. "Are you alright?"

"I don't know."

"Why aren't you still in the hospital?"

"I didn't go."

"Why not?"

"Calvin said we couldn't afford it."

"No shit!" She rushed into the dining room and came back to the kitchen with a chair. "Here. Sit down. You don't look so good. You best get to the hospital."

"Can't. No money."

"They can bill you."

"I would have to pay eventually. Besides, Calvin said I will only bleed for a few days and then I'll be back to normal."

"So, Calvin's a doctor now as well as a preacher."

"He said he knew a girl who miscarried once. He said it's no big deal."

"Not to him, obviously."

"I can't take off to drive you to the hospital. I'm tied down here without enough help. I don't know if you should ride the bus there either."

"I'm okay. I can still wash dishes."

"Are you bleeding much?"

"Not anymore. It's mostly over with."

"You just sit there awhile, and we'll see how things go. I can always call an ambulance if it becomes necessary."

Calling an ambulance was even worse. I would have two bills to pay off then.

"I'm okay," I told her, even when I didn't think I was okay at all. Something inside me had changed. It went beyond misery. It went deeper than my heart and soul. It had destroyed me and left behind a shell with nothing to fill it with.

Chapter 10

Calvin was right. The bleeding slowly eased up, although I was feeling weak. I kept the chair in the kitchen where I could sit down when I wasn't washing dishes. Iva Lee pretended not to watch me, but she did. Neither she nor I either one told the wait staff what was wrong with me. We let them think my weakness came from the fall I'd had.

Tuesday came and I rode the bus to class as usual.

"You're pale," Mr. Grason said when he saw me. "The fall must have hurt you more than you thought."

"I'm fine," I told him. I didn't have the small amount of money to give him for the books. I'd felt too weak to wait on tables that weekend. Thankfully, he'd never asked me for money – not one single time. After seeing the trailer, he most likely realized what little money I actually had.

"Should I take you to see the college nurse?"

"No," I told him emphatically. "I'm just tired is all."

I thought I saw all kinds of questions run though his mind, but he didn't comment on them.

"If you say so," he said gently.

Attending class was much more restful than being at the loud and busy restaurant. It was all I could do to keep my eyes open while sitting there. Being busy had kept me from realizing how exhausted I had become. I had an idea I could sleep for two days straight if I got the chance, which I never would.

For a teacher who was always a stickler for holding class to the last minute, he surprised every student.

"I'm going to end class thirty minutes early today in time for those without their own transportation to catch an earlier bus."

Every student in the room seemed happy about that, even John Greives. I didn't like the sneering grin plastered on his face when he looked from Mr. Grason to me. He lifted his brows when his gaze met mine. There was no doubt in what his devious mind was insinuating.

Mr. Grason didn't drive me straight home as I expected. He drove to a little park in the middle of town and stopped his car.

"Now, tell me what happened to you. I don't want to hear any more of your *I'm fine*."

I didn't want Mr. Grason, or anyone, to know that I'd miscarried, but I couldn't stop myself from telling him. I don't know why Mr. Grason brought out the truth in me, but he did. It seemed I couldn't keep my mouth shut with Iva Lee or him.

"How long were you passed out in the bathroom floor?"

"From around midnight until about time to go to work."

"Didn't your husband check on you?"

"He was asleep."

"You mean he went back to sleep while you were miscarrying?"

"He has no problem falling asleep," was all I could think to say in Calvin's defense.

"I'm taking you to the hospital right now," he told me firmly.

"Oh, no. I won't go. I'm just tired is all. It's been several days. Calvin said it would take a couple of weeks to regain my strength back. Appears he's right."

"How the hell would he know?"

"He said he knew a woman once who miscarried. He said it was no big deal."

Mr. Grason clenched his teeth and shook his head. It took several minutes for his teeth to unclench.

"Several days," he finally said. "You miscarried the night I took you home?"

"An hour or so after I got home."

"You were hurt worse than I thought. Didn't your husband realize you were hurt?"

I shook my head. I couldn't speak. Without expecting it, all trauma of the past week hit me. No matter how I tried I couldn't gain control of myself. I turned my head as though I was looking out the window as tears came to my eyes. I didn't want Mr. Grason to know I was crying.

The next thing I knew, he had scooted from under the steering wheel and pulled me into his arms.

"It's okay. I'm right here with you. Cry it out, honey. Cry it all out."

And I did. I cried worse than any baby as I clung to him. The feel of his warm body, his strong arms holding me, gave me comfort and at the same time I wished the earth would open up and I could crawl in. How would I ever be able to face Mr. Grason after making such a crying fool of myself?

"I'm sorry," I mumbled. "I'm so ashamed of myself. I don't know what's come over me."

"You have nothing to be sorry for or ashamed of. You've been through a traumatic experience. Not only the horrible fall you took but going through the shock of miscarrying. I'm surprised you were able to sit up much less going to work as though nothing happened. Most women would be taking a month off while she was being cared for. I know my sister did. She took a fall on metal steps and miscarried. She certainly didn't do any work or hardly get out of bed for three weeks straight."

His words were comforting, but I still felt guilty for letting him see my weakness. I wanted to be strong and capable and competent. I wanted a better life than living in a trailer with green mold on the outside and gray mold on the inside. I wanted a husband who was strong and dependable.

One who would take care of me instead of a bunch of church members I didn't know.

Fact was. I was not married to such a man. I was married to Calvin West and there was nothing I could do about it. As Mom had told me, I'd made my bed and now I had to sleep in it. I knew I couldn't go running back home. Mom would never allow such as that. Besides, the bed I would have to lay in back home would surely be worse than what I had now. I was stuck right where I was.

Someday, I consoled myself, things would get better. If I continued to work hard, I'd be able to bring in enough money to help Calvin pay off what he owed and be able to improve our living situation. Maybe, before long, he'd even get a better church to become minister of, one that had a nice house to live in.

"We'd better go," I said as I wiped my eyes with my hands and scooted away from him.

"You're still upset. What will your husband think if I bring you home in tears."

"He'll be asleep. He never knows when I get home."

"When do you see each other?" he questioned.

"Friday nights. He always wakes up when I get home on Fridays." I didn't tell him that Fridays were payday for me, but I think he might have guessed.

Chapter 11

I was shocked when I woke up one morning to see Calvin had a phone installed in the trailer. If we couldn't afford the bare necessities such as food and soap, how could we afford to pay for a phone? When I asked him that question, he became angry at me.

"Why can't you stop being so selfish. Surely you realize my congregation needs a way to get in touch with me. I don't know what's gotten into you that's making you so monetary. Don't you care for other people and their struggles?"

What did I say to such accusations? Of course, I cared about everyone's struggles. It seemed like Calvin didn't care in the least for my struggles, or that there were times when I needed my husband to care about me instead of *his congregation.*

"Selfish?" I questioned. "You are accusing me of being selfish?"

"You have always been selfish and self-centered. All you've ever thought about was yourself and what you want. Even your own mother realized that. It's one of the reasons she was willing to dump you off on me."

I was too stunned to say anything. I thought there was truth in what he said about Mom dumping me off on him, but not the rest of his accusations.

There was no need in arguing with Calvin. I knew he would only accuse me of other things that weren't true. I turned my back on him and walked out the door to catch the bus. In a way I regretted waking him up to ask him about the phone, and in another way I didn't.

I was experiencing a slow boil along with much confusion. I knew I was too tired and angry to think straight. I hadn't gotten over the miscarriage both mentally and physically. I needed to do some soul searching along with some deep thinking while I scrubbed baked-on grease off pots and pans.

"What has gotten you so down in the mouth this morning?" Iva Lee asked.

I needed to unburden my soul at least a little. I told about the phone and what Calvin had accused me of. Iva Lee stopped prepping food to look at me. She shook her head in disbelief.

"Holy shit," she said. "You're the least selfish person I've ever met. You're also the most blind and foolish person that's come down the pike. You're nothing like most teenagers I know. Did you date much before you married your so-called preacher?"

I shook my head. "Mom didn't permit me to date."

"Then how did you manage to get married?"

"He came to our church, and Mom decided a preacher would be a good catch for me." I couldn't remember if I'd confessed that to her before or not.

"Shit," Iva Lee said. "I'll telling you right now you've got to change, or you'll spend the rest of your life being nothing but a door mat. It's time for you to stop being a naïve, trusting child and turn into a knowledgeable young woman. I'm telling you right now, the man you marry can make or destroy your life."

I gave her a look.

"It's the truth. I'm being bluntly honest. Just because you're married doesn't mean you know a thing about adult behavior. That's why I have to tell you right out that you're married to the biggest asshole I've ever come across. He wants to work you to death to pay for his bills. Do you even know how much *he* owes, or what your money is actually paying for?"

I didn't answer.

"I didn't think so. It's time you started snooping around some. Find out a little about this husband of yours and what he does all day while you're working yourself into the bone yard. For goodness sake, Ellie. Surely you realize you're nothing but a skeleton of who you were when you started working here."

I was stunned, but she didn't stop there.

"You tell him I'm no longer letting you wait on tables, which I plan on letting you do more of. Every day I'm going to keep your tips until you have enough to open your own bank account. I'm tired of seeing you with worn out clothes and run over shoes with your toes sticking out. I tired of watching you eat only a small portion of your food so you can take the rest home to feed that no-account man you call a husband. It's borders on a crime when your husband refuses to let you go to the hospital with a miscarriage because you don't have money to pay the bill. I'm telling you right now, if you don't have the gumption to look out for yourself, I intend to do it for you. And I'll not hear a word from you. Understand?"

I nodded.

"Every payday on your break you'll go around the corner and deposit the cash I'll pay you, understand?

If I did what Iva Lee insisted I do, Calvin wouldn't take my deception well if he found out.

The longer I stood there washing dishes, the more I realized Iva Lee was right. It was time I learned a lot more about everything, including the man I had married. I knew he claimed to be the minister of a church full of people, but I didn't even know the name of the church. I figured he owed money, but I didn't know how much or what for. He claimed it was for our living expenses and his student loans. If it was true, how was I responsible for paying his student loans back? Wasn't he responsible or at least his parents?

As for his parents, I'd never met them. Didn't even know if his parents were actually alive. Never once had he taken me by his parents' house or shown me one picture. I wanted answers, but I didn't know how to find out one single thing.

"How do I find answers?" I asked Iva Lee as she dumped several greasy pots in the water for me to wash.

"I'm closing early Monday evening to have the place cleaned and fumigated. Pest control is required, and I find it easier to have it done on a regular basis. That way I stay ahead of inspections. Any of the staff that wants to clean can. They seldom do, but I thought you might stay. As soon as I close, you can catch a bus and go home. If he's home, you can come right back here. If he's not, go inside and snoop about like you should have already been doing. Go to a nearby grocery story and ask about the church. People who work with the public are full of information, but don't tell anyone your name or who you're married to. Secrecy, and I'll repeat, secrecy is one of the most valuable assets a person has. So, be smart and don't blow it."

I thought Iva Lee was being silly in what she told me I should do. I needed to stay at the restaurant and work. Calvin would be upset if I got less hours in. Besides, I'd be paying for extra bus fares. Still, after I thought about it, I would do as she suggested. I shouldn't blindly trust Calvin simply because he was my husband.

It seemed strange for me to ride the bus during the light of day. I always left the trailer before it was good daylight and returned around midnight. I got off the bus and just stood there looking about. It hurt to see what a run-down area this place actually was. It certainly looked better in the darkness than it did in the bright light of day. There were cigarette butts and unrecognizable trash scattered everywhere. Even the cracked sidewalks were caked with dirt. Weeds were growing in the many cracks where people hadn't walked on them.

Instead of going to the trailer, I decided to take a side street until I found the local grocery store. I had no trouble spotting it. It looked as rundown as every other building I passed, although it had been painted white once upon a time.

What paint was left had turned gray and was peeling. It looked a lot like some of the old stores back home. I loved to go into those old stores with all the interesting smells that been seeped into every fiber of the buildings for years.

I wandered through the isles letting old memories of home fill my senses. I remembered the happiness of being able to buy a drink and a nab after I'd spent the summer working in the bean fields. Those days seemed like a different lifetime ago – back when I was young and happier than I was now. I found myself wishing I could go back to that time. It was hard to believe it had been several months ago.

An attractive, young woman slightly older than me was pushing a baby boy in a shopping cart got my attention. The baby was so young he was having trouble sitting upright in the shopping cart. His mother had propped him up with blankets. She pushed the cart through every aisle of the store. Having a baby hadn't hurt her figure. She was shapely to the point of being over-blown.

Looking at her made me realize how much weight I'd lost since I'd married Calvin. I couldn't help noticing she had food and other things I wished I could buy. She even had a bottle of fingernail polish and a tube of mascara. I wondered how she could afford to be so wasteful of money. I picked up a banana, hoping I still had enough money to pay for it after paying for the bus fare, and followed her to the checkout where an elderly woman stood at the cash register. I don't know why I couldn't stop watching the woman. Maybe it was because she looked so different from me. I stood off to the side and listened as the clerk rang up her purchases.

"How are you today, Cleo?" the clerk asked politely. By the tone of her voice, I got the impression she wasn't overly fond of the young woman.

"Tired. This baby kept me up most of the night. Thankfully, I was able to take a nap this morning when he did. I'm thinking about putting him in day care when an opening becomes available."

"Are you getting a job?"

"Why would I do that?"

"To earn money. It's always rewarding to be self-sufficient."

She let out a slight chuckle as though it was a silly suggestion. "I earn money," she said with an attitude.

The clerk gave her a disgusted look. "That comes to fifteen dollars and twenty-six cents. Your bill is extra high this week."

"Put it on Calvin's account," she said.

"Okay. But tell Preacher West his account is ten days past due," the clerk told her. "If it's not paid by tomorrow, I'll have to stop his credit."

"No problem. You know he always pays for what I buy."

"He certainly is generous with you. Don't see many preachers like him," she said with what I took to be a slight insult in her tone of voice.

I watched as she pushed her cart out the door to a nice-looking car. She put her purchases and her baby in the back seat, got behind the wheel, and drove away.

"Is she married to a preacher?" I couldn't resist asking the clerk since she had said the name Calvin.

"Oh, no. She's not married to him or anyone else that I know of," the clerk made a disapproving face. "I've heard he already has a wife. Never came into contact with her, though. If you ask me ... I'll hush up. No need for me to gossip."

"Why haven't you seen his wife if he has a credit account here?" I asked, hoping she really did want to gossip.

"They say she's gone most all the time. Don't know why. Can't say as I blame her," she added in a slightly lower tone of voice.

"Why not?" I asked as though I wasn't too interested. I didn't want her to become suspicious of my curiosity.

"He's not the kind of man, or so-called preacher, I'd want to be married to."

"What kind of a man is he?" I continued to ask.

"Old enough to be a preacher, and young enough to be attracted to the likes of her. Don't know why any church would hire the likes of him to be their minister. He certainly knows a lot about sinning, if you ask me."

"Why's that?" I tried to ask as though I wasn't really interested, while I was actually glued to every word she said.

"Men are too easy to be misled. That woman is an expert at misleading men, if you get what I mean."

"What about Cleo's husband? Doesn't he pay for what she buys?"

The clerk gave a satirical grunt. "A man would have to be crazy to marry her. You've heard the old saying, why buy the cow when you get the milk for free. I can tell you for a fact the preacher's milk is not coming for free. Cleo Hampstead charges every sort of things to his account. If I didn't need the income so badly, I'd refuse to give him credit."

Another person came up behind me pushing a cart, ready to check out. "The clerk stopped her gossiping instantly. "You buying that banana or not?" she said to me.

The strangest feeling came over me. I felt lightheaded, almost as though I was floating. I placed the banana on the counter and walked out the door without buying it. Even looking at the banana made me feel worse. I didn't want the banana or for this woman, or anybody else, to know I was married to that *so-called preacher.*

I walked all the way to the trailer in what must have been a state of shock. I hardly realized where I was going or what direction I went in to get to the trailer, but suddenly I was going in the dented metal door. I had every intention of confronting Calvin with what I'd found out, but he wasn't at the trailer. I did as Iva Lee suggested and started going through the drawers. All I found was the underwear I'd washed and placed in the drawers. I searched in the kitchen cabinets and in the bathroom cabinets. It hit me how stupid I was being. These were the places I was responsible for. No way would Calvin keep anything personal in such places. I recalled what a mess of everything, including books and file folders, Calvin kept in his car before we were married. I'd not ridden in the car with Calvin since I'd started catching the bus to work. Most likely he would still keep things he didn't want me to see locked in the trunk of his rust bucket of a car. But his car wasn't here. It was always where Calvin was. How could I possibly get a chance to look in the trunk without Calvin knowing?

What was I to do? What could I do? My choice was to stay put and wait on Calvin to show up, or return to work. The restaurant offered me more comfort than the trailer did. I certainly spent more time there.

I was in a stupor as I walked out of the rusty, mold-ridden trailer. I found myself standing near the bus stop, waiting for the next bus to arrive. The only place for me to go was back to the restaurant, back to work, back to Iva Lee – the only person who seemed to care about me.

"So, you finally found out about him," said a voice. "Thought you were going to remain dumb as a rock the rest of your life."

I whirled around to see John Grimes standing there looking at me with an expression of *I could have told you so* on his face.

"Are you following me?" I demanded.

"No. I don't follow you or anybody else. It just so happens I live on the far side of the church house where your so-called husband is the so-called minister. I was in the store when you were following Cleo around. You were so engrossed in watching her that you didn't see me,"

"So-called?" were the words that came out of my mouth.

"Oh, I suppose he is the minister of the church all right, but he's not a husband to you. I'm sure you have already concluded that such from his actions even if you don't want to admit it."

I didn't know what to say or even what to think of his remarks.

"Don't look so stunned. I knew who you were the minute I saw you. You're the stupid girl who Calvin West has taken advantage of."

I just stared at him. *Stupid? Girl?* Why was he standing there calling me stupid? Could it be because I really was stupid?

"I attended several classes with Calvin. I got to know him well. You see, we both got our rocks off with the same old gal. Want to know her name? Don't matter if you want to know who she is or not. I'm going to tell you something else. The woman who he's spending all your money on is Cleo, Cleo Hampstead. But then you probably already know that since you were following her around."

I was stunned into silence. I stood there staring at him, not knowing what to say or what to do.

"Stunned speechless, are you? I just thought it was time you know the truth. Or do you already know the man you married has a baby boy by Cleo Hampstead. He's been paying her through the nose to keep her silent, but he's not paying me a plug nickel. So, I thought you ought to know he only married you to keep from having to marry her. Can't say as I blame him. No man wants to be married to the town whore."

I stood there staring at John's face as he talked. I felt as though I'd been burning hot and then dipped into ice water.

"Shut your mouth, John, before I shut it for you."

I turned my head to see Teddy Green, the gay guy from the restaurant.

"It's time she knew the truth," John said defiantly.

"Truth is something she needs to learn in her own time. Not yours."

Teddy Green reached out and took hold of my arm. I cringed and he turned loose.

"Get in my car, Ellie. I'll drive you back to the restaurant."

"No thank you," I heard myself say as I turned my back on them both and walked away.

I walked down the street and took back alleys that smelled like urine. I felt similar to the way I felt after seeing Grant's body tangled in the tines of the tiller. There was no Drake Lewis to sit me down and push my head down to return the blood to my brain. I didn't have Dad or Mom or any of the neighbors to share in my misery. Like with Grant, I realized life as I had known it was coming to an end. I didn't know what to do or which way to turn.

I saw a phone booth next to a service station and went to it. I wanted to call home – talk to someone who could give me comfort. But all the money I had with me was enough change to buy a banana.

Collect, I thought. I could call home collect. It would be Mom who answered the phone. Dad would be working in the field, pouring his sweat and soul into the crops he grew. Mom would be inside the house pouring her love on her baby, little Grant. She wouldn't want to listen to me tell her about Calvin and the whore. Most likely she wouldn't believe a word I said if she did listen. She had wanted me to marry Calvin, an upcoming preacher, a minister of God's word. Most likely she wouldn't even accept a collect call from me.

I picked up the pay phone and punched the O.

"Operator. How may I help you?"

I hesitated for a moment. Did I dare call home? Would it make me feel better or worse? "No one can help me," I said to the operator as I fought back tears and gently replaced the phone in the receiver.

Those were the truest works I'd ever spoken.

Chapter 12

I don't know how I got back to the restaurant, but I found myself walking through the back door. I must have walked all the way in a fog. It was getting dark, and I didn't remember riding a bus. I stuck my hand in my pocket to find the change I hadn't spent on the banana or bus fare.

"You've been gone a long time. What did you find out?" Iva Lee asked without looking at me. I wondered how she knew it was me, but then who else would coming in the back door this late?

"You have a certain way of coming in the door and tiptoeing about like a scared mouse," she answered my unspoken question. "Well, don't just stand there. Talk to me. Tell what you found out."

"I didn't find anything. No bank statements, nothing. He must keep everything locked in the trunk of his car." I had intended to unburden my soul on her. Tell her about John Grieves and Teddy Green, along with the whore and her baby son, but I didn't. My very existence consisted of silence. I couldn't find words to tell her any of it. If I did, then it would become truth and I'd have to do something about it, and I didn't want to be all alone while not knowing what to do. If I remained silent, I could deny truth and pretend nothing had changed – at least until John Grieves or Teddy Green told.

I helped Iva Lee clean until it was time for me to catch the last bus back to the trailer. I didn't want to go back to the trailer – back to Calvin, but what choice did I have? I no longer had a family, no friends, no place to run and hide. I could do nothing without money. I was stuck right where I was at. Helpless and afraid.

120

"Are you sure, you're okay?" Iva Lee finally asked me. "You've not seemed yourself since you got back."

What did she expect after telling me I needed to find out about my so-called husband and his debts. What I'd found out certainly wasn't what I'd expected. I found out he has a son by the town whore. That he was paying her bills with what was most likely the money I earned. That John Grieves lived near the church and seemed to know a lot more about Calvin than I did. Evidently, even Teddy Green also knew far more than I did. Could that be why he left me large tips when I waited on him?

"I realized I didn't know anything about the man I married. I really did think he was a Godly man," I told her instead of remaining silent. I didn't want to tell her anything more.

Iva Lee made a face. "Sometimes a so-called *Godly man* can be the worst kind. He thinks of himself as being better than anybody else. In his mind, he becomes privileged."

Did Calvin think himself better than anybody else? Did he think he was privileged? No, I thought. According to what little I had observed about Calvin, he seemed to think he was inferior to other people – as though he deserved what they had more than they did. According to the way he had lived, including his old rust bucket, he certainly wasn't privileged. But then, what did I know about how Calvin had lived before we were married?

Suddenly it hit me. There was a reason he was attending backwoods churches other than seeking free meals. He was looking for a solution to whatever situation he had gotten himself into, and I had become that solution.

Calvin thought I was so stupid I'd never question his motives for doing the things he did. That's why he married me. That and perhaps what John Grieves had said. He married me, a dumb country hick, to keep from having to marry the town whore, Cleo Hampstead. Was she the one who Calvin was talking about having a miscarriage? If so, she now had a baby?

My thoughts were interrupted by the bus stopping in front of the restaurant. The driver had become accustomed to picking me up late at night.

"See you in the morning," Iva Lee called as I hurried out the door as though she had to remind me I was to come in to work the next morning.

I suddenly realized it had taken every cent I had to pay the bus fare. I hadn't gotten any tips today or any change from where the other waitresses tipped me out, since no one else had been willing to help get ready for the exterminator. I hadn't even thought to ask Iva Lee for an advance for tomorrow's bus fare back to the restaurant. I had no idea what I would do come tomorrow morning when it was time to catch the bus.

As usual, Calvin was in bed snoring as I entered the trailer. I had an urge to grab the worn-out broom and start beating him with it until he told me the truth about all the things I didn't know. Instead, I went into the dingy closet of a bathroom and tried to shower in the trinkle of water that came out of the ancient plumbing. I wanted to get what little warm water there was before I put Calvin's dirty clothes in the washing machine. Every time I showered, I stopped up the tub and hand washed my uniform and then dipped out what little water there was to fill the old washing machine to wash Calvin's clothes or fill the bucket to flush the commode. The water hose in the washing machine only dribbled water. It took most of the night to fill up unless I dipped it out of the bathtub.

I hung my uniform up to dry and went into the bedroom to find Calvin's dirty clothes. I was trying to be silent as I felt around in the dark for the clothes he always tossed on the floor.

"What are you doing?" he demanded.

"Finding your dirty clothes to wash."

"It's about time. I've only got one clean shirt and pair of pants left. You're getting lazy, Ellie," he said as though it was his right to reprimand me. I washed clothes at night and ironed them while he slept. I wondered why he wasn't sleeping.

"Where's my food?" he questioned. Most always I brought left-over food home. Sometimes he ate at night, but usually he ate it in the morning.

"Didn't have any," I told him. "The restaurant was closed."

"Where were you all day?"

"Helping Iva Lee clean the restaurant."

"Is she paying you extra for that? Give me your tip money," he said.

I didn't answer. I now knew why he wasn't still sleeping. He needed money to pay for the whore's bill at the store. "I didn't get any tip money today. As I just told you, the restaurant was closed to clean for the exterminator. Iva Lee said she was also cutting back on my time as a waitress. She can get waitresses, but no one wants to be a dishwasher."

"Now wait a minute. If she won't let you waitress, then you'll have to get a raise in pay or find a job that pays more."

"What other place would pay me more under the table the way Iva Lee does. As you very well know, she doesn't even take out deductions like she's supposed to."

"Tell her if she doesn't pay you more, I'll turn her in for screwing over the government."

"That would go over good. Word would get around that I'm married to a whistle blower, and I'd never get another job."

He seemed to take that into consideration. "Then you'll have to stop going to classes so you can put in more hours."

"Why don't you ask your congregation to put more money into the collection plate?" I couldn't resist saying as I recalled him insisting I take classes so I wouldn't be an embarrassment to him in front of his congregation.

"I'm paid a salary. I don't get the money from the collection plate. It goes to pay all the churches bills."

"What are your bills, Calvin? How much do you owe?"

Calvin's face turned red in anger, but his voice became softer, more hurt sounding. "Listen to yourself for once. You're letting your selfishness show. Surely you realize we both have to contribute to our living expenses."

Oh, the things I could say to him, but I didn't. I needed to get the clothes washed if I was to get any sleep tonight. I'd have to get up early if I had to walk all the way to work instead of taking the bus. I knew Calvin would refuse to use his precious gas to drive me.

"I've got to put the washing in," I told him. When we were first married, Calvin had told me the responsibilities of being a wife. Keeping his clothes clean and ironed was only one of many. I was determined to be the best wife ever, so I tried my best to accomplish all he asked of me, but things could change in a hurry.

"Then do it. I expect you to bring home tip money tomorrow," he added as I fumbled around in the semi-dark room. He got mad when I turned on the bedroom light. He claimed the streetlights cast enough light in the bedroom for me to see.

Chapter 13

It wasn't easy for me to get up an hour early since I wasn't able to fall asleep after I finally got in bed. Our disagreements didn't appear to bother him the way it did me. I put on my only other uniform that Iva Lee thankfully provided and eased out the door without making enough noise to wake Calvin. I tried to assure myself that walking would be good for me. It would give me time to think, which I needed to do a lot more of.

It seemed to me the biggest problem between Calvin and me had been about money. At least it was until I found out that Cleo Hampstead had a credit account Calvin was paying for. Now there was even a bigger problem. That is if John Grieves was telling the truth.

Was Calvin the father of her baby boy? Was it true he married me to keep from marrying the whore? I found it difficult to believe such as that was true. Surely John Grieves was lying. Why would he do a thing such as that? Was there a reason he wanted to hurt me? Hurt Calvin? Destroy our marriage?

Admittedly, in the beginning I felt guilty for marrying Calvin when I wasn't sure I loved him the way a wife should, but that changed. I no longer felt guilty. I suddenly realized Calvin hadn't loved me the way a husband should. Ours was more a marriage of circumstances than of romance. Such realization didn't change that Calvin was my very own husband for the rest of my life and it was up to me to make sure our home was filled with as much love and respect as I could bring to it. I reminded myself I had given my heart and soul to Calvin once we were married, and it was my responsibility to continue. I assured myself that he was a good man. A preacher. A person even my critical mother approved of, but then mother had changed after Grant's accident.

I couldn't blame her for that. I could only imagine how traumatic it would be for a mother to lose the one person she loved more than anyone on earth, especially in such a horrible way right before her own eyes. I did know how it hurt when I miscarried. I had wanted Calvin to hold me, say comforting words of love and devotion, but he hadn't.

To Calvin it was only an everyday occurrence that I shouldn't make a big deal out of it. I thought of Mom and Dad. Evidently, they had needed each other and shared their need of comfort considering little Grant had been conceived. As for me, I concluded I had turned to Calvin.

I was only halfway to the restaurant when a car pulled to the side of the road beside me and stopped. It was Bret Grason. I felt embarrassment from the roots of my hair to the tip of my toenails. I didn't want anyone to see me walking on the side of the road.

"Miss the bus?" he said kindly. "Jump in. I'll give you a ride."

My pride wanted to tell him no and that I was simply enjoying an early morning walk, but I didn't. My feet were hurting, and lack of sleep made each step I took a struggle. A ride, regardless of where it came from, was nothing short of a blessing I couldn't turn down.

"Thanks," I managed to say after I opened the passenger door and got in.

"I have an early morning class," he said as I sank into his car seat. "Do you walk to work often?" he asked as he observed my face with a frown. I knew I looked as terrible as I felt.

"I usually sleep too late to enjoy walking," I told him, which wasn't exactly a lie.

"I see," he said. "I noticed the restaurant was closed yesterday when I drove past."

"Closed for pest control," I told him.

"You didn't work then?"

"I helped Iva Lee clean," I wished he would stop asking me questions. I didn't want to talk about anything. I needed silence. I needed to clear my mind enough to think. But then, I had silence during the night, and it hadn't helped.

He seemed to pick up on my need and said no more until we reached the restaurant. "See you in class tonight," he said.

I hesitated to answer. I did need to earn more money for my sake if not for Calvin's. But then, if I did earn more money, was it going to pay for what Cleo Hampstead blew money on instead of benefiting me? The only thing that benefited me was the classes I was taking. Education was the only thing neither Calvin nor women such as Cleo could take away from me. Bret Grason was a factor in giving me that education.

"Sure thing. Thank you for the ride." I reached for the door handle to get out.

"I'll be passing by the restaurant about the time you catch the bus. Want me to pick you up? It'll save you riding the bus."

I started to say no a moment before I thought of the bus fare I'd save. It would be a few more cents I could stash without Calvin knowing about it. Pennies make dollars, and dollars could be a key to my own salvation. As the old saying went, keep a woman barefoot, pregnant and penniless and you kept a woman controlled. At the same time the thought made me feel guilty of being selfish and greedy, but not enough to turn down the ride.

"That would be wonderful if it's not putting you out."

"It won't be putting me out," he told me in a voice that had gone more gentle than normal.

"Thank you," I felt tears sting the back of my eyes causing me to get out of the car faster than normal. I didn't need gentleness right now. I needed to get mad and stay mad. I needed to grow a backbone and do what was best for me instead of what was best for Calvin. At the same time, such a thought made me feel selfish.

~~~~

"You're early even for you," Iva Lee told me.

"I caught a ride," I told her.

"Who with?"

"Bret Grason."

"Humph," Iva Lee grunted and was silent for a minute. She finally said. "You ought to ride with him every chance you get. Saves you bus fare. It's not much, but every cent you can save adds up. I firmly believe a woman needs her own mad money. Money is a tool. Without that tool a woman can become trapped in a situation she can't get out of."

She didn't have to tell me about being trapped, or how much it cost me to ride the bus. I wanted to know more about Bret Grason. "You know Mr. Grason?"

"When a person is my age and runs a restaurant as long as I have, you get to know a lot about everybody."

"Really? Then what's the gossip on Calvin?" I couldn't resist asking.

"I already told you what I think of him. No need for me to repeat what I've already said. Calvin West isn't any of my business, but you are since you became my employee. What bothers me is that you're a good kid and he's not treating you right. I don't like seeing someone, as young and naive as you are, being taken advantage of."

Taken advantage of? I wasn't sure about that. Back home a good woman always did all the work they were capable of doing from the time they woke up at daybreak until they dropped in bed at night. That's what made a good wife. I wanted to be the best wife ever – unless what I found out about Calvin and Cleo Hampstead proved to be true. Then I didn't know what I would do.

"Did you know Calvin before I started working for you?" I couldn't stop asking her questions. I needed to know more about my husband. At the same time, I was fearful of what I would find out.

"Slightly. He came in here to eat on rare occasions. I got the idea he didn't have much money. Someone else was usually paying for his meal. He came in once to ask if would hire his wife. A few days later, you showed up and I hired you."

That wasn't news to me. I got the same idea of his lack of money when he was coming to church and eating Mom's cooking. And yet he had managed to attend college and seminary. I had to give him credit for that. It couldn't have been easy for someone who was a poor boy.

"Who paid for his meals?" I wanted to know.

"It was usually someone he was doing odd jobs for. He said he was working his way through college."

I had to admire him for that. "Did you know his parents?" I asked.

"No. Never met them or heard anything about them. Listen, I'm not interested in Calvin West. He is who he is and that's all there is to it. Who I'm interested in is you. Like I said, you're a naive kid who is easily taken advantage of. You need to open your eyes and see reality. You need to learn how to be street smart in order to survive in this day and age. You're no longer living in your isolated childhood with parents to protect you. You're in the real world now."

As soon as Iva Lee had prepped for the day, she unlocked the door and hung the open sign. Marie had called in earlier to say she was sick and wouldn't come in today.

"If we get a rush, I'm going to let you wait on tables. I'll help with dishwashing. I'm a cook, not a waitress," Iva Lee told me.

I didn't think I'd be doing much waitressing as breakfast seldom caused a rush. It was during lunch and dinner when the rush came. I was surprised when Judith came into the kitchen with a red face from anger.

"Teddy Green is refusing to let me wait on him. He's demanding for her to be his waitress," she told Iva Lee as she pointed her finger at me.

"The customer is always right," Iva Lee held in a grin. "Go take his order, Ellie. He always gets the same thing anyway."

I didn't want to wait on him after the confrontation with him and John, but he always left a good tip. Right now, money was more important than my feelings.

"Good morning, sweet girl," Teddy said as I stopped at his table. He was eyeballing me up and down in a way I couldn't determine. "I'll take the usual."

I nodded and walked away. I didn't like him calling me 'sweet girl'. To be honest, I simply didn't care for the man. He had a snoopy attitude, and I thought it was aimed at me. I brought him a glass of water along with a glass of orange juice.

"Thank you," he said politely. I rushed back to the kitchen thankful he hadn't said anything more.

He was still silent except for a *thank you* when I delivered his breakfast to him. After he finished his meal, he left the price of the meal plus a three whole dollar tip on the table, which was more than his meal cost. He left without saying another word to me. Why he wanted to leave me such a large tip, I didn't know. I was grateful for it.

"Well," Judith said. "If that don't beat all. He can't have a crush on you. You're not his type."

Once I was back washing dishes and scrubbing greasy pots, I turned to Iva Lee and whispered. "Why doesn't Judith like me?"

"It's not you she dislikes. It's herself. She's no longer has her youth. She thinks she's lost the ability to fulfil her impossible dreams, which in my opinion, is the gospel truth. When she looks in the mirror, she sees an aging woman who is stuck in a job she feels is degrading to her intelligence. Have to admit I know such a feeling, but I overcame it. She hasn't."

"Then why doesn't she do something about it?"

"The same reason you're not doing something about the situation you're in."

I gave her a questioning frown. I was working day and night to overcome the situation I was in, and she knew it.

"I'm sure you've heard the old saying that you can't drain the swamp while you're fighting the alligators. In other words, you're trying to survive the situation you find yourself in instead of getting yourself out of the situation."

I got the gist of what she was saying, although it didn't make a lot of sense. I didn't want to give up my job, going to classes, or being married.

~~~~

I shouldn't have been surprised when Bret Grason's car was parked near the bus stop since he said he was going to pick me up, but for some reason I was.

Hop in," he said after he rolled down the car's window.

I justified riding with Mr. Grason because it was a lot faster than riding the bus. The bus had to make a lot of stops to pick up passengers before it reached the school building. Plus, riding in a car was much more comfortable. After being on my feet for all the hours I worked, any kind of comfort was nothing short of a blessing. There were times when I was so tired, I didn't think I could take another step – but I always did.

"Have a hard day?" he asked as he pulled away from the curb.

I figured I must look like I felt. I was exhausted both physically and mentally. All I wanted to do was find a place where I could rest. That place certainly wasn't at the restaurant or in the rusty tin trailer. The soft seat of a nice car came as close as I was likely to get.

"I doubled up today. I waited on tables plus washed dishes," I tried to explain why I was exhausted.

"Why double up?"

"I need the money, so Iva Lee lets me keep tips along with my regular dishwashing salary."

"Does a minister make much money?"

I wished he hadn't mentioned Calvin or money. It only added to the stress I was feeling.

"He says not," I told him.

"That's what I suspected. His church is in the poorest neighborhood around. From what I've heard, they have a difficult time getting a minister to take it on. A lot of the congregation are takers instead of givers."

He was telling me what I already knew.

"Where are you originally from?" he asked.

I was glad he changed the subject, although thinking about my once upon a time home was almost as depressing as talking about Calvin and the church.

"I was raised at the end of a little, backwoods, country road. My dad was a farmer and my mother worked at a factory." At least she did after Grant and I started school.

"Where?" he wanted to know.

"A long way from here." I was sure he had never heard of the little community in which I had once lived.

"Do you visit your parents often?"

"No. I haven't been back since I got married."

"Why not?"

How did I answer that question? Did I tell him Calvin wouldn't spend for gas or waste his time on taking me home, or that my own mother might not welcome me? "There's many reasons," I finally said. "No time for visits. As you know, I work seven days a week from morning until midnight except on the nights I take your class. The rest of the time I do what has to be done and try to get some sleep in my spare time."

"What has to be done?" he questioned.

"Laundry. Housecleaning. As a preacher, Calvin is always needing clean clothes that are ironed nicely, And the place is always filthy. I can't seem to get ahead of mold and rust. I don't know how a tiny trailer gets so filthy."

Mr. Grason nodded as though he understood what I was talking about. "Do you ever do anything for yourself?" he asked in the kindest of voice.

In a way, everything I did was for myself. I had to survive, so I did what was necessary. Including turning a blind eye to what I knew I should take a closer look at.

"I'm taking your class," I finally told him. Although it was Calvin who suggested I take GED classes, it was the only thing I had to look forward to. That and the small amount of time I rode in the car with Mr. Grason. Odd, how a few minutes of comfort could mean so much.

"Calvin West is a lucky man to have you for a wife."

His words sounded like a real compliment. It did my soul good. I hadn't realized how much I needed a kind word – a compliment. I didn't want the car ride to end. If only I could stay in the car longer, but that wasn't possible. He had pulled into his usual parking spot in front of the college. I reached for the door handle.

"Wait a minute before you get out. I need to let you know there won't be class Thursday."

Disappointment hit me. I hadn't realized how much I looked forward to the break classes gave me until I would have to miss one.

"I'll be attending a job conference. I am the guest dinner speaker. I think it would be beneficial for you to attend. Could you possibly get away for a day?

"No," I answered. Missing work would mean less money, and Calvin would be furious if I brought home less of a paycheck. "I have to work." Surely, Mr. Grason realized that much by now.

"If not for the day, then for the time you would be in class. I have no doubt it would be a great opportunity for you.

Maybe more educational than attending class. I'll pick you up at work the same time you would be catching a bus to class. You can attend the dinner meeting, and I can take you home afterwards.

I was thinking about the extra money I could make by working. I would be able to ask Iva Lee to pay me in cash instead of adding it to my paycheck. It would be a little more to contribute to my meager savings that Iva Lee suggested I should have. And then I thought of the time I would be spending with Mr. Grason, while riding in his wonderful car.

"Experiencing the conference will be an education in itself. You need experiences beyond the restaurant and taking classes."

He was right. There was a different world beyond the tiny box I has spent my life in. Both Marie and Judith had harassed me about my lack of worldly knowledge. Maybe it was time for me to venture out if only for a short while.

"I have nothing against dishwashing and waitressing, but there are other opportunities you should know about. Like jobs that pay more for working eight hours a day. This will be an opportunity for you to learn about some of them."

He was right about that also, but I was still afraid. Afraid of Calvin finding out . . . afraid of what I wasn't sure of.

"I won't take no for an answer," he told me firmly.

"Okay," I finally said. I had time to think about it before Thursday. Mr. Grason couldn't force me to go if I decided against going.

Mr. Grason seemed pleased with my answer as we got out of the car and went into the building.

I had the math book open, and Mr. Grason was sitting in a seat beside me helping me with homework when John Grieves made his appearance. Usually, he was late, the last one to arrive. I knew he was early in order to continue taunting me about Cleo Hampstead. I didn't know why he took pleasure in harassing me, but it was obvious he did. He looked both me and Mr. Grason over with an expression between surprise and a sneer.

"Oops," he said. "Didn't mean to interrupt something, uh, important."

"Wait a minute," Mr. Grason said quickly as John turned to leave the room. "You would benefit from this as much as Mrs. West. Pull up a seat as I explain the math problem I assigned for homework."

"No need," John added with a challenging grin. "I happen to be exceptional at math. I already know what one and one add up to be."

"Your exceptional math knowledge could have fooled me. It would seem you're not applying your ability, or you are exaggerating your knowledge greatly."

"Ah, teach, I have many other ambitions besides excelling in your class. I only have enough time to pass this GED thing instead of acing it."

"Such a shame," Mr. Grason told him. "A wise person would choose excelling in at least one thing rather than being deficient in everything."

A grin came to John's face and his eyes glittered with amusement. He marched across the room and took a seat as close to me as he could get.

"Does Calvin know you are . . . uh, tutoring his wife?" John dared to ask Mr. Grason with a smirk on his face that Mr. Grason ignored.

"I tutor anyone who requires additional instructions," Mr. Grason told him. "It is not necessary to get approval from husbands, parents, or *boyfriends*," Mr. Grason put emphases on the word boyfriends.

Teddy Green came to mind. Teddy Green had told John to shut his mouth before he shut it for him. It didn't sound like the words and tone of voice used between lovers having a spat. But then, what did I know about relationships – especially with men such as Teddy Green?

~~~~

I was surprised to find Calvin awake when I got home.

"You're early," he said as he sat up in bed and turned on the lamp on his side of the bed.

"Class night," I reminded him. I was early because it didn't take as long for Mr. Grason to drive me home as it did when I took the bus.

"Bret Grason drive you home?" he asked in a normal tone of voice. It didn't appear he cared one way or the other.

"I was thankful for the ride. I didn't have enough money for bus fare," I explained.

"How much in tips did you make today?" he asked as he held out his hand for the money.

"None," I told him. "I washed dishes."

His eye narrowed. "That's not what I heard," he said all too gently. "I won't tolerate you lying to me."

I realized that he'd surely been talking to Teddy Green. I had better come up with something the best I could. "Oddly enough, I did have one person insist I wait on him. It was a man who I dislike, but he wouldn't have any of the other waitresses. He left a three-dollar tip."

"Hand it over," Calvin demanded. "I'll not put up with you holding out on your obligations. Makes me wonder how many times you've done that – and why," he added in that soft voice of his.

I had no intention of handing it over. "I paid it on what I owe for books. I've owed for them far too long. That's why I didn't have bus fare."

"You threw three whole dollars away when you didn't have to. Don't do it again, Ellie. Do you hear me?"

I looked him in the eyes. Something in me snapped. "Me holding out on you? Well, let me tell you something, Calvin West. I hear gossip the same as you. I've heard that you pay the bills for a whore. I also heard that she has a son and you're its daddy." I felt myself tremble as I said those words. Saying them out loud made them real.

Calvin looked shocked. "Who told you such as a pack of lies?"

"Who told you about the three-dollar tip?" I countered. "Could it be the same person who told me you are paying Cleo Hampstead's bills? Are you claiming you're not her baby's daddy?"

Calvin couldn't hide the surprised look that came to his face. He hadn't expected me to stand up to him, much less bring up Cleo Hampstead and her son. I usually remained silent without confronting Calvin. I'd listened to Mom ranting until I promised myself, I'd never be like her, but this time I couldn't help myself. What Calvin had done in the past was affecting me right now. The same as what he was doing in the present.

"I'm nobody's daddy," he told me harshly. "I'm not the one who pays her bills either. The church has a collection each Sunday to help out those in need. I've been instructed to use some of it to pay for her groceries as well as groceries for one or two other people in need."

"Really? Do you consider us not to be in need also? Why aren't you paying for our food and my bus fare with church donations?"

He opened his mouth, but I didn't give him time to answer. I rushed on.

"Are you saying a woman like her doesn't make enough money to pay for her food? She must not be good at her profession." Not only that. If a church congregation can pay for other people's groceries, it seemed to me they could pay their minister enough to buy groceries for his own family.

"I have no intention of upsetting myself by arguing with you. If you were selfish enough to waste money on books when it's needed to pay our bills, then so be it. But I'm warning you not to do it again, understand?"

He was trying to stop me from confronting him, but it wasn't going to work.

"I'm starting to understand things all too well," I informed him. "Now is your chance to tell me exactly what's going on with you instead of some stranger telling me."

Calvin shook his head in disbelief. "I can't believe you have turned into your mother. No wonder your dad tried to hide in the barn all the time. I don't want to hear another word from you," he said as he reached out and clicked off the lamp to signify he was through talking to me.

I turned my back and walked out of the tiny bedroom. I realized that silence had always been Calvin's best defense. He seldom talked to me. When he did, it was in a gentle tone filled with hidden criticism as though I was a dumb child who couldn't understand his real meaning.

I was now trying to figure out if what he said true? Was it the church that paid for that woman's bills? How could John Grimes know Calvin was the father of that woman's baby or not? Considering her profession, there could be many other possibilities. Was I jumping to conclusions that weren't correct? Was I like my mother? What exactly was so bad about my mother? Perhaps she had a reason for being the way she was – a reason I knew nothing about.

It was only normal for a mother to have erratic behavior after watching her beloved son be ripped to pieces. It did something to a person's mind that could never be recovered from regardless of what a person did, or how hard they tried to make the horrible accident stop replaying in their mind. It was worse than a silent scream that was always there.

Dad had erratic behavior and so did I. Mom agreeing for me to marry Calvin was erratic behavior. Me marrying him had to be the result of my confused state of mind. Desperation makes a person do strange things they would never do if they were their normal selves. I was desperate when I married Calvin. I was feeling desperation now.

Being desperate didn't change the fact that Calvin was my husband. I had promised before God *To love and to cherish him in sickness and in health until death we do us part.* I had to make the best of the situation I was in. No one had a guarantee that marriage life would be perfect. People had their ups and downs all the time. Why should I expect my marriage to be different?

But I did. I had expected a preacher – a man of God – to be as close to perfect as a mortal man could get – and that was what I wanted. A strong man I could always trust and depend on. Was Calvin that man? Were my fears about Calvin all in my head? If so, how did I get over such fears?

Chapter 14

I couldn't believe Mr. Grason's car was waiting at the bus stop. I was both relieved and disgusted with myself. Relieved that I didn't have to ride the horrible, diesel stinking bus. I was also disgusted because I wanted to ride in Mr. Grason's car. Not only that, but I took pleasure in being with Mr. Grason. I considered him the only *almost* friend I had other than Iva Lee.

"Good morning early bird," he said with a welcoming smile as I got into the passenger seat.

"Good morning. Got early classes again?" I asked.

"I do for the next several weeks. Have to admit I'm enjoying seeing the rising sun each morning. Watching the dawn arrive gives a man a sense of peacefulness when he doesn't have to fight traffic."

I knew what he meant. Riding with Mr. Grason gave me a few minutes when I didn't feel afraid of what life had waiting for me. Working from six o'clock in the morning until twelve o'clock at night was brutal. I wondered how Iva Lee survived it seven days a week for who knew how long.

"Have you had breakfast?" he asked.

"No. I can get something when I get to the restaurant."

"You don't cook breakfast for your husband?"

I shook my head. "He wouldn't eat it if I did. He says my cooking is terrible. He gets his own breakfast when he wakes up."

"What time does he usually wake up?"

I had no idea when Calvin woke up or what he did all day long. When I asked, he told me he was always overwhelmed doing church work involving sermons, bookkeeping, along

with visiting the sick and elderly, and consoling those in
need. I had and image of what needs women such as Cleo
Hamstead had for my husband. I wiped the images from my
head as fast as I could.

"I don't know," I told him.

"Is he home when you arrive late at night?"

"He's usually in bed asleep."

"He doesn't mind the long hours you work?"

"No. He would like for me to put in more hours if it were
possible. He regrets insisting I take GED classes."

"He's the one who wanted you to take classes?" he asked.

I tensed but told him the truth. "He was embarrassed that
I hadn't even graduated high school. He said it wasn't a good
reflection on him. His congregation expects their minister not
to be married to a high school dropout."

"Did you tell him about the dinner Thursday instead of
attending class?"

"No. If I did, he would insist I work. He says I'm not
bringing in enough income. He encourages me to work as a
waitress instead of a dishwasher,"

"Do you?"

"Sometimes, when the waitresses don't show up or they
get in the weeds. They have been there longer than I have, so
they get the preferred job. When I do waitress, I still have to
double up by washing dishes at the same time. Dishwashing
is a job no one else is willing to do."

"Yet you're willing to do it?"

"Work is work," I told him. "Calvin says as uneducated
as I am, I'm lucky to get a job as a dishwasher. He thinks
waitressing will bring in more money, but it isn't guaranteed.
Some people don't tip very well."

Mr. Grason's brows drew together for a moment. "This
job conference should be insight in what's available out there
for an ambitious, hard-working young woman."

"So long as Calvin doesn't find out. It might be best if I
don't go," I added, knowing I was taking a chance.

"Nonsense. If he finds out, tell him you're hoping to find a better paying job by attending the job fair."

Sounded reasonable, but I knew Calvin wouldn't approve regardless of the reason for me not working those few hours.

~~~~

I was a nervous wreck by the time Thursday rolled around. I even confessed to Iva Lee about the job fair dinner and my hesitancy to attend."

"Go," she told me. "I don't want to lose a dishwasher even for a few hours, but I think it will be good for you regardless if it helps you with a new career or not."

"I'm afraid Calvin will find out," I told her.

"So, what if he does? Will he beat you or something?"

"No. I just don't want to get him upset because I took off instead of working."

"Does he ever get you upset?" Iva Lee made a point of asking.

I didn't know how to answer her. I didn't want to admit I was always upset with Calvin. The fact he didn't give me details about his work or what it involved bothered me. Why he took every dollar I made without divulging what bills he owed bothered me, or how much he was being paid. Neither did I want to admit, much less confess, that I feared he really was using what I earned to pay off Cleo Hampstead debts. I was tempted to tell Iva Lee that John Grimes said Calvin was the father of Cleo Hampstead's baby, but my pride wouldn't allow me to do it. I feared once I talked to someone about it, the more it would become real. It didn't seem right that a woman such as her had Calvin's baby when my own baby didn't survive long enough to be born.

"I try hard not to get upset," I answered her question the best I could.

"If only such was possible," she said. "I used to have a husband," she added as though it didn't matter in the least. "He had the idea that it was a man's right to bed as many women as possible both before and after marriage. Made him feel more of a man, I suppose. When I discovered he was being unfaithful, I blamed myself. I thought I wasn't woman enough to keep my man faithful." She shook her head. "Took me a long time before I came to my senses and realized that wasn't the case. He was nothing but a cheat, a no-account fucking-about husband. One I had mistakenly thought was an honorable man."

"Did you divorce him?" I asked, although I had already assumed that was what she was going to tell me.

"Nope. I stayed married to old Hubert and made his life pure hell. He got shot and killed thirty years ago by a jealous husband who came home unexpectedly to find him in bed with his wife."

I was shocked as she stood there with a grin on her face. "Seriously?" I couldn't stop myself from asking.

"Seriously," she answered. "Unknowingly to him, I saved up enough to take out an insurance policy on him. I had an idea either some jealous man or jilted woman would get him sooner or later. According to the old saying, fool around with a man's girlfriend and you'll get the hell beat outta you. Fool around with a man's wife, and you'll get killed. I bought this restaurant when the insurance paid off. Goes to show a smart woman can make sweet lemonade out of a mighty sour lemon."

My mouth must have been hanging open. I didn't know what to think about her story, but I figured it had to be true. My next thought was why was she telling me. Was she suggesting I take out an insurance policy on Calvin?

She gave me a knowing nod as though she was reading my thought. "I'm telling you this because you need to know everyone has incidents that occur in their life that are both bad and good. It's how you handle them that counts."

Chapter 15

It's how you handle them that counts, kept running through my mind. How was I going to make the incidents in my life count?

I was both a nervous wreck and filled with guilt when Thursday rolled around. I had decided not to go to the dinner a dozen times. It was Iva Lea who stopped me from not going.

"You got any pretty clothes like a dress and nice shoes?" she asked me Thursday when I arrived at work.

Pretty clothes? My Sunday clothes were still at Mom's house. Mom had packed only a few changes of everyday clothes. She hadn't allowed me to take much with me after Calvin and I were married. She said I could get things later. I didn't argue because she had always pointed out that she was the one who paid for every article of clothing I had.

I shook my head. My best clothes were the uniforms Iva Lee provided. My shoes were a pair of runover sneakers with holes in the toes. I had been so worried about going to the dinner that clothes hadn't entered my mind.

"Didn't think so. Here," she held out her hand and stuck money in my hand. "You're to take off at 10:00 o'clock and go down the street to K-mart and buy yourself a nice dress and a pair of shoes."

I looked at the twenty-dollar bill she had given me. There was no way I could take it. It would take me forever to pay her back. It meant I'd have no *mad money* to open an account with in forever.

"Don't look so disturbed. I'm only your employer. I'm not trying to be your fairy godmother. I'm short on pumpkins and glass slippers. I'll take a dollar out of your paycheck each week. Now, get to work and don't argue with me."

I didn't argue. Until now, I hadn't realized I would need to wear a nice dress and shoes. I would do as she said because I didn't want to embarrass myself or Mr. Grason by not being properly dress.

A strange feeling came over me as I walked down the street. The sun was shining, and a delicate wind was carrying the scent of fall petunias that were blooming outside stores in window boxes. I hadn't walked down a street like this since I married Calvin. The streets I'd walked on near the rusty tin trailer were trash strown with rundown buildings that warranted caution instead of beauty.

A momentary sense of freedom came to me. I felt like a person. A real live person with twenty dollars of money in a pocket that had always been empty. I knew the feeling wouldn't last long. Soon I would be back to being a scared girl who was broke and disappointed in herself. One with a husband who would take every penny she made to pay for Lord only knew what.

I pushed the thought of Calvin aside. I didn't want to lose the wonderful feeling of freedom by thinking of Calvin. But I still felt guilty about spending money I didn't have and would need to pay back. I saw the K-mart up ahead. And then I noticed the building right beside it. The sign read *New to Me* store. Pre-loved items at discount prices.

My feet turned into that store without me having to think about it.

"Good morning," an elderly lady greeted me. "Anything I can help you with, my dear?"

"Uh," I mumbled as I looked about the store. There was a little bit of nearly everything filling every available space. "I'm looking for a dress and shoes suitable for a business dinner and yet not expensive."

The woman smiled. "You've come to the right place. Let's see. You look like a size 4, right?"

I wasn't sure what size I was, but I nodded.

"That's good. We have a lot of clothes in that size. Women tend to outgrow them fast. Let's see," she said again. "With your coloring, I'd say something in a vibrant purple, blue or green. Even black will look good with your brown hair and eyes. Most blonds need pastel colors so as not to overpower their coloring, but you can handle vibrant."

"I'm not sure I want vibrant," I told her. "I'd prefer something more Sunday like." And definitely nothing that would draw attention to myself.

"We've got that also," she said as she led me to a rack of clothes. I picked out a dusty rose-colored suit, a skirt and jacket along with a white ruffled blouse.

"Good choice," the clerk told me. "There is also a pair of shoes that match it perfectly. Plus, they are on sale for half price since they have been here for a long while. Like I said, not many women wear this size."

I spent a total of nine dollars and forty-nine cents. When I got back to the restaurant, I stuck my hand in my pocket and held out the money to Iva Lee. I didn't want to owe her any more than necessary.

"Keep it," she said.

"No, I don't want to owe you too much."

"Keep it until tomorrow then. You might need it for something tonight. You can give me what you don't use in the morning."

I agreed to that, although I would have to hide the money from Calvin tonight along with the clothes I had just bought. I would figure out how to do that later. Right now, I had to get back to work. I now owed Iva Lee more than simply being a good dishwasher.

~~~~

Iva Lee lifted her brows in surprise when I came into the kitchen dressed in the suit and shoes. I had used her hairbrush and a touch of the makeup she kept in her own private bathroom above the restaurant. I had not realized that she had a tiny apartment above the restaurant until today. There was a storage room in the back of the restaurant, a door in the back of the room leading to a narrow stairway. At the top of the stairs was a very nice apartment.

"I got a little place out in the sticks," she had told me with a grin. "But I don't go there all the time. I stay in my apartment upstairs a lot when I'm too tired to drive home."

That explained how she was always at the restaurant before I arrived each day.

"I trust you'll not mention anything to the other employees. I keep the door to the stairs locked and tell them the upstairs is for storage. Which it is," she adds. "I store things up there including myself. I like my privacy," she told me, making sure none of the others heard us talking.

Then, why did she take a chance on disrupting her privacy for me? I couldn't help questioning why she was doing so much to help me when she hadn't done the same for any of the other employees.

Iva Lee's eyebrows lowered as her grin increased. "You look good," she told me. "Like a young woman instead of a scared girl."

How true that description was of me. I was a scared girl.

"Doubt your own husband will recognize you when you go home tonight."

Her words tightened the knot in my chest and my apprehension increased. "I can't go home looking like this."

"Why not?" she wanted to know.

"Calvin wouldn't approve of me going to the job fair dinner instead of working. He would be furious about me spending money on clothes and shoes." He was always accusing me of being wasteful. Spending money I didn't have on clothes in order to take off work was wasteful, but I wanted to do both. I didn't realize how much I wanted this until I saw myself in the small mirror.

Iva Lee frowned. "Does he ever spend money on his clothes?"

"He needs decent clothes. He's a preacher," I told her in Calvin's defense. I didn't want her to think worse of Calvin than I suspected she already did.

"Humph," she grunted out a sound. "Don't forget I met him before you did."

"What do you mean by that?" I asked.

"It means I don't think he's treating you fairly. Seems to me you're trying mighty hard to make him happy when he's not doing the same for you. Seems to me you're too afraid of his criticism, which makes me wonder why. Does he beat you?" she asked me a question she'd ask before.

"No," I told her quickly. "He's a preacher. He's a good man."

"Humph," she grunted again. "Ever heard of Jim Jones and Jim Bakker?"

I shook my head. "Who are they?"

She rolled her eyes. "You surely were raised isolated. Those men claimed to be preachers, but we don't have time to go into that. Your ride just pulled into the parking lot. Don't keep him waiting."

I finally asked her what I'd been meaning to ask. "Can I change clothes here when I get back from the job fair dinner and leave my new clothes here?"

"Of course, you can," she told me with another roll of her eyes. "Get out of here before someone sees you and wonders why you're all dressed up."

She had a point. I rushed to Mr. Grason's car and got in as quickly as I could. I even looked around to make sure neither John Grimes nor Teddy Green was there to see me do it.

"You look different," were the first words Mr. Grason said.

I wasn't sure if it was a compliment or not until I got a good look at his expression. His eyebrows had lifted and so had the corners of his mouth, although he wasn't exactly smiling.

"You look more mature. It suits you," he added, as his gaze moved over me from head to foot and then back to my face.

"I hope I'm dressed suitable. Iva Lee told me I should wear something other than shirt and jeans."

"You are dressed perfect," he said, as he gave me another appreciative look.

His approval made me feel better about myself, but I still felt self-conscious about being dressed up and going somewhere with Mr. Grason when I knew Calvin would not approve. It felt like being back home with Mom. She had seldom approved of what I did, much the same way Calvin disapproved of me now.

I did my best to relax and feel the comfort of riding in Mr. Grason's car, but it didn't come. It didn't take long until I was feeling out of place and was regretting agreeing to attend this so-called job fair dinner.

"Where is the job fair being held?" I asked the question I should have asked when he first told me about the event.

"It's about an hour and forty-five minutes' drive from here in the small town of Cleveland," he told the name of the town and continued talking about the place. "The section of Appalachian land was granted to a Colonial Ben Cleveland for his heroic service at the battle of Kings Mountain. It's a small farming community where poverty is still rampant. The main purpose of the job fair is an attempt to bring workers and businesses to together. If we get enough people at the job fair, we may be able to get factories to move there. There is no better way to eradicate poverty than to bring in jobs."

I was both stunned and excited. I was going home – almost. The job fair was being held in my hometown. The small town where Mom had gone to shop once a month on Saturdays. She enjoyed sitting in her car watching people walk up and down main street. She always commented on what they wore, how they looked, and what kind of person they were. She always used people as an example of what I should or should not be like.

Dad and Grant had rather take a beating than go to town with Mom. Sometimes I felt the same way when Mom was determined to lecture me. Still yet, I enjoyed going to town. It was a break from the monotony of staying at the head of an isolated hollow.

"I used to live not far from there," I told him.

"Really? How far from town did you grow up?" he asked.

"About ten miles. My parents live at the end of Goins Road. The road was named after my great grandpa."

"What does your dad do for a living?"

"He's a row-crop farmer. He grows mostly beans. He will also grow a few other vegetables off and on, but there's not much of a market for anything other than beans. Cabbage sells sometimes, but you can't count on the market being good. Cabbage doesn't take as much labor as beans. Farmers tend to flood the market."

"And your mother?"

"She stays at home. I have a baby brother that she dotes on," I told him what I knew was the truth.

"No other siblings?"

I wished he'd stop asking questions. I didn't want to think about Grant, much less talk about him, but I felt I should give him an answer.

"An older brother, but he died. Enough about me. Tell me about yourself. What's your wife's name? How long have you been married?" I was quick to ask. He'd once told me his wife stayed home, but that was all I knew about her.

A sad smile turned up the corners of his lips. He stared at the highway for long moments before he spoke. "I prefer not to talk about my personal life," he said, and was silent for a few minutes. Finally, he seemed to make a decision and start talking. "My wife's name is Grace Anna. I married her fifteen years ago."

Fifteen years. I was a small child when he was married. It didn't seem possible he was that much older than me. It was obvious that time had made him far more intelligent than I was. Maybe when I was his age, I would feel more competent.

"Do you have children?" I wanted to know more about him, and now seemed as good a time as any to find out. I never had enough time talking to him while riding to and from class. When we did talk, it was usually about the GED classes I was taking.

"No. Grace Anna and I wanted children, but it didn't happen."

"Why not?" I was bold enough to ask.

He made a face and shook his head. At first, I didn't think he was going to answer, but he did.

"She had surgery before I met her, and it left her sterile." He was silent for a while before he continued talking. His voice grew softer and sadder. "She said she didn't know until after we were married."

"You didn't believe her?" I asked, surprised at the direction our conversation had taken.

"She had a hysterectomy. She knew she could never have children, but she convinced herself otherwise."

"Oh," I said. "You could adopt."

He shook his head. "Grace Anna is not capable of being a mother. I have full time help for her as it is."

This was something he hadn't told me before. I had thought his wife was a capable woman who was lucky to have a husband such as Mr. Grason.

"Grace Anna and I have a mutual agreement," he continued. "She's allowed to pretend she can still have children, and I'm allowed to pretend I have a wife who is normal."

"What's wrong with her?" I wanted to know. Hadn't he told me before that she spent her time being a housewife?

Was he telling me something different, or had I simply misunderstood him?

"She has both physical and mental problems, although her physical problems are not severe," he said, and then tried to add a happier tone to his voice. "Let's not talk about her. I prefer to dwell on happier thoughts. If we had more time, I could drive you by your parent's place." He was obviously changing the subject away from him.

My parents' place. I suddenly wanted to go back home. Wished I was a single girl again with Grant still alive - even if I wasn't Mom's favorite child. I would still have my dreams of having a wonderful husband and a happy future with children playing at my feet. My life wasn't turning out to be remotely like I had imagined it would be.

How different my reality was. I washed dishes day and night with only a few hours' sleep. I had lost a baby, while having a husband who cared more about the congregation of a run-down church than he did his own wife. Not to mention he could be the father of a child belonging to a prostitute. My next big problem was I couldn't get past wanting to know if *my hard-earned money was going to support her?* It certainly wasn't going to me.

That was my reality, and acknowledging it hit me harder than usual.

"Why the sad face," Mr. Grason asked me.

"Do childhood dreams ever come true?" I found myself asking him.

"Only if you work at making them come true," he told me gently. "That's the main purpose of job fairs. It helps give people a chance to realize their childhood dreams."

"How?" I asked, wondering how such as that would be possible.

"By showing people there are options to being stuck in doing the same thing or doing nothing at all. By showing people they have choices. That it is possible to accomplish their childhood dreams."

Seemed to me my childhood dreams were hopeless regardless of what I did or didn't do. "Are you living your childhood dreams?" I asked.

"Oh, no," he was quick to answer. "I can't claim to practice what I preach. I thought I would be a happily married man with children, a home, and a loving wife by this age in my life. I do have a house and a job I think is worthwhile," he added.

"Has a job fair ever helped you?" I wanted to know.

"Financially, yes. I get paid fairly well for helping with job fairs, but as far as my job goes, I am content with being a professor. I get satisfaction in thinking I help educate and guide worthy young people to meet their potential."

Did he think I was worthy and had potential? "Do you think I'm one of those young people?" I found myself asking.

"Not only do you have potential, you also have the greatest work ethic I've seen in a long while. Plus, you are above average in intelligence. Those three combinations can take you a long way in life."

"All it's taken me is to washtubs of greasy dishes," I couldn't stop myself from saying what I knew was true.

He smiled. "We all start somewhere, but we don't have to stay there."

~~~~

Once we drove into town, the more memories rushed at me. I was going home and yet I felt as though I no longer had a home. The minute I married Calvin I lost my home and my parents. I was cast out on a sea of unknown. A sea where a man I knew very little about was supposed to be responsible for me for the rest of my life. Mom claimed a wife's job was to be a helpmate to her husband, and yet it didn't seem like Mom practiced what she preached.

"Anything familiar? Mr. Grason asked.

"Yes. Everything is familiar."

"There might be people you know attending the job fair."

"I doubt it." I didn't think anyone I had grown up with would be seen going to a job fair. It was as though everyone was born in one of those old-time caste systems and wasn't allowed to step up. I could still hear Mom telling me "Stop trying to get above my raisin'," when I wanted something better than something my cousin's had.

"Why not?" I realized that Mr. Grason was asking me a question.

"We were taught to be satisfied with the lot God gives us." Was the answer I gave him.

He nodded as though he was finally understanding something. "It's that kind of rationalizing that keeps people seeped it poverty. It makes a person feel guilty if they make an attempt to better themselves, or even better the circumstances they live in."

I knew he was referring to me as well as the horrible trailer I was forced to live in. I also felt guilty that I had so much pride. I wouldn't want anyone who knew me to know how I was forced to live. Mom had always tried to keep up appearances. *What will people think* was one of her buzz words. What would she think and say if she knew how I was forced to live? Would she care, or would she think it was good enough for the likes of me?

"We're here," he said as he parked in front of a large building. "Did you go to this high school?"

"No," I told him. This was the most prestigious high school in the county. The one I went to was at the bottom. "There are a lot of cars here. Are all these people attending the job fair?"

"Yes, plus I imagine there are a few extra people who have shown up for the free dinner. You know the old saying, free food is good food. A few of the cars belong to those who are sponsoring the event."

"Who pays for all this?" I wanted to know.

"The cost is covered by the factories that are seeking employees. If there is enough interest, then they will build factories in the area. Hopefully, the companies can arrange with the county to provide the land to build the factories on for free."

"Why this town?" I wanted to know. Wouldn't it be better to have a job fair in a more prosperous area.

"It's simple. These companies do a study on the counties where there is little to no employment opportunities. That way they have a large supply of workers willing to work at the lowest wages possible. Plus, as I pointed out, the county, or some good Samaritan, will usually provide the land for free. It becomes a win-win for all involved."

That made sense to me. Especially the part about working for the lowest wages possible. At least getting paid under the table was a plus.

"There's a lot of cars," I stated the obvious.

"Free food always draws a lot of interest," he said. "That's why the job fairs always provide a free meal."

Mr. Grason got out of the car and so did I. By the time he had locked the doors I was beside him. Nervousness had hold of me. I wasn't sure where to go or how to act.

"The job fair is being held in the gym, while the dinner will be in the cafeteria." He lifted his arm and looked at his watch. "I think we'll have time to walk by the booths. They give away a lot of free samples of trinkets and pamphlets. Some of the things are worth getting although they are simple items."

Mr. Grason courteously guided me to the gym and opened the heavy door holding it for me to enter as he placed his hand on my back in a gentlemanly fashion. I was surprised to see the number of booths that had been set up. Several people were wandering around with plastic bags in their hands. Mr. Grason guided me to a booth where the plastic bags were being given out. He took two bags and handed me one.

"The bags are to put the samples in that you're interested in. Make sure you take the pamphlets also. They have a lot of job information in them."

At first, I was hesitant at taking samples until I realized the people who were running the booths really did want you to take a sample. It gave them a chance to talk to you personally while explaining what their factories were offering in the way of job creations and their benefits to individuals as well as the area. Oddly enough, I felt a bit insulted listening to them talk about the area I was raised in as being a poverty-stricken area. I wondered what they would consider the area in which Calvin and I now lived in?

Mr. Grason put his hand on my back to guide me around a crowd of people standing in the aisle near one of the exhibits. I brushed against the arm of a man and glanced up as I started to say excuse me. Much to my surprise I was face to face with Drake Lewis. For a moment, I was delighted to see a familiar face. I had an urge to throw my arms around him, but it didn't last.

He still had a tough guy appearance, but there was also something else about him that I couldn't quite interpret. Surprise at seeing me flashed over his face a moment before he grinned, looked from my face to my shoes and then back up.

"Well, well," he drawled out. "Fancy seeing you here. "Ditched your preacher already, humph? Can't say I'm surprised."

"Drake," I said. "There for a moment I was glad to see you."

He gave me a disgusted look before he took in Mr. Grason. "Is this the preacher's replacement?" he said, as he insultingly looked Mr. Grason up and down.

At Drake's obvious slur, I had expected anger from Mr. Grason, but it didn't happen.

"Mrs. West is still happily married to her preacher," Mr. Grason told him in a gentle tone of voice. "And no, I'm not his replacement. Actually, I am a professor who teaches the GED class Mrs. West is taking. I encouraged her, as well as the other students, to attend this job fair. Are you here in hopes of obtaining a better job, Drake?"

Drake looked surprised and then angry. He didn't appear to know how to answer. Oddly enough I felt sorry for him.

"Have you seen Mom and Dad lately?" I asked in hopes of breaking the tension in Drake. I also wanted to know more about my parents and baby Grant.

Drake's eyes left Mr. Grason to focus back on me. "Right often," he said as though Mr. Grason and I no longer mattered to him.

"How are they doing?"

"The new baby is helping with the loss of their beloved son. They never mention you," he added as he turned his back on me and walked off.

Mr. Grason placed his hand on my back again and guided me away from the crowd. Odd how that hand helped to comfort the ache I was feeling as all those horrible memories rushed me. "Who was that rude person?" he asked with obvious disapproval.

"He was our neighbor."

"And your rejected boyfriend?"

I wasn't sure how to answer that as I recalled him waiting for me when I went after the cows. Along with what he had said and the way he had kissed me.

"He was never my boyfriend. Drake's family made liquor and drank a large portion of it. Mom disapproved of him and his family."

"Appears he's trying to better himself," was the only comment Mr. Grason said.

"I hope he succeeds," I said. I should be used to Drake insulting me from all those years when I was growing up, but it still hurt. My first contact from a person from home had brought back painful memories.

"We best find our way to the cafeteria and take our seats. It wouldn't look good for the guest speaker to be late," he said a short time later.

I willingly and silently followed him from the gym clutching my half-full bag of vendor goodies. Seeing Drake had intensified the fact I had made a mess of my life. Coming face to face with him and his insults had overwhelmed me with guilt at never being able to live up to Mom's, and now Calvin's expectations of me. I'd made a big mistake by coming to this job fair. There was no way I would ever be able to better my situation.

~~~~

We took our seats near the front to make it easier for Mr. Grason to reach the podium when it was time for his presentation. There were several other people at the table who looked happy to be there as they chatted with each other.

The moderator finally walked up to the podium and asked for silence. He then called on someone to say grace over the meal. After the blessing, he asked everyone to get in line for the buffet.

I felt as though I was struggling through a cloud of fog as I got up from my seat to follow Mr. Grason through the buffet line. I took a small portion of several dishes. I wasn't in the least bit hungry. Once we were seated, I forced myself to eat the food without tasting it. I talked very little, although Mr. Grason did his best to keep up a lively conversation with the others at the table. Thankfully, I didn't recognize a one of them, and none of them recognized me. Drake was the only person there that I knew, although a lot of the attendees were my age. Most of them were probably from the school that was holding the job fair. As for Drake, I didn't see him at any of the tables. I had an idea he had too much pride to eat free food.

Mr. Grason was finally introduced. He made his way to the podium and did what I took to be an excellent job with his presentation according to the applause that followed. I had sat there with my eyes glued to him, but I hadn't listened to a word he said. I was lost in my own thoughts, none of which were pleasant.

"Are you his daughter?" One of the young ladies at the table leaned toward me and ask, while several people had delayed Mr. Grason by shaking his hand.

"No," I told her with a shake of my head.

"His wife?" she then asked.

"No. I'm one of his students," I said in hope she would ask no more questions.

"I'm willing to be his student. I'm sure he could teach me a lot," she said with a grin. "He's such a hunk."

I must have given her a disbelieving look for she turned away from me and started talking to the person beside her.

Finally, Mr. Grason returned to the table as the moderator took to the podium to end the dinner by thanking everyone for attending and attending the job fair.

"Are you ready to leave?" Mr. Grason asked me. "We've got a ways to drive."

I stood up so fast I almost knocked over my chair.

Mr. Grason never said a word as he walked beside me to the car where he unlocked my door first, opened it and placed his hand on my back as though he was helping me get in. I could feel the warmth of his touch through my thin suit jacket. Oddly enough, his touch was almost more than my misery could take. I felt the burn of tears behind my eyes as he got in the vehicle and pulled out of the parking lot. A few minutes later he spoke.

"What's bothering you, Ellie?" he asked gently as he reached out and squeezed my hand for a moment.

That act of kindness was more than I could take. Tears started rolling down my cheeks. "I'm sorry," I mumbled. "Bad memories," I managed to say as my tears increased.

He drove for another ten minutes before he pulled into the parking lot of a strip mall. He chose a secluded spot in the dimly lit section.

"Okay, Ellie. A heartache shared is a heartache halved. Tell me about it."

I surprised myself by telling him everything. From always knowing Mom didn't like the person I was, to describing Grant's horrible death, to Drake, and my marriage to Calvin. I even blamed myself for expecting more of Calvin than he was capable of giving me.

Mr. Grason didn't say a word as he reached out and took me in his arms much like he did the time I cried my heart out over my miscarriage.

Again, like a helpless child, I hid my face against his chest, gripped the material of his shirt in my clenched fists, and lost what little pride that remained as a flood of tears overtook me.

"It's all right, sweet girl. Cry it out. Cry it all out. It'll make you feel better."

He was wrong. I was even more ashamed of myself for crying like a baby. "I ... hate myself," I mumbled as I tried to sniff back my flood of tears."

"Oh, no," he said as his lips came close to my ear, his face buried in my hair. "Don't say that. You're a most wonderful person. You're special. Kind. Gentle. Moral. I knew that from the first moment I laid eyes on you."

Those words were what I wished were true, but I knew better. I didn't feel one bit better about myself. "I'm disgusting," I mumbled.

The next thing I knew his arms were holding me and his lips were showering kisses all over my face and neck. I lifted my face until my lips met his. The feelings that shot through me was something I had not expected. A burning need consumed my entire body. I couldn't get enough of his arms, his kissing, the hands that were touching me. I wanted more. Wanted to enter his very soul in order to become a part of him.

"Oh, Ellie," he mumbled as his mouth opened and his tongue entered my mouth with a desperation equal to mine. I felt him tremble a moment before he finally forced his mouth to leave mine. "I can't do this. You're still a child."

His words were like a slap in the face. Child? I had never been a child. I certainly didn't feel like one right now.

"I'm sorry, Ellie," he added as his arms loosened. "I don't know . . ."

"No," I told him firmly. "Don't be sorry. I'm not a child. I'm ..." I didn't finish what I had intended to say as I lifted my hands, buried my fingers in his hair and pulled his mouth back to mine. This time I kissed him with all the passion, all the desperation I was feeling.

He responded for fiery minutes before he pulled away again. "We can't do this. Not here. Not now."

He eased me out of his arms, started the car and drove out of the parking lot. I sat there stunned by the feeling of having lost what I had only moments before. I had wanted nothing more than for time to stand still, to remain in his arms forever. Have him never stop holding me, kissing me.

He took a handkerchief out of his pocket and silently handed it to me. I wiped my eyes, blew my nose, and put the used handkerchief in the pocket of my suit jacket. Too embarrassed to return a snotty handkerchief.

"It's best we forget this ever happened," he spoke softly as he stared at the road instead of looking at me.

Forget it ever happened? He was regretting holding me, kissing me. Did he also regret he brought me to the job fair? Did he regret having me as a student?

He drew in a breath and slowly let it out. "The moment I saw you something came over me. I knew you were the one I should have met a long time ago. The one I was meant to fall in love with. The one I should have married. And then I found out your age – and that you were actually married. Calvin West had already robbed the cradle. I wanted to take you away from him – and at the same time realized I would never do such as that. I care about you far too much to ruin your life, your marriage. Ellie, fact is each of us met a promise too late.

A promise too late kept running through my mind as we traveled in silence through the dark night.

"What God has joined together let no man put asunder," Mr. Grason broke the silence by saying as though his soul was suffering greatly.

"What God has joined together," I repeated. "Was it really God who joined me to Calvin West? I thought marrying him would join me to a person who would love me unconditionally, but I was wrong. He never loved me. Still doesn't," I admitted what I didn't want to be true.

"Did you love him?" Mr. Grason asked.

"I'm not sure. I expected to fall in love with him more with each day that passed. He was my husband. *My husband!* Instead, I find that I'm caring less about him every time I come home at night to find him in bed sleeping while I worked. I'm beginning to realize I don't have a husband. I have a master."

"Why don't you leave him?" Mr. Grason asked as though he was asking a question no more important than asking about the weather.

"I have no place to go." Marrying Calvin had put me in a trap I didn't know how to get out of. What God had joined together, I reminded myself.

"You earn enough money to rent a small place. Iva Lee might even be willing to let you rent a room in her house. She appears to be fond of you or she wouldn't be trying to help you the way she does. From what I've observed, she doesn't treat any other of her employees the way she does you."

"Why don't you leave your wife?" I couldn't stop myself from asking.

"Responsibility," he was quick to answer. "I feel responsible for her. She's not able to take care of herself – mentally or physically. I can't simply walk away from her even when it's exactly what I want to do."

I was sure Calvin would be able to take care of himself. I wasn't sure if I could take care of myself.

Chapter 16

It was after midnight by the time we got back to the restaurant. I asked Mr. Grason to drop me off there. I had wanted to ride the bus home in hopes it would appear to Calvin I was working instead of being at the job fair – if he happened to be awake. Iva Lee had the open sign turned off and the closed sign up. Thankfully, she still had a light on at the back entrance. She opened the door when I knocked.

"Back a little late," she said and looked to make sure Mr. Grason was waiting on me. "The bus left thirty minutes ago. You look beat. Didn't things go as you planned?"

No, they hadn't, but I wasn't about to tell anyone about it. "I hadn't realized the job fair was being held in my hometown. It brought back a lot of memories," I said, as I took off my suit jacket and unbuttoned my blouse. "I'll change fast. I don't want to keep you here any longer or keep Mr. Grason waiting on me. Oh, here is your money," I told her as I took the money from my pocket. "Thank you," I added with heartfelt appreciation. At the same time, I regretted spending money on myself. "I'll pay you back a little each week."

"I know you will," she told me. "Some people deserve help. Others don't."

I didn't question her statement as I rushed into the bathroom to change into my work clothes.

"Unless you want to take them home with you, I'll put your nice suit, blouse, and shoes upstairs in case you should need them again," she told me.

"I best leave them here for now," I told her.

164

As much as I didn't want to, it was time to return to the rusty, mold ridden trailer – and Calvin.

Mr. Grason dropped me off as close to the trailer door as possible. It was as though he wanted Calvin to know I'd been with him.

"I'll pick you up in the morning," he told me as he reached out and squeezed my hand.

"No. Please don't. It'll be best if I ride the bus," I told him as I pulled my hand away.

"I'd like to see you in the morning. At least to take you to work."

"Not tomorrow," I told him. I'd kept enough change from Iva Lee's money to pay bus fare to and from work tomorrow.

"Ellie ..."

"Please, Mr. Grason. Not tomorrow."

"Okay," he told me.

I heard him drive away as soon as I closed the trailer door.

"So, he brought you home," came Calvin's voice from the bedroom.

By the tone of his voice, I realized someone, such as John Grimes, had informed Calvin about the job fair.

"Obviously," I returned as I walked into the bedroom without turning on the light. "I'm exhausted."

The bed springs groaned as Calvin moved enough to turn on the lamp light and gave me a harsh look-over. "You found riding around with *your* teacher exhausting?"

I didn't like the way he said *your* teacher, but I wasn't about to let him make me respond in the way he wanted me to.

"I was hoping attending the job fair would lead me getting a better paying job, but I don't think it will happen. Who told you about the job fair?"

"Who told me isn't important. Why you didn't tell me is important."

"I didn't plan on going until the last minute."

"Really?"

"Really. I ended up feeling out of place. I wish I hadn't gone. I hadn't realized it was being held at Cleveland High School. It brought back memories of Grant being killed."

"You've had time to get over that," he told me.

"I'm trying."

"You better try harder. I find it unpleasant living with a brooding woman."

I turned my back to him and went to the tiny bathroom where the tub, sink and commode were all crammed together. Calvin's dirty underwear was lying in the floor. I started to pick it up to examine what kind of stains might be on it. Instead, I stomped my feet on it and left it there.

When I returned to the bedroom, the light was still on, and Calvin was stark naked. I tried not to show my revulsion at what was about to happen. I'd always tried my best to be a good wife to Calvin by letting him do what he wanted when he wanted. I'd even tried to do the things I hated because Calvin like it that way.

"Take off all your clothes," he told me. "I want to get a good look at you."

I gritted my teeth as I took off my uniform and folded it carefully. I would have to wear the uniform again tomorrow.

"Tell that teacher of yours you're my wife. No man touches my wife other than me. Got it?" he said as he reached for me.

Afterwards, I couldn't fall asleep as silent tears slid down my cheeks. Calvin had no such problem. His snores vibrated off the walls. I simply couldn't believe that a just, loving God had joined me together with this man. I way lying there thinking he was sadistic, even borderline cruel. He had just used me for his own pleasure.

Was God punishing me for being born? For being the kind of person even my own mother dislike?

~~~~

"Didn't sleep much last night, did you?" Iva Lee said as soon as I walked through the back door. I wondered how she always seemed to know things about me without giving me so much as a good look.

"No, I didn't."

"You have hickies all over your neck, which weren't there when Bret Grason dropped you off last night. I take it Calvin made a point of leaving his mark on you."

I felt my face blush. I had dressed and combed my hair without looking in a mirror.

"There's makeup in my private bathroom if you want to try covering them up. Some women would be proud to show them off. The choice is yours."

I wasn't some woman. "Thanks," I mumbled as I went upstairs to her private bathroom. Much to my regret, I looked in the mirror. A sad girl was looking back at me. Her eyes were red, her mouth and cheeks appeared rubbed raw from beard stubble. There were several purplish bruises where Calvin had made a point to bite and suck on my neck obviously to mark me. Problem was none of it had been done with love.

I did the best I could with my appearance. I even used some of Iva Lee's eye drops in an effort to take the red out of my eyes.

"You look better," Iva Lee said as I entered the kitchen. "A little paint and plaster can improve the looks of any old shack. I ought to know being I've used a lot of paint and plaster on myself."

I looked her over. Never had I noticed any kind of makeup on her. Cooking food in a hot kitchen would sweat off any makeup she might wear, so why did she keep a good supply in her private bathroom?

"I've not always been this old and fat," she continued talking to me as I silently listened. "I was once young and pretty. Youth doesn't last forever, and unfortunately, beauty is in the eyes of each beholder. There are times when I buy

makeup and fancy things simply to jog pleasant memories –
regardless if I use it or not."

Okay, but that didn't make good sense to me. Why waste
money on buying things you might never use?

"When you get my age, you'll better understand the needs
of a woman my age," she answered as though she had read
my mind. "My needs are not much different than yours," she
grinned as she said that. "I told you briefly about my husband
and finding out he was cheating on me. Instead of giving in
to killing him myself, I decided what was gravy for the goose
was also gravy for the gander. In other words, if my husband
could screw his brains out with other women, I could do the
same with another man. I might add that I only had one man.
One special man."

I was stunned by what she said as I watched her chop
vegetables with expert ease using a razor-sharp meat cleaver
as she talked.

"You actually . . .?" I didn't know what word to use to
describe the image that came to my mind.

"Had a lover," she gave me a nicer word than I was
thinking. "I did and still do."

Still do? I couldn't believe such as that. She was too old
to behave in such a way. Only young people did such as that
– women like Cleo Hampstead.

"After ole Hub died, my lover and I chose not to get
married. One of the things I know for a fact is married life
gets boring fast. It also makes spouses expect more of each
other. Having a lover ... well, it remains intriguing."

I was speechless. Was she suggesting I take on a lover?

She stopped chopping and raked the vegetables in a bowl.
"I have learned a lot of things during my life. One of the
things is that the young jump into marriage expecting life to
turn out to be *happy ever after*. It seldom if ever does. Living
with another person can be difficult even when the couple is
in love with each other. You've heard the old saying, when
hardships come in the door, love flies out the window."

I couldn't believe Iva Lee was on an advice roll. I just couldn't figure out what that advice was – not to mention figuring out who her lover could possibly be.

"Why are you telling me all this?" I had to ask.

"You remind me of being young, and it was not so long ago, I might add. I want you to know you have choices in what you do or don't do with the rest of your life. Make sure those choices are wise choices."

"What are you gabbing about?" Marie asked as she came in the back door.

"The weather," Iva Lee was quick to answer. "You got here on time for once. Something must be wrong with you."

Marie made a face as he glanced at me and then took a good look. She laughed right out loud for a moment. "Makeup," she said. "Trying to cover up a wild night? Didn't know preachers believed in passion. Those hickies surely did come from your preacher."

"Hush up," Iva Lee told her. "I haven't seen a hickie on your neck in years. Wonder why?"

Marie snorted out a huff. "You wouldn't know a hickie if you saw one."

Iva Lee only grinned and told her to get to work prepping the dining room.

A short time later, the phone rang. Iva Lee lifted her brows in question. It was early for anyone to be calling the restaurant.

"Good Eats," Iva Lee said in her southern drawl. "Yeah, she does. She is. Okay, just a minute." She pressed the phone's mouthpiece to her chest as she turned to me. "She says she's your mother."

Excitement rushed over me. Finally, after all this time, Mom wanted to talk to me. I was so happy I could cry. Instead, I hurriedly took the phone from her.

"Mom, is it really you?" I said as I felt a smile that spread over my face.

"I want to know what you think you're up too?" It was Mom all right.

"Uh," I mumbled, not understanding the anger in her tone of voice. "I'm at work," I told her. My smile disappeared.

"I know that along with all the rest you're trying to hide," she accused.

"Hide?" I questioned. "I don't know what you're talking about."

"Don't give me that. I heard about you being all gussied up and running around with a man who wasn't your husband. I've never been so ashamed in my life."

"Are you talking about me attending the job fair last night?" Someone had wasted no time gossiping to her.

"Is that what you're call it? I'm not that stupid. You have no business slutting around in the middle of the night with some man. You've got a good husband. A preacher. I know what you were doing with that man."

"For goodness' sake, Mom. I wasn't slutting around with anybody. He's the teacher where I'm getting my GED. I rode with him because I didn't have a car."

"Don't you lie to me. He couldn't keep his hands off you."

I recalled the gentlemanly way he would place his hand on my back. Where I came from a man never touched a woman unless it was sexual.

"Who told you such a lie?" I demanded. "Was it Drake Lewis? You know better than to believe a thing he says."

"Drake Lewis never said a word to me. I heard about it from more than one little bird."

Oh, sure. Those *little birds* who always gossiped to Mom about things they knew nothing about. It had to be those *little birds* who also told her where I worked. Never before had she cared enough to find out anything about me. She didn't even know I'd miscarried.

"I've never been so embarrassed in all my life to hear how fancy you were dressed with your face all painted up like a jezebel."

I was speechless. Someone sure had to be jealous of me to exaggerate so much to Mom, but then, it came as no surprise. I didn't know how to explain further or even if I should try.

"I have a good mind to drive down there and tell Calvin what you've been up to. It's time he put his foot down on you."

"Mom," I said as I tried to hide my exasperation with a bit of reason. "I would love for you and Dad to come for a visit. I'd like to see you both as well as little Grant. As you know, I've never seen my little brother."

I didn't realize Iva Lee could hear every word Mom was yelling at me until she leaned closer the phone and gave me a wink. "Get off the phone, Ellie. It's time to get back to work before I dock your pay."

"Sorry, Mom. I've got to go," I told her.

"I better never hear another bad word about you," she told me.

Iva Lee took the phone from my hand and hung it up. "Now I have the answer to why you married Calvin West," she told me.

I worked the rest of the day in relative silence. Iva Lee didn't say another word about Mom's call. I was thankful none of the other employees had come in time to hear the conversation and that Marie had been in the dining room where she couldn't overhear the phone call. In a way I feared Mom would come charging through the door of the restaurant to lay into me. In another way I hoped she would show up. I wanted her to see how the *good preacher* forced me to live. She just might have more to be embarrassed about than me attending a job fair.

~~~~

Mr. Grason was parked near the restaurant entrance when I came outside to catch the bus to class. Mom's accusation caused me to hesitate. I felt like she had eyes right there watching me. That thought made me mad as heck. I could ride with Mr. Grason and save bus fare if I wanted to. I hadn't done anything wrong, other than the few minutes when he had tried to comfort me, and I refused to think about that. I certainly wasn't going to let a few gossiping *little birds* dictate how I would live my life.

I walked to his car and got in with determination. I couldn't stop myself from feeling self-conscious from what we did in the parking lot after the job fair. Thinking about it made my heart speed up. I had to admit I wanted to experience that feeling again.

"What's got you in a snit?" he asked right off.

"I'm not in a snit," I informed him.

He grinned. "Get it off your chest. A problem . . ."

"Shared, is a problem halved," I finished what he was about to say."

"Right. So, what is it?"

"Who did you talk to about me at the job fair?" I wanted to know since the only person I recognized was Drake. Mom said she hadn't talked to him, which I believed. They always disliked each other too much to ever become gossiping buddies.

He looked puzzled for a minute as he drove out of the parking lot onto the highway. "No one, really. Wait a minute, come to think on it, there was one woman who asked about you. I told her you were my student, and you hoped the job fair would help you get a better job than washing dishes at a restaurant."

"Did you tell her the name of the restaurant?"

"Come to think back on it, I believe I did say you worked at Good Eats."

I now understood how Mom knew where I worked, and why she was coming down hard on me. Some woman had started gossip, and it reached Mom in record time. Mom feared a scandal was brewing. One that reflected back on her.

"Tell me what happened, Ellie?"

I told him about Mom's phone call.

"I'm sorry I caused you a problem. You are the one person I would never put in a compromised position. I care too much about you for that."

He *cared* about me. Those were magic words I'd longed to hear all my life. Words from someone who cared instead of a mother who was responsible for me, or a husband who needed what he could get from me. I took a closer look at Mr. Grason to see if he meant what he said or was it just another meaningless comment. The way he was looking at me warmed me from my toes to the top of my head. I had never had anyone look at me that way before.

My breath caught in my chest when he reached out his hand to caress my cheek with the tip of his fingers.

"Time is a cruel barrier in what could have been. If only I could flash back to a time before I was married and met you before Calvin West did, both our lives would be different right now."

That was true in so many ways, but it didn't happen. He couldn't go back in time, and neither could I. "We're right where we're at," I told him.

He started to say more, but John Grimes was standing against the building watching us as we pulled into the parking lot.

"I think he's stalking me," I said what came to my mind. "He and Teddy Green are telling Calvin every move I make."

"I wouldn't put it past John Grimes, but why would Teddy Green do something such as that?"

"I don't know why either of them are so interested in my life. What would either of them have to gain by it?"

"From what I've observed of John Grimes, he enjoys harassing those he deems weaker than him. As for Teddy Green, I don't know him well enough to even take a guess.

Oh well," he let out a long breath. "We best go in or John will make something out of us sitting in the parking lot."

He was right about that. If we lingered, Calvin would know about it, plus it would be exaggerated greatly, before I got home tonight.

As soon as Mr. Grason and I got out of the car, John Grimes came up to us.

"Say Teach, I need to get home early tonight. How about giving me a ride after class."

"No," Mr. Grason told him.

"You give her a ride," he nodded his head toward me with a sly grin. "I deserve the same privilege."

"No, you don't."

John tried to act offended. "Then you best tell me why not," John demanded.

"You're not pretty. She is," Mr. Grason told him as he held the door to the building open for me.

As soon as I walked in, Mr. Grason closed the door. Leaving himself and John standing face to face on the sidewalk. I couldn't hear what Mr. Grason was saying, but it had to be enlightening. John Grimes looked taken back and completely speechless. It was easy to tell he had not expected whatever Mr. Grason was saying. His face turned red. He hung his head and looked at his feet. Mr. Grason said a few more words before he opened the door for John Grimes. He hurried past me."

"What did you say to him?" I dared ask Mr. Grason.

"A few words his father should have said to him a long time ago. I don't think he'll be insulting toward you again."

~~~~

When Mr. Grason dropped me off at the trailer, Calvin was waiting up on me.

"That teacher dropped you off, right?"

"That's right," I told him calmly.

"That's good," Calvin surprised me by saying. "It's faster than taking the bus. It will give you time to catch up on my laundry. I'll be going out of town tomorrow to attend a refresher course in ministry. I'll need my clothes washed, ironed, and packed before you leave for work in the morning."

I was speechless for a few minutes as I tried to understand what he was saying. "Your good suit and shirt are clean and pressed," I told him. I always kept his clothes as nice looking as I possibly could. His only dirty clothes were what he had on or what he'd worn today.

"I'll need both suits and several shirts and pairs of underwear and socks. Pack them carefully. I don't want them to wrinkle. You'll need to polish both pairs of my shoes."

"Why?" I asked.

"Because I'll be gone for several days. I'll also need all the tip money you got today, and I don't want you holding out bus fare on me. You can get that teacher of yours to haul you around, which won't be much of a problem since he's already doing it."

The way he referred to Mr. Grason as that teacher of yours made me madder than him expecting me to stay up most of the night doing his laundry. "Why didn't you let me know before now?" I demanded.

"I told you two days ago," he said. "You've had plenty of time to do your job. Good thing I checked on my clothes before morning."

There was one thing I knew for a fact. He hadn't told me one word about a refresher course or him being gone two days ago or any other time. That was something I would definitely have remembered. "How long will you be gone?" I asked as I tried to hold my temper.

"I've already told you I'll be gone for several days."

I didn't like the hateful way he said that. Neither did I like the way he was assuming I was his servant. I wanted to be a good wife doing what a wife was supposed to do, but I didn't like being treated as though I was his door mat. Someone who he could blame as he wiped his feet on me.

I was up for hours as I repressed shirts that I had ironed before. I took a damp pillowcase to Calvin's suit and used the iron to press sharp creases in his pants. I then carefully folded his clothes in the worn suitcase Calvin had left open in the front room.

It was three o'clock in the morning before I got to lie down beside the sleeping Calvin. I would be lucky to get three hours sleep if I counted on Mr. Grason to pick me up. I could never count on him being there before the bus arrived. I hoped he would be because Calvin went through my purse as well as the pockets of my uniform. He took every bit of the change I had tried to hide from him. One thing was for sure, I'd have to find a better hiding place if I was to have a penny of my own. Once I got back to restaurant, I would tell Iva Lee how thankful I was that she insisted I open secret a bank account even if I could only add a handful of change to it each week.

I woke up tired and irritable. I reached out and shook Calvin awake out of spite more than out of curiosity.

"What time are you leaving?" I asked as sweetly as my irritation would allow.

"You woke me up," he stormed. "Why did you do it?"

"I wanted to know what time you are leaving."

"Shit," he said. "I about forgot. "It starts at eight o'clock. It's a two-hour drive."

The revengeful part of me almost wished I'd not woke him up.

"Get my things together," he demanded.

"Your shirts and suits are on hangers, and your underthings are in the suitcase."

"Put them in the car for me. I have to shower, shave and get dressed."

"It'll make me late for work," I told him.

"Doesn't matter. Your job isn't as important as mine. Besides, that old hag who runs the place won't fire you for being late. Nobody with any brains is willing to be her dishwasher. It's a brainless job," he said as he hurried toward the tiny bathroom.

I jerked my uniform on without washing, brushing my teeth, or combing my hair. I carried Calvin's shirts and suits to the car and hung them on the ceiling's grab bar. I then went back inside and got his suitcase. Once it was in the car, I ran to the bus station. I didn't have bus fare, but I'd rode the bus so much the driver trusted me to run inside to borrow the money from Iva Lee.

Much to my relief Mr. Grason got there just as the bus was pulling up. I wasted no time getting into his car.

"Oversleep?" he asked with a slight grin.

"Under slept is more like it. I got about three hours sleep."

"Why's that?"

"Calvin had to go to some kind of refresher course today. He didn't tell me until I got home last night. I had to press his clothes and pack his suitcase for him."

"How long is he going to be gone?" he questioned.

"He didn't tell me exactly. Said several days."

"Umm," he kind of grunted and ask no more questions.

I hadn't realized I'd fell asleep with my head resting against the passenger window until he stopped the car at the restaurant.

"Wake up," he said as he gave my shoulder a gentle shake.

"I must have fallen asleep," I needlessly said. "Thanks for the ride."

"See you tonight," he told me as I got out of the car.

Chapter 17

I didn't mention to Iva Lee about Calvin being gone. I don't know why I wanted to keep it to myself. Most likely because I wanted to know how it would feel to be on my own for a little while. Then it occurred to me there would be little difference in the way I was already living. I was always on my own until midnight. I basically had a husband in name only for most of my waking hours. Now, for a day or two I would know what it was like to have no husband at all.

The phone rang and Iva Lee answered it. "Take it easy then," she said and hung up. "Marie just called in sick," she told me. "You'll have to double up today."

When I asked Iva Lee why, she shrugged her shoulders. "She does that right often when life becomes too much for her. She has to take a sick day to build up enough determination to keep going."

I had been working there for what seemed like forever and I had yet to take a day off except for classes and the job fair. Both Marie and Judith took off regularly, and yet Iva Lee said nothing to them.

"Do you think Marie is really sick?" I asked Iva Lee.

"Oh, yes. Without doubt. Probably not physically, but both her and Judith get sick in their own way. I find it works out right good to let them think they've pulled something over on me. That way they try to be good in order to make up for their lying. Her absence will give you a chance to wait on tables today. Add a little more to your mad money while *he's* away."

Which would be precious little. Calvin would be back by my payday.

~~~~

Mr. Grason drove me home that night the same as he did most nights. The only difference this time was that he turned off the engine and got out of the car instead of waiting long enough to see me enter the trailer. I must have given him a questioning look for he said, "I'll walk you to the door and make sure no one is inside."

"You don't have to do that," I was quick to tell him. I was embarrassed for him to see the outside of the trailer. The inside was worse. What little furniture that had been left inside the trailer was worn out many years before. Plus, everything smelled of mold and decay that I couldn't get rid of no matter how much I tried to scrub before I went to bed at night. Maybe if I didn't work both day and night, I might make the place look better. But then, I was a long way from being a miracle worker. Water and a rag could only do so much.

He seemed to know what I was thinking.

"I'll wait outside the door while you make sure the place is safe," he said.

His words didn't help with my embarrassment, but they did touch something inside me. He cared about my safety. It gave me a warm and fuzzy feeling toward Mr. Grason.

I used a key to unlock the door, something I never did when Calvin was there. No one in their right mind would think there was anything worth stealing inside such a despicable trailer. There was nothing of value inside, but it made me feel better knowing the door was locked once I got home. It was better to be safe than sorry.

I flipped the light switch on, walked through the tiny living room, into the pitiful excuse of a kitchen, into the bathroom and then the bedroom. The bed was unmade. The cover tossed aside just as I had left it. I pulled aside the plastic curtain that hung over the closet door. My few things were still on hangers. Calvin's clothes weren't. No one was hiding. Nothing had been disturbed.

I went back to the door, opened it and told Mr. Grason that everything was okay.

"Good," he said, and looked at me as though he had more to say but didn't. Finally, he said, "Lock the door."

The door clicked closed as I leaned against it and made sure it was locked as though it couldn't be forced open easily. Glass windows could be broken if someone wanted in. I flipped off the light and moved to a window to watch Mr. Grason get in his car and drive away. I felt a tremendous loss. How weird it was to be in that trailer without hearing Calvin's snores.

When I crawled into the bed all by myself without Calvin, I pulled up the quilts around me. They were not enough, not nearly enough to warm the chill I was feeling. I looked out the trailer window at the darkness of the night. It would be the first time I had slept alone since my marriage. At least Calvin had always been there at night. Oddly enough, I missed Calvin, although I had gotten to take a warm shower without having to use the hot water to wash Calvin's clothes or mine. The good part was that I didn't have to hand over what few tips I'd made that day. Having a couple of dollars in my pocket made me feel more secure.

What I didn't like was the feeling of loneliness that came over me. Never in my wildest dreams did I think my marriage would turn out to be like this. I felt deserted. Not because Calvin was gone, but because I had a husband in name only. There hadn't been so much as one day that we had spent together. We never simply talked to each other, never laughed together, or did anything together. It wasn't often that Calvin woke up long enough to crawl on top of me once I got home.

It was difficult for me to understand what he did left me feeling worse than if he'd never touched me. After those times, silent tears came before I finally fell asleep.

Once I fell asleep, it wasn't Calvin I dreamed about. It was Mr. Grason. The things I refused to let myself imagine when I was awake came to me in my dream. I felt the strength of his arms and the warmth of his body as he held me against him. I reached up my hand and traced the shape of his face, felt the roughness of beard that hadn't been recently shaved, caressed the softness of his lips with my fingertips. Felt the chill of the air on my flesh as he removed my night gown. I undid the buttons of his shirt moments before he took off his pants. I felt the pleasure of his naked body against mine. I rested my face on his chest to hear the racing of his heart. My heart was racing also.

I woke up. Reached out my hand to find my bed was empty except for me. I cried for the loss of something I never had.

I wiped my eyes on the bed cover and looked out the window. My breath caught. My body tensed. Had I seen the reflection of a face peering in the window or was it only a shadow cast by the far away night light? I had never noticed a shadow before, but then I had always been so tired once I finally got in bed, I hadn't noticed anything.

I got up, took the pillowcase off Calvin's pillow and hooked it on the two nails that someone had once used to hang curtains on. If a peeping tom was out there, he couldn't see me now. Still yet, it took a long time for me to fall back asleep.

The next morning Mr. Grason was parked at the trailer instead of at the bus stop. He was a good thirty-five minutes early, which meant I would not have the pleasure of taking my time in getting ready for work. I quickly washed my face, combed my hair and put on my work clothes and rushed outside.

I did take time to walk by the outside of the bedroom window. There were scuffed up marks in the dirt, plus one clear large footprint. A renewed chill crept over me. I thought it best not to mention it to Mr. Grason.

"Why are you waiting outside the trailer this early," I wanted to know.

"Hope you don't mind too much. I wanted to pick you up early. I thought that we might stop for breakfast before work."

I started to remind him that I worked at a restaurant but didn't. There was food available there. Free food for me but not for him.

"Okay," I said.

"I thought it would be a nice break for you and me both."

"Yes, it will," I said as I recalled last night's dream. My insides fluttered. A need arose in me much like it did when we kissed in the parking lot. I felt guilty for allowing myself to want something that wasn't mine to have.

"Why are you doing this?" I asked.

"Because I'm hungry, and I didn't want to cook my own breakfast this morning.

"I mean why do you take me to work and back almost every day?"

"Because I like your company," he answered in the same tone of voice he used about cooking his own breakfast. "Plus, it gives me company and saves you a little time and money."

"It takes your time and your money," I pointed out.

"I can't think of a thing I'd rather do with a few extra minutes of my time," he said.

I thought of the parking lot along with my dream. I feared I was blushing at what I'd rather do.

"When will Calvin be back?" he asked as though he and Calvin were the best of friends.

I had already told him I didn't know, but I would tell him again. "He didn't tell me for certain. Why do you ask?"

"I don't like the idea of you staying in that place alone. I've told you before it's not the best neighborhood for a lone girl, especially when she is as pretty as you."

As pretty as me. Those words were good for what little ego I had left, but I knew he was being kind instead of being truthful. Since I'd married Calvin, I tried not to think about how I looked. It was all I could do to keep myself clean.

Making an effort to be one of those pretty girls who curled their hair every night and spent time putting on makeup in the morning was more than I could manage. I knew my hair had gotten long and ratty with me having to put it in a hairnet when I waitressed. It was tied down my back with a rubber band when I was washing dishes. Working double shifts seven days a week, not including the two nights I was in class, had caused dark circles to develop around my eyes along with drooping exhaustion showing in my face. I had also lost enough weight until the uniforms Iva Lee had provided now hung on my body. Calvin hadn't noticed or said anything about my appearance. Having a husband who never really looked at me, didn't encourage me to spend time on appearance. I tried my best to avoid a mirror. I knew I was becoming as decrepit as the old trailer we lived in and so exhausted I didn't care.

"Everything is run down, but I've seen no evidence of it not being safe," I told him what I hoped was true. I couldn't hide the fact this section of town looked like a garbage dump, but I had too much pride to admit we lived in an area that might be riddled with crime even if that was the case, which I didn't think it was. Just because people lived in poverty didn't make them more dishonest than those who were rich. Maybe less so. Mom had always claimed the way people got rich was by taking advantage of other people. In my opinion, she had a point.

Mr. Grason drove to a restaurant I wasn't familiar with. From what I could determine, it was located across town from Good Eats. I feared he chose the place because he didn't want anyone to see him eating breakfast with me. But then, he was seen taking me to and from class, which meant a lot of people saw him with me. Most likely he wanted to treat me to a different place than I was used to. I had to grin thinking anyplace other than Good Eats would have accomplished that.

I opened the door and got out of the car at the same time
he did, but he hurried to my side and placed his hand on my
back in a similar way he did at the job fair. When we got to
the restaurant, he opened the door and held it open for me to
go inside. His gallant behavior was something I wasn't used
to. Growing up the only time I saw men treating women in
such a manner was on television. I was used to women doing
most everything for themselves. Having Mr. Grason being so
gentlemanly made me feel special. I tried not to show that I
liked the feeling, but I was sure I couldn't hide it from him or
anyone else.

A hostess ushered us into a dining room with tablecloths
along with fancy settings on all the tables. It looked elegant
and expensive. I cringed at the thought of what this was going
to cost, but he didn't seem concerned. "I'm not hungry," I
told him as an excuse not to run up my bill. The tip money
from yesterday wouldn't pay for more than a cup of coffee at
a place like this.

He grinned. "You'll be hungry when the meal arrives.
Their food is wonderful."

"You eat here often?"

"Not as often as I would like. I don't like eating at a
restaurant alone. Grace Anna refuses to leave the house
unless she wants to. What would you like?" he asked as he
picked up the menu.

I wondered about his comment about his wife, but I didn't
want to ask questions. I looked at my menu and gasped out
loud when I saw the prices. "People actually pay these
prices?"

"It's worth it. This is my treat for you."

"Uhh . . ." I started to object with the excuse that I never
ate this early.

"No arguing," he interrupted. "I'll order for you."

Stake, eggs, hashbrowns, butter biscuits, apple butter
along with coffee with thick cream. He ate it all, but I couldn't

eat much of my meal. He asked for a takeout bag for me to take home.

"You can put this in Iva Lee's refrigerator until I pick you up for class tonight."

"Okay. Thank you," I told him, still feeling out of place as we left the restaurant.

Iva Lee's eyes widened when I placed the takeout bag in the refrigerator. "Bret Grason?" she questioned.

I nodded.

"Does Calvin know he took you to breakfast?" she asked as though she could read my thoughts.

"Calvin is taking a refresher course?"

"In what?"

"In ministry," I told her.

"Where is this refresher course being held?" she asked.

"He didn't tell me where."

Her eyebrows lifted. "Out of town then?"

"Yes."

"When will he get back?"

"He said several days."

"Did he take extra clothes?"

"Yes. He had me press and iron both suits and extra shirts for him."

"Everything?" she questioned.

I nodded.

"Including his everyday clothes?"

I thought back to looking in the tiny closet when checking for intruders. I hadn't looked on the shelf where I kept his everyday clothes folded and put up. "I only packed his suits, shirts, and underwear," I told her. "Why do you ask?"

"How much a man takes with him tells how long he plans to be gone."

"Makes sense," I told her. I would remember to check when I got home after class tonight.

Iva Lee appeared to have more to say, but Judith came rushing in through the back door.

"I get sick and tired of having to get to work this early. I want to work the lunch to dinner shift," she complained without so much as saying good morning.

"And I want a waitresses who doesn't whine and complain all the time," Iva Lee came back at her. "If you don't want this job, others will."

"I doubt that," Judith sniffed.

"Had three girls put in their applications yesterday. Pretty girls who should bring in customers just to get a look at them. Customers don't like grouchy waitresses."

Judith grumbled under her breath as she marched to the bathroom.

Iva Lee chuckled under her breath. "Some people aren't early birds. I do get tired of listening to complainers. Give me girls who comes to work and are thankful to have a good paying job. Girls like you, Ellie."

I didn't know how to respond, so I mumbled thank you as I searched for any kind of utensil Iva Lee had used so I could start washing dishes.

~~~~

When it was time to leave for class, I got the takeout bag from the refrigerator and left the restaurant. I had expected Mr. Grason to show up to drive me to class. His car wasn't parked in its usual place or anywhere else that I could see. He hadn't shown up when the bus arrived. I didn't want to take a chance on having to walk all the way to the college, so I got on the bus thankful that I had enough money to pay for the fare. I took a seat right behind the bus driver.

"Well, well, look who's riding the bus. Your boyfriend dump you the same as Calvin did?" John Grieves said as he used his hip to push me over as he sat down beside me.

"Do you always have to be so insulting?" I demanded. "Please, return to your own seat. I plan to read a chapter in English, and I would like to do it in peace."

He laughed. "Oh, you're a cool one, alright. Old Calvin has left you stranded, and your boyfriend has stopped chauffeuring you around, while you stick up your nose and act like nothing has happened."

"John," said the bus driver. "Go back to where you were sitting and leave the lady alone."

"I'm only trying to tell her how things stand."

"You heard me. Move it or I'll band you from riding this bus."

"Well! So that's the thanks I get for enlightening the lady. I have you know I always pay bus fare the same as everyone else," he grumbled as he stood up and stomped down the aisle.

"Sorry about that. He can be irritating," said the bus driver.

"I find him disgusting," I said as I opened my English book to pretend I was reading for the time it took to get to the college.

I was the first to get off the bus and hurried toward the building. I heard the bus driver tell John to hold on a minute and sit down in a seat. I assume he did.

I was seated in the classroom opening my math book when John came marching in as though he owned the place. As I feared, he sauntered up to my desk and sat down beside me as though nothing had happened.

"I guess you've noticed your boyfriend's car isn't in the parking lot. Do you suppose he ran off with your so-called husband?" John laughed as though he found his comment funny.

"Why do you make a point of being insulting?" I asked as calmly as possible, when I would have preferred shoving my math book down his throat.

"Because I feel like educating snobby broads, and you are a tight-assed snob."

It was then that Mr. Grason came into the room. It was obvious he had heard John's comments. He rushed to John, grabbed him by the back of the shirt, lifted him out of his seat and practically dragged him out of the classroom and down the hall.

"Appears Mr. Grason reached his breaking point with John," Harry, one of the other student's, said as he came into the room. "What happened?" he asked as he turned to me.

"John's big mouth got him in trouble," I said.

"I'm not surprised. Mr. Grason has taken more off John than most professors do. Last semester Mrs. Taylor lost it and beat him over the head with a staple gun before he could stop her. The nurse at the infirmary took eleven staples out of his head. Doubt he'll be allowed to attend classes here again. Don't think he'll be given another chance."

"Eleven staples," I said, and wished I'd had a staple gun handy. I would have aimed it at his mouth.

"Don't know exactly what came about, but Mrs. Taylor is still a professor here and John is allowed to attend classes. It seems there was some sort of mutual compromise that took place."

"I don't understand why there are hateful people such as John," I said.

"He's always had disciplinary problems even during grade school. I think his dad beat him on a regular basis, but he never admitted to such."

"You went to school with him?"

"I did, but I kept my distance. No one wanted to be friends with him."

"I can understand why."

"If he wasn't the way he is, I might feel sorry for him," Harry admitted. "I hope he's expelled permanently this time. Some of us come to class in order to better ourselves. Say, I've noticed that you usually ride with Mr. Grason. Are you related to him?"

"No. He drives by my place on his way home. He's kind enough to give me a ride so I won't have to take the bus."

"He's good like that," Harry said. "One of the best professors here. He cares about the students."

I thought that was probably true. He'd always been kind to me.

A short time later Mr. Grason returned to class without John Grimes. Harry glanced at me but didn't say a word and neither did I. Mr. Grason continued with class in the same manner as usual. I thought his jaws appeared to be clenched tighter than normal when there were moments of silence. Other than that, nothing had changed.

~~~~

"Why didn't you wait on me?" Were the first words Mr. Grason said once we were in his car after class.

"I didn't want to miss the bus in case you didn't show up."

"You should know by now that I'll always show up."

No, I didn't know that. How could I even assume such a thing? "Why were you late?" I dared ask.

He let out a breath of air. "Grace Anna was having difficulties that required my assistance."

I wanted to ask him what kind of difficulties, but I didn't think his wife was any of my business.

"She's not well," he said. "Mentally," he added after several moments of hesitation."

"I'm sorry about that," was all I could think to say.

"Not nearly as sorry as I am. Grace Anna's condition leaves me feeling helpless. I've tried to do everything possible for her, but nothing helps." He shook his head and was silent for a few moments. "Helpless and hopeless," he added. I have very little to look forward to and neither does she. Grace Anna will never have a normal life, and I'll never have a normal wife. She freaks out at the oddest of times. She'll want all of my attention and at the same time she'll freak out if I so much as touch her hand. She takes screaming fits for no apparent reason."

"Why is that?" I asked.

"I wish I knew."

"Has she seen a doctor?"

"Many doctors, over and over again. It has changed nothing."

There wasn't anything else I knew to say that might give him comfort. I reached out and gave his hand a squeeze. His fingers closed over mine and held on. My touch appeared to give him comfort.

"What happened with John Grimes," I wanted to know.

He seemed relieved to talk about someone other than his wife.

"The Dean hadn't left his office, so I took him there. John had been in so much trouble he was put in probation last semester. John was expelled. He won't be allowed to attend classes at this college again."

It seemed a shame that he needed an education as much as anyone I had ever known, and now he would not be able to get it.

"That's sad," I found myself feeling sorry for him.

"It's sad that John is a troublemaker. He does everything he can to make other people's lives as miserable as his."

"He lives somewhere near the trailer," I said.

"Actually, he stays with whoever will give him free space. I've heard he stays with Teddy Green off and on."

"The gay man?" I blurted out.

"That's what I've heard. Teddy Green appears to have a good heart. I try my best not to judge a man for what he does in his private life as long as it's consensual and doesn't hurt anyone else."

"I didn't know people like that existed," I told him. "Marie and Judith at the restaurant have been trying to educate me, so they claim. In my opinion, they're laughing at how dumb I am."

"Dumb doesn't apply to you," he said. "You haven't been subjected to the profane side of life. Too many kids in this day and time have their innocence ripped away from them at an early age."

I didn't want to talk about such at that with Mr. Grason. He obviously didn't want too either.

"Have you heard from Calvin?" he asked as we neared the trailer.

"No," I told him.

"Do you think he'll be home when you get there?"

"I don't think so. He took at least two days' worth of clothes with him." I thought about what Iva Lee had said about clothes.

"Today is the second day he's been gone," Mr. Grason pointed out.

He was right. Calvin could be in the trailer right now. Different emotions ran through me at the thought of Calvin being in bed snoring away. Part of me wanted him to be there and part of me didn't. What kind of wife was I to have such mixed feelings?

Mr. Grason stopped his car as close the trailer as possible. The place was pitch dark as usual, but there was a police car parked nearby. When Mr. Grason and I got out of the car, a police officer got out of the black and white.

"Something's going on," Mr. Grason said as we stopped to meet the officer who was headed toward us.

"Good evening, Bret," the officer said to Mr. Grason. "Had classes tonight?"

"Good evening, Rob. I have classes every night. What's going on?"

It was evident the police officer and Mr. Grason knew each other. The officer didn't answer as he turned toward me.

"Mrs. West?" he questioned.

"Yes," I told him.

"I hate to inform you of this." His words were polite and practiced as though he had said them many times before.

Those words brought ice cold fear to me. I grabbed hold of Mr. Grason's arm. I needed more strength than I had to hear what he was going to say next.

"I have an eviction notice. The owner of the trailer wants the premises vacated immediately."

I was stunned into silence. No one was dead. No one had been in a horrible accident. I was weak with relief. I turned loose of Mr. Grason's arm. "There's not been an accident?"

"No accident. An eviction notice," he repeated.

"What's an eviction notice?" I asked.

"According to the owner of the trailer, the rent on the place has not been paid in the past three months."

"But it belongs to the church. My husband is the minister there. He said the trailer comes rent free."

"Not according to the owner."

"Who owns it if the church doesn't?" Mr. Grason asked.

"The name on the eviction notice is a Harold Cummings. He resides in the state of Florida and has this mobile home for times when he vacations here, which he hasn't done in several years. It states he was paid the first month's rent, but nothing since then. It also states that a Mr. Calvin West has been notified several times of the impending eviction but has not responded or paid the rent. He was notified three days ago to vacate the property, which hasn't been done."

"I'll pay the back rent," Mr. Grason told the officer.

"I'm sorry to inform you that Mr. Cummings won't agree to that. I was told to wait here as the renters remove what belongs to them. None of the household furnishings belongs to the renters."

I didn't know what to do or what to say. I stood there dumbfounded as I stared at the officer.

"Can we have a copy of the eviction notices?" Mr. Grason asked.

"I was given copies to provide you." He handed the papers he was holding to Mr. Grason instead of me. Mr. Grason put them in his pocket.

"I'll help you gather your things," Mr. Grason told me. "We'll put them in my car."

The policeman followed us to the trailer. "I'm to observe everything that's removed," he told us.

I actually laughed at that. "There's not one thing in the place that has any value. It's nothing more than a tin box full of rust and mold," I said as I unlocked the door and flipped on the light.

The officer and Mr. Grason looked about but said nothing I went to the bedroom. I pulled the plastic curtain away from the closet and gathered my few clothes that were on hangers in my arms and then looked at the shelves. All that remained belonged to me. Calvin had taken every article of clothing that belonged to him. I put my underwear in my arms along with my other clothes and went to the tiny bathroom. I took my toothbrush and a bar of half-used up bar of Ivory soap. Calvin had taken the toothpaste, shampoo and my hairbrush.

"I'm ready to leave," I told the officer.

He looked at the few things I held in my arms, looked about the place and nodded. "The bed clothes and towel doesn't belong to you?"

"They were here when we moved in," I told him.

"Where shall I take you," the officer asked as he made sure the door was locked. He put the key in his pocket.

"She'll ride with me," Mr. Grason told him.

"Good. My job here is finished. Have a good night," he said politely as he headed to the black and white and drove away.

I followed Mr. Grason to his car. I was too stunned to cry, too devastated to talk.

"Do you have someplace to go?" he asked as he took my things out of my arms and held the passenger door open for me.

I shook my head. "No."

"Put your things in the back seat. I can take you to your parents' house if that's where you want to go," he told me.

I shook my head again. I would be about as welcome back home as I was now welcome in the horrible trailer. "Take me back to the restaurant," I mumbled. "Maybe Iva Lee is still there.

She wasn't. The lights were out, and her car was gone from the parking lot. She wasn't staying in her little apartment tonight. I wouldn't be able to stay there either.

"I'm going to get you a motel room for tonight. We'll figure out what to do in the morning," Mr. Grason told me.

"I don't have money for a motel room," I admitted as I fought back tears.

"I do," he said.

I had no other choice other than to agree. "I'll pay you back."

"I know you will. I would take you home with me if it wasn't for Grace Anna. She has problems when a stranger is near her. She barely tolerates the woman I've hired to help her."

"It's okay," I said. "At least I now know why Calvin left in such a hurry."

"There are people who choose to hide from their problems rather than solve them," he said. "What I can't come to grips with is why Calvin didn't take you with him."

I was wondering the same thing. I concluded I wasn't a likeable person, much less a loveable one.

"I can only assume he thought you would borrow the back rent money from Iva Lee, and all would be solved by the time he returned."

I hoped that was what he thought, but I doubted it. "He took everything he owned. Including the toothpaste and shampoo. I don't think he's coming back."

"He might not, but I think he will," Mr. Grason said as he pulled into a Motel 6 parking lot. "This is the least expensive motel in town," he told me. "You wait in the car. I'll go in and get you a room for the night."

I sat there numb from the tip of my toes to the top of my head and thankful for it. I just might take a screaming fit when the reality of the situation finally hit me full force. It didn't seem possible that Calvin had left me behind. What kind of husband would do a thing like that because he was behind on rent?

Out of the blue, John Grimes' words came back to me. *Your boyfriend dumped you the same as Calvin did.* John Grimes knew Calvin had run out on me, and that he wasn't coming back. How did he know when I didn't. Mom used to say, *the wife is the last one to know.* She was right.

Mr. Grason returned to the car and got in. He drove around the back of the motel and stopped. "I got you a room for two nights just in case it takes me that long to find you a place to rent. After class in the morning, I'll see what I can find."

"I don't want to be a bother to you," I told him. "Iva Lee might help. She seems to know a lot of people."

"How much money do you make each week?" he wanted to know. "It will determine what you can afford."

I told him and his brows crept halfway up his forehead. "I looked at the amount owed on back rent. A month's rent didn't amount to more than a week of your income. What did he do with all the money you and he earned?"

"I have no idea. He always took my paycheck along with tips. I had to hide change for bus fare. That was why he never complained when I rode with you."

Mr. Grason's teeth clenched. His jaw muscles twitched. Finally, he said, "I'll check things out for you tomorrow."

"John Grimes knows what was going on. He said Calvin dumped me." I didn't tell Mr. Grason what else he said.

"Let's go inside." He got out of the car and took my things from the backseat. I went around the car to him. I didn't know which room he had rented for me. I followed him to a room on the second floor. He balanced my clothes in one hand and unlocked the door with the other. He opened the door and flipped on the light before he let me enter in front of him. The room smelled musty with a lingering odor of cigarettes. At least it smelled better than the trailer.

He closed the door behind him and laid my clothes down on the bed before he closed the curtains.

"Keep these curtains closed, the door locked, and don't go outside until I come to pick you up in the morning. Motels are never the safest places in the world."

I thought it was probably as safe as the trailer had been, but then, Calvin had always been there when I was – except for last night.

I was surprised when Mr. Grason turned to me, took me in his arms and held me tight against him.

"Don't worry. I'll take care of you," he whispered in my hair. "I won't leave you stranded."

It was all I could do to hold back my tears. His kindness was getting to me faster than anything else would have. "I'll manage," I said in a shaky voice.

"I know you will," he said as his hand stroked my back. "I'll help you if you'll let me."

It wasn't like I had much choice in the matter. I felt him let out a breath he seemed to be holding a few moments before he turned me loose.

"Take yourself a nice hot shower and try to get some sleep tonight. I'll come by early to take you to breakfast. Look through this peep hole in the door before you open it."

"Okay," I told him. The feeling of shocked numbness still lingering.

"Lock the door behind me," he said.

I made sure the door was locked and looked toward the motel key he had placed on the dresser.

"What now?" I mumbled to myself. "Take a hot shower and try to sleep."

I went into the bathroom, turned on the light, took off my clothes and got in the shower. Unlike in the trailer, there really was hot water. There was also a tiny bar of soap, a miniature bottle of shampoo and wash cloths and towels. Things I hadn't seen much of since my marriage to Calvin. Married life hadn't been too good, but I feared being dumped was going to be worse.

No one could see me now, so there was no reason not to let the tears flow. I stood under the spray of hot water and cried until I was exhausted. My dream of living happily ever after had caved in around me. My marriage had failed. I was a deserted woman.

I turned the covers down and crawled between clean sheets. It was the most comfortable bed I'd slept in since I left home, but I didn't think I could possibly fall asleep.

I must have, for I woke up to the sound of someone pounding on the door. I jumped to my feet and rushed to the peep hole. It was Mr. Grason. I was still in my underwear.

"Just a minute," I called through the door as I grabbed the uniform I'd lain on the dresser after I had taken a shower last night. I put it on as fast as I could and hurried to the door. I opened it, and he came inside. He looked me up and down and then looked toward the unmade bed.

"Are you ready for breakfast?" he asked. "The maid will tidy up the room and make the bed."

"She will?"

"It's her job. It's done in all motels and hotels."

"Oh," I said. "I've never stayed in a motel before."

"So I gathered."

"Do you happen to have a comb. My hair is a mess. Calvin took the only hairbrush."

He reached in his back pocket and handed me a comb. Interesting how men always seemed to carry a comb in their back pockets.

It was still early by the time we had finished breakfast. Mr. Grason had taken me to a different place to eat. One that wasn't as expensive as yesterday.

"I hope Iva Lee will be at the restaurant. We need to tell her what happened before any of the other waitresses show up," Mr. Grason said.

"She's usually there very early of a morning," I told him. I was already feeling guilty for not being able to take care of myself. At this time, I had four days' worth of pay Calvin hadn't been able to take from me, but it wouldn't amount to enough for me to rent a place. I thought of Mom and Dad, but I knew without asking they would never loan me enough money to get me out of the fix I'd found myself in. To make matters worse, they would blame me for Calvin leaving. They would think I wasn't woman enough to keep my husband. I'd heard Mom make similar comments about other women.

Iva Lee was in the kitchen prepping for the day when we came in the back door. "You get earlier every morning," she said as she turned her head to glance at me. "What has happened?" she asked when she saw that Mr. Grason was with me.

"Calvin took *all* his clothes," I managed to say.

"Seems he skipped town," Mr. Grason said. "Owing three months of back rent. Rob Blevins was waiting when I drove Ellie to the trailer. He fulfilled the eviction notice. I took Ellie to a motel last night. She needs to find a place to stay right away."

"I see. At least you were there to give her a hand. Got any place in mind?"

"We were hoping you might know of a place."

"Wish I could let her use my storage room, but I can't do such as that. What about your place?"

"Grace Anna would go wild at having someone there. You know how she is."

His words surprised me. It meant he and Iva Lee knew each other better than I realized. Iva Lee saw my surprise and explained.

"My place and Bret's places are less than a half mile apart," she said. "We don't come into contact with each other often, but I do know about his wife's condition."

"What about the space above that storage shed on the backside of your farm?" Mr. Grason asked.

"You're talking about the one in the edge of the woods not far from our property line?"

"That's the one that came to mind. It's been empty for a long while, hasn't it?"

"It's been ten years since anybody stayed in that place. It's gotten run down some."

"Then it's available," Mr. Grason said.

"I suppose it is, but . . ." she hesitated a moment. "Come to think on it, the place might be better than that trailer."

I didn't like them discussing a place for me to stay in without my input, but I wasn't in a position to do a thing about it. Actually, I should be thankful to have them looking out for me. Without them I would be left on the street with nowhere to go and no one to turn to.

"I'll be able to pay rent now that Calvin's gone," I told them.

"There's the catch," Iva Lee said. "I won't rent the place to Calvin West."

"You won't be renting it to him," Mr. Grason pointed out.

"I'll let Ellie stay there for the time being, but when he returns that's it." She turned toward me. "Understand?"

I understood all right. "I don't think he'll be coming back," I told her, wondering if he had deserted the church the same as he had deserted me.

"You're wrong there. He'll fall flat on his face again and come running back to you expecting you to forgive him and take him in. He treated you like his slave and he'll do it again. Men like him never change. I know. I was married to one."

"She has a motel room for tonight. After class, I'll go by the storage shed and see what needs doing. With luck, she can move in tomorrow night."

"Stop by my place. Don can help you. I'll call him and tell him to find some extra sheets and things. What's still in that place probably isn't fit to throw away."

"I don't know . . ." I began.

"How to thank us," Iva Lee said for me. "Remember when Calvin shows up, be it tomorrow or a year from now, you'll be out of there if you take him back."

"I understand," I told her.

"I don't want the other waitresses to know anything about you staying there. It's nobody's business but ours." She turned to Mr. Grason. "Come back by around three o'clock. That's slack time and I can take care of things while she's gone. She needs to see the place in the light of day."

"I'll do it," he told her.

"Now go, before Marie and Judith get here."

Mr. Grason left without saying anything further.

Iva Lee gave me a look. "His cutting out is for the best. You're too good for the likes of him."

I felt tears sting my eyes.

"You buck up and put some grit in your craw. Don't you say a word to anybody about anything. When somebody, like Marie and Judith, drills you about him being gone, say life happens and let it go at that, understand what I'm telling you?"

"I understand," I told her for the second time. But I didn't understand anything. Why hadn't Calvin paid the rent? What had he done with the money? What about the church? Why had he run away and left me behind?

"Muddy water clears up with time," Iva Lee said as she plopped dirty dishes in the sink for me to wash.

Chapter 18

Mr. Grason showed up at three o'clock sharp parked in the same spot he always parked in. I was glad that Marie and Judith had already left. The second shift would arrive at any minute.

"Go on," Iva Lee said to me. "Tell him to have you back no later than four-thirty. I expect you to put in as much time as you always do. At least you'll be able to put all your earnings in your secret bank account. I'll warn you not to let anyone know you have it. This thing with Calvin West isn't over yet. You don't want to be left standing in hell's door ever again."

She was right about that. Standing in hell's door was an adequate description of where I'd been if she and Mr. Grason hadn't been willing to help me.

"Iva Lee said to have me back between four and four-thirty," I told him. He no longer looked like the polished college professor. He more resembled the hard-working men back home. His hair was wind-blown, and he had dirty streaks on what looked to be his work clothes.

"I'll do it," he told me. "The shed needed a lot of cleaning. I'm glad Don was there to help."

"Don?" I questioned.

"He's Iva Lee's . . ." he hesitated a moment. "Friend," he finally said.

"Is he the man she told me about? The one she's been with all these years?"

"She told you about him?" He sounded surprised.

I didn't want to break her trust in what she told me, so I only nodded.

"She doesn't usually talk about her private life to anyone. I'm surprised she did with you. I'm also surprised she agreed to you staying in the shed. She likes to keep her private life private. She surely thinks a lot of you."

I could almost hear the words he didn't say. That both he and Iva Lee felt sorry for me. The realization hit me hard. It must be more evident than I thought how stupid and immature I really was. In their eyes I was surely nothing more than a helpless child who had gotten herself in a fix. One I didn't know how to get out of. Which was true. Never in my wildest dreams did I think Calvin would desert me the way he did.

A flicker of hope came. Maybe he hadn't deserted me. It was possible he really did have to take a refresher course. It was also possible he hadn't read or received those eviction notices. Perhaps it was the church that hadn't paid the rent on the trailer. Calvin could return today and discover that the trailer was empty. Why hadn't I thought of that sooner? Why had I been so fast to jump to conclusions?

Still yet, I had to have a place to stay. Sleeping on the streets wasn't an option I wanted to consider while I waited on Calvin to return. If he did return, he and I both would be on the street. Iva Lee had made that clear.

We left the buildings behind and drove into the country. I was amazed there was still such places this close to town. I had thought the town would surely go on forever instead of being cramped together in one place, but the buildings had ended, and farms appeared. The rural landscape reminded me a lot of where I was raised, except there were no deep mountain hollows, or towering hardwood trees. It was more scrub brush and rolling hills instead of high mountains straining to reach the sky. It all made me long for home, the place where I was raised. The only place where I had ever belonged.

"I took it upon myself to stop by the church," Mr. Grason told me and then he became silent as though he was debating if he should tell me more.

"What did you find out?"

"I'd rather not tell you this, but I think it's something you should know," he rushed his words together. "I talked to an older woman who lived across the street from the church. I got the impression she was a snoop as well as a member of the church. She didn't mind telling me what little donations the church had managed to acquire had disappeared along with their minister. She also mentioned there was gossip going around that the resident prostitute and her baby had also disappeared. She said the young woman had recently confessed her sins and was trying to get redemption from the church and God. Then entire congregation had been trying to help her including their new minister. She said the minister had allowed the woman and her baby to move into the parsonage while he rented a trailer for him and his wife. The entire congregation had thought it was a Godly thing for him to do until a couple days ago."

I thought it was impossible for me to be hurt more than I was already hurting. I was wrong. Not only did my eyes fill with tears, my heart was now crying tears of blood. The hateful John Grimes had been the only person who had told me the truth about the man I had married.

"Are you okay?" Mr. Grason asked.

How could I be okay after receiving some of the worst information a wife could get? "I'll never be okay again," I told him.

~~~~

We both rode in silence the rest of the way to the shed. What more could either of us say without making everything worse?

A man came around the corner of the building as Mr. Grason stopped his car. I recognized him immediately. It was the man named Don who always asked for me to be his waitress. I would never have guessed he was the man who was Iva Lee's lover. If either of them had given any indication, I hadn't picked up on it.

"Welcome to your new abode, Ellie," he said as I got out of the car. "You looked surprised to see me."

"I am surprised. Iva Lee didn't tell me."

He grinned. "For a snoopy old woman, she likes to hold her privacy close in hand."

"So it seems," was all I could manage to say.

"She mentions you often. You remind her of herself when she was your age."

"I do?"

"Of course, she was many years younger along with many pounds lighter way back then," he said with a grin. "She enjoys sampling her own cooking. Go on inside. Bret and I have worked wonders with this place in the few hours we've been at it, if I do say so myself. All it lacks is a lot of soap and water along with elbow grease and a woman's touch. I think you'll like it here. I know I did the few times I stayed in the shed."

"You stayed here?" I knew I sounded surprised.

"Iva Lee doesn't get mad at me as often as she used to," he said with a mischievous grin. "I think it has something to do with her change of life. Calms a woman down, it does. You don't have to contemplate such as that for another thirty years."

What was it with these people? Where I came from folks would never talk about such things. Especially coming from a man. How was I to respond to that remark? I turned to Mr. Grason. "We best hurry," I said.

"That we had. Iva Lee gave orders to hurry back with Ellie."

"She's a great cook, but she never did like washing dishes," Don said with a light chuckle. "I'm heading back to the house unless you need me for something."

"I think we've done enough for today. I'll tidy things up tomorrow before Ellie moves in."

"Sounds good. Bye for now, Miss Ellie."

"Bye, and thank you," I called out as he walked away.

"He's a fine person," Mr. Grason said. "I never did understand why Iva Lee refused to marry him."

"Once bit, twice shy," I told him.

~~~~

It was the next day during lunch when Teddy Green came in the restaurant and asked for me to serve him. I didn't want to, but he tipped good. I owed Mr. Grason for two nights stay at a Motel 6 and Iva Lee rent. All tips were a blessing.

Teddy Green was looking at the menu when I came to his table with his water and orange juice. He didn't look up.

"Calvin is a fool. You didn't deserve being tied to the likes of him, but you lucked up when he took flight. I'll take a salad with avocados and stuffed olives."

I returned with his order and placed it before him. "Thank you, Ellie," he said politely as he looked at his salad. "A wise girl never makes the same mistake twice," he added as he unwrapped his salad fork from the napkin.

"You think he'll come back?" I couldn't resist asking, although Iva Lee had warned me never to say anything to anybody.

"Squalling tom cats always return regardless of how far away they're dropped off."

"Where was this tom cat dropped off?"

"Don't know. Don't care."

I returned to the kitchen and left him with his salad.

"What did he say to you?" Iva Lee wanted to know.

"He said Calvin was a fool. He also warned me that no account tom cats always return."

"Not so fast if they're wanted for stealing church money," she said. "I heard the sheriff is looking for him."

She'd made a good point.

"It's time for you to file for a divorce on the grounds of desertion."

I was stunned. I hadn't thought of doing such a thing.

"If you don't, he can come back years from now and claim half of the assets you've earned. He might not have a legal right to anything, but he can make your life hell until you give in just to get rid of him."

I was speechless. Me get a divorce? I hadn't been married long, and she was suggesting I get a divorce. All my life I had been told once you got married it was for the rest of your life. If a person was divorced, they were looked down on forever. Yet, I didn't want to be married to a thief, especially one who had run off with a prostitute who had most likely given birth to his baby.

~~~~

Mr. Grason was waiting in the usual place at closing time. I left the restaurant and made my way to his car. I had spent the entire day going through familiar motions. I washed dishes when needed. Waited on tables when it was necessary. Responded to conversations automatically in the same way I always did. And yet I felt as though I no longer existed. I was only a shadow moving through a cold cloud that surrounded me.

"How did the rest of your day go?" Mr. Grason asked, as he turned the key in the ignition. The engine started up, and we drove away from the restaurant.

"Go?" I said. "Like usual I suppose."

"I don't suppose Calvin got in touch with you, did he?"

"No." Did he really think he might? If it had been Friday, a pay day, it might have happened. "Why did you think he might?"

"You're pale, and you're acting different. Something must have happened."

"Iva Lee said I needed to get a divorce from Calvin."

"You don't want a divorce from him?"

"For better or for worse," I repeated words from my wedding vow. "I have no idea what I should or shouldn't do. I don't even know for sure if Calvin ran away. He might come back tomorrow with a reasonable explanation."

"Do you want him to return?"

"I do if what they say about him stealing the church money and running off with Cleo Hampstead isn't true." I didn't tell him how desperately I wanted to have a husband of my very own. I wanted the good preacher that I had kept telling myself he was. The perfect husband to share my life with. The one who would be the best father in the world to our children and husband to me.

"You haven't had time for what has happened to settle with you. You're still in a state of shock. You're finding it impossible to accept what happened, which is only to be expected."

"You're right. I tell myself I'm having a nightmare I'm going to wake up from any moment."

"Ellie, my sweet girl, I know this is going to sound condescending, but sometimes bad things happen for the best."

"A lot of bad things are always happing to me," I told him. "I lost my brother. I lost my baby. I was evicted from where I lived. And now I've not only lost my husband, I've discovered he's a liar, thief, and cheater. I'm left alone with nothing and nobody. How can any of that be for the best?"

He shook his head and gave me a bewildered look. "You still have your job and a paycheck that will no longer be taken from you. That's something good. As for having nobody, you have Iva Lee and Don. By tomorrow night you'll have a better place to live than you had before. Plus, if I may say so, you have me."

I turned to get a better look at Mr. Grason. He was staring straight ahead at the road, his face solemn. I feared I had hurt his feelings.

"I didn't mean to sound ungrateful. I can't begin to tell you how thankful I am for you and Iva Lee. It's just that my life has turned out nothing like I thought it would be."

"Life doesn't always turn out how people expect. I learned that for a fact."

His words made me think of him and his wife. His life hadn't turned out the way he expected either. "What can we do?" I asked and hoped I didn't sound as desperate as I felt.

"Make the best of what we do have, Ellie." He reached out and took hold of my hand. The warmth of it was comforting. I didn't want him to ever turn loose, but he did. We'd arrived at the Motel 6. My space for one more night.

Mr. Grason parked and sat still. Saying nothing. Doing nothing. I didn't want to get out of his car and go inside that musty room with the lingering odor of cigarettes, but I didn't have a choice. Not tonight. Not when Mr. Grason had paid for another night.

"One more night here and you'll be in your own place tomorrow. Things will seem better then," he assured me. "I'll see you to your room."

My room. My own place. I wondered what my room back home was like right now. Did it still have my clothes in the closet? Was my bed made up just the way I liked it? Had Mom changed everything and turned it into the baby's room? I knew nothing had changed in Grant's room. Mom had made it into a shrine. She had gotten upset if I'd so much as set foot in Grant's room.

As for my own place, I feared I would never have such a thing as my own place.

"Where's the key?" Mr. Grason ask.

"Oh. It's in my pocket." I reached into my pocket where I had the few dollars of tip money. The feel of that money gave me a small amount of ease. It was more money than I'd ever had in my pocket. It was security. My security.

I pulled out the key and tried to insert it into the lock. My hand was trembling. Mr. Grason took the key and opened the door. Like last night, he flipped on the light and looked about before he put his hand on my back and guided me inside.

"I'll have a look in the bathroom before I go. I know you're exhausted."

He was right I was exhausted, but I didn't want to be left alone for the third night in a row. Once he was gone, I'd take a hot shower and cry myself out again. When morning came, the same unhappiness would be waiting for me.

Mr. Grason came out of the bathroom. "All clear," he said. "The maid has done a fair job of tidying things up."

"It doesn't smell as much like cigarette smoke as it did last night," I told him.

"That's a good thing," he said as he headed toward the door.

I stood there, not moving, watching him leaving me alone.

"Try not to be so sad. I can't stand the thought of leaving you looking that way."

He reached out took hold of my arm and pulled me against him. His arms closed around me, giving me comfort.

"You know I don't want to leave you here by yourself, but I must. I don't dare stay with you any longer. It wouldn't seem right. It wouldn't be right."

It might not seem right, but that didn't stop me from wanting him to stay if it was only another minute or two. I couldn't remember anyone ever holding me close, comforting me. Mom certainly hadn't. Neither had Dad. Calvin wasn't the holding kind of person. When I tried to snuggle up to him, he'd push me away. He claimed having someone touching him made him to feel claustrophobic.

"I don't want you to leave," I admitted out loud.

He squeezed me tighter for a few moments, let out a long, drawn-out breath before he turned me loose. "We met one promise too late," his words came out in a kind of whisper. "I'll pick you up for breakfast. Lock the door."

And he was gone.

Chapter 19

I wouldn't get to the take another look at the place where I was to stay until I got out of class that night. The college had some kind of special function and the restaurant stayed in the weeds from breakfast through dinner. I feared I'd not make it to class on time considering the pots, pans, and dishes stacked up. I scrubbed and ran them through the Hobart dishwasher faster than I thought possible. Still, there was a pile of greasy everything to wash.

"Go on," Iva Lee told me. I've handled such as this before. He's waiting on you. Don't make him late for class."

"Thank you," I told her with heartfelt sincerity. I hurried to the bathroom and got my small bag of clothes I'd put in the motel's plastic trash bag and my books. Iva Lee had told me to include my good suit, blouse and shoes in the bag. I had.

"Busy?" Mr. Grason said as I got into the car and put my clothes in the back seat. I held my books in my lap as usual.

"Extremely. I feel guilty for leaving Iva Lee with it."

"That woman can handle whatever is thrown at her. She can get the waitresses to pitch in if necessary."

I believed that. "I got lucky in working for her."

"Luck is opportunity you make the best out of."

He was right, but I believed in opportunities that were good for you along with those that were bad for you. Luck was when you unknowingly chose the right one. "Is the shed ready for me?" I asked.

"It's ready for you. Don did his best to include everything he thought you would need. What is she charging you for the place?"

"One week's salary a month which includes electricity. I'm to keep one week's salary for my own needs and save the rest. I'll be able to pay you for hauling me back and forth for work and classes."

"That comes for free. I enjoy your company," he said.

The thought of having money of my own took some of my fear away. A person without money wasn't able to better their situation.

I wondered if he had ever enjoyed anyone else's company. Surely, I wasn't the only person he'd ever helped.

"Did Teddy Green come in today?"

"I don't think so. I washed dishes all day. We were overrun with visitors to the college. Does she ever call Don in to help her out?" The only time I'd seen him was when he came in to eat. Never once had he appeared to know Iva Lee.

"Like I told you before, she likes to keep her private life private."

"Is she ashamed of living with him all these years without marrying him?"

"I once heard her say a piece of paper didn't make a person married. It's only a tool to be used by the law."

"Do you agree?"

"I agree," he said. "That piece of paper says I'm responsible for Grace Anna for life. I'd do the same without the paper, but I'd do it because it was the right thing, not because I signed that piece of paper."

For better or for worse, in sickness and in health till death do us part, I thought. Words that bind.

"In my opinion Iva Lee wanted Don to have freedom of choice. If either of them wanted out, they could call it quits without never-ending legal battles. If they chose to stay together, they would. I'm sure you've heard the old saying, *set a bird free and if it comes back it belongs to you,*" he told me.

I'd heard a similar saying, but I wasn't sure if I agreed. That little bird might get lost and never be able to find its way back. "What about adultery and living in sin?"

"A person's sins are something they'll have to take up with God on judgement day. Take animals for instance. I don't believe God condemns them if they couple with more than one mate. Why should he condemn people for doing the same?"

I didn't comment. I would need some time to think on that a while.

"Do you think God expects me to be tied to Calvin for the rest of my life?" I dared ask what had been bothering me all day long.

"No," he told me firmly. "I don't. He broke his commitment to you, not the other way around. I believe in a God of love and compassion, not of one sitting high on his throne ready to condemn at every opportunity."

His words made me feel a little better, but still yet, I wasn't so sure.

"Time to encounter the hallowed halls of education," he said as he pulled into his parking space. For the first time ever, I noticed *Mr. Grason* was printed on a weathered, wooden sign. This had been his assigned parking spot for years.

~~~~

For the first time I smelled the hint of summer in the air as I got out of the car at the shed. Everything was silent and in darkness. There were no streetlights shining on trash filled streets. No sounds of vehicles trudging along revving their engines or banging of metal things against other things. No strange sounds echoing from building to building. No stench of poverty and rot. I could almost believe I was back home again. Back to a place where I felt secure, a place where I wasn't afraid all the time.

"It's isolated here," I said out loud.

"There's nothing here to be afraid of," he said, taking the wrong meaning to my words. "You'll be a lot safer here than you were at the motel or the trailer."

"It's dark," I said. Again, he mistook my meaning.

"I should have left a light on when I left, but it didn't occur to me. You can leave one on when you leave of a morning if it will make you feel better, but we'll be bringing you home every night."

He would bring me home every night. Not once had Calvin met me at the bus stop to make sure I was safe walking to the trailer. Most nights he would have slept until morning without knowing I had or had not returned - except for the times he knew I would have a paycheck or tip money. He never met me at the bus stop on those nights either, but he would stay awake long enough to collect.

"I like the darkness. I couldn't see the moon and stars in town." There weren't even lightening bugs to be seen on hot nights. The only animals were rats, stray cats, along with an occasional hungry dog.

"You're right about that."

He and I both looked up at the sky. A glimpse of the moon could be seen between rapidly moving clouds. "I don't think it will rain," I told him. "The tips of the halfmoon are turn upward. It means they are positioned to hold rain. When the tips are down it's called a dripping moon."

"Haven't given it much thought," he said as he led me to the stairs that led to the top of the shed where I would be staying. He had shown me yesterday that the bottom part held stored equipment and such. Most all of which was no longer in use.

"Did you know a creek will have more water flow between the new moon and the full moon than at other times? Dad used to say never to dig potatoes or store food during that time of month because it would have too much moisture in it to last long."

"Didn't know that either."

"Us hillbillies are intelligent about things like that."

"Among other things," he added as he unlocked the door with a key and flipped on the light. Someone had put in some elbow grease. The place was much cleaner than yesterday. An attempt had been made to make it look like a place a woman would like. The living room, dining room and kitchen were all one large room. The bedroom and bathroom had doors opening to them from the living room area.

"It's nice," I told him. "Did you do all this work today?"

"I did some. Don brought the bed and bathroom things up from the main house. He said you'd have to provide your own doodads." He opened the door to the bedroom and the bathroom for me to see inside.

There was a bar of soap, a full bottle of shampoo along with a new hairbrush and comb lying on the bathroom sink. I had an idea Mr. Grason had furnished those little things Calvin had taken with him.

I bit my lip to hold back tears of gratitude to people who didn't owe me a thing. I wondered if I would ever be able to repay their kindness.

After Mr. Grason left, I snuggled up in bed with the sound of peep frogs hollering at the little pond not far from the bedroom window. If I tried really hard, I could almost pretend I was a girl in my bed at home. If I pretended just a little bit harder, I could almost hear my dad snoring as he lay in bed beside Mom. Try as I might, I couldn't bring anything to my imagination about Grant other than the sound of Grant's screams as he fell under the tiller. For a moment, I heard Drake Lewis telling me to close my eyes and not to look at what happened seconds before the sound of sirens filled the air.

I jumped straight up out of bed to find that I had been dreaming. My feet hit the bedroom floor of the shed instead of my old bedroom floor at home. I hurried to the window to look out into the dim light of early morning. Much to my amazement a man was riding a tractor and mowing a large field of grass. No wonder I had dreamed of Dad and Grant.

I opened the window and stuck my head out. I wanted the smell of fresh mown grass. For some reason, it gave me the feeling of having a second chance at starting my life over. I could be happy if I chose to be, or I could wallow in misery.

"I'm not a wallowing kind of person," I said out loud as a peptalk to start the day with. I looked at the clock someone had left on top of the dresser in the bedroom. I had ten minutes before Mr. Grason showed up.

I was on the bottom step when he drove up.

"Did you sleep okay?" he asked once I was seated in his car.

"I did," I admitted without mentioning the dream the mowing woke me up from.

"Don got an early start on mowing the first cutting of the hay field for the year. Hope the noise didn't wake you up."

"I love the smell of fresh mown grass."

"Me too," he said. "Don's a farmer at heart. He has a few head of registered angus cattle, plus a few chickens and ducks. He provides the restaurant with fresh eggs along with an assortment of vegetables from his garden. He's a retired police officer who literally worships the ground Iva Lee walks on."

"Do you have a farm too?" I asked him.

"I have a considerable amount of land, but Grace Anna doesn't like animals of any kind. She has a phobia of everything from a bug to a bear. She freaks out if she sees a dog or cat. A mouse got in the house two weeks ago. I caught it in a trap, but it took two days before she was exhausted enough to sleep. I had to hire cleaners to wash every item from the basement to the attic. She's convinced everything is covered in deadly germs. She can't stand to get one speck of what she thinks of as dirt on her or her surrounds. She's almost as bad about noise. I had her bedroom sound proofed.

Her caretaker has to put soothing music on while she naps so I can mow the lawn."

Sounded to me like a miserable way to live for both Mr. Grason and his wife. "Is there no way of helping her get better?"

"The doctors say not. They warned me she will only get worse with time, which came as no surprise. There has been a tremendous difference from the time we were first married until now. I dread what she'll have to go through in the years to come."

"It has to be tough on her and you both," I tried to say something comforting considering how much he had already helped me.

"It is. Got any idea if you'll like living in what Don has started calling your she-shed?"

I understood he was trying to turn the discussion away from him and his wife. I wanted to escape thinking about my situation with Calvin for just a few minutes if possible.

"I'm sure I will. The peep frogs sang me to sleep last night."

"They're music to the ears this time of year. Ellie, I know the last three or four days have been a whirlwind you never expected to happen but look at it this way. You have been given a clean slate to start a new life," he said as he reached out to give my arm a gentle squeeze. "I know I'm butting in where I don't belong, but I've been thinking about what Iva Lee told you. If you'll allow me, I'd like to consult a friend of mine, who happens to be an attorney, about you getting a legal separation from Calvin. I've been told it takes a year of separation before finalizing a divorce."

"Have you ever considered divorcing Grace Anna?" I couldn't resist asking him.

"I think of it all the time. Divorce gets complicated when the person you want a divorce from is mentally impaired until they wouldn't understand the outcome of a divorce. It's not that I don't want to be responsible for her for the rest of her life, it's that I want a different kind of existence for mine. I don't want to spend the whole of my life without the loving relationship of my woman. I even want to raise my own children. I hope that doesn't make me sound like a selfish person to you."

"It sounds reasonable. Like something everyone wants. I know it's what I want."

"Then you'll allow me to talk to my friend about your situation?"

"Yes," I said as a chill crept up my spine at the thought. A divorce meant I'd failed at being a wife.

~~~~

A whole week passed without one word from Calvin. I gave up all hope that the talk about him was merely gossip. It shook me up was when the sheriff showed up at the back door of the restaurant to ask me questions.

"Mrs. West, would you please step outside and get into my car where we can talk in private?" he made a point of asking.

I looked at Iva Lee for permission. She nodded as though she knew in advance the policeman was coming that morning, which most likely she did. The only good thing was that Marie and Judith hadn't arrived yet.

I was shaking all over. I had the same feeling of guilt and fear I had when Mom was going to rake me over the coals for doing something she didn't approve of. At least the officer wouldn't be cutting a switch to give me a whipping.

"I want to ask you a few questions about your husband," he told me after he'd gotten into the driver's seat. "As you may already know, he's been accused of stealing money from the church he was minister of. Do you know anything about that situation?"

"No," I told him. "I didn't know a thing about that until Mr. Grason told me what the woman across from the church told him."

"What did Mr. Grason tell you?"

I told him the best I could.

"You didn't talk to the woman yourself?"

"No."

"Why not?"

I thought about my answer to that question. "I didn't want to hear the bad things she had to say about Calvin."

"As to the woman he supposedly left with. Did you know anything about his relationship with her?"

"No," I told him firmly. I had no intention of spreading gossip about my husband even if it was true.

He continued asking me all kinds of questions that I had no answers for. I didn't know if he was just being snoopy or if he was trying to trick me into admitting I was involved.

"You expect me to believe you're this uninformed about your husband's activities?" he said as though Calvin was nothing other than a common criminal.

"My husband was going to seminar to become a minister when I met him. I thought he was a good, honorable man whose main goal in life was to give help to those who needed it. Now," I told him firmly. "I've answered all your questions the best I know how and told you every single thing I know other than what I ate for breakfast. If you don't mind, I'd like to get back to work."

The officer almost grinned. "By all means go back to work. I may contact you with more questions later, Mrs. West. I have one more question before I let you go. Do you have any idea where your husband is now?"

"I do not," I told him firmly.

"What would you do if you did know where he is?" he asked a second question.

He stared at my face as I thought about an answer. What would I do? I shook my head. "I don't know."

"Would you take him back?"

The answer to that question came with certainty. "No." I told him.

"Why not?"

The answer to that came crystal clear to me. "I'm better off without him."

It was a relief when he dismissed me. Yet, it was all I could do not to burst into tears. Instead of going back to work, I had the urge to start running down the street and run all the way to the shed. Might have if it hadn't been such a long distance. I stiffened my backbone, clenched my teeth and went in the restaurant door.

"How did that go?" Iva Lee asked.

"I don't think I told him a thing he didn't already know."

"He grilled me earlier this morning. I made a point of assuring him you knew nothing about his activities and weren't involved. I also pointed out the hours you worked and went to school. He'll talk to Bret next."

Marie came rushing through the door with a look of *got you* on her face.

"Though he'd be taking you away in handcuffs," she said.

"Marie," Iva Lee said with authority. "You go out that door and come back in showing respect."

"I wasn't being disrespectful," she declared.

"You better not be. No one has the right to kick dirt in another person's face, especially when they have their own big pile."

Marie downed her head and rushed to the bathroom. She hadn't expected the tone of voice Iva Lee had used. I hadn't either.

"Thanks," I said.

"Not needed. It's time to get to work."

That evening right before the three o'clock waitstaff left, Iva Lee shocked everyone.

"I'm going to close the restaurant at one o'clock on Sundays."

No one ask why or applauded. Sunday evenings were the slowest time of the week. There was a rush right after church ended, but tipping was sparce. I was the only one who didn't mind waitressing during that time. A little money was better than no money.

Saturdays and Sundays were the two days Mr. Grason didn't have classes early of a morning or at night. There was no bus service all the way into the country where the shed was. Iva Lee volunteered to drive me to and from work. She refused to let me pay for the ride. The only drawback was that she went to work at five o'clock in the morning and didn't leave until twelve-thirty at night. With me there, she never stayed over in her little upstairs apartment.

Watching everything she did convinced me she had to be super-human. She was many years older than I was. Extra weight and gray streaks in her hair had a hold on her, yet she did more work than any two people put together. I did everything in my power to do enough work to ease her load. At first, I only cleaned up during the early morning prepping. As time went on, she showed me how to assist her with the preparation of the food.

"Never skimp on food preparation. Always use the freshest and the best even when it costs a few dollars more. Slow, is the key word. Prep slow. Cooking the food slowly makes it taste better. Short order cooks fail to do exactly that. They cook the food in short order without taking time to give food that little something extra. You've shown an interest, so I'm willing to teach you all you want to learn."

I didn't tell her I was trying to show gratitude more than I was showing interest. I did want to learn though. Mom always told me I was the snoopiest child she'd ever seen. She claimed I had to have my nose in everybody's business.

Mom. My thoughts often went back to her. Should I call and tell her that Calvin had taken off, or did I continue taking the chance she wouldn't find out he was a thief and cheater? I wasn't sure how fast the grapevine of gossip could travel all the way from Good Eats to the little town of Cleveland and then all the way to the end of Goins Creek.

Sooner or later, she would find out. I feared I would get as much blame, if not more than Calvin got. Back home women always carried the load regardless of what the load contained. Men were privileged for a reason I never understood. Some things were expected to be accepted, not explained.

~~~~

It had been a busy Friday night when Mr. Grason pulled into the parking lot to pick me up after work. I would have felt guilty for leaving Iva Lee with all the cleaning up if I hadn't been exhausted. I had prepped, washed dishes, bussed tables, and waitressed all at the same time.

"Your hind end has been in high gear all day long. Go out there and let him take you home. I can handle this," Iva Lee told me.

"Thank you," I told her and wasted no time in leaving.

Mr. Grason had a solemn look on his face. I didn't know if he'd had a rough day at the college or if Grace Anna was having one of her bad days. He'd admitted teaching classes was his relief from having to contend with Grace Anna.

"What a day. We've been in the weeds since the doors opened this morning," I told him instead of asking what was bothering him. I thought we both could use the restful silence of leaving the college town behind and driving far out into the country. The day was in full splendor. The air was warm and refreshing. Blossoms were everywhere. The birds were busy gathering food for their young as they flew filled the air with their songs.

"This time of year holds its own special beauty," he said as though he knew what I was thinking. "And yet there is a sadness that comes with it. All too soon, the beauty of spring and summer dies back to allow fall to show her blazing glory before it lets the coldness of winter intrude. Winter is the time of hardship, a time of dying. At the same time, it allows a period of rest and recuperation. It makes the joy of spring more welcome when it finally arrives."

"Spring is my favorite time of year," I told him. "There's something inspiring about new life starting all over again."

"You're right about that Ellie. You've been given spring. You are getting a chance to start a new life over."

I started to question his comment, but he didn't give me time.

"Let's go inside," he said all too seriously. "I have something to tell you."

Okay. So, he had finally gotten information from his lawyer friend about me divorcing Calvin. From the solemn expression he had worn all the way from the restaurant, I wasn't going to like what he had found out.

I followed him up the stairs, he took the key from my hand, unlocked the door and flipped on the light as usual. His hand was firm on my back as he guided me inside. He didn't do his usual check of the bedroom or bathroom as he usually did before he hurriedly left me alone. He sat down on the small couch and patted the cushion for me to sit beside him. I sat and waited for him to start talking.

"You're not going to believe what my attorney found out about Calvin," he said as though he was trying to find the right words.

He stopped talking long enough for me to imagine all sorts of things from Calvin being dead to him being a child serial killer while using the guise of being a minister.

"My attorney found evidence a young man by the name of Joseph Gerry married a young woman by the name of Cloetta Hampstead a little over two years ago. You might know her better as Cleo Hampstead. A short time later he left her sitting high and dry without any explanation.

They had been living in a small community of South Carolina. She had no idea what happened to him. She had no evidence of him being killed. Sadly, both her parents had been killed a short time before she met Joseph Gerry. They had left her a small life insurance policy, which she received. My attorney discovered a short time later Joseph Gerry skipped out and left her with an over drafted bank account. Her insurance money disappeared the same time her husband did.

"A few weeks after his departure Cloetta discovered she was pregnant. Her only close relative was an elderly aunt on her father's side. She had no choice other than to move in with her aunt in a small, rented apartment to have her baby. The elderly aunt had a fatal heart condition. She died right after the baby was born. The young woman used what little money her aunt had managed to save to track her missing husband down."

I felt as though I had been dipped into ice water and frozen solid as he stopped talking. I didn't want him to tell me more, but he did.

"A few months ago, Cloetta found him. He claimed to be the minister of a church and was living with you, although he was legally married to her. To make a long story short, he somehow managed to hold Cloetta off until he gathered up all the money he could come across and then left town with his legal wife and baby."

I sat there staring at Mr. Grason.

"Calvin?" my lips moved to say the word.

He nodded. "Joseph Gerry is his real name. He was raised in foster care. The children's home had no background on him. All they knew was that he was left there at the age of five years. He went from foster home to foster home until he was old enough to run away. It seemed every foster home he went to had money disappear. On two occasions it was a substantial amount of money. No one could prove he was the one who had taken it."

"Calvin," I said his name again.

"Is not your husband. He committed bigamy when he pretended to marry you. My attorney found out more if you want to hear it."

I nodded.

"He did have a roommate right before he met you."

"Teddy Green," I said when he paused.

Mr. Grason almost grinned. "No. It was a woman. It appears women are easier to scam. She was considerably older than him and lonely to the point of desperation after her husband died. She wised up quick and left him high and dry. After the woman left, he was in need of financial support in order to finish his requirement to become a legit minister. It appears he thought being a minister was an easy way to rake in large amounts of money from good intentioned people. So, he went that route, but he needed a new source of income while he finished preparing himself to become a minister."

"I had no money," I told him.

"He feared the last woman would report him to the law as a scammer, so he came up with a different plan. He already had a job lined up for you. He must have thought you would earn enough to get him the rest of the way through seminar."

"What about college loans?"

"He was afraid to apply for one as he was using an alias. He didn't want his deserted wife to find him, but she did."

"His wife nor the woman didn't report him?"

"No, the woman didn't, but my attorney tracked her down. All she wanted was to get on with her life after the lesson she had learned. As for his wife, at first, she thought he was living with a girl. When she found out he had actually gone through the pretense of marrying you, she threatened to sue him as a bigamist. He must have convinced her to allow him time to gather enough money to leave town with her and their baby."

"Where did John Grimes come in?" I asked.

"I assume John found out something was going on between Calvin and Cloetta. I'm assuming Calvin made up some kind of story to hold John off. My attorney didn't delve into anything concerning John Grimes."

I sat there frozen numb as I tried to think of how much more I needed to know. "What now?" I finally said.

"What happens now is up to you. Do you want to take action against him for committing bigamy? If so, my attorney friend can handle it. If you decide not to open yourself up to a scandal, he will see that your so-called marriage is annulled."

A vivid image of my mom came to me. She would go crazy when everyone found out I had lived in sin even when I thought I was married. She would never be able to live down the scandal, nor would she ever forgive me for ruining what joy she now might have in her life.

"I don't want anyone to know," I told him. "Can I keep it a secret?"

"As you were underage when the so-called marriage occurred, it can probably be arranged to keep your name out of any legal matters that might arise. To my understanding, the amount of money he stole from the church was a minimal amount. The church may choose not to press chargers. It happens often when the embarrassment of their negligence would be too great."

"What does annulled mean?"

"It means there is no longer a marriage that took place. By law you will be considered single again."

"What do you suggest I do?"

"I suggest you get the annulment regardless of whatever else you decide. You can always take legal action against him later. I would also suggest you say nothing to anyone about the annulment. Not even to Iva Lee for a while to come. Not that it would change anything with her, but it's always best to have fewer people knowing what's going on with you."

"What if she insists I go forward with a divorce?"

"Tell her my attorney is handling it."

"Will I have to return home to my parents after the annulment?"

"Not if you choose not to. Things can remain as they are right now, if that's what you want."

"I can live here and continue working at the restaurant and going to class?"

"Yes, you can."

"You'll still let me ride with you."

He grinned. "You can ride with me until the end of time, if that's the way you want it."

"I want it that way," I said as the ice that held me started to break apart. I was unable to remain strong. Unable to hold up under the tremendous truths that had been dumped on me. I was shaking all over as tears ran down my cheeks. I didn't want to cry, didn't want to grab hold of Mr. Grason to bury my face in his shirt. But I did.

He held me against him. Rocked back and forth with me in his arms much the same as he had done in the parking lot after the job fair.

"It's okay, Ellie. Everything is going to be okay. You'll get through this just fine. I promise you'll not have to go through this alone. I'll be right here with you."

His words of kindness were as devastating as knowing what my so-called husband had done to me. I was flooded with a desperation so powerful I feared I would no longer be able to exist. At that moment, Mr. Grason was the only person in existence. The only person who was there when I needed him. A whirlwind of confusion swept over me. It brought with it an avalanche of need to hold onto him for dear life. If I turned loose, I feared I might disappear into a void of darkness I would never come out from.

My reaction was all powerful, all consuming.

My mouth was on his. My hands ripping at the buttons of his shirt. I had to get closer to him. Had to feel my body next to his.

He wanted to say something, but I feared what it might be. He couldn't turn me away. I wouldn't let him stop doing what we were doing. I had to belong to him regardless if it destroyed us both. I was a raging fire that needed to be put out. He was the only one who could do it.

He must be feeling similar to what I was feeling because he wasn't making me slow down or stop.

~~~~

We were lying in the floor with our bodies entwined when some kind of sanity returned to me. Mr. Grason was breathing softly, but he wasn't asleep.

"Are you okay," he whispered near my ear as though speaking out loud could not be allowed.

"I'm okay," I whispered back.

"It's getting late," he finally said, and our bodies began to untwine from each other.

We found our scattered clothes and put them back on. He put on his shoes. I didn't.

"Can you forgive me?" he asked.

"Can you forgive me?" I repeated.

"We best pretend this never happened?" he suggested.

"We best pretend this never happened," I agreed.

"I don't want to leave you," he finally said.

I didn't repeat those words, but I felt them. I didn't want to be alone with all the truths I now knew.

"It's best I be alone," I lied. He had a wife to go home to. I had nothing other than the feel of him holding onto me.

"If you need me . . ." he hesitated. "I'll get you a phone put in tomorrow."

"No need. I have no one to call."

"You've got me," he said as he reached for the door. "You'll always have me, Ellie."

I said nothing as I listened to the door close and his footsteps going down the steps. The car engine started up. I went to the window and watched his car's taillights grow smaller in the distance until they were out of sight.

~~~~

I slept some and woke up early. I didn't want to get in the shower and wash the feel of Mr. Grason off me . . . but I needed to get into the shower and wash the feel of Mr. Grason off me. Iva Lee would show up soon. I had to look and seem as normal as possible.

I laughed at the thought of normal.

I got into the shower. I ran all the hot water out of the tank and stood under the cold spray until I was covered in chill bumps. It was almost time for work.

I was waiting on the bottom step when Iva Lee pulled up. The peacefulness of early morning had worked a bit magic on me. I felt more at peace, or at least more tranquil. Knowing the truth about Calvin, or be it Joseph Gerry, was supposed to set me free. Perhaps it would in time, but it would take time. Time for me to accept what happened as fact, as well as time for me to become a different person. Different in the fact that I was no longer Mom and Dad's little girl. I was now my own person with my own responsibilities. I just hoped I would be able to draw enough strength to become me before Mom found out the truth.

"This place is beautiful early of a morning," I told Iva Lee once I gently closed her car door behind me.

"I love early mornings too," she said. "That's part of the reason I go to work this early."

"What's the other part?" I found myself asking for lack of anything better to say.

"Money," she said without hesitation. "I am determined to die a very wealthy woman. To do that I have to work like the dogs of hell are nipping at my heels."

"Why would you want to *die* rich?" Hadn't she rather enjoy spending her money while she was alive.

"Because I was raised without so much as a pot to piss in. Do you know where that expression came from?"

"No."

"Hides used to be tanned in pee. Poor families would save all their pee to sell to the tanneries. They only got pennies, but pennies helped keep their bodies from eating their brains. Did you know when the body is starving, the body will eat its own brain."

"That's gruesome," I said.

"Poverty is gruesome. I wish it didn't exist."

"Me too," I told her.

"The sheriff stopped by after you left last night. He said the only Calvin West who could be found died at eighty-nine years of age, which was fifteen years ago."

"Really?" I said.

"You don't seem nearly as surprised as I'd expected. Did Bret find out the same information?"

I nodded, but I wasn't sure she could see the movement in the darkness of the car. "He did," I told her.

"I thought he might have hired someone to do some research. Is that why his car was parked in front of the shed when I drove by last night?"

"Right. I knew he had something he was debating telling me when he didn't leave the minute he dropped me off the way he always did." I hoped she hadn't lingered or came up the steps.

"What are you going to do about it?" she was straight forward in her question.

"Nothing," I told her.

"Wise decision. Some secrets should remain hidden for the betterment of all involved."

An old familiar chill inched up my spine.

"Time erases memory faster without gossip being spread around. Pretend you know nothing more about Calvin West. Rumors will settle down soon. Neither you nor he had enough notoriety to keep gossip going for long. I took it upon myself to do something last night that I thought was for the best. You see, I've known the sheriff for a long time. I asked him to make a deal with the church. He's going to check with them today. I'm going pay what this so-called Calvin West stole from them. It was a minimal amount. They will have to sign a no disclosure form if they accept the money, and then there will be no more investigation or warrants put out. Do you agree with my proposal?"

"Yes," I told her.

"Will you also agree for me to take another dollar from your paycheck every week until I'm refunded what I had to pay the church?"

"Most definitely."

"Good. Seems like you'll be working for me for a long time to come."

"I'll agree to that also."

"Good," she repeated and said no more.

Chapter 20

The church was more interested in getting their money back than finding and prosecuting their wayward ex-minister. Neither did they want the embarrassment of admitting how desperate they had been in finding someone to take on the job as minister of their church.

"Appears you're one unlucky girl who hit a lucky streak," the sheriff told me. "You owe Iva Lee Keys a lot of gratitude. I don't know anyone else who would have done what she has done for you."

I agreed.

Mr. Grason also expressed his gratitude to Iva Lee. She only shrugged and let it all drop without further ado.

A week later she took me by surprise as I waited for Mr. Grason to pick me up.

"I've thinking about your predicament," she said. "You've hardly mentioned your parents. I assume they will think you are still married to him. You'll need to tell them something if they find out he's no longer in the picture, right?"

"Right," I certainly would.

"I know your so-called marriage was silently annulled."

"How?" I found myself asking.

"Like I told you before, I have my ways of finding out almost everything."

"Right," I said again.

"So, I took it upon myself to have a friend of mine prepare and brilliantly put something on record at the courthouse. Seldom does anyone go through those huge books of records unless they have a specific reason for searching for something. If a question arises, well we'll deal with it then."

She handed me a folded sheet of paper. I opened it and my eyes popped and my mouth surely fell open. It was a death certificate for a Calvin West. He had died on the day he disappeared. I looked Iva Lee in the eyes. She was looking right back.

"I won't be taking any money out of your paycheck for that. It didn't cost me a thing." She went back to cleaning.

I showed the paper to Mr. Grason once he stopped at the shed. I had debated showing it to him all the way there. I thought it best if I did so.

"What's this?" he asked.

"Turn on the overhead light and read it."

He hadn't dared go up the steps to check that the shed was safe since we did what we did.

"My temptation will be too great," he told me.

My temptation was just as great – and so was my guilt. How was it I could want to sin so badly when I knew it was wrong. Yet, somehow, what Mr. Grason and I did hadn't seemed wrong at all.

Mr. Grason burst out laughing when he read the death certificate. "Iva Lee knows how to get things done."

"She does," I agreed.

"She is a genius. I hadn't thought of doing such a thing," I told him.

"How did she manage it?" If anyone knew, it would be Mr. Grason."

"Don't know, but if I had to guess, I'd say it has something to do with the man who shares her bed."

"Don?"

"He's a retired police officer. He knows how to get favors from those who he's given favors to."

"Do you think she and Don are living in sin?" I couldn't stop myself from asking a second time.

"No. Remember my animal theory?"

I remembered all too well.

"You know there is going to come a time when we can't fight it any longer, don't you?"

He was right as long as we were close to each other. He was my magnet. I was fighting not to add any more sins to the pile I already had. The only way to stop the inevitable was to put at least of hundred miles of distance between us. I couldn't do that until I paid my debts off to Iva Lee, and I didn't mean in money only.

"Can I come up?" he surprised me by asking.

"No," I was quick to tell him. If I'd hesitated that wouldn't have been the answer I would have given him.

"I'll be here early in the morning as usual," was all he said.

"Okay."

"Ellie,"

"What."

"I'm glad Calvin West is dead." He slowly got out of the car and waited on the bottom step until I hollered out the window.

As usual, I stood there and watched his taillights disappear.

~~~~

Sunday came. Iva Lee and I both breathed a sigh of relief as she closed and locked the back door to the restaurant.

"I wouldn't say this to anyone other than you, but there are times when I do get sick and tired of being here."

I almost laughed in surprise, but I caught myself in time. "I'm thankful you allow me to be here with you, but it'll be good to take a small break if it's only a half-day off."

"Once I'm rich enough, we'll take Mondays off too," she added with a slight smile.

"Advertise for more business," I told her. "If you doubled your business, you could get rich enough faster.

She grinned. "And die sooner. Have you told your mother about Calvin West's death?"

"No."

"Why not."

"Dread."

"You should."

"Why?"

"She'll have to find out sometime."

"What if she tries to make me come home?"

"You think she'd do that?"

"The only reason she might want me back is if she wants a babysitter for baby Grant." I told her what had been sneaking into my mind even when I didn't want it to. Mom was used to earning money. She wouldn't like being without it regardless how much she loved her baby boy.

"Has it ever occurred to you that you're now considered a grown woman. Your mother can't make you do anything you don't want to do. Has she even contacted you since you've been gone, other than the one time she called the restaurant?"

"No," but that didn't mean she never would. Or did it?

"On the other hand," she said. "There are times when a person should let sleeping dogs lie. You mother might represent one of those dogs."

"I agree with that."

We got into her car.

"Do you know how to drive?"

"No. My brother was the only one Mom would allow to drive."

"Your brother?" she questioned.

I took a deep breath. I suppose it was time I told her what still haunted me. The main reason I had married Calvin West."

"My older brother was killed in the most horrible way."

"When?"

"It was on a beautiful spring day. The birds were singing, and the sun was shining."

"How was he killed?" she prompted after I had gone silent.

I told her every gruesome detail. I left out nothing other than meeting with Drake Lewis. He was as much of my past as the man called Calvin West. I wanted both men to be put in my past. Done and over with. Never to rise again.

"I'll get Don to teach you how to drive," she told me without commenting on what I had just told her.

Her silence made it easier on me.

"Do you want to start learning today or next Sunday?"

"There's no time like today," I told her.

~~~~

I laughed out loud when I looked out the window and saw what Don had drove into the yard. It actually had to run if he drove it there, but that didn't mean it could be started and driven again.

"Get yourself down here, Squirt."

For some reason he'd started calling me Squirt.

"My black beauty awaits you."

He was stretching it a lot to call coats of Bondo and Rust-oleum a black beauty. An orange rusted disaster would be more correct.

He had a huge grin on his face by the time I got down the steps. "My woman has given me marching orders," he said. "You are to be proficient in driving this masterpiece before I leave you with it this evening."

"That's a tall order," I told him.

"A feasible one none the less. She has told me often what a quick learner you are. I'm going to drive it through that gate into the field. We'll change places, and you'll be driving with proficiency before an hour is up."

I laughed. He didn't.

After an hour was up, I was changing gears smoother and using the clutch without being as jerky. The freshly mown hay field was flat enough and big enough for me not to worry about running over anything I shouldn't. The cows were in another field.

"I want to learn how to drive, but it'll be a long time before I can afford a car," I said lightly. Besides, I was already working day and night except for these few precious hours on Sunday's.

"Ever hear of taking out a loan?" he asked.

"I have. I'm paying Iva Lee each week on what she loaned me."

"She loaned you money?" His words sounded with true disbelief.

"She did."

"Was the loan your idea or hers?"

"Hers," I told him.

"Well, I'll be a monkey's uncle. "That woman trusting someone with her money is like trusting someone with her life."

"She takes some out of my pay each week," I clarified.

"Does she charge you interest?"

"What's interest."

"The extra you have to pay for using someone else's money."

"I don't know if she is or not."

"Either way, she's grown soft. Don't tell her we talked about this. She wouldn't want me to know her hard shell has cracked a little."

"I won't tell if you won't."

He held out his callused hand and we shook on it.

"Your next lesson will be next Sunday," he told me after two hours of driving in circles in the hayfield. "We'll change places before we get to the gate. I've always hated replacing gates."

"Lost your confidence in your own driving instructions, huh?"

"You could put it that way if it makes you feel better."

I got out at the shed and watched Don and his Black Beauty disappear down the gravel driveway. I didn't get the *left alone* feeling it gave me when watching Mr. Grason drive out of sight.

The sight of the brightly colored wildflowers swaying in the gentle wind did give me a very lonesome feeling. Soon, their blossoms would fade. Back home the smell of wood smoke would be filling the air as people built fires to cook supper. The weather was at least ten degrees warmer here than back home. It was much higher in the mountains than here. Altitude like attitude made a difference. Here there was mainly electric stoves instead of using wood stoves to cook on. But that was the diversity of life.

Instead of going back inside the shed, I chose to take a walk through the woods behind the shed. There was something about being in the woods that brought peace and contentment.

I was almost out of sight of the shed and hay field when a sound startled me. I whirled around to see where the noise came from.

"I didn't mean to scare you," said Mr. Grason. "I've been watching you drive Don's Black Beauty around in circles. If you wanted to learn to drive, I would've been willing to teach you."

"This was Iva Lee's idea," I told him.

"A good one at that. I should have thought of it myself, but I like driving you about."

I smiled. I bet he had never liked hauling me about as much as I liked the comfort he and his car gave me.

"I missed seeing you yesterday and today. That's the real reason I'm here sitting on a log."

I missed him too. Oh, my goodness, how I longed to be with him.

"Come closer. Sit down beside me," he said.

"I should go back to the shed," I told him.

"And I shouldn't be here, but we are here."

I walked over and sat down beside him.

"I don't know which is worst, being without you or being with you and trying not to take you in my arms."

I understood only too well. My entire body was on fire from wanting Mr. Grason.

"Mr. Grason," I said his name, only his name.

"Don't you think it's time you started calling me Bret?"

"Not as long as I'm taking classes under you."

"Under me. Oh, hell, Ellie. Don't say such as that. The very idea makes wanting you grow stronger."

"Mom used to tell me just because I wanted a piece of candy didn't mean I was going to get it."

"Logic such as that makes me dislike your mom, but I bet it never stopped your wanting. Neither does it stop mine."

I looked through the trees to where I had made circles in the hay field. "What would it accomplish if you crept into my bed every night? Would I hug my pillow to cry myself to sleep after you had to get up and leave me. I would still be alone when I woke up each morning because you belonged to someone else."

"I don't belong to someone else. All I have is a piece of paper. A responsibility that I can't turn my back on. Ellie, it's been years since I've slept with Grace Anna."

"Maybe you should," I said as the thought of him being in bed with another woman ripped at my insides.

"I cringe at the very thought."

"Who did you sleep with before I came along?" I couldn't stop myself from asking.

"Only my imagination," he told me. "I don't need to ask the same question of you, do I?"

"No," I admitted.

"Please don't turn me away any longer," he said.

"We'll end up hurting each other," I tried to sound logical and wise. "Such as that never works out for the best."

"It worked out for the best with Iva Lee and Don. It'll work out for us."

"Give me some time to think about it. Surely you can understand I want desperately to be a wife and mother, not someone's concubine."

"You would never be my concubine. Don't you ever use that word to describe yourself again," he said with feeling. "You've become my world. Surely you realize that."

I didn't want to realize that. I couldn't accept what I would become if I agreed.

"Give me some time," I repeated.

"I don't want to, but I will," he finally agreed. "Remember each opportunity we have to be together is an opportunity we'll regret not taking some day. Life is too short to give up our chance at happiness."

I put my arms around him and kissed him long and hard before I stood up and walked away. He tried to stop me leaving him at first, but he finally turned my arm loose and let me go. I would have given in if he hadn't

~~~~

Time passed day by day, week by week, and month by month. My days were all the same. I left the shed and went to work. I left work and went back to the shed. The leaves were all down and the trees were bare and gray. Winter was coming on for real and I still hadn't given in to what Mr. Grason and I both wanted. I had made a horrible mistake by thinking I was marrying Calvin West – better known as Joseph Gerry. I didn't want to make a mistake equally as bad when I knew the truth of what I would be letting myself in for.

Another Sunday finally came, and I got in the car with Iva Lee.

"Don says you have become a pretty good driver," Iva Lee said.

I didn't comment on all the time I'd spent practicing in his black beauty.

"In a few days I'm going to tell him to take you to one of his friends that has cars for sale. He'll get you a good deal on a used car."

"I don't have the money to buy a car."

"Yes, you do. I know exactly how much you have in your secret bank account. I also know you don't have time to spend much money. You don't even buy many groceries. You eat at the restaurant, the same as I do."

"I don't need a car. It's easier on me to bum rides," I tried to make a joke.

She didn't take the joke up. Instead, she became gravely serious. "What are you going to do about the baby?"

"What baby?" I asked innocently.

"The one you're trying to hide from everyone including its daddy."

"I don't know what you're talking about."

"You're a horrible liar, Ellie. Surely, you realize I've always kept pads and tampons in the restroom for the waitresses to use. I check them almost every day and replace them myself. I know when every single girl who works for me has her period. I know when your last period was. That excuse for a human being wouldn't even allow you enough money to buy a rag for you to use."

I didn't say a thing as her words shot to a place in me that was still hurting.

"I'm just thankful he isn't the father of the baby you're carrying, for what it's worth. Have you told Bret yet?"

There was no need for me to lie to her. She really was too smart for that. Besides, I needed someone to confide in. Someone to give me advice.

"He doesn't know. I've refused to let it happen again."

"It only happened that one time?" she asked in a tone of disbelief.

"Yes, but we both wanted it to happen every night, but I've refused."

"Talk about powerful resistance. You and he have more will power than Don and I ever had. Why haven't you told him about the baby."

"He's got a wife."

"And I had a husband. That didn't stop me and Don from loving each other."

"You weren't carrying his baby," I told her.

"I carried four of Don's babies, but never to full term. I miscarried with each one of our babies. After the second miscarriage, the doctor advised me to never become pregnant again. He said I was risking my own death with another pregnancy. I tried two more times. Came within a hair's breadth of dying with both of them. After the last one I lost, my doctor cut my tubes without telling me. It was years later that I learned what he'd done. Don knew. He wanted me alive more than he wanted to become a father."

I was sad for her. Sad for her four dead babies. Sad for the one I lost. That realization hit me hard. Somehow this pregnancy had nothing to do with my other one.

"You've miscarried once. I don't want you to end up like me."

I didn't know what to say to that. I had wanted my other baby, but not nearly as much as I wanted this one.

"Why haven't you told Bret?" she asked again. "Tell me the truth this time."

"I'm afraid," I said, and realized I was telling her the truth.

"What are you afraid of?"

"That he won't love me enough to divorce Grace Anna and knowing that would devastate me. I'm also afraid that he might actually divorce her and marry me. If he did that there's a chance he would resent me for making him divorce a helpless woman."

"Let me set you straight on something, Ellie. Grace Anna isn't a helpless woman. She is crazy, but she's crazy like a weasel. It didn't take long for Bret Grason to discover he'd made a horrible mistake by marrying her. Her parents knew she was as wild and worthless as a bed bug. The went out of their way to set Bret up with her. Poor Bret, he realized what had happened soon after they were married, but it was too late. I'll give the stupid man credit for trying as hard as he has to make things work out. I dare say things would have been different if he'd met someone he loved the way he's in love with you."

"He's in love with me?" I couldn't help being surprised at hearing her say those words.

"Don't act so surprised. You know he is."

"I thought Calvin was in love with me too," I confessed.

"And there lies another of your problems. You shouldn't be judging Bret by what Calvin was like."

"Once bit, twice shy," I repeated what I'd once said about her.

"When you meet Bret in the woods today, tell him about the baby. You'll make him the happiest man in the world. Plus, he needs to take you to see a doctor, and I don't mean the school's doctor this time."

I was amazed what Iva Lee knew about everything, but then I shouldn't have been.

Iva Lee dropped me off at the shed and I went straight up the steps as she drove away. I was in a hurry to take a shower and meet Bret. This time I was going to bring him back to the shed with me. Afterwards I was going to tell him about the baby – unless he'd already realized my little poochy belly didn't come from being fat. I opened the door and rushed inside. It suddenly dawned on me that I hadn't locked the door when Iva Lee picked me up, or had I?

I was reaching for the door to go back outside when a hand suddenly grabbed hold of me from behind. I turned around hoping it was Bret. The hurtfulness of that grip on my arm told me it wasn't.

"You knew I would find you," he said.

"You better get back where you came from," I told him. "The sheriff has been after you for stealing from the church."

"No, he's not. I can go where I want as free as a bird. I happen to know that old woman fixed things up for you."

"What happened to your wife and baby?" I demanded to know.

"I like you better, so I've come back to you loving arms."

"My loving arms nothing. I despise the very thought of you." I jerked my arm free from his hand. Leave right now. I never want to set eyes on you again."

A sly grin came to his face. "How bad do you want to get rid of me? How much money can you come up with, little Ellie? You best start coughing up all that money the old lady has been paying you all these months."

"I'll never give you another dime," I told him. "If you don't leave here right now and never show you ugly, filthy conniving face again, I'll take out a bigamy warrant for your arrest."

I must have hit a nerve for his hand slapped me across the face before I saw it coming. The force of it knocked me against the door. I grabbed to stop myself from falling. My hand clutched the doorknob. I managed to get the door open and ran outside. He grabbed hold of me again before I got to the top step.

"Give me your money now or I'll beat you to death and find it for myself."

"I don't have money," I told him.

"Where is it then."

"Iva Lee keeps it. This is her place. As you already know, she paid off what you stole from the church. She's keeping my pay until I've paid back everything you stole, including three months of back rent."

"You lying bitch. I know how much you get paid. I also know how much that pitiful excuse of a church had in their stupid little coffer. No way would anybody pay back rent for that rusted out piece of shit."

His hand slapped me across the face again. I caught myself on the railing to keep from falling. I kicked with my right leg and grazed him in the groin with my foot. He yelled out in pain, but I didn't get a direct hit good enough to stop him. He leaped on top of me knocking me flat of my back on the tiny landing. He had me by the hair ready to beat my head against the floor. I had hold of his wrist with both hands when he was suddenly jerked off me.

The anger I saw on Mr. Grason's face made him look like a raging lunatic. His first blow broke Calvin's nose. His second punch landed on his chin. He didn't strike again. Instead, he had hold of his hair as he rammed his head against the railing with a force that shook the landing. The wood was old and weathered by the elements. It splintered. A needle-sharp piece of wood the size of a broom handle went through the back of his neck and came out near his Adams apple.

Mr. Grason dropped his head with as a look of disbelief on his face.

"Did he hurt you bad, Ellie?" a voice that didn't belong to Mr. Grason asked. Don was standing on the steps looking at me and then at the large sliver of wood sticking out of Calvin's neck.

I think I answered him. Mr. Grason was still staring at the jerking body in disbelief.

"I saw what happened," Don said. "He deserved what he got."

I managed to get to my feet and reached for Mr. Grason. I clutched him in my arm and burst into tears.

"I have to call the sheriff," he mumbled as his arms closed around me.

"Hold on a minute," Don said. "I was a cop long enough to know what's gonna happen when the laws that be finds out about this. I'm a witness to it being an accident. I also saw him beating Ellie. You won't be convicted with an intentional murder, but you'll lose your job. You'll also be known as a man who committed murder. You'll have a cloud hanging over your head for the rest of your life. One you don't deserve. Doing what the law requires always has consequences. Most of the consequences are bad for the victim."

Don shook his head and kicked Calvin's twitching leg with his boot. "This piece of shit will have a real death certificate if you call the Sherriff. Somebody is going to get in trouble since there's already a death certificate on record even if it is in an alias' name. There'll be no doubt about Calvin West and Joseph Gerry being the same man. They'll know Iva Lee had something to do with it. I won't allow my wonderful girl to get into trouble." He let out a huff of air. "Bret, Ellie, do you think you both are capable of keeping this a secret for the rest of your lives.

We must have said yes, because Don said "Good. Bring me the sheet off the bed, Ellie."

I reluctantly left Mr. Grason's arms, made my legs move as I got the sheet and brought it back. Don spread it over the top of Calvin's dead body and rolled him in it.

"Have you regained enough strength to help me carry him?" Don asked Mr. Grason.

"My adrenalin is still pumping along with my anger," he told Don. "Lead the way. I'm willing and able."

"Good," Don said again. "Ellie, do you still have that gallon of bleach I put under the sink?"

"I should have. I've not used any."

"Get it and make sure you pour it on every speck of blood. It's soaking into the wood. We don't want that to happen."

I went back inside and got bleach, detergent and the broom. I tried not to look at Don and Mr. Grason carrying off what was wrapped in the sheet. I tried not to think of the time I'd spent with him thinking I was his wife. I had no idea what was going to happen next. I did know I had to get rid of the blood stains.

I scrubbed for hours. Carried gallons on top of gallons of water from the sink and kept pouring it on the landing as well as the steps. Both should have the same amount of cleaning. A clean landing and dirty steps would be a dead giveaway. I had no idea if the bleach, soap and water would do the job that needed doing, so I kept at it.

The sun had set by the time Don and Mr. Grason returned. A cold wind was blowing downed leaves in a circle. I felt chilled to the bone as I watched the two men. Don rummaged in the bottom of the shed until he found what he was after. A trunk containing old clothes. He pulled out pants and shirts and gave some to Mr. Grason.

"Give me your clothes, take a shower and put these on," Don told him. "I have to burn our clothes and scrub our boots with diesel fuel and gas. Give me the clothes and shoes you're wearing, Ellie."

Mr. Grason and I did as we were told. A short time later I smelled the smoke from a fire. Don was no fool. He'd obviously been a cop long enough to know how to cover up most everything. I hoped.

Don came back an hour later. He had a hammer, rusty nails and a plank identical to the one that got broken. He wasted no time taking the broken board off and replacing it with the other board. I couldn't tell any difference in the railing when he had finished. He inspected the board and the wet landing as closely as he would have searched for a splinter in his hand.

"Good," he said again. "Bret, you stay with Ellie until Iva Lee gets here. I'll toss this board on the fire before I go to the house and brief Iva Lee on what has happened. She'll bring you another sheet, Ellie."

He looked me and Mr. Grason over closely and nodded. He was satisfied neither of us were going into hysterics. And then he was gone.

"I don't believe this happened," Mr. Grason said. "Are you sure you're okay? There are places on your face that's starting to bruise." He clenched his fists. "I'd like to kill him all over again. Slower and more painful this time."

"Don't talk about it ever again. We've got to make ourselves believe it never happened."

"You really believe we can do that?"

"I believe it's what we need to do," I burst into tears.

He took me in his arms and held me close. "I love you, Ellie," he said. "I'll do anything for you."

"I love you too," I said as I realized how true my words were. Never again would I try to push him away from me. This was a man who had killed for me, whether he intended to or not. Come to think of it, Iva Lee had done similar with the same person in faking his death certificate. Don had allowed himself to become an accomplice by destroying evidence along with the body.

How could I ever think I was alone again.

Chapter 21

"**W**ill you tell me what was done with him?" I asked Mr. Grason after we'd both settled down a little.

"We dug a deep hole in the barn stall until we hit solid rock. We rolled him in naked and then took four bags of burnt lime and dumped the bags in the hole. Don climbed down, ripped the bags open and climbed back out with the empty bags. When that was done, we scattered some hay and shoveled all the cow manure we could find into the stall. We left the stall door open so the cattle could go inside to tromp the manure and hay together. Then we came back here."

He was silent for several long moments before he spoke again.

"I shouldn't have told you that. It might be best you didn't know what we did."

"It won't make any difference," I told him. "It's time to forget," but I knew we couldn't. Not now, not ever.

Mr. Grason was still holding me in his arms when Iva Lee arrived in her car. She came in the door acting as though nothing had happened. She looked me and Mr. Grason over.

"I think it best you go home and get some rest. You'll need to teach classes tomorrow morning the same as always."

She reached out and took his hands in hers.

"Skinned knuckles," she said. "I'm sorry they got skinned when you were helping Don castrate some calves today. I'm sure you and those four calves will heal all right especially since you and Don used diesel fuel to pour on their cut. It always seems to splatter on shoes. I have yours and Ellies' new shoes in the car. I'm hoping she has similar size feet as mine."

"I'd rather not leave for a while," he said.

"I know, but you should. Grace Anna's hired help will be expecting you. Don is making sure those calves are all right. You know how protective he is when it comes to his animals."

Mr. Grason took his arms from around me and stood up to leave, hesitated.

"She'll be fine," Iva Lee said. I'll be here for a while discussing the possibility of changing the menu for the restaurant. She's worked so many extra hours, I might have to give her tomorrow off. Then again, I might not. Good night, Bret."

He left to walk back home.

Iva Lee turned to me. "Is your stomach upset?"

"No. It feels okay."

"Are you sure? I can take you to a doctor if necessary. It's easy to fall down steps and land face first on the hard ground."

"Landing face first hurt, but my stomach didn't get hit," I said, playing her game of words. I suppose she was in the process of showing me and Mr. Grason never a word of what happened should be spoken about by either of us.

"Trauma can cause stomach problem too."

"If I feel unstable, I'll let you know."

"I'm going to stay here for a while if you don't mind."

"I welcome your company," I told her. "I'm still shaken up by the fall."

"No doubt about it. Falling on your face causes a lot of stress. Did you tell Bret about the baby?"

Evidently, we didn't need to pretend my baby didn't exist. We could talk about it. "No. It wasn't the right time or place."

"I agree, but don't make excuses for not telling him. It's his baby the same as yours. Don't deny him that right."

The point she made hit home. He had the right to know, but it might not be for the best. Plus, I didn't want him to have a claim on my baby? It was mine, all mine. I feared I would always feel that way regardless of how much I loved a man."

"What about Grace Anna?"

"It's best she remains in the dark about everything. She's crazy not stupid. She's also vengeful beyond belief. She knows how to use people to her advantage. The good Lord only knows what would happen if she found out Bret fell in love with you. Especially when you are such a young thing with nothing to offer him other than yourself along with his baby."

"If he knows, how can she not find out?"

"You've heard the old saying that if one person knows, it's a kept secret. When more than one person knows, it's no longer a secret. Still yet, I'm convinced four separate people can keep a secret when they are equally involved."

I hoped she was right.

"I don't understand why he hasn't left her long ago if he hates living with her.

"You might say she has him by his short hairs."

I must have given her a confused look, for she explained.

"Everything he owns and cares about is in her name. Her daddy saw to that. Her daddy's wasn't crazy by a long shot. He was just plain devious. He figured out how to make Bret marry his daughter while keeping him walking on a mighty thin line."

"Looks to me like not having to live with someone you don't love would compensate for losing material things."

"Why didn't you leave Calvin. You didn't love him, plus he made you miserable."

"I didn't have any other place to go and no money to go on."

"In other words, you didn't know you could do better without him."

Thinking back on it, she was right.

"That's exactly where Bret Grason was – until he met you. I've been sitting on my haunches waiting to see what a man does when what he thinks is the right thing doesn't coincide with what he needs to make his life worth living. She's not going to walk out on him, Ellie."

"And he sees himself as being too honor bound to walk out on her."

"Perhaps that's the case, perhaps not. In the morning when Bret comes to pick you up, come in to work unless you're spotting or having stomach pains. I'll tell those gossiping women I saw you take a face-first fall down the steps. They found out you're renting the shed from me. So far all they know about Calvin West is that he deserted you. With luck, it will stay that way long enough for gossip to settle down. Of course, gossip will raise its head when they find out you're having *his* baby, but it won't amount to much. Having a baby is an everyday event."

Not when you're the one who's having the baby, I wanted to say. But I didn't.

"Think you're stable enough to be left alone? It takes a strong person to endure the fall you've had."

"I'll be okay."

"Are you sure?"

"Yes." But I wasn't sure. How could anyone expect me to be okay? I didn't think it possible to be okay ever again. But I was going to pretend."

Iva Lee surprised me further when she went outside and came back with sticks to put in the windows.

"I know you keep the door locked, but the windows don't have locks. Sticks work good enough. The sound of breaking glass gives its own warning. I'll got a pistol in the car I'm going to loan you. Keep it under the pillow you don't sleep on."

"Why? Do you think Grace Anna might show up?"

"No, but a woman named Cloetta might. She allowed her own husband to sleep with you in order to steal enough money to take off. She'll likely know he returned for the same reason."

She had a point.

~~~~

I watched Iva Lee drive away. I didn't know exactly what to think of her, but I was certainly appreciative of her.

I made sure the door was securely locked and Iva Lee's sticks were securely established in the windows. I even took the pistol into the bathroom with me where I stripped off my clothes and turned the water on. The shower I'd taken earlier wasn't enough. I needed to wash myself again. I felt dirty.

The warm water ran out too soon. I wasn't satisfied yet, but I would shower again come morning. I used a clean shirt for a nightgown and took the pistol to bed with me. I'd seen Dad and Grant shoot guns often. I knew how to shoot even when I wasn't practiced at it. I slipped it under my pillow. *Try not to think of a thing,* I told myself.

I had fallen asleep, but it was a restless sleep. From Grant's accident to what just happened kept flashing through my dreams. I awoke to the sound of a horn blowing. I got out of bed and looked out the window. Mr. Grason was getting out of the car.

"Give me a minute," I hollered through the closed window.

He heard me, looked up and nodded, turned around and got back in the car. He knew I needed a few minutes to myself.

The first thing I checked was my underwear. There were no blood spots. Next, I put my hand on my stomach. There was no pain or soreness. My baby was okay. Next, I looked in the small bathroom mirror. There wasn't as much bruising as I expected, but both sides of my face were bright red from being slapped hard. A fall would be more convincing it there were some scrape marks, but there were none.

I washed my face and put on my only other uniform. Don had taken the one I had been wearing. I hoped Iva Lee washed it instead of Don burning it. From midnight to morning a washed uniform didn't have time to dry.

I made sure the door was locked and got in the car with Mr. Grason. "The fall I took off the steps didn't bruise my face much," I told him when I realized he was staring at me.

"I'm relieved," he said.

"It's turning colder," I changed the subject. "It's probably snowing in the high mountains. I can remember it blowing snow on Halloween night."

"It comes with the altitude."

"I'm pregnant." Talk about choosing the right time.

His foot hit the brakes and he skidded to a stop on the gravel driveway.

"What did you say?"

"I'm pregnant."

I saw him doing mental calculations. He didn't question it being his.

"Have you seen a doctor?"

"No."

"I'll take you to one right now."

"No need. This baby is secure. I'll not miscarry it," I said with more confidence than I was feeling.

"We need to make sure."

"I'm sure."

"I want this baby," he said.

"So do I."

"I want you too. You know that, don't you?"

"I know."

"Does Iva Lee know?" he surprised me by asking.

"Doesn't she know everything?"

"That she does."

"She insisted I tell you."

"Why didn't you tell me sooner?"

"I didn't want to jinx anything."

"Is that why you kept me at arms' length all this time?"

"Partly."

"And the other part was?"

"My marriage was annulled, but yours wasn't."

"I'll get a divorce."

"No, you won't," I told him what I knew to be true. Never would he be able to get away from such a woman,

"How can you say that?"

"I don't want to be a home wrecker."

He laughed, but not with amusement. "How many times have I got to tell you. I no longer have a marriage. All that's left is a piece of paper."

"The tie that binds," I told him. "Drive on. We'll discuss this later when the dust has settled some."

"I want to discuss it right now. Get things straight with us right now."

"Too much had happened for us to be able to think straight today, much less make plans. Let's get on with our day. We'll have time to talk tonight."

"At twelve o'clock at night?"

"If not tonight, tomorrow night. You can let class out a little early."

He started the car. His silence told me he accepted my suggestion even if he didn't agree with it.

He drove to the door of the restaurant, stopped and leaned toward me as though he was going to kiss me bye. I placed my fingers on his lips. "Tonight," I told him.

"Promise?" he insisted.

"Promise," I repeated and got out.

The kitchen was empty, but I could hear voices in the dining room. Iva Lee was talking to someone. I hoped it wasn't the sheriff. Surely, he hadn't discovered what happened yesterday this this fast.

"Come in here, Ellie," Iva Lee called out.

I put on my most innocent look, tried to wipe the fear off my face, poured myself a cup of coffee to have something to do with my hands, and went to the dining room.

"Look who's here, Ellie," Iva Lee said with enthusiasm.

My hands jerked. I sloshed hot coffee on them before I could control my reaction.

"Mom, Dad, this is certainly a surprise. Oh, you've got my baby brother with you. I've been longing to see him." I looked at the cute little fellow sitting in Dad's lap. Dad had him playing with the car keys.

"Not enough to make a trip back home," Mom accused.

I didn't tell her I felt unwelcome. Never once had she contacted. There was only that one call to the restaurant. It certainly hadn't been an invitation home.

"I've kept her busy seven days a week," Iva Lee spoke up. "She mentions all of you and going back for a visit often. Did you say you had a reason for this sudden visit?" Iva Lee was running interference by reminding them and me that she was right here.

"We've been hearing gossip," Mom said.

"About what?" I asked as innocently as possible.

"We heard you ran Calvin off," Mom stunned me by saying. Her eyes shot to Iva Lee as though her glare could make her leave us alone. Iva Lee didn't budge.

Mom didn't believe in running around a bush. She came straight to her reason for being here.

"I never ran him off. He left to take a refresher course for ministers."

"Why isn't he here then?" Mom continued. "I heard he's been gone a long time."

"Who told you that?" I asked.

"Never you mind what little bird told me."

"That's a cruel and insensitive thing to ask, or haven't you heard?" Iva Lee was coming to my rescue again. She didn't trust me to handle the situation as she thought I should.

"Heard what?" Mom demanded.

"He was in an accident. Both he and the other driver lost their lives." Iva Lee didn't beat around the bush either.

Mom was stunned. A tiny bit of color blanched from her face.

"Oh, honey," Dad said. "Why didn't you let us know. We would have been here for you."

"We deserved to know about it," Mom said.

"Shock," Iva Lee continued talking. "She went into such a state of shock she hardly remembered her own name. She's just now coming back to herself. You know how tragic accidents affect people."

Iva Lee's story almost had me believing what she was telling them. What she was saying had a lot of truth to it. Still yet, I'd never met anyone who could weave such outrageous tales and make people believe her every word.

"When did it happen?" Mom managed to ask.

Iva Lee told her the day he left on his so-called refresher course.

"He's been dead and buried that long?" Mom asked in disbelief.

"Not buried. He was cremated." Iva Lee said before I could respond.

She didn't know how vehemently Mom rejected cremation. To her it was as bad as burning in hellfire.

Mom gasped. "You disrespected a preacher. How dare you?"

"It's what he said he wanted if he passed before I did. Neither of us expected it to happen so soon." I couldn't resist adding a little truth.

"I don't believe it. A man of God would never request such a thing. You didn't want to pay out money for a real burial. That's the real reason."

Iva Lee's jaws clenched. She was holding back what she wanted to say.

"It's true there wasn't enough money for a regular burial. There was never a penny to spare, but I would have gone into debt to see him buried," I wasn't lying about that. "But how could I go against what he said he wanted?"

"You should have," Mom was firm.

"How have you managed?" Dad asked.

"I continued doing what I've done since the day I married Calvin. He got me this job before we were married."

"As you can tell, she's still working here," Iva Lee told Mom.

"Not anymore. She's going back home with us."

"No, I'm not," I told her firmly. "I've made a new life for myself, and I don't plan on it changing."

"You're obviously not capable of making decisions after such a tragedy. We're your parents, we know what's best for you."

I opened my mouth to object, but Iva Lee spoke up before I could.

"You could be right about that. It's likely she'll be needing your financial support along with a place to live. I've been letting her stay at my place and working here to earn her support. I'm not sure she'll be able to do that after the baby is born. To be honest, it would be a relief on me if you were willing to support her and pay off what she borrowed from me. Medicine and doctor's treatments takes ever cent she makes. Did you know she had a miscarriage early on. She has to take things really easy now. I can't allow her to lift anything that weighs over ten pounds. Not to mention the fact she's still paying for his cremation and the accident. It was his fault. His insurance didn't cover everything. There's still a possibility that the other person's family will sue her for damages. Her being his wife and all. They'd already have done it, but they know she doesn't have a dime to her name. Can't get blood out of a turnip, regardless of how hard you squeeze it."

Mom looked stunned. I could see the wheels of her mind turning. It didn't take her long to realize my baby and I could be a never-ending expense on her. One I didn't want her to have, plus one she didn't want to have. It would be a high expense to pay for a babysitter.

"When's it due?" Mom wanted to know.

My hand automatically went to my belly. I told her I was farther along than I actually was.

"You're not big enough to be that far along," but she could still see the baby bump when I rubbed the loose material against my belly.

"She's not been able to keep food down. No surprise considering what all she's been through."

Mom nodded like she understood. "Oh, dear. I did so want my little girl to come home with us, but considering the circumstances, it might be for the best not to make her move just yet. I don't want to put added stress on her. We'll give her a little more time before we make sudden changes in what she's used to."

Dad's eyebrows raised, but he said nothing.

"Wait a minute here. It's obvious you've not had time to come to such a conclusion. Taking her home with you might be for the best. Since her first miscarriage, the doctor suggests she spend a lot of time in bed. There's always a chance she'll have to spend the last two or three months of her pregnancy basically bedridden. She'll need a mother to wait on her hand and foot. I can't do that and work here. She can't afford full time care. Going back with you be the best thing for her."

Mom was on her feet, taking a step backward. "We'll see what can be arranged," she mumbled. "We'll get in touch with you soon," she said to me. "Come on Ben, little Grant needs a clean diaper."

Dad stood up, looked at me and said, "If you need me, call."

"I will, Dad. Thank you for coming. It was time you and Mom knew what happened to Calvin."

"Come back soon," Iva Lee called to them as they went out the door.

I said nothing.

"I'd laugh if it wasn't so pitiful," Iva Lee told me.

So would I if I could. "Tragedies come in threes," I said. "What do you suppose will happen next?"

"Not one bad thing. I'm glad they left before Marie and Judith got here."

So was I.

"Mom's not really a bad person," I tried to justify the impression she had surely given Iva Lee.

"You don't say."

"She had a rough childhood. It has haunted her ever day of her life."

"What happened?"

"I don't know. She refuses to talk about it. I think Dad knows, and that's why he coddles her the way he does."

"Selfish," Iva Lee said.

"Actually, she was a good mother to Grant and to me. She went out of her way to protect me from every bad thing that could befall me. She was more lenient with Grant since he was a boy."

"She didn't protect you from Calvin West."

"She thought he was a preacher. A man of God. She and I both believed he would provide me with a respectful life."

"And to think we let her leave here still thinking he had."

"It's for the best." I know I sounded as disappointed as I was feeling.

"Are you sure you don't want to go back home with her?"

"Positive," I told her.

"Then get back to work."

Both Marie and Judith noticed my face.

"Who beat you up?" Marie asked with a laugh.

"I fell down the steps," I told her.

"That's what they all claim," Judith chimed in.

"I was there when she did it," Iva Lee said from where she was stirring several pots on the stove. "Tripped over her own feet."

"Hard to believe," Marie smart mouthed.

"Sure is. Her feet aren't nearly as big as yours and Judith's. Neither of you have ever tripped and fell, have you?"

Oddly enough, neither of them had anything else to say.

~~~~

Mr. Grason showed up early before closing time.

"Go on. Won't get a lick of work out of you if you stay here," Iva Lee said with a grin.

"I'll make it up to you," I assured her.

"I'll see to it."

"I was hoping you could leave early. I couldn't stand waiting any longer."

"The others went home not five minutes ago."

"They have nothing to do with us."

"They have a lot to do with gossip." Good grief. I sounded too much like my mother.

"Who cares about gossip."

"Your wife."

"For goodness sake, Ellie. Will you stop bringing up my so-called wife."

He had no idea how much I wished I could.

"My parents showed up today."

"At the restaurant?"

"Yeah. They came to find out why I ran Calvin off."

He looked surprised. "How did they know he was gone?"

"That's what I would like to know. Have you seen John Grimes lately?"

"No, I haven't."

"Me either. Looks to me like there has to be a grapevine connection somewhere."

"Did you set your parents straight?"

"Iva Lee did. Don't think I've ever met anyone as savvy as she is."

"She can read people like they're an open book."

"She told them Calvin died in an accident."

He looked stunned.

"She said both people died in the car accident he had caused, and that I had him cremated."

Mr. Grason's eyes twinkled. "I hope she stays on our side."

"She says four people can keep a secret when all four are involved."

The twinkle went out of his eyes. "What does she say when two people and a baby are involved. That's what I want to know."

"She says it's best if your wife doesn't find out anything about what's going on."

"Will you stop calling her my wife."

"I will when she stops being your wife. Anyway, Iva Lee says she's crazy not stupid."

"Iva Lee told the truth that time."

"What might she do if she finds out about us?"

"Wish I had an answer to that question."

"Have you thought about having her committed to an institution?"

"I tried everything I knew to do to get her help, but she convinced every doctor she's went to that I'm the one who's crazy instead of her. They believe I want to get rid of her, so I'll have control of her estate."

"Her estate?"

"Her father oozed power instead of sweat. He was one of the most dangerous and vindictive men I ever had the displeasure of meeting, and the apple didn't fall far from the tree. He once told me if I ever left his daughter, I'd have a fatal accident in less than an hour."

"He actually threatened to kill you?"

"Me along with everyone I cared about, including my dog."

I found that hard to believe. "Is he still alive?"

"No, but his daughter is."

"How did he die?"

"The backside of his evil heart blew out one night. He bled to death before the chambermaid found him. Not that he would have survived if he'd been in the hospital when it happened. The heart attack was too massive."

"And his daughter inherited his estate."

"Along with his worst qualities."

"Is she rich?"

"She hoards millions the way some children hoard candy."

"You're rich," I said

"Oh, no, my dear Ellie. I'm one of the poorest men who ever existed."

By the time he stopped the car in front of the shed, he'd talked himself out of spending intimate time with me. He'd also talked me out of wanting him to.

What if someone saw his car parked in front of the shed when it shouldn't be there?

What if a crazy woman found out the truth about my baby?

Four people now knew the man who called himself Calvin West wasn't my baby's father. I had no doubt Iva Lee had told Don the truth.

Only two of us had anything invested in keeping the secret.

Mr. Grason waited in the car while I went upstairs, turned on the light and looked about. He didn't leave until I went to the window and waved. Again, I watched his taillights fade away.

I was standing in the kitchen when a horrible sound scared the living daylight out of me. I whirled around and looked in the direction the sound was coming from. A black telephone was sitting on the kitchen counter. My first thought was to grab a skillet and beat the thing to pieces. My second thought was to pick it up and say hello.

I took the second option.

"Ellie," came Iva Lee's voice. "I take it you're home."

"Been here about five minutes. There's a phone on the counter." I remembered Mr. Grason telling me he was going to have one installed. Seems he did.

"Right. I thought it best you have one considering you might need to call me. My number is written on the pad near the phone."

I saw a small pad of paper along with a pen.

"I had Don meet the man from the telephone company and let him in the shed to hook it up. There used to be a telephone in there some years ago."

"You had it installed?"

"It was so busy today I forgot to tell you about it. I also forgot to tell you Don also hung your clean work uniform in the bathroom. I knew you would need it for work tomorrow."

"You washed it?"

"Don did. He likes keeping things clean and in order."

Obviously.

"Is Bret there?"

"No, he dropped me off and left."

"Good. Did you tell him?"

"Early this morning."

"You shook the tree. Now we'll see what falls out."

"What?"

"Never mind. See you in the morning." She hung up.

I didn't like the idea of someone having a key to the shed other than me. But then glass was easy to break. As Dad used to say, *locks are only to keep an honest person honest. A villain can always find a way in.*

I hurried to the bedroom, lifted the top of the bedspread and looked under the pillow. The pistol was exactly as I'd placed it.

~~~~

Mr. Grason was acting slightly different when he picked me up the next morning. "What's wrong?" I asked him.

"Nothing," he told me as he reached out and took my hand in his. "Things are finally right."

"What makes you say that?"

"After all these years, I can see blue sky peeping through the storm clouds."

"You sound like Iva Lee. I prefer straight talk." At least most of the time.

"I can see a chance of having the life I always wanted. In the meantime, I have to make sure you're taken care of. I don't want my action to put you and my baby in jeopardy."

I knew he was talking about what happened with the so called Calvin West. Did he think one of us would tell? Iva Lee was the only one who might claim innocence. I wasn't so sure about me. Both of us could be charged with conspiring to cover up a crime and so could Don.

"Iva Lee had a telephone installed in the shed," I told him.

"I called the telephone company. Whoever I spoke with said one had already been ordered. Iva Lee is always on the ball."

"She called as soon as I got home. It almost scared the life out of me."

"You didn't know it had been installed?"

"Iva Lee forgot to tell me. Don let the telephone company in. How many people have a key to the door?"

"Have no idea."

"How many people have lived in the shed?"

"Only Don that I know of, but I've only lived here for about fifteen years."

"Since you married Grace Anna."

"Right."

"The house and farm belong to her."

"I'm afraid so."

"If you divorce her, you'll lose it?"

"That's an understatement."

"Meaning?"

"Meaning I now have more than a house and land to lose. I have to be extremely discrete in how I treat you. I can never take a chance on her knowing what you mean to me."

"Never?" I questioned.

"Not for a while yet. I've got to see about setting up a few things now that I've got a reason to do what I should have done years ago."

I wanted to ask more questions, but I was afraid of the answers. Even worse, I didn't want to get my hopes up by things I knew could never happen. What I needed to do was look at things with a realistic eye to the future.

I'd lain in bed last night thinking about what Iva Lee had said to my parents. It was the hard, cold truth. What would happen when I had this baby? I didn't want to leave it at some kind of daycare so I could earn enough money to survive. Would Iva Lee be willing to let me stay in her shed forever while I brought my baby to work? Such as that would get old on her part in a hurry.

"I plan on supporting you and my baby even while I'm setting things up," Mr. Grason was saying.

"Supporting us?"

"Right. I'm going to give you as much money each week as I can get together without Grace Anna finding out. I don't want you to let anyone know, even Iva Lee. There's always a chance she'll unknowingly give something away that could get back to Grace Anna."

"You're afraid of her, aren't you?"

"No one can predict what a crazy woman might do. She has found out I pick you up in the mornings and drop you off each night. I think she's hired someone to watch me, and perhaps even you. Don't get upset if I ask Iva Lee take over giving you rides even when it will just about kill me. At least I'll be able to see you in class for a while longer."

"Are you serious?"

"I'm serious, all right. I've got to stay away from you as much as I can make myself. As for being afraid, we both need to be afraid of her. She's gotten worse since you showed up. The only person who has ever scared me worse was her father."

"What about her mother?"

"Disappeared when Grace Anna was a young girl."

"No one ever found her?"

"Neither hide nor hair or fingernail," he said.

"He killed her?" I squeaked out in disbelief.

"Who knows."

"You're scaring me."

"I don't want to scare you. I want you to keep both eyes open and trust no one."

"Not even you?"

"You can trust me, but I might not be there when you need me. That's why I want you to have more money than what Iva Lee pays you."

"For someone who doesn't want to scare me, you're doing a mighty fine job of it. So is Iva Lee. She gave me a pistol."

"Good. I'll see if one of the students who deals in black market trading can get a DeSanctis belly band holster for you."

"Sounds like what I've always wanted." I couldn't resist the sarcasm.

"Want and need are two different animals. We're here," he said as he stopped in front of the restaurant closer to the entrance than usual.

"Right. You're dropping me off now that you've got me paranoid of just about everyone without telling me why."

He patted my hand. "Better safe than sorry."

"Sure," I mumbled as I got out and went inside. Iva Lee had been wrong. I should never have told Mr. Grason about my baby.

~~~~

That evening, when Mr. Grason picked me up, he drove straight into traffic without saying anything. "Open the glove compartment," he finally said.

I did. There were two thin shoe soles along with an envelope.

"Open the envelope."

I did. There were two one-hundred-dollar bills. Not crisp and new but worn and wrinkled.

"Put a bill in each shoe, then put the shoe sole over them."

"That's a lot of money," I said in astonishment.

"Not nearly enough. Do as I say."

I put them in my shoes.

"Under your seat there's the belly holster I told you about. Get it out when I take you home tonight and put it between your books. Don't let anybody know you've got it. Start wearing the gun in it."

"Okay," I mumbled.

I had never met Grace Anna, but she *might* be right. Mr. Grason was the crazy one.

"I'll most likely shoot myself."

"You know how to put the safety on, don't you?"

"I came from a family of hunters."

"Is that a, yes?"

"It's a yes."

"Keep the safety on. It's easy to slip the safety off while you're pulling the pistol out."

He surprised me when he reached over and touched my growing stomach. "Our baby might help to camouflage the belt and pistol."

Those words made me think there was no *might* about it.

Chapter 22

Mr. Grason hardly glanced at me the entire class. If anyone noticed, they didn't show it. I found myself looking at each student trying to decide which one could be a squealer. Perhaps, even a plant to report back to Grace Anna on what Mr. Grason did in class.

Had John Grimes been a plant? No, I didn't think he was reliable enough for that. Besides, he was too mouthy and insulting. A plant would have to be silent enough not to draw attention to themselves.

Good grief. I was putting bats in my own belfry. I was making myself see things that weren't there. But then, I hadn't seen the man who called himself Calvin West setting me up either. I had been stupid enough to marry him. Stupid enough to think we were husband and wife.

I even miscarried his baby. He didn't seem to care in the least. Even refused to take me to the hospital. A sudden thought hit me. Did he have a reason for not taking me. Would a doctor have discovered something he didn't want anyone to known? I remembered the bitter taste of the coffee he'd given me to drink. I'd never tasted coffee like that before or after. Come to think back on it, he never made coffee again. Had I missed the step on the bus because I was dizzy from running, or was it because the door was closing too fast? Or was my miscarriage caused for a different reason?

I lagged behind as Mr. Grason unlocked the door from the driver's side. I got into the passenger seat before he had a chance to open the door for me. I wondered if the change in his actions would be a giveaway, or whoever might possibly be watching us think he wanted to be rid of me?

What was it Iva Lee had said about me shaking the tree and seeing what fell out? She knew more than she was telling me. I would ask her a few questions come morning.

The ringing of the telephone woke me up from a deep sleep. I rolled over and looked at the clock. It was two o'clock in the morning. I had been asleep for less than two hours. I jumped out of the bed in a panic, rushed into the kitchen and grabbed the receiver. I knew something awful had happened.

"Hello," I said. There was no answer. "Hello," I said again, and held the earpiece tighter against my ear. Still no answer. "Hello. Can you hear me?"

Nothing.

I decided to stay silent and listen. In a few minutes I heard the sound of breathing, a kind of low excited breathing.

Then came a woman's voice. Rough, authoritative.

"You stop playing with that phone. Put it down and go back to bed."

"No. You're not my boss," said a whining voice. The whine grew louder right before the receiver was slammed down.

I got that old warning chill crawling up my backbone. I had no doubt it was Grace Anna who called. How did she get my phone number.

I went back to bed. How did I get myself into this predicament? Did it come from one needy kiss after a job fair, or had my self-esteem gotten so low I needed someone to lift it up?

"Dummy," I whispered. I was right here because of a man who claimed to be Calvin West, along with my willingness to marry him. I might as well admit the rest since I was being honest with myself. I had no right to do what I did with Mr. Grason regardless of the reason.

Sunday came and Iva Lee did something no one had expected. She closed before time for church to let out. She surprised me again when she drove to a church and parked her car in an area where it would be concealed by trees and shrubbery. She hadn't said a word about why she was doing what she did.

"Why are you stopping here?" I asked as I looked at the impressive church with stained glass windows and towering steeple. Nothing like the little church I grew up attending. Money was involved here.

"I want you to see someone."

"Who?"

"Grace Anna. Her mother took her to this church ever since she was a little girl. When her mother disappeared, her father took her here every Sunday. She still attends. I parked here because I prefer neither she nor Bret know we are here."

"Why not?" I asked.

"He has some tough decisions to make. I don't want to influence what he does in any way."

"What kind of decisions?"

"One is what he's going to do about you and his unborn baby. Another is if he chooses to untangle himself from the travesty of his marriage to Grace Anna."

She seemed to think I had no say so in what Mr. Grason choose to do about me and my baby. Perhaps I didn't where he was concerned, but I certainly did where I was concerned.

"I see I chose the timing right. Church is letting out."

The congregation was filing out. Some hesitating to speak with others, but most marched straight to their cars. It crossed my mind some of them would be surprised to find Good Eats closed, but most of them would be dining in more elegant places.

"There she is." Iva Lee said.

She didn't have to point her out. Her arm was tucked possessive in the crook of Mr. Grason's arm. She was tall, slender and dressed in an expensive pale lavender suit.

"Her suit is made of the finest wool since its winter. She wears silk during the heat of summer. She has her clothes tailor made to fit perfectly. A hairdresser comes to her house on every Saturday to do her hair. Her caretaker does her makeup every morning before she goes downstairs. If one thing happens out of her customary order, she freaks out. You'll notice no one is talking to her or Bret. Definitely not getting too close to her."

I could understand why. The queen of England could not have shown as much arrogance as this woman was showing. Her back was ramrod straight. Her head held high with her chin arrogantly lifted. Mr. Grason marched beside her accordingly. In my opinion he looked miserable.

"Poor Mr. Grason," I said.

"He didn't choose to marry her. She saw him, wanted him, and her daddy saw that she got him. I brought you here so see her along with the iron clad control she has over him."

"I thought she was Crazy."

"Believe me she has more mental problems inside that head of hers than in a lunatic asylum. At the same time, she is borderline brilliant and as conniving and vicious as a pack of hyenas."

"Why can't he divorce her now that her father is dead?"

"That's a multi-million-dollar question. I've not been able to find out how her daddy managed to get Bret roped and hogtied and you know how snoopy I am."

"What can he do?"

"In my opinion, up until now, he thought living was easier if he stayed married to her than trying to free himself. I'm not saying he's not in love with you, I'm pointing out that he just might be the kind of man who would risk his life for a baby of his own."

For a moment I was stunned. And then I realized I would do the same thing. My baby was more important to me than anyone else in the world.

"Does she have a high pitched, whiney voice?"

"Definitely not whiney. More of a normal woman's voice. Why do you ask?"

"I've gotten two telephone calls late at night with only breathing, other than on the first night. That first call while I was silent and listening, I heard a woman with a gruff voice tell a woman to stop playing with the phone. A whiney, high-pitched voice said, 'You're not my boss'."

"Why didn't you tell me before now?"

"I wanted to pretend it didn't happen. It only happened those two days after the phone was installed.

"Nothing recently?" she asked.

"No, nothing recently."

"Good. I can assure you neither voice came from Grace Anna. For one thing, Grace Anna takes both sleeping pills and tranquilizers at night or she would never sleep. Once she's asleep, she doesn't wake up until morning when she has to take another pill before she can fully wake up."

"How do you know all that?"

She grinned. "I just told you I'm snoopy. Plus, I've known her since the day she was born. I also know what medications she takes and when she takes them. Domestic help have their own little grapevine. It's rumored when she was a child, her mother had gone against her husband and was trying to get a professional diagnosis of her mental condition. Before that could happen, her mother disappeared, and her father took over making all the decisions in his daughter life."

"Why Mr. Grason?"

"As I said before, she saw him, she wanted him, and her daddy made sure she got him."

~~~~

I got another late-night phone call with no answer when I said hello. I told Iva Lee about it the next morning.

"It's her," she said.

"Her who?"

"Calvin's wife. She's probably trying to find out where he ran away to this time. She's thinking he might be with you. She most likely took a chance on him answering the phone."

That made sense. Come to think of it, her whining voice did sound a lot like her voice that day in the store.

"Don't worry," Iva Lee continued. I'll get in touch with the sheriff and have him track her down. He can scare her into not calling you again."

Two days later the sheriff was waiting on me at the restaurant. He motioned for me to get into his black and white as soon as I got to the restaurant.

"I've got a restraining order for you to sign."

"A what?"

"A piece of paper stating Cloetta Gerry cannot contact you again. She won't even be permitted to get close you. If she does, she can be arrested."

"It was her calling me?"

"It was. She'd find all night bars to call you from. One of the bartenders got suspicious of her calls and reported to the local sheriff. As it was a long-distance call, he was able to confirm it was your number she called."

I signed the restraining order, went into the restaurant, and hoped that was it.

"I'd say she's needing money," was the first words Iva Lee said to me.

"The restraining order was your idea?"

"It was."

"Thank you."

"Most likely she reported him as missing, but the law won't be looking for him. He's skipped out on her before. I'd say she's wanting at least child support from him or you one."

"Me?"

"Doesn't matter where money comes from when you're wanting some."

"I was taken in by him worse than she was."

"Right, and you're the one with a job. I dare say she will lay low, at least for a while."

"What should I do?"

"Nothing. You signed the order. Help me get prepped."

Why was it my stupid mistakes were there to haunt me forever.

Chapter 23

The bone chilling cold of winter set in. Everything seemed to stagnate as it huddled down into its own cubby hole. The only thing changing with me was the size of my belly. I was finally showing enough that my uniform didn't hide it. Iva Lee gave me two large, black colored aprons to wear. She made a point in letting everyone who was interested know that my baby's father was Calvin West, the minister who died in a car accident.

Every week Mr. Grason kept his word. On Thursday's he had me get two hundred dollar bills out of the glove compartment and put it in my shoe.

One Sunday when Iva Lee drove me home, there was a small two-door dark blue Honda sitting in the driveway.

"Who could that be?" I questioned as I sat in the passenger seat. The things that Iva Lee told me along with Mr. Grason's warnings, had me cautious.

"Nobody," Iva Lee said. "It's yours."

"Mine?" I must have sounded as surprised as I felt.

"I had Don get it for you."

"You did?" I was totally taken by surprise.

"I did. He'll come by after while and ride around with you as you drive. He'll take you Tuesday to get your driver's license before you go to class."

"I don't have enough money to pay for it," I told her.

"From what I can tell, you spend almost no money on necessities. You can use one week's money each month to make a car payment. There won't be a need to take it out of your bank account."

"One week's salary is enough to pay for a car?" I was skeptical about that.

"Once a week's salary every month. This is a used car. It didn't cost much, but it should be reliable enough. I wouldn't advise cross country trips, but short distances should be fine."

"It will save you and Mr. Grason from having to haul me about."

"It's time you became more independent."

That was true, but it also meant I wouldn't be riding with Mr. Grayson five days a week. I had no doubt that was why Iva Lee had Don get me that car."

"Who do I pay for it?"

"Don. He bought it."

I wasn't surprised.

Don came by later that evening to ride with me while I drove up and down the driveway. He had me backup and parallel park.

"I'm pleased with myself," he told me. "I taught you well. I might even give you credit for your speed of learning."

"Am I supposed to thank you for that comment, as well as for the car?"

"Nope. Thank Iva Lee for the car, but keep in mind you're paying for it. She doesn't give her money away. When she gets something into that hard head of hers, it can't be gotten out."

"I sure was lucky to find a job with her."

"She's always been willing to help the underdog when they are willing to help themselves. As I mentioned before, she sees something of her younger self in you. Now that you're expecting, she's become even more protective. She would have given up all her accomplishments to have a baby of her own."

"Why didn't she adopt?"

"It seems adoption agencies discriminates against a woman living in sin. Plus, considering who she was married to back then was a drawback. After her husband's murder red flags started to fly. When she bought the restaurant, she worked twenty-four seven, and didn't have time for a baby even if the agency had approved her."

"You never had children?"

"My wife and six-month-old son were killed in a car wreck. Can't say I ever got over it. I'll pick you up tomorrow around three o'clock to get your driver's license."

He had me drop him off at their house. I'd never seen the place before. It was not the kind of house I expected to see. Iva Lee had spent a considerable amount of her hard-earned money on this place. It was a large farmhouse style home framed in by trees, shrubbery, and gardens I had never imagined. Even during the middle of winter, the grounds and garden were impressive.

"Maintenance of this place is my responsibility. In return for my work, I get to farm all five-hundred acres of her land and keep the proceeds. Our arrangement works well for both of us."

"It's beautiful," I said.

"It's her dream come true. The only thing lacking is the patter of little feet," he said as he opened the passenger door. "Drive carefully on you way back home. It wouldn't pay to have an accident when you've not got your driver's license. Ride with Bret in the morning and I'll see you at three o'clock tomorrow."

I drove back to the shack thinking about the beautiful place Iva Lee lived. How could she possible enjoy her home when she seldom saw it in the light of day. At least she was now taking Sunday afternoons off. And then it hit me. The only thing lacking to make Iva Lee's dream come true was the patter of little feet.

I could provide that part of her dream.

Was that one of the reasons she was willing to help me? Was I to provide her the baby she never had? Would the patter of my big feet be allowed? Iva Lee had already proved she could get a death certificate for someone who wasn't dead.

Don had proved he was willing to go against the Law to secretly bury a body. I was a nobody. I was easily disposed of. My parents could be told that I died and was cremated if they asked about me.

Those thoughts wouldn't leave my mind. I tried telling myself I was nothing other than paranoid. My hormones were causing me to have stupid imaginations. Iva Lee had been nothing but kind to me. How dare I have such thoughts about her.

However, my mind continued having such thoughts until I finally dropped off to an exhausted sleep. My dreams were filled with worst possibilities.

I woke up with Mr. Grason beating on my door and calling out my name.

I rushed to the door wearing only the oversize shirt I always slept in. The relief on his face was evident when he saw me.

"Thank goodness you're alright. Whose car is that?" he asked, as he pushed past me to enter the room and looked about.

"Mine," I told him. "Iva Lee had Don get it for me. I'm paying him back monthly."

"I don't believe it," he said. "She just took away my only chance of being with you."

"How did Grace Anna arrange that?" I wanted to know.

"She didn't arrange it, Iva Lee did. No one tells Iva Lee what to do.

He was right about that. "She said I should have my own transportation in case I needed it."

"That part is true, at least."

"You don't trust her motive?" I asked him.

"You and my attorney are the only two people I trust, and I don't entirely trust him. Back a person in a corner and it's surprising what they'll be willing to do to get out of it." He rubbed his fingers through his hair. "I've got to do some thinking about our situation, Ellie. I've got a terrible feeling that's scaring me."

I didn't tell him about my own fears. "I'm to ride in with you today. Don will take me this afternoon to get my driver's license."

"At least that's for the best. Make sure you don't drive if the roads get slick. I'll have an excuse to drive you around then."

He seemed to relax some.

"I'm going to wait in the car for you to get dressed."

He pulled me against him and kissed me like a starved man finally getting food. His hands were all over me. I was clinging to him when he finally pulled himself away.

"We can't. Not yet. There *will* come a time, Ellie. I promise you that."

There was something in his tone that made me wonder if he actually believed what he'd said.

~~~~

I was a nervous wreck by the time Don drove me to the driver's license place. He was driving his Black Beauty which puzzled me.

"You're more familiar with driving this piece of junk than you are your Honda," he told me when I asked why he was in this rust bucket.

"I didn't practice with this car yesterday."

"I already knew how you handle this car. I wanted to see how you'd handle the Honda. You're a natural."

It almost made sense, so I said no more.

After I passed the written test, Don waited in the office while a man got in the car with me.

"Hoped you get paid enough for having such a dangerous job," I told him.

"Not nearly enough," he said without the grin I had expected. "A man does what he has to do."

I had no trouble getting my license. Don had me drive back to the restaurant.

"Bret can drive you home tonight if he shows up. If not, Iva Lee will drive you home. After tonight, you'll have your own ride. Make the best of your navigational freedom," he said with a grin as he patted my arm.

My navigational freedom. I could come and go as I pleased. I didn't have to depend on anyone. It was something I'd never had before. There were my parents, then Calvin, then Mr. Grason, and Iva Lee.

Freedom. I almost cried.

That night Mr. Grason gave me the usual two hundred dollars although it wasn't a Tuesday class night.

"Just in case we don't get a chance to be alone without watching eyes," he said. "Don't know why, but I think I'd better rush getting away from Grace Anna. I'd leave out with you before morning came if I thought we had half a chance of Grace Anna not tracking us down."

"You're really afraid of her?"

"You bet I am."

"You believe she would hurt you?"

"Hurt me, you'd better believe it. She knows the best way to hurt me would be by hurting someone I love. Her father used that tactic all his life and so does his daughter."

"You're saying. . ."

"You and our baby. That's where she would aim her revenge."

I gasped.

"I didn't mean to scare you. Just warn you. She has money to see that a person disappears. That's why I have to be careful and bide my time."

He might not have meant to scare me, but he did. I got even more scared after he dropped me off and left. I didn't know what to do or which way to turn. I didn't dare say anything about what Mr. Grason told me to Iva Lee. Fear about her wanting a baby was still simmering inside me.

Trust no one, Mr. Grason had warned. I was taking his advice.

I tried my best to think of what I should do. I fell into a restless sleep without coming up with anything.

Sometime near morning I tried to come awake but couldn't get out of my sleep-fog. Grant's ghost came and sat down on the bed beside me.

"I'm here, Ellie. I've always tried to protect you, but I've not been able to do much considering what happened to me."

"I'm dreaming," I said.

"Not exactly. I'm here because I must do a better job of protecting you and the baby this time. At least your so-called husband can't get rid of this one. You're going to leave this place. It's no longer safe. You've already realized that on your own, but you can't linger. It's now or never."

"How? I have no place to go unless it's back home."

"That's possible, if that's what you want, but they will know where you are."

"They?" I questioned.

"The baby's dad and his wife. She can't have a baby of her own. She wants an heir. A baby belonging to her husband will suffice."

"Iva Lee will protect me and the baby," I tried to argue.

"She can't even if she wanted to. He'll have a claim on his baby. He has enough money to take the baby away from you if, and I stress if, you survive its birth. An evil woman with an unlimited amount of money is a dangerous thing."

I wanted to argue with him, but I knew he was right. "What can I do."

"I'll guide you step by step, but it's up to you to carry it through. I can't physically help you."

When I did come fully awake, it was time to get up and go to work. I remembered every word my brother had told me. He was right. I had no choice other than take his advice.

Iva Lee gave me a few minutes off on payday to deposit my check. The bank was only a five-minute walk from the

restaurant. I always made the trip on Fridays during the three
o'clock shift change. I had gone over what Grant had told me
every minute of every day until Friday came. I had his plan
fixed in my mind so firmly I could make it happen with my
eyes closed – as long as nothing went wrong. If it did, I would
have to take the hit on the chin and accomplish my escape
regardless.

It was difficult to act normal when I knew what was about
to happen, but I thought I was doing a good job of it. I don't
know if it just happened or if my brother's spirit might be
with me for real. A rush hit the restaurant ten minutes before
three o'clock. A bus arrived with fourteen hungry young men.

"Can you help with them and go to bank right before it
closes?" Iva Lee asked me.

"No problem," I told her.

I almost laughed out loud with the relief I felt. I had
worried about drawing all the money out of my account other
than what I owed on the car, which was half of what I had
after working all these months. I was glad for the car. Without
it, leaving would be more difficult. I feared the bank just
might call Iva Lee about my withdrawal. I was sure everyone
knew her. If I made the withdrawal at closing time, perhaps
the employees would be in too big a hurry to get home to stay
long enough to make a personal phone call.

I was hoping Grant's spirit was still protecting me as I left
the warmth of the restaurant and went out in the cold. Winter
had brought cold and light snow flurries but no ice. I'd never
driven on ice, or much of anywhere else.

I made the deposit and told the teller exactly how much I
wanted to withdraw. She gave me a look I didn't like.

"Why are you withdrawing that amount of money?"

I thought about telling her it was none of her business,
instead I said, "I'm buying a car."

"Really. Do you know anything about cars? I hope you
don't get taken since you're paying cash."

"Not much. Don picked it out for me."

Seemed like everybody in this area knew everything about everybody.

"What model is it?"

How I would like to tell her to mind her own business.

"It's a used blue Honda."

I was relieved when two customers came up behind me in their last-minute rush to do their banking. Reluctantly the teller put the money in an envelope and handed it to me. She didn't realize it, but she'd just given me an excuse for withdrawing the money if Iva Lee caught me.

I happened to see some brochure in the lobby of the bank advertising sunny vacations down in Florida. Perfect, I thought and grabbed one. I went out the door and around the corner where she couldn't see me and quickly stuffed the envelope through the buttons of my shirt into my bra and the brochure in the pocket of my apron. All I had to do now was act normal until closing time.

I must have succeeded. Iva Lee didn't comment about anything other than what we normally talked about. Mainly work.

"See you in the morning," Iva Lee told me as she locked the door and we both got in our cars. I drove behind her until we reached the driveway to the shed. She blinked her lights as she always did as a way of saying goodbye. I blinked mine and breathed a sigh of relief. Grant's plan had worked up to this point. The only thing different was a scraped spot in the road where a chug hole had been. Don had filled the hole.

I stopped the car and got out. *Easy. Act normal,* Grant seemed to be whispering to me. *Don't rush. Don't act in a hurry.*

I got out and made my slow time up the steps, unlocked the door and went inside. I turned on the light and did as usually and checked the bedroom and the bathroom. No one was there. I took my few clothes out of the tiny closet and my underwear out of the drawer and laid then on the bed. I changed from my uniform and put on jeans and the darkest

colored shirt I owned. *Put all your things in a trash bag,*
Grant said. *Put it in the trunk of your car as though it's trash
then go back inside and write Iva Lee a check for the
remainder you owe for your car.* That way they couldn't
claim I tried to steal the car.

I gathered everything I owned, which was only a
hairbrush, comb, soap, shampoo, and toothpaste and put them
in the bag with my clothes. I put my pair of shoes in the bag
and wore boots I'd bought at the secondhand store. I carried
the trash bag out to the car and put it in the trunk, locked the
car and back went inside.

I nearly jumped out of my skin when the phone rang. I
almost didn't answer it, but thought it was best if I did. I
certainly didn't want to hear the breathing again.

"Just checking to make sure you got home okay," Iva Lee
said. "Don filled in that chug hole up and it's still soft. Didn't
want you to get stuck or go in a ditch trying to avoid the spot."

"I noticed it. I drove around it as usual."

"Good. Just checking. Sleep well. See you in the
morning."

"I will. Thanks for calling," I hung up with relief. It
wasn't unusual for Iva Lee to call after I got to the shed. She
did it often. Hopefully she didn't suspect a thing.

I turned off the living room lights and went into the
bathroom an turned on the shower, but I didn't get in. Grant
had told me to do everything I normally did, like take a
shower when I got home. I didn't want wet hair. I only
washed my face and hands before I turned off the shower and
the light. I went into the bedroom and turned off the light the
same I would do if I had gone to bed. I gathered all the hidden
money I'd gotten from Mr. Grason and stuffed it inside a little
pouch I'd fastened onto the belly holster. He was right. My
growing belly hid the pistol I carried along with the extra clip
and bullets. I didn't think I needed the pistol, but I took his
advice anyway. I sat on the bed for twenty minutes watching
the hand of the clock creep away each minute. If anyone was

watching, they would leave thinking I had turned in for the night. At least, that was what I hoped.

"Please, Lord," I whispered to myself. "Let everything go as it should."

Now, get in the car and leave. Grant was telling me.

I put the check on the nightstand with a notation that said, *Thank you for everything* on the bottom of the check. I hoped that would be enough to let them know that leaving was my choice.

The night was clear with a new moon high in the sky giving faint light as I went down the steps to the car. The air was freezing cold without a sign of snow or ice. I unlocked the car door and got in. I turned the key and the engine started up. I turned around without turning on the headlights and eased down the driveway with them off. Thankful that the moon was giving me enough light to see the road. I was glad Iva Lee had reminded me about the soft dirt and gravel Don had filled the chug hole with. I certainly didn't need to get stuck.

Once I reached the highway, I still dared to drive a mile without the headlights on. It was easier to see the highway than the driveway. I was relieved when I finally turned them on. I did my best to remember every instruction Grant gave me when he sat on the side of my bed.

Don't go south, Grant had told me. *Go north, but not in the direction of home.* He didn't have to tell me that. Again, I knew that would be the first place Iva Lee and Mr. Grason would look for me. I hoped the brochure I left in my apron pocket would throw them off, a least long enough for me to find a safe place to hide.

West Virginia, Grant had told me. "Go into the high mountains and find a place where nobody knows you, or cares who you are. I thought that was a good advice, but the lure of warmer temperatures was still drawing me. I didn't want to be cold, but it was better than being afraid.

I drove all through the night on the highway I thought Grant had told me to go. I did wonder how Grant knew those road numbers when he had never traveled them. The sky was turning a light gray when my gas was getting low. I had left with a full tank of gas. I was thankful the little Honda wasn't a gas guzzler. I stopped at the first gas station that was open. The place was busy, but I had no choice other than to stop. I was running on little more than fumes. The car in front of me paid the attendant for her gas and drove on. The attendant filled up my tank. I didn't have the right amount of cash.

"You'll have to go inside to pay. I don't have change. I can only take the exact amount," he told me.

I didn't want to go inside. The more people who saw me, the more likely I would be found. I needed to disappear without a trace. I considered giving him the money and telling him to keep the change, but I dared not waste a single dime. I had no idea when I'd be able to earn more money. Besides, I was hungry. I could buy a few groceries to sustain me for a while.

I was relieved when no one questioned me or even looked at my face. The checkout lady was still sleepy and only doing her job with blurry eyes behind a pair of thick glasses. I happened to see a map of West Virginia and added it to what I was getting in case Grant's instructions stopped coming in clear. Or I took the wrong road somewhere. Both were likely to happen any moment. I had never traveled before. The north, south, east and west directions were still confusing to me, as were road numbers. I'd never seen a map, much less read directions on one.

Sometime during the evening hours, my adrenalin started to fade. My eyes grew heavy, and I became so sleepy it wasn't safe to continue. I pulled off the highway into the parking lot of a small shopping center and parked as far back as possible. I leaned my head against the headrest and fell right to sleep.

I woke up two hours later, drank some of the chocolate milk I had bought and ate a pack of crackers. I drove on, only stopping once again to fill up with gas and use the restroom.

The sun had set some time ago, and twilight was diming the narrow, crooked road I was traveling on. I hadn't seen another car in a while. I didn't know where the road would end up, but I had a feeling it was the road I should be on.

I almost jumped out of my skin when bright lights reflected in my rearview mirror a moment before a car passed me going at breakneck speed. Much to my horror, the car didn't make the sharp curve and slammed into a rocky embankment beside the road. I slammed on my brakes and came to a stop opposite the wreck. I pulled my car to the edge of the narrow road a little ways from the wreck and turned my car off. I left my headlights on to be able to see better, along with making it easier for other vehicles to see my car, and got out. I ran to the accident fearing what I would find.

It was worse than I feared. Hitting the rock had crumbled the car in on itself. The car's engine was in the driver's seat along with the woman. My breath caught at what I saw. There was blood spraying from her neck wound. I wanted to help her. Wanted to get her out of the car, but the crumpled metal along with the engine had her trapped. I jerked on the door, but the metal was twisted so badly opening the door was impossible. I reached through the broken window, grabbed hold of her arm where the blood hadn't reached and yanked in hopes I might be able to pull her out the window. I only moved her upper body slightly. From her chest down, she was entwined in twisted car parts.

She opened her mouth as though she was going to speak, nothing but a stream of foamy blood ran down her chin and mixed with the blood coming from her neck.

The smell reminded me of Grant's horrible accident.

A strange feeling came over me. It was almost like I was watching what was happening from a great distance.

The woman was dead and there wasn't a thing I could do to save her any more than I could have saved my brother.

My headlights allowed me to see inside the car. The accident had shattered every window in the car, and smoke was starting to rise from underneath the crumpled hood of the car. The smell of gas was strong. I saw her purse on the back seat. I don't know why I reached in the broken window and got her purse, but I felt it was something I should do.

I took out her billfold wanting to know who she was and got out her driver's license. Her name was Mary Tracy, and it stated she was single. She was near my age.

Mary Tracy's life had just ended.

Flames were starting to rise from the car's engine.

I had no idea why I did what I did next. I don't think Grant told me to do it, but something did. I stuck her driver's license in my pocket, pulled out mine, and put my driver's license in her billfold. She had a considerable amount of cash. I took the money out of her billfold, but I couldn't make myself take her money. But then, what would a dead woman need with money?

Flames shot into the air. I jumped back from the sudden surge of heat, dropping her purse in the edge of the road next to her car. I ran to the open door of my car as another car drove up behind me.

"Get the hell outta the road," the man yelled at me. "She's gonna blow any second."

I got in my car. I couldn't back up because the other car was behind me. I drove forward past the burning car as the man drove backward fast to get out of range of the coming explosion. I had driven around a curve when the explosion sounded. I looked down and found I had dropped her money in my lap when I jumped in the car seat.

Keep going, I heard Grant say. *There's nothing you can do now. If you stop, they'll find you.*"

He was right. If I stayed there, the police would want me to testify to what happened. I would no longer be able to keep my whereabouts a secret. There was a man there to do what was necessary.

I drove as fast as I dared in order to put as much distance between me and the car accident. I turned off the road and drove on a different highway to make sure my car wasn't spotted on the same road as the accident. I drove into the night until I got low on gas. I found a gas station, filled up with gas and continued on.

By the time daylight came I realized my body had gone numb, and I could no longer think straight. My brain was nearing a state of comatose. I had to get some sleep. I saw a shopping center in what appeared to be a farming town and pulled into a far corner of the parking lot. I let the seat go back as far as it would, lay my head on the headrest and went to sleep.

I woke up five hours later with a stiff neck and aching back along with the need to use the restroom. I got out, stretched and went inside the shopping center.

I found a restroom, used it and washed my hands and face. I looked in the mirror and raked out my hair with my fingers. I looked as bad as I felt. I had no idea how far I had traveled or where I was at.

On my way back to my car I saw a newspaper vending machine against the side of the building. On the front page was a picture of an accident. Flames were shooting skyward. Police, firetrucks, and ambulance were on the scene. I put money in the machine and took out the paper. I had no doubt it was the accident I had witnessed. FATAL ACCIDENT was the headline.

I opened the newspaper the moment I got in the car. It told of the horrible accident that had happened. It stated that the car and the person inside, assumed to be a woman, were charred beyond any recognition. Evidently the car had a full tank of gas which led to an explosion along with a fire so hot it was impossible to put it out.

The only thing to identify the assumed driver of the car was a driver's license burned, but still readable.

The newspaper stated it appeared her purse was on fire when the explosion happened. It blew her purse down the road from the burning car. One man, who arrived on the scene minutes after the accident, stated he found the purse blown away from the burning vehicle to within feet of his car. He stomped out the fire in the purse and retrieved it. He said he found a few bills of money blowing along the side of the road along with her slightly melted driver's license.

The identity of the woman would not be revealed until the next of kin were notified.

I stuck my hand in my pocket. I still had Mary Tracy's driver's license along with the money I had gathered up in the dark. I took the money out and counted it. There was fifteen one-hundred-dollar bills. I now had more money on me than I had ever hoped to accumulate.

"What am I to do now," I whispered out loud, hoping Grant's spirit would come to me. My driver's license would let everyone interested know I hadn't headed south.

I checked the odometer to discover I had traveled almost five hundred miles. Not a far distance considering how long I had been driving, but I had gone slow not wanting an accident or a speeding ticket. It wasn't as though I was accustomed to driving long distances.

My next question was would the newspaper reach Iva Lee and Mr. Grason? My address was at Iva Lee's shed. The law would surely let my parents know what happened. I knew they would be devastated.

Would I have a death certificate the same as Calvin West did? Was I also destined to have an alias? Could I pull it off for the sake of my baby?

What choice did I have?

"None," I answered.

Keep going, Grant seemed to tell me. *West Virginia is too close to here. Head into the hills of Kentucky. A herd of*

Elephants can hide for nearly forever if you find the right place in the hills and backwoods.

I didn't know where I was or which road to take to get to West Virginia or Kentucky. I had dozens of questions rushing through my mind. I didn't have an answer to a one, so I kept on going.

Chapter 24

I drove the rest of the day. Darkness was setting in. I was hungry, exhausted, and smelled as dirty as I felt. I was ready to burst into a flood of tears by the time I saw a motel built against the side of a tall, rock bank. Actually, everything I had seen was built against rock banks. The road had taken up just about all of the land in the narrow valley. Every building I saw appeared shabby and in need of maintenance. The buildings I'd passed reminded me of the neighborhood where the rusty trailer was located.

I pulled into the motel, went inside and asked for a room.

"You sure do look beat, honey," the old woman said. "You been traveling long."

"Long enough for one day," I told her. "How much for one night?"

Her mind went to money, and she seemed to forget further questions. I reached into the opposite pocket from where I kept Mary's money and gave her the cash. She handed me a small amount of change along with a key.

"Thank you," I said and got back in the car and drove a few doors over to the room that was mine for the night.

I didn't carry the trash bag in. I got out clean pants with elastic waist and shirt along with the bathroom things and the map. I had noticed it showed parts of adjoining states. Maybe if I studied the map long enough some place would draw me to it.

I locked my car door and unlocked the motel room door and clicked on the light before I closed the door. The room was small, but clean enough. I checked the bathroom before

I closed and locked the door. Mr. Grason's caution had rubbed off on me.

The water was only lukewarm but that was okay. I washed and scrubbed until I felt clean again, and then I hit the bed without studying the map as I had intended.

I didn't open my eyes again until the sky was turning gray. I could have slept until the sun was high in the sky, but I knew better.

It was time to hit the road. I didn't know where I was going, but I wanted to get there fast. Plus, I wanted to be gone before the old woman or anyone else woke up. I took my dirty clothes and my bathroom supplies and put them in the back seat. I was in such a rush to get away I couldn't wait long enough to open the trunk.

It was bitter cold. Much colder than it had ever been at the shed. At least the road was empty of traffic as dawn broke into daylight. It felt like I was the only person left in the world. I turned the heater on high to warm the car up and noticed there were more buttons.

For the first time it dawned on me that the car had a radio. I didn't know if it worked or not. I turned the knob, and radio came to life. The five o'clock morning weather and news was on.

"For all you out there in radio land, you best gather up your firewood and your dogs along with all the blankets and quilts you can find. It's going to get colder as the day moves along. We're going to have a freezing cold three dog night. A winter storm will set in with a vengeance before this time in the morning."

I shuttered at the thought of it getting colder than it already was. "Okay, Grant. Coming here was your idea. You best be telling me where to go."

I didn't get an answer.

There was one thing I did notice, besides the ominous looking sky and narrow roads. Houses were becoming far and

few between. The ones I did see spoke of a better time and
needed repairs.

I kept traveling, stopping at any gas station I saw. I feared
running out of gas and being stranded in the middle of
nowhere.

After hours of driving, I was exhausted. My back hurt,
and my arms and legs ached from the same kind of constant
use. The high mountains became higher, and the road became
narrower. And yet I continued on searching for some place I
hadn't found.

After more miserable hours of driving a slight drizzle of
rain started misting my windshield. I needed to find a motel
soon. Thankfully, I came to a wide place in what seemed the
middle of nowhere. There was a general store next to a gas
station and a restaurant of sorts.

I was glad to fill up the tank with gas. It wasn't on empty,
but I feared I might never see another gas station unless I
headed back in the direction I had come from, which I
planned on doing. It appeared I'd come to a dead end in this
part of the world. The paved road had ended and there was
only a gravel road leading away from the place.

"You lost, Missy," the old guy who filled up my tank
asked. What few teeth he had were worn down to nubs and
stained brown with tobacco juice. He wasn't the homeliest
man I'd ever seen, but he came close.

"Mostly hungry," I said trying to evade answering his
question.

"You're at the right place then. Go on over there and fill
your belly up on some good home cooking. My wife's the
best cook far and wide if I do say so myself. Now, where did
you say you were heading?"

"Actually, I've been looking for a nice place in the
mountains where I might settle down and raise a family."

He gave me a strange look. "Your man not with you?" he
asked as he pretended he was not looking at my belly.

"No, he isn't. He was killed in a car accident a few weeks before we knew a baby was on the way. I couldn't stand being in the same place I had always been with him. So, I packed up my things and headed out. Haven't found any place that called to me, so I've just kept searching."

"Odd you've ended up in this neck of the woods. Strangers don't often come here. It's mostly the folks who live here abouts. Best get on over there and get some food afore she closes down. There's a storm brewing."

"I heard that on the radio earlier."

After I ate, I would head back the way I had come. I had obviously taken a wrong road.

"Ask me, the radio fellow's wrong. He claimed it would come tonight, but my bones say it will come sooner," the old man told me.

I drove the car in front of the restaurant and parked. I got out and locked the car door. I wasn't sure what kind of place this was or what kind of people inhabited it. I went inside to the warmth of the room filled with the smell of food. It made me think of a miniature Good Eats.

There was a lone, gray-haired man eating at one table and an elderly man and woman eating at another table. They eyed me over when I came in but made no attempt to acknowledge me.

"Find you any seat you please, honey," called a woman from somewhere in the kitchen. "I'll be right out as soon as I find what I did with my oven mitt."

"You lose that thing again, Betsy? You'd lose your own head if it wasn't attached."

The way the woman said that made me think of Marie. I didn't miss her one bit. I sat down facing the kitchen.

A plump woman as round as watermelon came out holding a pot of hot coffee with her hand in an oven mitt. She walked over to the man and woman and filled their cups before she filled the lone man's cup.

"Thanks, Betsy," the man said. Can't beat your coffee or your food."

"Thanks," she said as she sat the hot coffee pot down on a plate at a vacant table and strode over to me.

"What can I get for you, honey?" she asked as she eyed me up and down. I could tell she wanted to ask me questions, but she didn't.

"Uh," I stuttered a little. She hadn't given me a menu or had anything written on a board.

"You want a plate of food, or just coffee and a sweet roll?"

"A plate of food. Do you have milk?"

She looked at my stomach. "Good choice," she said, and went into the kitchen and brought my food back out in less than five minutes

By the time I was nearly finished eating, the man from the service station came in. He went straight to the kitchen. I could hear words being exchanged every now and again, but not what was being said.

The gray-haired man drank his coffee, got up, went to the counter and placed his money on the counter and left.

The man and woman followed suit. "We're leaving now Betsy. We best be gettin' on home. It's startin' to put it down out there."

I turned to look out the window. Snowflakes the size of quarters were filling the air. I jumped up and rushed to the counter where the people had left money.

"How much do I owe you?" I called out. "I've got to leave now. I've never driven in snow before."

Both the woman and man from the service station came out of the kitchen. The woman picked up the money left by the others and told me how much I owed.

"Honey, where are you heading?" the woman asked.

"To the nearest motel."

"Land's sake. That's a good forty miles away. Don't know if you'll make it considering the way it's snowing out there. These back roads get mighty dangerous when it snows. Not only that, but Hoke said a skiff of ice has already frozen on the roads."

"Looks like I'll have to be on my way in a hurry," I said. "It's too cold to sleep in my car like I've been doing," I said what I was thinking. The woman's eyebrows lifted as she glanced at her husband.

"Honey, most likely you'll get stuck or slide off this road and tumble into a ravine before you get off this mountain. Might not find you until the spring thaw. Like I done said, this here road gets mighty tricky when it's slick."

"Then I best leave right away before it gets any worse." I headed for the door.

"Now, hold on a minute," the man said. "Me and Betsy can't let you head out in this. You'll get your killin' for certain. Then it'll be on our minds forever."

"I . . ." I began, but the woman interrupted me.

"You don't want to take a chance on wreckin' and killin' that baby you're carryin', now do you?"

"No, of course not. I'll drive really slow. I've got fairly new tires."

"You got chains?" the man asked. "Course chains don't do no good on ice."

"Chains?" I questioned before I realized what he was referring to. I'd seen my dad put chains on his truck once or twice during deep snows.

The two exchanged another glance and the man kind of nodded his head at her.

"We were just discussin' the storm that's set down on us," the woman said. "We can't let a woman in you condition go out in this kind of weather. It wouldn't be Christian of us. My Mommy died back during the summer, and we've not put nobody in her little place. We decided it would be best to let you stay there for the night and see how the roads are in the morning."

The man held up his hands when I started to object. "We'd let you stay with us, but we've only got one bed. Maw's place is a might of a distance up the holler from here, but the place is solid and safe. I'll drive my truck and you can follow me in your car before the roads gets worse. I'll get you a fire going in the stove and set a bucket of coal inside, so you won't have to tote anything in during the night."

"I done fixed you up a sack of food to take up there with you. Mommy still has some canned food in the root cellar but it's not handy to get in there this time of year."

I wanted to refuse. Wanted to scream. Wished I'd never come this way in the first place. I shouldn't have listened to what I thought was Grant's spirit directing me. As Dad used to say, it appeared I'd jumped out of the frying pan into the fire.

"We best get going, Missy. It's gonna get deep out there afore long 'less I miss my prediction."

I looked out again and was stunned into silence as well as further resistance. I wasn't even sure I would be able to drive the car around the corner in the snow that had already fallen outside. It appeared I didn't have a lot of choice in taking them up on their offer. I couldn't risk driving down those twisting roads, and I couldn't sleep in the car now that the temperature had dropped.

I followed the man outside and got in my car as he disappeared behind the gas station building. In a couple of minutes, he came around the building driving an ancient jeep truck. He motioned for me to *come on* as he drove behind the restaurant building.

Now would be a good time for Grant's spirit to speak up, but he didn't. It was my decision to tackle a road that was getting deadlier by the minute or trust the old man and woman to do right by me.

My car slid a little as I backed out of the parking space. It was obvious there was ice underneath the snow. I put the car in low gear and tried to keep my tires in the tracks his jeep was making. Fine time to find myself in this predicament.

I thought I had driven up a mountain before, but this climb upward was something else. I was really testing the little Honda's ability on what couldn't be called a road. It was a goat path twisting its way around trees and large rocks. Snow was sticking on everything as I followed the jeep through a world rapidly turning white.

Finally, we were driving on what appeared to be a ridge straight toward a small, crudely built log cabin nestled in a cropping of trees. The man circled the cabin and I followed. He stopped in what appeared to be the back of the cabin. He got out of the jeep and stomped a path through the snow to a porch at the back door. When he had the door open, he motioned for me to get out and come inside. I followed in his tracks trying not to get much snow in my shoes. My feet were already freezing, along with the rest of me. There was a considerable amount more snow on this ridge than there was down below.

Much to my surprise he switched on a light in the rustic log cabin. There was a single lightbulb in the center of the room. The place didn't look anything like the Iva Lee's shed did. The cabin was bigger than I thought with two large picture windows in front of the cabin and a door to the outside between them.

"Maw Wiseman was determined to have a cabin on top of this hill. She wanted to look out the windows and see the valley below. Some of the neighbors helped Pa and us build it for her about ten years before he died."

He pointed to the side of the room. There was a fireplace built into a wall of solid fieldstone. "Maw Wiseman insisted on putting that in, but we had to close the fireplace off to keep the cold air from blowing down the chimney. Fireplaces don't heat worth a lick. We hooked up a coal stove to it. Draws mighty fine. You can check out the bedroom and bathroom. Pa didn't want a bathroom put in. He said a body ought not to eat and crap in the same place. After Pa died, we went ahead and added on a bathroom, along with running water and electricity. Maw Wiseman pert near had a fit, squalled like a drowned cat, but she got used to easy living in time. Didn't use the bathroom hardly a-tall, though. We also had electricity put in. She had a fit about that too. Claimed the bright light hurt her eyes."

I walked over to the windows and looked out. I could see all the way down into the valley. I could make out the general store, gas station and restaurant. Smoke was rising straight up from the gas station and restaurant chimneys, but there was nothing coming out of the general store's chimney.

"What a view," I said. "Where do you and Betsy live?"

"We live up above the restaurant. It was Betsy's idea to have a business and house together. Saves money. Between the gas station and the restaurant, we manage to get by. You've probably noticed the general store was closed down. Cost too much to haul supplies up this mountain."

His answer made me think of Iva Lee's little apartment above Good Eats. In a way I missed being there, and in another way I didn't. If I was honest with myself, I had never been happy working there. I was always exhausted, ill at ease, and disgusted with Marie and Judith's vulgar talk. The second shift waitresses weren't as bad, but I'd had little contact with them. Only Iva Lee, and the GED classes had made it bearable for me. And yet, I had questioned both Iva Lee's and Mr. Grason's motives in helping me.

"It's a view, alright. Maw Wiseman loved looking down in the valley. She claimed it made her think of how God must feel looking down on the world. She got really religious the last few years of her life. Not that she wasn't afore. All of us living here on this mountain live mighty close to God. He's about all we have to count on when things get tough."

He took a large box of matches down from the fireplace mantel, bent down and opened the door to the coal stove. "I've always kept dry kindling in the stove in case I was up here and needed to warm the place up in a hurry. Wet kindling ain't worth a plug nickel. I sheltered in here some during deer hunting season. Killed three big bucks a while back afore deer season was over. Got enough meat out of 'um to winter us. Ever eat deer meat?"

"All the time when I was little. Dad and my brother liked to hunt. Got a deer now and again, but mostly squirrel."

"I like squirrel gravy mighty fine, but my Betsy don't like picking the hair off after I skin 'em. Ain't none of my business, but considering your condition, why ain't you with your parents after you man died?"

"There was a horrible accident before I got married. It's still hurts too much for me to talk about it." I bit my bottom lip fighting tears. The last few days alone along with being stranded had been too much for me.

He nodded and grew silent.

I stood there fighting tears and shivering while he struck a match to the kindling. I was familiar with starting a fire. Mom and Dad burned wood and coal to heat the house. Mom always used a wood cook stove. I got pretty good at starting a fire for Mom to cook our food. Dad most always kept a fire in the heating stove during winter.

"Kept this place just like Maw Wiseman had it. My Betsy couldn't bear to change a thing from the way her maw had it. Her and Maw were mighty close. Two peas in a pod if you ask me. Bout done her in when her maw died. It was harder on her than when her Pa died. My own folks have been gone a long time, but sometimes I feel like they're right here with me."

My baby would be an only child.

There was no way I would ever get married again – not that I'd ever been married. Calvin had done a good job of ruining me on such as that.

I couldn't stop myself from thinking about Mr. Grason. There were times when I was sure I was in love with him, but was I? Maybe I'd turned to him because I was desperately longing for someone to care about me. I still believe he did care, but not enough to go through whatever it would take to divorce Grace Anna.

Would a man who didn't love me secretly slip me all the money he'd given me? It was as much as I'd earned the entire time I'd worked at the restaurant. I had enough money to get by on for a while if I was careful, but it wouldn't last forever.

I wouldn't think about that right now. I had to get through this snowstorm and figure out what I was supposed to do next. It sure would be easier if Grant would come back to me with some kind of advice. It was obvious I hadn't done so good on my own.

The man kept talking as he worked on the fire. "We had three children. One boy and two girls. They moved away as soon as they were old enough to go after good jobs. They don't come around much anymore. Breaks Betsy's heart not havin' 'em underfoot. Can't say as I blame 'em, though. Nothing in these mountains other than peace and quiet. Young folks want a little excitement in their lives. I know I did when I was young, but things change when you're old."

I watched the kindling blaze up hot. The fire reminded me of the fire when Mary Tracy wrecked her car. I wondered if there was any more in the newspapers about the accident. Had the sheriff contacted my parents? Did they think I was dead? Did Cloetta, Iva Lee and Mr. Grason think I was the one who burned to death? Since my address was at the shed, I was sure Iva Lee would most likely be notified first. Would a sheriff's deputy or Iva Lee tell Mom and Dad what happened? Would Mom suffer worse because she thought the fire had cremated me? Would she think it was my punishment for supposedly cremating Calvin?

"I'll bring in another bucket of coal and set it on the porch, so the snow won't melt in the floor. Betsy is mighty particular about this place. That bucket of coal ought to be enough to do you all night and tomorrow morning, Maw always insisted on havin' a mighty big pile of coal delivered.

She never did like doin' without what she needed," he told me. "You'll be safe and warm here, so I'll leave you to it. My Betsy won't like me stayin' with a pretty woman for long. She's the jealous type, you know."

I wasn't sure if he was serious or joking. He wasn't exactly dead-old, but he'd gone over the hill years ago. The fact that he hadn't cracked so much as a grin made me lean toward him being serious. I watched him go out the front door and disappear around the side of the house where I could barely see a large hump covered with snow.

He kicked at the pile with his heavy work boots until he had most of the snow off a spot, filled the coal bucket he'd picked up on the porch full to running over. He brought it back to the porch and sat it beside the door where it was protected by the porch roof. He walked around the side of the house, got in his jeep, circled the rest of the way around the house and headed down the mountain in the same tracts his jeep had made coming up.

I was left alone in a strange cabin on top of a mountain. I was warm and safe due to the kindness of these strangers, this couple who didn't know me at all. There were still good people in the word. Calvin, Cloetta, and Grace Anna were the exception.

I went outside, got my trash bag and dirty clothes from the trunk of the car and dumped it inside the cabin door. I went back to the car, got the heavy sack of food. I made sure I stomped the snow off my shoes and took them off before I carried them inside. I would respect Betsy's wish to keep the place pristine.

I looked in the bag to discover there was a loaf of homemade bread, a large hunk of cheese, and six thick slices of country ham all wrapped in plastic wrap. I had enough food for two or three days if I ate sparingly.

It suddenly dawned on me that they had done all this for me when they didn't even know my name.

I opened the bedroom door so it would warm up. The small room had a single lightbulb in the center of the ceiling. The bed was a double with a handmade quilt on top. There was a dresser, but no mirror. What looked like a small hand knotted rug was on the floor. Other than that, the room contained nothing else.

I opened the bathroom door next. The space was tiny. It had a commode, sink and bathtub all within an arm's reach of each other. Two towels and a single washcloth were on a shelf above the commode. There was a small mirror above the sink. I looked at myself. I could see why they wanted to help such a pitiful young woman. I was little more than a pale sunken face with huge, frightened eyes. I reminded myself of a scared little girl just before she burst into tears.

~~~~

Morning came. I got up and rushed to the stove. The cabin was cooling off. I hadn't woken up during the night to fill the stove with coal. I found some kindling in a wooden box and placed it on the remaining live fire coals and then carefully put small pieces of coal on the kindling. I was relieved when it flamed up. I went to the bathroom, washed the black coal dust off my hands before I used the commode.

When I was finished, I went to the picture windows and looked out. There had to be more than a foot of snow out there. Perhaps a foot and a half. At least no more snow was falling. The sky was dark with ominous clouds hanging low.

Everything was coated in a blanket of white including the trees. Their limbs were hanging low. Some limbs were bent so low they almost reached down to the snow. It always amazed me how snow blanketed everything in an eerie silence. I stood there looking at the picture-perfect winter scene. The kind found on postcards.

I could see smoke rising from the chimneys down in the hollow. The general store appeared a bit forlorn without any sign of life. If anyone cared to look, they should be able to see the smoke rising from the cabin's chimney. One thing was for sure, the Jeep couldn't make it up the winding road. My little Honda couldn't make it out. Until the sun shined hot enough to melt the snow, I was stranded.

The good thing was that no one would ever find me here. A strange kind of sadness washed over me as I realized what I'd done. When I left my driver's license behind, I'd made sure no one would be looking for me.

But I knew where they were. I could always go back someday, or so I told myself.

Chapter 25

The second day in the cabin I had to go outside and break a path to the coal pile thankful for the boots I'd bought at the secondhand store. I filled both coal buckets and set them on the porch. I took the broom I'd found and swept the snow off as best I could.

I had eaten most of the food Betsy packed for me. There were a few odds and ends of food in my car I'd bought when I filled up with gas. Again, I had to tromp a path from the back door to the car. I had no idea what I would do when my food ran out. I couldn't possibly walk down the mountain with snow up to my knees.

I came back inside, took my shoes off and sat close to the stove to warm myself up. It would be a while before the sun had enough heat to melt snow.

I was still stranded.

I never should have left the main highway.

Why was it that I always seemed to make bad decisions.

My stupidity was greater than I had ever imagined.

Why couldn't I do something right in my life?

Going back home to Mom and Dad would have been better than starving to death on top of this mountain. At least there would have been food to eat, and neighbors close enough to help out if needed. I was now isolated with nothing other than a view.

I was sinking into a pity party made up of desperation when a knocking sound came at the back door moments before the door opened. A man walked in wearing artic boots, canvas pants, thick coat and fur lined cap with ear flaps tied below his chin. On his back was something like a big sack. I gasped and jumped to my feet. I didn't have a thing to defend myself with

"Dad burn, if it's not cold out there," he said as he looked toward me. "Ma'am, I didn't mean to scare the life outta you. You've gone plum pale."

"Who are you?" I demanded as though knowing his name would aid in my self-defense.

"I'm Nash Smith. Hoke Reeves sent me up here to check on you. My mom sent you a sack of food to do you until I can get the road cleared enough to get you off this mountain. None of us expected to get this much snow. Everybody is snowed in solid. Had myself a time getting to you. There's right at two feet of snow out there. Might take me a day or two considering how many roads I've got to clear before I get to this one."

Relief rushed over me. I wasn't forgotten to starve to death in this cabin or freeze to death trying to get down off the mountain. It was all I could do not to burst into tears.

"I'm going to leave this sack of food for you and then be on my way. Don't want to melt this snow off me in Maw Wiseman's floor. Betsy would skin my hide."

I watched as he shucked the sack from his back.

"Are you doing okay? Is there anything you need?" he asked as he looked at my stomach, and then quickly gazed at my face.

"I'm very comfortable," I told him, which was true. What I needed was to be off this mountain, but where could I go once I got off? "Thank you for bringing food. I don't know how you walked in this deep snow."

"No problem a-tall. I roam these hills all year around. Takes more snow than this to make me hole-up," he said as he placed the sack by the door.

I tried to see his face beneath the fur cap and thick dark beard and mustache. All I could see were lively eyes the color of which I couldn't describe. They weren't blue, green, or brown. More like a deep slate gray and yet not. His eyebrows where thick and dark. I couldn't tell how old he was, but there was no gray mixed in with dark hair. Yet, I could tell he was older than I was.

"Say, what's your name? Hoke said he forgot to ask."

"Ellie," I said before I caught myself. "Mary Ellen Tracy, but everyone calls me Ellie," I quickly added in hope of cover my slip-up.

"When is the little one due," he boldly asked, which surprised me. Most men didn't talk about such things.

"About two months."

"Where were you headed when you got lost?" he didn't seem reluctant in asking personal questions about private matters.

"Nowhere specific," I answered.

"Nowhere," he grinned though his thick mustache. "Looks like you've arrived here then," he chuckled slightly. "I've heard folks claim this is God's country because no one other than God would want it. They're wrong. The folks who live here love every inch of this wonderful place."

I certainly wasn't loving it.

"Hoke said your husband was killed and you're trying to outrun your hurting."

"That's one way of putting it." Actually, I was trying to outrun my fears.

"Then this is the right place to lay-up and heal. Folks are willing to give a helping hand to those in need. The rest of the time they'll leave you be to heal in your own time. Folks here-abouts believe in letting folks live their own lives."

I didn't know if *heal* was the right word for me. Hide might be better.

"You see that light switch over there by the front door? The one with a dot of red paint on it?"

I saw it.

"Hoke forgot to tell you about it. If you get in trouble or need me to come back before I get the road clear, turn that porch light on. It's a right powerful light. Hoke and Betsy put it there in case Maw Wiseman needed them. Betsy didn't like her staying up here all by her lonesome, but they couldn't do one earthly thing with her. Independent until the morning she didn't wake up, she was. Just turn that light on and they'll see it and send for me," he said as he went to the front door to look out the big window.

"Thank you," I told him.

"I see you've broke a path to the coal pile. Both buckets are full. Put the food in Maw's refrigerator," he grinned slightly. "After it thaws out some. Froze solid, most likely from me toting it in this weather. Don't reckon I need to remind you how cold it is out there."

He seemed to have forgotten about walking on the cabin floor as he came closer the heating stove as though he wanted to get a better look at me.

"It's warm in here, so stay inside," he told me as he turned around and headed to the back door. "Don't worry about a thing. We're used to deep snows on this mountain. Hain't never killed nobody with enough sense to stay in out of it."

Before I could ask him more questions, he opened the back door and was gone. I rushed to a window to see him disappear in the woods, following in the same tracks he'd made coming here. Evidently, he lived on the backside of this mountain. I wondered if there were more people living nearby.

I grabbed the broom and the rag mop to clean up the melting snow he'd left on the floor. When it was all cleaned, I opened the sack. There was enough food to last me several days. I wasn't going to starve or freeze to death and that was reassuring.

I opened the sack of food to find it contained different food this time. There was a bag of potatoes wrapped in a towel to keep them from freezing, another bag of dried soup beans, a glass jar of flour, another jar of lard, a large chunk of ham and what appeared to be a jar of instant milk powder. All were wrapped in towels. No sandwiches this time. I would have to cook my own food, which was all right with me.

~~~~

The next evening, I heard the sound of a loud engine grinding away. I looked out the window to see a man on an old tractor clearing snow from around the gas station and restaurant. I wondered if it was the man, Nash Smith, clearing the roads. I also wondered who would come out to fill up with gas or eat at the restaurant in this weather?

I'd had enough time to do some thinking on what I would do once I was able to get off this mountain. Where would I go? Did I continue to stay in this snowy section of land, or did I head south toward South Carolina, Georgia, or the warmer state of Florida. After being stranded in the snow, I longed for sunshine and warm weather. I could close my eyes and imagine the green grass and flowers that were surely blooming down south.

I had always heard it was easier to hide in a crowd of people. High numbers made people invisible. Being the only stranger in a thinly populated area made me stick out like an elephant in a cabbage patch. I knew Florida was a desirable destination especially in the wintertime when all the snowbirds headed south.

Iva Lee said most all the vegetables and fruits she got for the restaurant during winter came from Florida or California. I wondered what it would be like to live year-round in warm weather. Did I dare find out?

I also wondered what had happened to the real Mary Tracy. Did she have a family looking for her? Had the law discovered the car that burned wasn't a Honda, or the woman wasn't me? If so, would there be someone looking for me. Even law enforcement might get involved in a search since my driver's license was found at the scene of the accident when Mary Tracy's wasn't.

The brochure I left in my apron pocket might have thrown them off for a while but finding my driver's license this far north would let them know I was traveling in the opposite direction.

Being alone in the cabin for days had also given me time to think about Mom and Dad. Their world had been ripped apart with Grant's death. Thinking I was dead would have hit them hard even when I wasn't their favorite child. I was still their child, their only daughter. I knew I would be devastated if something happened to my baby even when it hadn't been born.

Allowing them to think I was dead was nothing short of cruel. Mom practically forcing me to marry Calvin was also cruel, but could I place all the blame on Mom? She did what she thought was best for me. If Calvin had turned out to be the man he pretended to be, it really might have turned out for the best.

It was water under the bridge, so to speak, and there was nothing anyone could do about it now. I had let the past go and do my best to provide a good future my baby. My baby. Not Mr. Grason's. I certainly didn't want him to have a claim to my baby even when he claimed to love it and me. I had no doubt how much he wanted my baby with or without me.

Stay put, I seemed to hear Grant say. *It's easier to spot a rabbit on the run than one hiding in the weeds.*

I almost laughed at the thought Grant's ghost was now haunting me instead of my parents. I couldn't see him like they did, but I could hear him speaking loud and clear. He was right. Who in their right mind would ever think I would be stranded in a cabin on top of a mountain in nearly two feet of snow?

Even I didn't know where I was at.

The tractor driver worked all day scraping the snow up in a pile a little bit at a time. It would not be possible to clear more than a narrow road, which nobody had used and most likely wouldn't for a while. When lunch time came, he filled up his tractor from the gas station's diesel pump, and then parked the tractor in one of the cleared spots in front of the restaurant. He and Hoke Reeves would be the only people eating Betsy's good cooking. I wish I was there. I'd found a pot and put the dried beans on the heating stove to slowly cook. I'd made pancakes for breakfast - but no syrup. I'd sliced the slightly frozen potatoes and placed a slice of ham in a skillet to fry. I wasn't going to starve any time soon.

"Be thankful," I told myself. I was warm and I had food to eat. I had everything I needed in Maw Wiseman's little cabin, at least for a while.

The sun came out, but it had little to no warmth in it. I couldn't tell if any of the snow had melted, but it had formed a hard crust on top. Nash Smith had started clearing the road to the cabin, but he was having trouble finding a place to put all the snow. The road was so narrow there wasn't room to push the snow to the side in order to get my car out. From what I could tell from the cabin, it would make my leaving even more difficult. The pilled-up snow would take longer to melt.

By the end of the day, Nash Smith had scraped his way to the cabin. He shut off the tractor behind my car, got off, and came to the back door where he stomped snow off his feet. He knocked on the door.

"Hello, Ellie. I'm coming in to get warm. It's colder than an Eskimo's hind end in a January blizzard."

I'd found a coffee pot and a can of coffee grounds in the bottom of the cabinet and put it on top of the coal stove to perk. I never liked the taste of coffee, but I loved its smell. It reminded me of home. I had started sipping it for the last few days. It gave me something to drink and helped warm my insides.

"Do I smell coffee?" Nash said as he came through the door. "It would be a cup of heaven right now."

"Freshly perked," I told him.

"I brought more food from Betsy. She's having cooking withdrawal since nobody can get to her restaurant. Need your coal buckets filled up?"

"No, they are full." I had filled them early that morning. It was something I did in the morning and before darkness set in.

I watched as he took off his boots, coat and furry hat as though he intended to stay a while.

"Is the road wide enough to get my car out?" I made a point of asking as I poured him a cup of coffee and handed it to him.

"It's wide enough to take you out on my tractor if you don't want to stay here any longer. Betsy doesn't have an extra bed on top of the restaurant, but she said she'd make you a pallet on the kitchen floor."

A pallet on the floor would not be comfortable considering how big my baby was growing. I was going stir-crazy alone in the cabin, but I was warm and comfortable enough.

"Don't think I could get up and down?" I told him.

"I figured that," he said as he leaned toward the heat of the coal stove. "I've got an extra bedroom at my place. You're welcome to stay there. But keep in mind I'm a single man and folks might talk dirt about us."

"I doubt they'd claim you're my baby's daddy," I couldn't resist saying.

He grinned. "I have been known to leave this mountain right often. Some might claim you've tracked me down."

"In that case, I'd better stay put. I would like to be on my way, though."

"On your way to where?"

"Someplace that feels like home."

"Sounds to me like you're running away from something. What is it?"

"Sad memories," I told him as he turned his backside to the stove to warm. "Is Betsy and Hoke tired of me staying here?"

"They understand the predicament you're in. They're concerned about you going into early labor up here all alone. That's why they had me scrape the road all the way up here. I can get to you in a hurry, if you turn that light on."

"You can see the light?"

"Not from my place. They'll let me know if need be. I'm a Jack-of-all-trades around here. The youngster who didn't move away as soon as he donned long pants. Seems most of the young folks headed out to seek fame and fortune instead of staying put. Me, I love the place I'm living in. This has always been home to me," he said with a touch of nostalgia.

"You didn't want to see what lay beyond this mountain?"

"When I was seventeen, I lied about my age and joined the army. For the next four years, I saw more beyond this mountain than I wanted to see. I promised myself if I ever got back here, I wouldn't leave again. And I haven't."

"I thought you were known to leave the mountain right often," I couldn't resist repeating what he'd told me.

"Only for day trips and on rare occasions overnight to pick up supplies and things. I don't consider it leaving here. Care if I set down for a spell, I ought to thaw out a bit before I start again?"

Of course, he could sit down. He had more of a right to be here than I did. "Please do," I told him.

He sat down on the couch like he was used to doing just that.

"Want more coffee?" I asked.

"Don't mind if I do. After that, I best be on my way. Uncle Jeb wants me to scrape his road as soon as I get through here. He has a craving for Betsy's cooking."

"I'll pay you for scraping me out," I told him.

"No need. I trade work with Hoke for gas. It's not your fault you got stuck in this cabin."

"It's my fault I took the wrong road."

"Where again did you say where you were heading?" he asked as though I had confused him.

"Home," I repeated similar to what I'd told him before. "I'm looking for a forever home for me and my baby."

"Your husband didn't provide a home for you while you were married?"

"No, he didn't."

"Must not been much of a provider."

I wasn't sure how I should answer that. I decided to be truthful. "He left behind a lot of bills he hadn't paid."

"Were you able to pay them off?"

"I worked long enough to pay everything I owed before I left. If you don't mind, I'd rather not talk about him. He's dead and I must make a new life for me and my baby." I decided to turn the table and ask him a few personal questions.

"Why isn't a man your age married?"

"Never met but one girl I wanted to marry, but it didn't happen. These days seems like all the pretty girls in courtin' distance are my cousins."

"I though all the young people left as soon as they wore long britches."

"Pert near all of them did. There's still a stray here and there."

I wondered if he considered himself a stray, but I didn't ask.

"Well now," he said as he got to his feet. "I best get at it. This snow won't scrape itself.

I felt deserted as I watched him put his warm things back on, go out the door, get on the tractor, and drive off scraping the snow as he went. I grabbed the broom and swept the floor. Took the mop and went over it although it wasn't dirty. Only the spot where his boots set was slightly damp.

The next morning, I was surprised to see Nash Smith coming in the back door again. He hadn't even bothered to knock.

"Get your things together," he said. "I'm going to drive you out."

"But the road?" I started to question.

"I think I can drive your car out if I'm real careful like. I checked and your car's not too wide to drive it out. I know you won't want to leave it on this mountain."

He was right about that.

"Good. I can be on my way," I told him, even when I didn't feel confident I could drive to a major highway in this snow.

"Nope, you won't be able to leave yet. Another snow is gonna hit any minute. That's why I walked all the way up here to get you off this mountain."

I didn't want a pallet on Betsy's floor, and he must have read my thought on my face.

"I'm taking you to my place. I have two bedrooms."

"What about the dirty talk?"

"Mom said she would supervise us."

"Mom?" I questioned, still not gathering my things.

"She lives up the holler a jump from me."

"Why can't I stay here?"

"The last time a storm such as the one that's coming hit us, we were snowed in for a solid month. Couldn't even get my tractor out. Had to fashion me some snowshoes to get to the barn to feed the animals. Can't chance you staying here alone for that long. Mom said some babies get impatient and come early especially if the mother gets stressed."

I got my things, while he gathered what food stuff I had left and carried everything to my car as I put on my warmest clothes.

"As cold as it is, I feared the battery would be dead," he said. "It started right up even in this cold. I'm clearing the snow from the car's back door so you can get in. Too much work to get all the snow tromped down to the front seat, and you're too big to crawl under the steering wheel."

I could have done it, but it wouldn't have been the easiest thing I'd ever done. I had gotten rather large in the last few days. My baby had been kicking like crazy. My belly actually felt sore. I settled into the back seat.

"Hang on tight. There might be places where I'll have to gun it," he warned as he stepped on the gas.

The car shot backward a few feet and then stopped. Disappointment seized me. He put the gears in forward and eased forward as far as the car would go, and then put it in reverse and shot backward.

"I've got to get it over the snow drift I couldn't reach with my tractor. I'd rather not take the time to shovel us out."

After five tries, he'd packed the snow down enough to back over it and turn around in the space he'd cleared.

I think every hair was standing on my head by the time Nash got my Honda maneuvered down the narrow excuse of a road. Both sides of the car were scraping against the snowbanks. I feared there would be nothing but bare metal instead of paint on both sides of my car. He stopped in front of the restaurant.

"Need to let Hoke and Betsy know we got out. I'm sure Betsy has something ready to eat before we go to my place."

"Oh, thank goodness," Betsy said as we walked in. "I'm so relieved to see you. I was plum worried about you up there all by yourself. If something had happened to you, it would have been my fault."

"I was very comfortable in your mother's cabin. Thank you for letting me stay there. How much do I owe you?" I asked, wanting to pay my own way instead of taking advantage of helpful people.

"Oh, my, honey, you don't owe me a thing. Mommy would have been so happy if she knew you were there."

"Got any hot food for a couple of cold and hungry folks?" Nash asked.

"I sure do. Take yourselves a seat."

Betsy brought us two plates of food, a cup of coffee for Nash and a glass of milk for me. She sat down at the table across from me.

"I'm so glad Nash got you out before the coming storm hits. Lord only knows how long it will last. Sometimes we get snowed in for weeks on end."

"That's what Nash was telling me," I used his name for the first time. "I can't believe he's walked through this snow twice to help me, plus scraped the road and managed to drive me out."

"Nash is good like that. Don't know what folks on this mountain would do without him."

"Ah, shucks," Nash drawled in mock humility.

Betsy smacked him on the shoulder lightly. "None of that, Nash. I'm being serious. You've always been willing to help your neighbors when they are in need."

"My neighbors are willing to help me in return."

Betsy went back into the kitchen as we ate our good home-cooked food. It tasted even better since I didn't have to cook it.

I glanced out the window and a feeling of da ja vu took hold of me. Big snowflakes were falling.

"Guess we better be getting on," Nash told Betsy as she came to our table with a coffee pot in her hand. "It's starting to come down out there."

"How much do I owe for our meals," I asked.

"Oh, honey, I'll put it on Nash's tab as usual."

"Please, I'd rather . . ."

Betsy held up her hands to silence me. "I won't hear no more, honey. Nash has done taken you under his wing, so you're part of our family now. As some of the younger folks keep saying, just *pass it on.*"

I couldn't believe what she was telling me. Just because I foolishly got stranded in a snowstorm didn't make me part of their family. It made me an idiot. Nash grinned at what must

have been my expression as he stood up and scooted my chair
out like a southern gentleman.

"Ellie is determined to stand on her own two feet. I'm
only assisting her a little bit."

"I thank you both, and your husband too," I made a point
of telling them again.

She patted me on the back. "Nash and his mother will take
good care of you. When the weather breaks, stop by again."

I had a feeling I was being nicely dismissed, and I
couldn't blame her. It had to be a relief to have me out of her
mother's cabin.

Once we were in my car, I turned toward Nash. "I think I
should try to leave regardless of the weather. I've been an
imposition." I was feeling close to tears. "I had no intention
of causing all this trouble."

"Think nothing of it. It makes people feel good when they
get a chance to help others. It's called goodwill toward
mankind."

It didn't make much difference in what I wanted. The
snow was peppering it down too hard for me to have a choice.
I no longer had my own freewill. I was dependent on Nash
and these people – at least for a while.

"This little car goes right good in the snow," Nash said,
breaking the silence. "Look at those snowflakes. They're the
size of quarters. Did you ever let the snowflakes fall on your
sleeve and look at all the different patterns? They remind me
of a kaleidoscope of white. No two are ever the same. People
are like that too. No two will ever be the same even if they
are twins."

I knew he was making conversation to break the silence
of uncertainty that had consumed me. He was taking me from
one situation to another, and yet I was still trapped in a
mountain of snow. I wanted to scream, cry, push him out of
my car and get the heck away from there.

"You're gonna like my Mom. She's rock solid. She was
born and raised right here. Her grandma was a full-blooded

Indian. Took Mom under her wing to teach her everything she thought she should know in life. Mom is what's known as a medicine woman."

"That's good," I said, although I was only half listening. I was too lost in my own thoughts to care about what he was telling me.

"It can be good where you are concerned. She's delivered just about every baby on this mountain."

I heard what he was implying. Did he think I'd take a chance on letting his mother deliver my precious baby? No way. I intended to have my baby in a hospital with a qualified doctor and nursing staff. I was taking no chances.

It was then that the truth hit me. Staying put in the shed would have been taking a chance with my baby. Leaving had also been taking a chance. Being stranded on this mountain was taking another chance with my baby's life. I was already a horrible mother, and my baby wasn't even born yet.

"My baby means everything to me," I said out loud.

"That's how it should be," he told me gently. "A mother and her baby have a love bond with each other even before it's born. That's why I'm taking you to my house. You and your baby will be safe there," he said as if he knew I was running away from more than a dead husband.

"You said you lived alone."

"I do. Mom lives in the old home place a ways up the holler from me. With the storm that's on us, I thought it best for her to stay with me."

"You only have two bedrooms," I pointed out. Did he expect his mother and me to share a room?

"I'll sleep on the couch. It's right comfortable. Believe me, I've slept on a lot worse."

"No . . ." I started to object, but he stopped me.

"Enough feeling bad about not being that independent, self-sufficient woman you're striving to become. I have no doubt you'll get to that place soon enough. Until then, show a little gratitude you ended up with wonderful people such as me," he said with a touch of humor.

His words made me feel even worse. To my horror, I started crying.

"Dad, blast," he said. "Just my luck. I've got a crying woman on my hands, and I can't take a chance on stopping this car to take you in my arms. Suppose you can hold out until we get home?"

I didn't know if I should laugh or cry harder.

"Seriously, Ellie, all joking aside. We're here to help you, or anyone else who needs help. As Betsy said, if the need ever arises, just pass our kindness on to the next person. Until then, have yourself a good cry if it makes you feel better."

He took a blue bandana handkerchief out of his pocket and handed it to me.

"It's clean," he said. "Pulled it out of the drawer this morning and hain't used it once today."

I took the handkerchief and wiped my eyes and blew my nose and handed it back to him.

"Keep it. We're not home yet. I'd rather hold a woman in my arms when she has a clean nose."

I didn't think that remark was a bit funny, but I could see him grinning big through a face full of hair.

Chapter 26

Traveling through an almost whiteout was so slow that I had completely stopped crying by the time his house came into sight. It wasn't a log cabin as I had expected, but a regular looking house painted a cream white. It had a large picture window in front and two chimneys puffing out heat waves on each end. One chimney for the heating stove and one for the cook stove.

"Mom gets cold easy these days. She likes to keep the place good and warm. That's one of the reasons I insisted she come here until the weather breaks. Didn't want her having to wade through the snow to get coal and cook wood. Your company will be a bonus for her. She loves to mother everything she can get her hands on. So, try not to get irritated at her hovering over you. It'll keep her from hovering over me so much."

Winter was just setting in good, and I was already fed up with snowstorms. I cringed at the thought of how I would be feeling by the time spring came. Again, I regretted not heading south. How wonderful it would be to feel the sunshine on my arms instead of a kaleidoscope of white snowflakes.

"I'll get you settled inside, and then I'll come back to move your car and get your things."

"Thank you," I said.

He had stopped my car so the passenger door opened to a shoveled path leading to the front steps of the house. He hurried to my side to take hold of my arm.

"I don't want you to fall," he told me. Crusted snow can be slick as wheel grease. Especially when you're wearing those slick bottomed boots. We'll have to get Betsy to order you some work boots along with a thick wool coat if she doesn't have some stored in the general store. You'll go stir crazy if you can't get outside some, regardless if it's winter time."

"Okay," I readily agreed. I was cold to the bone already. "Let me know . . ." I begin when he finished what I was going to say.

"And you'll pay for them," he chuckled slightly as we came to the steps that showed signs of recently being swept with a broom. "Careful. Step easy," he warned still holding my arm.

A wave of welcome heat hit me in the face when he opened the door and allowed me to enter in front of him.

"Mom, we're home," he called out loud enough to make me jump. "Mom's a little hard of hearing," he whispered near my ear, but she reads lips in case you need to know later on."

A woman, short and slight in weight came rushing to greet us. She had salt and pepper hair with a lot of gray at her temples and on top. At the nap of her neck was almost black hair. A shade darker than her son's. Her face had few wrinkles and was a healthy shade of tan that surely came from her Indian heritage. I wondered if Nash's complexion would be the same beneath all that beard, mustache, and bushy eyebrows.

"Welcome home," she said as she stretched out both hands to take mine. "I admit I've been waiting impatiently for you to arrive."

It kind of sounded like her words had a double meaning to them, but I chose not to question what it could be. "Thank you," I said. "Everyone had been more than kind to me. I can't possibly express my gratitude."

"Not necessary," she was quick to say. "Not necessary in the least. Are you feeling, okay? Come sit by the fire and get warm. I'll bring you a nice cup of my own sweet tea. Nash isn't too fond of it, but I can tell you it's been a lifesaver for me in cold weather."

"Please don't bother," I told her as she sat me down in a rocking chair next to the fire.

"No bother. Here, let me take your coat before the snow melts and gets it wet."

I let her take my coat off like I was a child in need of help."

"I see your baby is growing good," she said as she looked at my stomach. Two months you say?"

"Yes," I told her. "There abouts." Seems Nash had told her all about me.

"Nash was the only baby I know of who came exactly on time. He's been on time ever since," she said with a chuckle. "He does tend to try and rush things, though. I'm always telling him things happen in their own time."

I watched her scuttle out of the room, remembering what Nash had said about her mothering everything. My own Mom was never the over-maternal type toward me. I wasn't sure if I'd like having Nash's mother doting over me, if that was really what she would do.

Nash came onto the porch stomping the snow off. He came in the door with my suitcase and bag of food in one hand and his boots in the other hand.

"Mom won't let me walk in my own house with my boots on," he said.

"No need for me to clean up your mess when I don't have to," she was quick to tell him. "Put her things in her bedroom. Are you two hungry?"

"No. Betsy fed us."

"I figured she'd do that. I'll get to feed you two supper though. To tell the truth, I'm a better cook than Betsy is."

"Betsy is Mom's sister. There's a lot of sibling rivalry between them, just telling you so you'll be forewarned."

"There is not," his mom informed me.

"Whatever you say, Mom."

"He's a sassy one," she said to me. "I have to smack his butt every now and again."

Oh, boy, I thought. Another mother and son worshiping each other the way Mom and Grant did. Somehow, I didn't think it was as bad a thing as I once did.

"Honey, once you've warmed up, go in the bedroom and rest up some. You've got to be exhausted considering what you and your baby have been through. "Maw Larkin, my grandmother, used to tell me an unborn baby goes through every emotion it's momma goes through."

I hoped that wasn't true. I wanted my baby to be happy and at peace with the world around it. I was willing to do everything in my power to see that it had every good thing I could provide for it.

"I've rested a lot in the last few days," I told her. "I had little to do other than sit by the fire and read a book."

"Good. That's what you need to do during this time. Nash can show you where your bedroom and the bathroom are before he goes out to care for the animals. Reckon you know we're going to get a snow blizzard."

"Yes," I said as I looked out the window. "I think it's here."

"Oh, no. Not yet, honey. It's going to hit hard during the night. Snow'll be three feet deep come morning. That's one of the reasons I insisted Nash bring you off Mommy's mountain.

Her mother's mountain? I suppose it was if she and Betsy were sisters. Nash said his mother lived in the old home place. Made sense.

"I best get the wood box filled before the snow gets worse," he told me as he headed to put on his outside clothes.

I hoped he would hurry back. I felt more comfortable with him than with his mother.

Shortly, he came inside shaking show from his clothes.

"I see Mom's already got you sitting beside the heating stove. She's even put you in her favorite rocking chair." He leaned closer to me and whispered, "It means she likes you a lot. I don't get to sit in her special chair – ever."

Mrs. Smith came rushing from the kitchen with a mug in her hand. "I didn't make it too hot. It's the right temperature for comfort."

Nash glanced in the cup. "Tea instead of warm milk?" he grinned at his mother.

"I'll get you some if you like," she told him with twinkling eyes. "It'll warm you up."

"I'll pass. It appears to be warming up a little. The right temperature outside will soon be warm enough for a big snow to hit," he said to his mother and me. "It's right at freezing."

I'd heard Dad say many times that it was too cold to snow.

"I'm going to get the animals fed and settled in the barn before the snow gets deeper."

He surprised me by reaching out his hand and gently touching my chin before he turned and headed toward the door where his coat, hat and boots waited.

"That boy can't stop working," Mrs. Smith said as she fondly watched her son leave the house. "It been a mighty long time since I've seen him set down longer than to gulp down his food. Your arrival will be good for him."

Her last words confused me. How could my arrival be good for him? I wanted to ask, but decided it was best not to do so as I sipped on the tea. It was a bit too sweet for me. It was both minty with a slight taste of root beer.

"I love that tea," she said as she took a seat in another rocker across from me. "I drunk it all the time when I carried my babies. I was sick the whole enduring time with all of 'em. That tea was all that helped me. You been sick any?"

"No, I haven't," I told her. Actually, I felt better being pregnant than I did before. I didn't tell her I'd miscarried one baby. Putting it into words scared me even when I knew this baby was safe.

"You're the lucky one. God meant you to have a lot of babies," Mrs. Smith told me as though she knew what she was talking about. I hoped she did.

"I'm only having this one. I don't plan on ever getting married again," I told her what I considered to be true. I wouldn't take a chance on marrying my baby's daddy, Mr. Grason, even if he suddenly became a widower. I had convinced myself what happened between the two of us was compensation to replace the baby I had miscarried. Mr. Grason hadn't really been in love with me, while I had been desperate for his attention. At least, that's what I had been telling myself while holed up in Maw Wiseman's cabin.

Mrs. Smith nodded as though she understood. "That's what most women say after they've lost the man they love. It takes a while, but they get over their hurtin' and take another chance on love. The second time around is always special. They know what it's like to lose a loved one, so they make sure they shower more love on those remaining in their lives."

"My baby means everything to me," I told her. "That's why I was trying to find us a good home before it is born."

"I understand that. If you don't mind me saying so, you couldn't have found a better place than right here. God surely was guiding you because this is the best place on earth to raise a child. It's not one of those places where you have to be on the look-out all the time. Everybody looks after the children and treats them like they are their own."

I had only seen two houses and Maw Wiseman's cabin. There couldn't be many people or children about.

"To be honest, most of us who live on this mountain are kin to each other," she added. "We really are one big, happy family. I think's that's one of the reasons why Nash picked a woman from off to marry."

"He's married?" I asked. I thought he'd told me he never had a wife.

"No, honey. He never got a chance to marry her. She had a blood cancer. Died before they said their wedding vows. To this day Nash claims he'll never love another woman, but I know better than that."

"Oh," I said. "He must have met her while he was in the armed service."

She looked surprised. "He told you about that time?"

"Not really. He said he joined up right after high school."

"That he did. All boys had to enlist or be called up to serve our country sooner or later. You finish up that tea and go lay down a while."

I didn't want to take Nash's room away from him. "I'll sleep on the couch instead of him," I told her.

"My gracious, no. That wouldn't be right a-tall. You'll need some privacy. He don't."

"I feel bad about putting him out of his bed and causing you to leave your house to stay here."

"Nash's bed is wherever he lays his head. As for me, Nash wouldn't let me stay alone in my house during this snowstorm. He likes to see that people and animals are safe and well cared for.

I wanted to ask her questions about Nash and the woman he had planned to marry, but I didn't want to sound too snoopy. Afterall, they were doing me a kindness instead of opening up their life history for me to probe.

I placed my hands on the arms of the rocking chair and hefted my growing bulk up out of the rocking chair and followed Mrs. Smith across the living room.

"This is the bathroom," she said as she pointed to a door centered between two other doors. This is Nash's bedroom I'll be sleeping in. And this is your bedroom."

She opened the door to a small, dimly lit room with only a single bed and a dresser. It had one window with thick curtains pulled over it.

"We keep the doors shut and the curtains closed during the day to keep most of the heat in the living room and kitchen. You can open your door at night if you get cold. Both

Nash and I like I bedrooms to be rather cold. Makes snuggling under the quilts feel better."

I could only nod at what she was telling me. I never did like being cold regardless if I was asleep or awake.

"Why don't you go in there and take you a little nap until supper time. I'll wake you up when it's ready if you fall asleep. Mommas need a lot of sleep if they want nice plump babies."

"Okay, thank you," I said as I went into the room and closed the door. I didn't want to sleep, but I didn't want to seem rude by refusing to do so. I saw my trash bag of things sitting in front of the dresser and considered putting my things in the dresser drawers but doing that felt as though I would be preparing to stay here for a while. I wasn't going to do that. I would leave here as soon as the roads were clear enough for me to drive off this mountain. I had every intention of finding a warmer place to raise my baby.

~~~~

I woke to the smell of coffee perking. For a groggy moment, I thought I was back home in my bed with Mom cooking breakfast. An instant later reality hit. I was in a strange bed in a stranger's house. I got out of bed, dressed, went to the bathroom, and then made my way to the kitchen.

"Good morning," Mrs. Smith said with a bright smile on her face. "Did you sleep good?"

"I did," I told her. I was surprised at how good I had slept.

"You look more rested than you did last night when we ate supper. Have you looked outside?"

I shook my head as I went to the kitchen window. "My goodness," I gasped at what I saw. The path that was shoveled from the kitchen door to the barn and woodshed had to come to Nash's waist or above. I guessed he was a head and shoulders taller than me. Six feet tall or maybe an inch or two more. His mother was about my size but weighed less than I did.

"Like I suspected there's about three feet of snow out there," she said.

I couldn't believe it. I had never seen so much snow in my entire life. "I don't believe this," I found myself saying what I thought. "How are people supposed to survive this?"

"Oh, honey, we've had more snow than this every few years or so. It always snows a lot on this mountain. Sometimes we get drifts reaching the roof of the house. Sure makes it rough on us to get out and about."

I didn't want to seem dumb, but I didn't know the name of the mountain I was on. I had been too concerned about out-distancing my fears to make sure where I was going. "What's the name of this mountain?" I asked, wanting to know where I was without admitting how lost I had gotten myself.

"Roan Mountain," she said as she gave me a look. "I thought everybody knew where this mountain is. It was a resort destination in the late eighteen hundreds. The Cloudland Hotel closed down around 1910. Rich folks came up here to escape lowland heat before they discovered air conditioning. Where did you come from?"

I didn't want to tell her the truth. I didn't want to lie either, but I didn't have much of a choice. I had heard very little about the state of Georgia, but I'd once waited on a couple from Preacher's Gap, Georgia. I had been intrigued by the name.

"Georgia," came out of my mouth before I took another breath.

"Where at in Georgia?"

She would have to ask. "Preachers Gap," I told her.

"Never heard of it. What town is it near?"

Again, I had to rely on what the couple told me. "There's Miller's Gap. Ever heard of Suches, Ga?"

"No, can't say as I have."

I was saved from more questions by Nash coming to the kitchen door and doing a job of stomping his feet. He came inside before taking off his boots, coat, gloves and fury cap.

"Nash," his mother scolded.

"Now, Mom, it's too cold to undress outside. It's dropped to below zero out there. Thank the Lord for a winter beard or I would have frozen my chin off. Wish I could grow hair on my nose instead of inside it. Got any hot coffee?"

"You and Ellie sit down at the table, and I'll take up breakfast. How are the animals?"

"They're okay. The deep snow keeps the wind from blowing through the barn. As long as wind don't hit 'em, they'll be fine."

Mrs. Smith busied herself taking up food and placing it on the table.

"It's a treat to have Mom here cooking for me. I'm a rotten cook, but a man needs his own home by the time he reaches my age."

"A man needs a wife and children so his mother can be a grandmother."

"You're already a grandmother."

"Right, but you're the only one of my young'uns who still lives here."

"I planned it that way. I get special attention along with great food."

"Compliments get you more food," his mother said with a smile. "Ellie says she from Preacher's Gap, Georgia. Ever heard of the place?"

"No. I traveled through some of Georgia's towns once when I was picking up supplies."

"She didn't know we're located on Roan Mountain, Tennessee either."

"I got on the wrong road and had no idea where I ended up," I tried to explain as I felt my face burning red. I didn't like answering questions. I shouldn't have asked questions.

"That's easy to do. Goodness knows how many times I've taken the wrong road to places," Nash said as though he was sticking up for me. "Did Mom tell you about the headless mule of Roan Mountain?"

"No."

"That's foolishness," his mother was quick to say.

"Maybe, maybe not. Anyway, the story goes that an old prospector had struck a motherlode of gold and put his findings in sacks. He strapped it on his old mule and headed through Teaberry to go down off the mountain in order to buy himself a fine home to live the rest of his life as a rich man.

"It so happened that all the gold he'd mined was extremely heavy. The old mule could barely walk under the weight. A hard rain had come during the night making a muddy sink hole in one spot on Grassy Ridge. It just so happened that the old mule chose to walk on that exact spot. When his weight hit the mud hole, he sank up beyond his belly.

"The old prospector was said to be half drunk on liquor and the other half drunk of the idea of spending the rest of his life as a rich man. He wasn't thinking what was the best for him and his mule. He tried everything his befuddled mind could think of to get the mule out of the mud hole, with no luck.

"Finally, the old man took a cussing fit and blamed the mule for his predicament, pulled his hunting knife from its sheath and cut the mule's head off.

"He then managed to unload his gold a little at a time. It was too heavy to carry so he found a safe place to stash it, while he headed down the mountain. He'd pocketed enough gold to buy himself another mule or perhaps a horse and wagon in order to climb back up the mountain to retrieve his gold.

"Well, the old fellow never made it off the mountain. Nobody ever knew what happened to him. But the headless mule remained on the mountain. Folks claims there are times when the headless mule can be seen rambling over the Roan. They say they first hear the clump, clump of feet before the animal appears. Kept us boys from camping near those places."

"Poppy cock. You boys camped up there a lot."

"Not in the places where that headless mule had been sighted."

"Poppy cock," his mother said again. "Don't you listen to him, Ellie. And Nash, don't you be telling Ellie such foolishness when she's in her condition. You don't want to mark her baby."

"Mom believes in old wives' tales," Nash said with a grin.

"Don't make fun of what's proved itself, right?"

Nash decided to change the subject. "According to my measuring stick, there is thirty-eight inches of snow when we got up this morning. As cold as it's getting it will most likely crust on the top. I shoveled a path to the barn and shed about daybreak, but we'll have to stay put for a while."

"I'm glad Ellie isn't in Mommy's cabin," Mrs. Smith said. "Lord only knows when we'd be able to get her out. And with a baby on the way."

I felt guilty. "I'm sorry I got lost," I told them.

"Don't be sorry about that. I've no doubt God planned for you to end up right here with us," she told me. "By the way, do you have any baby clothes?"

Baby clothes! Such as that hadn't occurred to me. I thought I had two months before I would need baby things. I planned on finding a tiny house to rent or hopefully buy before then.

"No," I admitted. "I was going to buy things when it was near my time."

"That will give us something to do while we wait on the thaw. I brought some of my material and yarn down from my place. I like to keep busy when we get snowed in. Instead of me piecing together quilts, we'll make baby clothes."

I wanted to object that I wouldn't be here long enough to make clothes, but I wasn't sure considering the snow was to the windows.

"I would enjoy that, but . . ."

"I know. You never learned how to sew or knit. Don't you fret. I'll teach you everything you need to know."

Chapter 27

Mrs. Smith made a point of asking me to call her mom, or at least Laurel, which was her name. I chose to call her Laurel. Mom felt too personal. She kept a calendar hanging on the kitchen wall. I looked at it every day along with checking the depth of snow outside. Every time the sun came out to melt the snow a little, more snow would come that night. I was standing in the living room looking out the window at the falling snow when Nash came up behind me. He must have known how despondent I was feeling. He reached out and placed a hand on my shoulder.

"I know you're going stir crazy, Ellie. I'd open the roads if I could. I can't even dig the tractor out of the barn," Nash told me. "Much less scrape a road. Folks are all right though. Everybody knows to prepare for weather like this. Sometimes it's March before the roads are clear."

"March?" I squeaked out. "My baby is due before then."

"Like I told you, Mom delivered most all the babies on this mountain. She's the best mid-wife a woman could have."

I didn't want a midwife. I wanted a doctor and a hospital.

"I guess you've noticed that it's Christmas next week," he said as though that should make me happy.

"I noticed."

"Maw will start cooking up food and baking cookies, cakes and pies. It'll help pass the time if you settle in and help her with all the preparations. I usually go out and find a little pine tree to decorate, but they are buried in the snow so deep even I couldn't put on snowshoes and go hunt one. I know it's hard, but time will pass easier if you settle in and try to be patient.

"I've never been snowed in before," I told him. At least, I had never been snowed in so completely.

"I thought it snowed in the mountains of Georgia."

"Not like this," I told him as tears came to my eyes.

"I know how you're feeling," he said as he took out his blue bandana handkerchief and wiped the tears from my eyes before replacing the handkerchief in his pocket. "Try not to be so sad, although being the first Christmas without your husband has to be hard on you."

I was surprised at his reasoning for my sadness. I wasn't thinking about Calvin. I was thinking about being a young girl and how excited I would get at Christmas time. Mom and Dad would make a trip to town a day or two before Christmas to buy us gifts. It would usually be oranges, apples, nuts and Christmas candy. Grant would get whatever he'd been longing for. I would get a doll when I was little, and clothes when I got older. I was disappointed that I didn't get what I wanted when Grant usually did.

"I don't miss him," I surprised myself by saying. My words surprised Nash even more.

"What did you say?" he questioned.

"I miss being a little girl a Christmas time. I always wanted to believe there were reindeers. Santa Claus, and gifts slipped underneath a tree, but I never did. I always knew fairytales never came true.

"I was right with you on those things but believing in fairytales is okay if it makes you happy. Say, what did you mean by saying you didn't miss him."

"I don't want to talk about him. He wasn't a nice man."

I could tell he wanted to ask questions but didn't. He reached out and put him arms around me, holding me against his solid body – until his mother came into the room. He took his arms from around me even though his mother was pretending she wasn't watching us.

"Ellie was remembering her childhood Christmases," he explained, somewhat embarrassed.

"I always get a little sentimental myself this time of year. Folks can't get out to go to church. We have a nice church here. When the roads clear, we'll all go together."

"I'm going out to the barn," he said. "I'll bring in a load of firewood when I come back."

"Good idea. Best bring in another bucket of coal," Laurel told him. "Heard on the radio that it's gonna be another cold night."

"Maybe it'll be too cold to snow," Nash said. He reached out his hand again and gave my shoulder a gentle squeeze.

Oddly enough, his gesture of comfort made me feel just a mite better. I told myself surely, this snow would melt before my baby was due

~~~~

After stuffing ourselves with another of Laurel's suppers, I sat down near the heating stove along with Nash. I no longer sat in Laurel's personal rocking chair. Nash had pulled up a leather chair near the fire. All three of us would sit in chairs as we waited for bedtime. Lucky enough, we still had electricity regardless of the snow.

We all three sat in silence, staring at the stove as though it was important, for a long while. Suddenly Laurel broke the silence.

"I guess you know you're carrying a girl baby," Laurel suddenly said.

"Really?" was what I said. I had no idea if my baby would be a boy or a girl, and I didn't think she did either.

"I can tell by the way you're carrying it. It's all in the front of you. A boy baby fills out your sides as well as your front."

"She's usually right with her predictions," Nash said. "Folks claim Mom is a seer. Her ability was handed down from her Indian grandmother."

"I don't claim to be a seer," she said. "Sometimes God sends me insight into things. Sometimes I pass it on, sometimes I don't. Depends on what God tells me I should do."

"That's what a seer is, Mom."

"Poppy cock," she said. "I'm tired. I'm going to bed. You and Ellie can keep this warm stove company as long as you want. I'll be asleep as soon as my head hits the pillow."

She got to her feet and marched to her bedroom as though she was mad at something. Nash grinned as he watched her go.

"She wants us to be alone," he whispered. "She thinks God brought you here to be my wife."

My eyebrows shot up and my mouth must have hung all the way to my chest. I didn't know what to say.

"Don't look so shocked," he said with a chuckle. "I don't think the way Mom does. I have to admit I'd make a wonderful husband."

"I... I," I stammered.

"Don't get upset, Ellie. I only want to give you insight into how Mom thinks. I know you'll leave as soon as it's safe. Until then, I want you to feel as safe and content as possible here in my home. Mom and I both welcome you to stay as long as you want. If you find this is the place you want to call home, we'll help you find land and help build a small house for you."

I didn't know what to say or what to think. Did he really mean what he said? Would these people be that kind to me? They didn't know me from Adam's dog, and yet those I'd met had taken me under their wings. Tears came to my eyes and ran down my cheeks.

"Oh, honey," he said soft and low. "I'm always making you cry."

He got up from his chair and came to me. He lifted me up and hugged me in his arms. I hated being so emotional, but his comfort was real. I remembered the times when I needed Mr. Grason's comfort. I had been foolish to allow what happened. I could have stopped it. Yet, if I had, I wouldn't be carrying my precious baby. I couldn't make myself regret him – and yet did I want to go back to a man I didn't entirely trust?

Fact was if not for Mr. Grason, I'd still be working at Good Eats and living in the shed. I would most likely spend my life being miserable. Either that or I'd likely be forced to return home to Mom and Dad. As things stood, I had money I'd earned along with Mr. Grason's guilt money. I even had a dead woman's money, and a safe place to stay for the time being, along with hope of a future.

"You don't make me cry," I whispered as I pulled away from him. "I'm feeling helpless, and it makes me emotional. You won't believe it, but I'm not a person who cries."

"We all cry at times," he whispered near my hair. "Expectant mothers are supposed to be emotional. Their hearts grow bigger along with their midsections."

"More old wives' tales?" I whispered back.

"More like my crazy thinking. Oh, Ellie, you're such a sweet girl. I have no idea what happened to you, or why you chose to run away the way you have, but I want you to know you're safe here. You don't have to run any longer if you don't want to."

"I'm not running away from anything," I said, while knowing I was lying. "I'm running toward something better than I had." And that was the truth.

"That's a good way to put it. I ran away from my hurt after Jolie died. I loved her with ever cell in my body. She was my world, my life, my hopes for a future. She wasn't feeling good and decided to see a doctor a few weeks before we planned to be married. She discovered she had leukemia. I wanted to get married right then, but she refused. She thought it would hurt me less to lose a girlfriend than to lose a wife.

"She was wrong. I wanted her to belong to be for as long as possible. I gave her all my love and all my support, but she wouldn't marry me. I still dream about her at night, but there are times when I have trouble remembering her face, the sound of her voice. I feel guilty about that. What I would give to have a baby from her. A little one who was a part of her, but it never happened."

"My baby is the most precious thing I have," I told him. "I would do anything to keep it safe."

"As a mother should," he told me as he moved us both to the couch instead of the chairs next to the fire. "Let's sit next to each other for a while. Commiserate in our mutual misery," he added with a grin.

I didn't feel nearly as lonely, or nearly as afraid sitting next to him on the couch.

Sometime later I opened my eyes to discover I had fallen asleep with my head resting on Nash's shoulder. He was awake and trying not to move enough to wake me up.

"I fell asleep," I said in surprise.

"That you did."

I sat up, leaving the warmth of him. "It's getting cold in here."

"The fire has burned down. I didn't want to wake you up to put wood in the stove."

"I'm sorry."

"Will you stop saying you're sorry. I'm not. It's been a long time since I held a sleeping woman in my arms. I liked it," again I saw his grin through all that hair.

I reached up and rubbed my fingers through that pile of beard. It felt courser than I thought it would. "I've never touched a man's beard and mustache before," I found myself saying.

"Do you like it?"

"I'm not sure," I said, although I didn't like the feel. I was sure kissing a man with all that face hair would not be pleasant.

"I always shave it off come spring. It keeps my chin and lips from freezing off during long, cold winters."

He picked up my hand and rubbed it against his beard. He surprised me when he kissed my palm. His lips were warm and soft.

"I best fill the stove up with coal. You'll sleep a lot better in your bed, but you're welcome to sit here with me as long as you want."

He hesitantly turned loose of my hand. I stood up and went into the bedroom.

I slept well that night.

~~~~

Day after day passed and the snow didn't melt. December was gone and the middle of January came on.

"We usually have a January thaw," Laurel told me. "It's unusual for all this snow to refuse to melt down a little. I guess God knows what's best for us," she added. "I wonder how the neighbors are getting on?"

"I'm thinking about finding my snowshoes and making my way to Hoke and Betsy's," Nash said. Not that I think they aren't safe and snug as a bug, but I'd like an excuse to get out and about."

"Why don't you wait a few days. We've got to have a thaw soon," Laurel insisted.

"Don't mean to be negative, but I'm beginning to think this snow is going to stay until spring."

Their talk made me want to scream. I had to get out of this house. I was going stir-crazy.

"I'll go with you," I was quick to say. "I can't stay inside any longer."

"No way," Laurel was quick to say.

"I know how she feels," Nash said. "Let's you and me compromise. You can put on Mom's boots and warm coat, and I'll take you to the barn with me. Ole Wimpy had her calf last night. It's a wonder its little ears didn't freeze off. Probably would have if I hadn't helped rubbed it dry."

"How long were you out there? I thought you were in the house sleeping," his mother asked.

"It was after midnight when I got back inside," he said.

"My goodness. I'd sleep through a tornado."

I hadn't heard him either.

"You're welcome to use my things," Laurel said. "I don't plan on going out in this weather anytime soon. But only if Nash promises not to put on those snowshoes and take off on his hairbrained idea."

Nash laughed softly. "Once a mother, always a mother regardless of how old her baby boy is."

Nash helped me put on boots, coat, gloves, along with his mother's winter hat. He treated me as though I might break if I extended any body parts. His mother tried not to grin as she watched. One part of me liked his gentle caring, while another part wanted to tell him I wasn't helpless.

Finally, satisfied with my wrappings, he opened the kitchen door for me to go outside. A few steps onto the porch and I was grateful he'd seen that I was wearing warm clothes. I knew it was cold out, but I hadn't realized that cold could cut like a knife.

Nash made sure I was walking in front of him. "Take small steps," he warned. "Don't fall on the ice."

He seemed as relieved as I was once we reached the barn. He forced the door open and motioned for me to go inside.

"It's good this snow had formed a hard crust," he told me. "Otherwise, I'd have to shovel snow drifts away from the door every time I entered."

It was cold inside the barn, but not anything like outside. The icy wind wasn't hitting in here. He put his hand on my back and guided me to the back of the barn where two cows, a calf, a horse, along with a number of chickens, ducks, and geese were shut up in a stall. All were huddled down in the hay.

"The little calf is over here with its momma."

He led me to an inner stall where a brown cow with huge eyes lay in the hay beside a little calf that reminded me of a baby deer. "She's a Jersey," I said. "We had a Jersey. I milked her all the time."

"Jerseys are the gentlest of cows, but the bulls are hell on hoofs. You never know when one will turn on you and kill you."

"You have a Jersey bull?"

"No. One of the neighbors does. I take my cows to his bull."

"I've only seen two houses beside Maw Wiseman's cabin."

"There's a lot of houses in every nook and cranny. Folks around here own a right smart of land. They don't like living in sight of each other. They claim if a neighbor has a chance of seeing you piss off the porch, you're living too close to each other."

"I tend to agree," I told him.

"You do," he said in surprise. "I didn't take you to be a country girl."

"I'm country all right."

"And yet you're surprised at snowstorms."

"Surprised at this much for this long."

"Are you still determined to leave here when the roads are clear?"

"I am," I told him.

"Why?" he asked as he looked me in the eyes.

"I don't know how to answer that."

"You have a place in mind? Perhaps go back to Georgia where you were raised?"

I let out a little sound I hoped sounded like a laugh. "I don't know where I'm at, much less were I'm going."

"That's what I was afraid of. If the weather turns warm, I'll drive you wherever you want to go."

"Thank you, but I can't let you do that."

"Why not?"

"It's something I'll have to do on my own," I tried to explain. "I suppose I'm trying to find myself as well as find a home where my baby and I belong."

"I traveled some when I was in the service. I'd see houses with people rambling about. It made my soul hurt to think what had been and what now was. People had lived and died in those places. It was a continuation of life and death. No one lasts forever, even when the land did. I realized I wanted to find my home too. It wasn't until I returned here that I realized this had always been my home."

I knew what he was trying to tell me. How could I make him understand that the place where I was raised was never my home. I hadn't owned one inch of anything. It all belonged to Mom and Dad. They planned on it eventually belonging to Grant. Now, it would belong to little Grant instead of me even if they knew I was still alive.

"I want to buy my own place. A small piece of land and a little house that can never be taken away from me."

"You've had a lot taken away from you?" he asked.

"Not taken away. It's what I've never had."

"Is it safe to say you're searching for something you never had?"

"I suppose so," I admitted.

"Then perhaps you can find it here,' he suggested lightly.

"There's nothing here for me."

"Oh, Ellie, you're wrong on that. There's everything waiting right here for you."

I thought of the land and house he talked about earlier. "Who has land for sale?"

"A lot of people have a small plot of land they would sell a decent woman to build a house on."

"Would you?" I couldn't resist asking.

"If that woman is you, I would and so would my mother. She often talks about selling a parcel to keep from paying so much on taxes. As you might have noticed, she's no longer young and healthy."

"She's not healthy?" She seemed healthy to me.

"Nothing like she used to be."

I looked from the calf with only its head sticking out of the hay to the face of the beardy man. The way he was looking at me was confusing. It appeared he liked me, but I wasn't so sure.

"Why would you want me to stay here?" I had to ask.

"Because I'm starting to think Mom might have a valid point. The longer you stay in my house, the more it seems you belong here with me."

"Oh," I said, a bit puzzled. "You surely like sleeping on the couch."

He laughed, reached out and hugged me against him. "Let's just say I like the idea of you sleeping in my bed."

I pushed him away.

"Don't you dare take that the wrong way. I'm just saying in an awkward way that you're the only woman I've met since Jolie died that I'm interested in."

"That's because we're isolated in a snowstorm. Besides, all the other women are your cousins."

"I can't win with you, can I?"

"You've had time for your hurting to heal some, I've not."

"I'll accept that," he finally said. "But first, will you give me permission to kiss you. Just in case it'll help with your healing."

I looked up at him and didn't say a thing. It wasn't that I wanted him to kiss me. It was more like wondering how being kissed by a beard and mustache would feel."

He took my look for an answer.

His lips were warm against mine, but his beard and mustache had a smattering of snow mixed in. His arms held me strong and firm against him. It felt okay, but there was no sudden thunder and lightning.

His lips left mine and he just held me against him. "You sure have a cold nose," he said.

"You sure have a lot of frozen snow in all that beard."

We stayed in the barn that way longer than it took to see a calf. There was a comfort in that old barn with all those animals trying to keep warm.

"You'll love it here during the springtime," he said. "There's something special about new life starting all over again. It makes the winter worth enduring."

His words triggered memories so strong it was all I could do not to burst into a flood of tears. If I cried, my eyes would probably freeze shut. That thought made me smile instead of cry.

"That's a girl," he said. "I have a whole mountain of beautiful things I want to show you."

"I would like to see beautiful things," I made myself say through chattering teeth.

"I've kept you out here long enough," he said as he noticed how cold I was. "Let's get you back inside and warmed up."

"Thank you," I managed to say. "For getting me out of the house."

He bent his head and kissed me on the tip of the nose. Its effect was stronger that the kiss on my lips.

"Get over there by the fire," Laurel scolded. "Nash should be ashamed for keeping you outside so long. He never feels the cold."

I dropped her clothes at the kitchen door and hurried to the stove. I was chilled to the bone. I laughed out loud. "It did me good to get outside. It also made me realize how good it is to stay inside by the fire. How that little calf didn't freeze to death is amazing to me."

"If there had been any danger of it freezing, Nash would have brought it in the house."

I didn't doubt that.

~~~~

Two weeks later the sun came out and the three and a half feet of snow slowly turned into two and a half feet. Still, Nash claimed he couldn't get the tractor out of the barn. He pointed out there would be solid ice beneath the hard crusted snow. His mother agreed with him.

"It's right at February. You can't get on the road even if all the snow melts. Your baby could arrive any day."

"Mores the reason I need to get off this mountain and closer to a hospital," I told her.

"I'll have you know I'm still capable and competent. I've delivered more babies than most doctors have."

"What if something goes wrong?" I was quick to say.

"Nothing is going to go wrong with you and your baby. I'd know it if it was."

Her so-called seer's ability didn't reassure me in the least.

"It'll be another week or two before the roads are clear enough to get off this mountain," Nash made a point of telling me."

I looked at him with pleading eyes. His expression told me there was nothing he could do about it, and I knew he was right. Another week was more than I could possibly take. I was so miserable I didn't want to think about another week much less two or three weeks from now. I couldn't find a comfortable position when I was asleep or awake. The only thing I did better than normal was peeing. Seemed I had to do that every two hours both day and night.

"You got no choice other than to settle down and wait it out," Nash told me. "Your only other choice is for me to put you on my back and tote you out."

"No thanks," I told him, not the least impressed with his attempt at humor. "You're not that tough or strong."

"Thanks, but I might be," he added. "I know I'd give it a try if necessary."

I felt instantly guilty for complaining. What more could these people do for me. And here I was gripping about my discomfort and wanting to get off the mountain.

"I know. I'm just miserable," I said as an apology.

"It's to be expected. I'll make you a cup of my special tea. It'll help calm you a little."

"Thank you," I said.

Nash came over to me and took me in his arms right in front of his mother. "We're here, honey. We'll take good care of you and your baby. I promise."

I lay my face against his chest and let him hold me for a few minutes. His strength did help calm me, but it didn't do a thing for my need to pee.

I went to bed early and got up in the middle of the night to use the bathroom. I looked out the window. A moan escaped me. It was snowing again.

I was embarrassed when Nash opened the door.

"Are you okay?" he asked.

"No," I told him. "It's snowing out there."

"You're not in pain? You're not in labor?"

"I'm not in labor, but I'm in mental pain. I don't know how much more snow I can stand. If I hadn't got on the wrong road, I might have been in Florida by now."

I could see the white teeth in his grin of relief.

"Much more of this snow and half the people on this mountain will go with you. Finish up what you're doing and come in the living room with me," he said and closed the door back.

He was waiting on me when I came out of the bathroom. He led me to the couch and sat me down beside him with his pillow at my back. He wrapped the quilt around us both even when the room was warm.

"This will most likely be the last snow of the season," he told me. "I'll help you get off the mountain when it's safe."

"Are you sure about the last snow."

"No," he answered. "I've seen it snow here in late April."

I let out another moan. "How do you stand it?"

"It's lonely, I'll admit. Having you here has helped. Mom being here has helped too. I know she misses being in her place. Like I told you, she's not as strong as she used to be. I worry about her."

His words didn't give me more confidence in his mother's ability. "We've been snowed in for two months," I pointed out.

"It's to be expected. That's why the women put up all the food stuff they do. They grow big gardens and gather wild berries to can. The men kill deer or a beef and hog if they have them. We know what to expect and how to survive."

My parents and neighbors did the same thing. We simply weren't snowed in forever like we are here.

He cuddled me up and I must have fallen asleep. The room was light when I woke up. He was still holding me in his arms.

"I've got to use the bathroom," I whispered.

"I've got to build a fire in the kitchen stove and then go to the barn," he whispered back, and kissed the top of my head.

I finished in the bathroom and was dressing in the bedroom when I heard Laurel's bedroom door open. She went to the bathroom and then to the kitchen. I heard her putting more wood in the cook stove. I left the bedroom and went to the kitchen.

"Didn't sleep too good, did you?"

"No, it snowed again."

"I noticed. Might as well settle down and take it a day at a time. Getting upset isn't good for your baby. It's your job to be happy instead of moaning about the weather all the time."

She was right. I was determined to be happy from here on out if possible.

I knew it was easier said than done. I felt inadequate all the time. I was responsible for my baby when I couldn't take care of myself. I hadn't gotten to Kentucky or West Virginia as intended. If I really was in Tennessee, I was in the same state where Calvin had taken me. I had simply doubled back for goodness knows how long and climbed higher into this mountain range.

We got several more inches of snow every night for the next week. I smiled and talked and made baby clothes. Laurel had allowed Nash to put on his snowshoes long enough to go to her house and bring back her old sheets to make diapers out of.

"I can't tell you how excited I am at the thoughts of having a baby in the house again. Nash won't be able to force me to go back home as long as you're here."

"I can hardly wait to see my baby," I told her.

"I know what you mean."

"Babies are the truest gift from God."

We had finished ripping the sheet up and hemming the edges when I realized my back hurt. It's what I got for sitting so long. I stood up, stretched and looked out the window again. "The sun is coming out," I told her.

"I'm glad. My old bones could use some warmth from the sun. Wood heat is a good thing, but it doesn't heal the body like sunshine does."

"You're religious," I told her. "My mother was too. She went to church at least three times a week."

"You lost them both?" she questioned.

"There was an accident," I told her again. "I've lost my brother, my parents and a husband."

"You poor child," she said. "Sadness comes in threes. It's now time for your blessings to arrive."

"I hope you're right," I told her as I stretched again. "I sat still too long," I told her. "All my parts went to sleep."

"It'll be over soon," she told me. "You'll have you baby in your arms. I can tell you there will be times when you wish it was back in your womb where it was safe, and you didn't have to stay awake at night trying to stop it from crying."

I knew she was wrong about that. I would never want it back inside me, but I didn't point it out.

"Heat wave," Nash said as he came in the kitchen door. "It's above freezing right now."

"How long before the roads are clear," I wanted to know.

"You sure are obsessed with clear roads," he said. "But it'll be a while depending how fast this snow melts."

Relief flowed over me. How wonderful it would be to leave this mountain. To no longer be cooped up.

"We're all suffering from cabin fever," Laurel said. "I dare say everyone on this mountain will get down on their knees and kiss bare ground when they are able to see it."

"And then the plowing begins. I love the smell of rich freshly turned earth," Nash said as he all but danced across the floor to me. He grabbed me in his arms and gave me a hug. "You'll soon see what a handsome man I am once I shave this winter beard off."

He actually scrubbed his chin across my face as though he had the right to do so. I pushed him away.

"He's always been a farmer at heart," Laurel told me. "He used to eat dirt."

I laughed at that. "A neighbor of mine used to eat dirt when she was little. The doctor said she had a vitamin deficiency."

"I liked the taste of dirt," he told me. "Still do," he said as he pretended he was going to lick my face.

"Stop being silly," I told him, embarrassed. "What's gotten into you?"

"You sound like my mother. I'm trying to snuggle with you and you're pushing me away."

"For good reason," Laurel told him. "Stop aggravating her. We both know you're excited the weather is turning warm. We are excited too."

A pain shot through my back hard enough for me to grip Nash's arm.

"What's wrong?" he asked with concern.

"Nothing is wrong. I sat too long."

"She's in labor," Laurel told him. "Been that way since she got up this morning. She's been as restless as a cat in season. She started feeling uncomfortable about the time I sent you for the sheets."

"Why didn't you tell me." He asked me.

"She doesn't know what labor feels like," Laurel said. "She'll know before the night is over," she added.

"I've got to get to a hospital," I said in a panic.

"Can't, so settle in and think about holding your baby girl in your arms. What are you going to name her?"

I had been thinking of names ever since I knew there was a baby on the way. I haven't decided on one. I need to see her face to face first."

Laurel grinned. I had referred to my baby as being a girl.

"Lettie Ellen, after you," Nash said. "Sweet little Lettie, just like her mother."

"I rather not name her after me." My real name was Ella Lynn Goins. I suppose it still was since I had never been legally married. That's when it hit me. Did I put my real name on my baby's birth certificate? What about the name of my baby's father? If I was in a hospital, I couldn't avoid either telling the truth or lying. If my baby was born here, I would have some time to get things straight in my mind.

I should have done this kind of thinking before now, but I hadn't. My only concern was to make sure my baby was safe.

Never in my life had I realized what pain giving birth involved. It felt as though my insides were being ripped out.

"It'll get a lot worse before it's over," Laurel kept telling me after each pain hit. "You might as well expect it."

Nash was walking the floor, going from the kitchen door to the living room door and back again.

"Will you just lay down and go to sleep," Laurel said to him. "Your pacing is driving me crazy. You're worse than any man I've ever seen. You'd think that baby is yours," Laurel called from the bedroom where she sat beside me.

She had put an oil cloth on the bed mattress to keep it clean along with a ragged sheet she hadn't cut up for diapers. A fairly good sheet was spread over my lower body even when I was sweating all over. I had a few moments between contractions. Long enough to see the expression on her face. It was as though she had thought of something that made her happy.

It was then that I gripped the sheet covering me and bent my body with a push. If she told me again the pain would only get worse, I just might come up from there and slug her.

"Let me check you," she said instead as soon as the contraction eased slightly.

She lifted the sheet and spread my knees.

"It's crowning," she said. "You're a fast one. Push when I tell you to push and ease up when I tell you to ease up."

Sure thing. Easy for her to say when I was the one lying there in agony. I was determined not to scream out with my pain, but how I wanted to do just that. One thing was for sure, the pain wasn't worth what little pleasure I had putting the baby in. And then I thought of my baby instead of the pain.

"It's worth it," I mumbled. "My baby is worth the pain."

"Push with all your strength during the next contraction," she said as I felt her hand probing me down there. It hurt.

The contraction hurt worse. I did as she said. I pushed so hard I raised my upper body off the bed. I didn't moan, I squalled out with the ripping pain as my baby came out.

"Good. I've got her," Laurel said. "Nash, get your hind end back in the other room. You don't need to be in here."

He rushed to the head of the bed and grabbed my hand. "You okay, Ellie? You alright?"

"She's just fine. Now, get out."

"No, way," he told her firmly. "I'm staying right here."

Laurel didn't argue as she held clamped the cord, cut it, and held my baby up by its feet. She patted it firmly on its back and rear end as fluid came from its mouth. A moment later she drew in a breath and let out a scream.

"Hear that, Ellie? Your baby has a set of lungs on her."

She laid my baby on my chest. "Hold onto her while I tend to you."

I pulled my hand out of Nash's and grasped my baby. I didn't want her to fall off.

"She's beautiful, Ellie. She has your hair. I'll get a towel and help clean her up," Nash told me.

I couldn't keep my eyes off the little miracle lying on my chest yelling to the top of her lungs as Nash's gentle hands cleaned the bloody mucus off my baby. I gave him a quick glance only willing to take my eyes off my baby for a moment. The expression on his face startled me. I saw love along with pride on his smiling face.

"What is your maiden name," Laurel surprised me by asking.

"Goins," I answered her.

"That's an honorable name," she said.

I could feel Laurel's hands pressing on my belly while pulling and tugging on me. There was a sharp pain causing me to gasp.

"I've got the afterbirth out," she said. "I need to rub your womb until it knots up. Don't want you to bleed."

Chapter 28

The birth of my baby brought sunshine. The snow was finally melting, but a few inches of snow still fell most every night. Laurel refused to let me do a thing other than take care of little Lettie Ellen. I had named her what Nash suggested, at least for the time being. When I filled out her birth certificate out later on, I could change her name if I so chose.

"She's such a good baby," Laurel told me. "So far, she's not colicky. You give good milk."

Everything about my baby was perfect from her little toes to the top of her head. I looked for a sign of her father in her, but I didn't see one single thing that reminded me of Mr. Grason. She was my baby alone, and that was how it was going to stay.

For a while, I was so wrapped up in loving my baby, I forgot all about leaving the mountain. It was April when the snow was all gone, even in the shady spots. Green grass was starting to show itself. Birds had returned to the mountain. They woke me each morning to the sound of their singing. One morning, I overheard Laurel talking to Nash when she thought I was still asleep.

"I want to go back to my own home," she said.

"Then go back."

"How can I do that. People will claim you're living in sin."

"Folks might claim such as that, but you and I will know different."

"What we know won't matter. Your reputation will be ruined. No decent girl will ever be willing to marry you."

"Mom, do you really think your being here would make a difference between Ellie and me if we chose to enjoy sinning."

"Nash, I don't like the way you said that."

"Then what do you suggest?"

"I suggest you haul that girl to the preacher's place and marry her right away."

"I see. You'd force us into a marriage just so you can avoid gossiping neighbors."

"You're twisting my intentions into something I don't mean. I've seen how you look at that girl. It's all you can do to keep your hands off her. You'd lay down at her feet and let her walk all over you if she asked. Not only that, you love that baby of hers as though it was your very own."

"Okay, Mom, I'll ask her to marry me if that will make you happy."

"It will."

"I'll wake her up right now and propose."

"Stop being silly, Nash. You have to find the right time and place. Surely, you've got a little romance in you. After breakfast, I'll tell her I'm going to walk up the holler to my house. That ought to give you some time alone with her."

I grabbed my trash bag from the dresser drawer where I had placed it when I arrived. I packed my clothes, along with all the baby clothes and diapers in it. I wasn't about to stay where I wasn't wanted. Neither did I intend to marry a man because his mother wanted me to in order to avoid a scandal. I would leave as soon as I got a chance. I would pull another exit the same as I'd done before.

Laurel was the only one who seemed happy as we ate breakfast. Nash was too silent as he kept glancing at me. As for me, I didn't have much to say to either of them.

"Why are you so quiet?" Laurel asked me.

"I'm barely awake," I fibbed a little. "Lettie kept me awake most of the night," which was true, but I didn't mind. I could have spent all night long holding my baby in my arms.

"I'm going to make a trip up the holler to my house after I wash the breakfast dishes," Laurel finally said. I won't be gone long."

"I'll go with you just to make sure everything is okay," Nash told her.

"No, you won't," she was quick to tell him. "I'm perfectly capable of checking everything out myself."

"I won't stay a minute," he continued. "I'll hurry right back here. Now, don't argue with me, Mom."

She pinched her lips together but didn't object. I suppose Nash needed time to decide how to be romantic.

"I'll do the dishes," I offered.

"No, you won't," Laurel said. "I've told you often enough that I don't like anyone in my kitchen."

I didn't remind her it was Nash's kitchen, and neither did he. I wished they would both leave so I could. It was then that Lettie whimpered. I rushed to the bedroom to let her breastfeed. I wanted her to be full and asleep when I made our getaway.

Lettie had eaten and burped by the time I heard both Laurel and Nash go out the kitchen door. I rushed to the kitchen window to see them walking up the narrow holler. I wondered why Nash hadn't driven his truck. The goat path of a road was wide enough, but then she might not live far away.

I quickly placed the note I had written earlier on the pillow. I eased my sleeping baby in my arms and the trash bag in my hand and rushed outside to where my car had been parked all winter long. Nash had made sure the battery was charged not long ago. He said he might need to jump it off and charge the battery before it went completely dead from sitting so long in the cold. It would be my luck for the battery to be dead when I needed it most.

I carefully placed my baby in the passenger seat, tossed my trash bag in the back seat and got behind the wheel. It started right up. I tried not to think about anything as I drove away from the place where I had known nothing but kindness.

I couldn't repay them by permitting a forced marriage only Laurel wanted. Not only that, but I had also overstayed my welcome. Laurel's words convinced me of that.

I found the road I had arrived on and drove back down it. I had no idea where I was going. I only knew I had to get away.

"Well, Grant," I said out loud. "Want to put your two cents in this time?"

I wasn't sure if I laughed or cried when he didn't say a thing.

I stopped twice during the day to nurse my baby and change her diaper. I filled up once with gas and bought a pack of crackers and a jar of peanut butter along with a large bottle of water. I wasn't hungry, but I needed to eat in order to give milk.

The sun had long set, and twilight was fading to darkness. I stopped in a motel when I became exhausted and carried my baby in with me to pay for a room. I wasn't about to take my eyes off her even for a minute. Once we settled in a room, I took out the map I should have studied to begin with. The first thing my eyes were drawn to was the name Cleveland. The town near where I was raised.

I spent hours studying the map and memorizing the roads and their road numbers along with the north and south directions.

I had the strongest urge to drive back to my hometown. For some reason I needed to touch base with my roots before I could make a new life for myself. No one had ever seen my car and wouldn't recognize it as being mine. Not only that, but I was also thought to be dead. I had no doubt my parents had held a funeral service for the charred remains of the real Mary Tracy.

My baby woke up and I put the map down to care for her. I enjoyed giving her a warm bath, putting clean clothes Laurel and I had made on her and put her in bed beside me. How I loved the feel of her little warm body sleeping next to mine.

She was the most important thing in my world. It was my responsibility as her mother to find a home where she could grow up safe and happy.

As usual, my little Lettie woke up before the break of day. During the night a decision had firmed itself. There was no question about me going back home. Not to stay, but to aid in getting my new life started all over again. I didn't want my new life to start from the place Calvin had taken me. A place where I had always been afraid and unhappy even when there were kind people such as Iva Lee and Mr. Grason.

Mr. Grason. What was I going to do about him? Regardless of how much I didn't want to admit it, he was the father of my baby. Did he not have rights? No, I was quick to answer my own question. Just because he deposited a sperm inside me shouldn't automatically give him claim to my baby. He had a wife. He had responsibilities to another woman. It wasn't my fault that woman couldn't give him a child he had a right to claim as his own.

He didn't know Lettie had been born alive and healthy. To him the baby he had sired died in the fire along with me. That was the way it had to stay.

I left the motel as soon as I'd taken care of Lettie's needs. As Laurel said, she was such a happy baby I had no problem with her crying or sleeping. Plus, she was growing and smiling when I talked to her. My heart was filled to the brim with love.

The early morning air smelled fresh and crisp as I put Lettie and our things in the car. For some reason I thought of Easters when I was a child. It was time for daffodils and yellow bells to start blooming. Spring. The time when new life was starting in full swing. The time when my brother had been killed. I wondered if Dad still tilled the garden spot where Grant had died. What grew in the spot where his blood had fertilized the ground?

The sky was barely showing a little grayness as I drove away from the motel. It was five o'clock on Saturday morning. If my estimation of driving time was close to correct. I would be arriving at Cleveland around two or three o'clock in the afternoon. Mom always went to town on Saturdays regardless if she needed to buy something or not. Going to town on Saturdays was a tradition almost every person with transportation indulged in. There were times when Mom sat in the car watching people walking up and down the street. She would comment on everything about them from their dress to what purpose they had being there.

I no longer questioned my decision as I followed the roads I had memorized. I didn't want to get lost again even when I didn't regret doing so. By now, Laurel would be moving back into her own home up the holler, and Nash would be getting on with his own life. Perhaps he would find himself another Jolie to love, marry and have children. He would make a wonderful father. He had dotted on Lettie. Held her in his arms as much as I would allow.

He was almost as bad at making sure she was still breathing as Laurel and I were. We'd all heard about SIDS that was recently been diagnosed as causing babies to stop breathing during their sleep. I had no doubt both Laurel and Nash had fallen in love with my baby. For some reason I remembered Nash staying awake on a cold night to make sure he rubbed a baby calf dry, so its little ears didn't freeze.

The next time I filled up with gas, I carried Lettie into the general store with me. I bought food for me along with a cap and a pair of the lightest lens of sunglasses I could find. My disguise for when I arrived in the town of Cleveland. I didn't want to take a chance on being recognized by snooping eyes.

I had made better time than I'd expected. It was two o'clock in the afternoon when I arrived at Cleveland with my hair tucked under the cap and sunglasses on. I feared the sunglasses might draw attention if someone looked at me sitting in the car but wearing them was better than being recognized.

I found a place to park near where Mom and Dad always parked. All I could do now was wait in case they kept the same habits as they had two years ago.

I was not disappointed. In less than an hour, I saw them come walking up the street side by side. Mom was carrying a plump baby boy in her arms. Dad was carrying two brown bags holding their purchases.

Mom looked happy. Real happy and proud of the baby wiggling in her arms. She said something to Dad causing him to smile down on baby Grant. They continued walking up the street until they were right in front of my car.

Much to my surprise, they met up met up with Aunt Guinn walking in the opposite direction. They stopped only about two feet from the bumper of my car. I panicked, and then grew unexpectedly calm. I carefully rolled down the window a couple of inches so I could hear what they were saying.

"Fancy meeting you here today," Aunt Guinn said as though she hadn't seen them in ages. "The one time I've come into town in a month of Sundays, and I run into both of you. My, my, how little Grant has grown. It's been almost six months since I've seen him and you both. Lordy mercy, how time flies."

"He certainly has," Momma said proudly. "I'm glad to see you are well enough to go shopping. I've been meaning to stop by and visit with you, but you know how time passes you by when you're trying to hold up under things."

"I do. I thought I was a goner for certain. It's a thousand wonders I didn't die when my appendix ruptured. You talk about pain. I suffered something awful. I still hurt so bad I can barely get about. The doctor says I'm a walking miracle. If you ask me, God is the one who let me live."

"No doubt about it," Mom said.

"Listen to me talking about myself when you and Ben have had your share of suffering. Reckon we all go through hard times, but God is always walking beside us. He gets us through if we believe in him. I plan on going to church this evening being I'm better. I reckon you and Ben will be there as usual."

"We will," Mom said.

"I want you to know I'm still praying over the way Grant and Ellie died. I know parents never get over the death of their children, but it's a comfort to know we'll meet them again in heaven."

"That kind of suffering never ends, but we have no other choice other than to bear up under the sorrow," Mom said. Her lips puckered and her eyes narrowed. She had heard enough from Aunt Guinn.

"Just to think, both your children died in such a horrible way. Did you ever discover what Ellie was doing driving on that road? I heard she had to be going at top speed considering how the car was mangled up causing the gas tank to explode. They said you only had a few ashes to bury."

I saw both Mom and Dad stiffen as they looked away from Aunt Guinn.

"We have no details on what caused the accident. All we know is that we lost our darling daughter," Mom told her. "It was good to see you after all this time. We best be getting along."

"At least God gave you another baby at your age none-the-less to make up for your loss," she continued.

It was evident Mom was trying to get away from her and all her gossiping questions.

"Glad you're doing good. We best get along now," Dad finally spoke up.

"See you at church tonight," Aunt Quinn made a point of saying again.

"I'm sure we will," Mom said as she and Dad walked away from her.

I watched my parents backs until they were out of sight. I had my answer. They thought I was dead, and they were getting over their loss.

I had finally gotten to see my baby brother for a second time. I wondered what Mom and Dad would do if I had gotten out of the car and shown them their granddaughter? I could only imagine the fury they would have at my deception. There would be no warm hugs, no tears of joy to find out their daughter was still alive. I was dead to them, and it was best I remain that way. But I didn't want to be dead. I wanted my parents. I wanted grandparents for Lettie. I wanted a place where we both could belong.

I wanted to go home.

I sat there for hours watching people walk up and down the streets. I tried not to feel anything, and yet I was feeling everything. My emotions had gone crazy. I laughed and I cried. I loved and I hated. I longed, oh, how I longed for something I didn't have, something I couldn't find.

Suddenly I remembered sitting inside the car with Mom, while Dad shopped on Christmas eve. Dad had bought Grant a sled that I had begged for, but I never got. He got a rifle a short time after I had begged for one. Dad taught him how to shoot it, but not me. Grant had even gotten the horse I had begged Dad to buy for me. I'd been told I wasn't allowed to ride Grant's sled, shoot his gun, or ride Grant's horse. I thought of the clothes Mom had bought me during all those Christmases. I wondered if any of them were still hanging in my closet?

Now, my little brother could get all the things my parents had denied me.

It was Lettie who brought me out of my pity stupor. What had I been thinking to allow myself to delve in such a depression? Hadn't Laurel told me my emotions could affect my milk supply?

In reality I still had parents and a baby brother. Mom and Dad still had a son. They also had a daughter and a granddaughter even if they didn't know it. That daughter was going to get a new life, a better life than I'd ever had.

I started the car and drove to the school I had attended. The buildings appeared unkept and run down. I let myself run down memory lane from first grade until the last day I spent there. I was always laughing with the other students. We shared jokes and funny stories that may or may not have held any truth. We listened and told tales about the teachers, while we did our best to make their lives miserable.

It was hard to believe I had been there only two years before. I felt like I'd lived a lifetime during those two years. I was tired to the bone and still saddened at how my life had turned out. I wasn't even voting age, and I knew my own dreams had come to an end. I would spend the rest of my life trying to give Lettie all the things I had wanted for myself. And that was okay.

I had gotten old before my time.

When it was time for church to start, I headed toward the place I once called home. The one thing I had left to do, was drive up the road, see the places I saw most every day of my life before Calvin appeared. I had to look at the house I was raised in. And then I had to let it all go and drive away.

I released the breath I'd been holding as I turned onto Goins Road. I felt as though I was seeing the place for the first time. Seeing houses and barns and fields that were different from what I remembered. Things had changed and yet they hadn't. The road was narrower and the houses shabbier than I remembered. Interesting how perspectives changed once you'd been away for two years.

A lump came in my throat as old memories rushed me. I could almost hear the thudding of my heart as Mom quarreled at me when Grant and I got off the school bus to be driven home in her car. It seemed everything I did was the wrong thing. From talking to the wrong boy, to saying the wrong thing to an adult made Mom mad. I was always getting my clothes too dirty. My hair was always hanging in my eyes. I never seemed able to behave like the lady Mom wanted me to be. I was her disappointment. Grant was her pride and joy.

Odd that not one single person was outside their houses, but I knew many of them would be looking out the windows as usual. When their day's work was done, they looked out their windows to see who was coming home and who was going out.

I wondered how many of them would tell about seeing a girl drive by who held an uncanny resemblance to Katie and Ben Goins' dead daughter. Would they think my spirit had arrived, or would they say a stranger drove by.

And then it occurred to me. Most likely no one would be looking out their windows. It church time on a Saturday night. Most everyone would be inside the church house singing old hymns from memory.

I came to the end of the road and parked in front of my parent's house. It was older and equally as small as Nash's house. It seemed Iva Lee's house was the exception. She had made sure she overcame every hardship life had thrown at her.

I was determined to do the same.

I don't know why I did what I did. I jumped out of the car, locked the doors and left Lettie sleeping inside. I rushed to the back door where Mom always kept a key hidden. For some reason, she kept the doors locked although no house on our holler had ever been broken into. I unlocked the door and went inside.

Nothing had changed other than the baby bottles sitting on the counter. The yellow and metal kitchen table and chairs were the same. There was still a wood cookstove, an almost new electric stove and a white wooden Hoosier cabinet sitting against the wall. Across from the stoves was Mom newer plywood cabinets with their heavy coating of shellac and polyurethane. I recalled the day she had the sink put in. I no longer had to carry her buckets of water from the spring house.

I hurried to the bedroom where I had once slept. The bed was neatly made up. Everything looked spotless and deserted.

The room seemed to welcome me back, but the room and I both knew my being there couldn't last but a few minutes more.

I opened the closet door. My clothes were still hanging there musty smelling and forgotten. I grabbed at least half of them. The ones that had been my favorite, left a small crack in the door so the rest of my things could get a breath of fresh air, and hurried out the back door. I locked it and placed the key exactly as Mom had left it. I unlocked the car, tossed my clothes in the back seat with my garbage bag and got behind the wheel. I started the engine, turned around and drove away.

Someday Mom would see the crack in the closet door and investigate. Would she think someone had stolen my clothes, or would she fear my spirit had returned to reclaim my Christmas presents?

There was one more place I had to go before my quest for closure came to an end.

Chapter 29

It wasn't too long of a drive to Good Eats, but it was after midnight when I drove past the restaurant. The main lights had been turned off with only the security lights on. Iva Lee's car was gone from the place she always parked. Wish I could stop, walk to the back door and place my hand on the doorknob, but I'd never do that again.

I'd never catch the bus that stopped nearby to ride to the horrible mold ridden trailer where Calvin would be in bed snoring.

I would never again long for the time I'd spend with Mr. Grason. The time when he'd make me feel like my life mattered. He had given me the attention I desperately needed. He brought my soul back from being nothing, to being a real live person. He had also given me Lettie. A treasure even he wanted so badly he'd given me enough money to buy a small home somewhere.

I drove on. I needed to take one last look at Iva Lee's fancy house. I also needed to see where Mr. Grason lived with his rich wife, Grace Anna. I also needed to say goodbye to the shed where I hadn't been ashamed to stay in. A place where Calvin West ended for all time.

There was a light in one of the upstairs windows at Iva Lee's house.

"Thank you," I whispered into the darkness and hoped she would know what her kindness meant to me.

I then drove to the road that led to where Mr. Grason lived. I knew what kind of chance I was taking. Of all the people in existence, he was the one that could do the most harm if he knew I still lived.

Turn around, Grant seemed to say.

I turned around. Seeing where Mr. Grason lived wasn't worth any chance I would be taking.

I dared to drive up the gravel road to the shed. My baby was conceived in that shed. Calvin West's blood fertilized the grass. I would now leave all that far behind me.

I passed Iva Lee's place again. I knew it was my imagination, but I thought I saw her standing in her bedroom window looking out with a huge grin on her face as I passed by.

Good going, girl, she seemed to be telling me. *It'll be what you make of it.*

I drove another fifty or sixty miles before I stopped at a motel for the rest of the night, or should I say morning. Lettie thrived just fine sleeping to the movement of the car, but I was exhausted.

I must have needed the rest more than I realized. I went back to sleep after feeding Lettie. It was nearly nine o'clock in the morning when I woke up.

As usual, I gave Lettie her feeding and a bath, put on my favorite Christmas dress of all time, left the key on the dresser, packed everything in the car and drove away.

"Now what?" I asked myself. "You've touched your roots. Found out you're still considered dead and wasn't recognized by one person. It's time you decided on a place to call home.

What I did now would determine the rest of my life. I couldn't afford to make a bad decision.

"Well, Grant, you told me to turn around. Have you got anything else to say for my own good?"

As expected, he was silent.

My destiny from here on out would be up to me. I drove on, only stopping when it was necessary to fill up with gas or tend to Lettie. I didn't need to look at the map again. I knew exactly where I was going.

~~~~

The sun was setting when I finally parked my car and shut off the engine. I took Lettie in my arms and walked into the restaurant.

"Find yourself a seat," called a voice from the kitchen.

I pulled out a chair at a table and took a seat. Several people were at tables eating their suppers. The aromas that filled the place started my stomach growling. I was starved. I needed to eat to make milk.

Betsy almost dropped the pot of coffee when she saw me sitting there.

"Lands sake alive," she almost shouted. "Let me have a look at that beautiful baby," she said as she sat the coffee pot on a plate and moved the blanket from her face. "I thought you had left out forever. Why did you come back?"

"I'm looking for a home. I want to buy Maw Wiseman's cabin if you'll let me."

Every person in the place was looking at me and Betsy. They waited to see what her answer would be, and so did I.

"Law me, honey, let's get some good food in your belly and then we'll talk. I can't tell you how glad I am to see you. I've worried myself sick about you and that baby," she told me as she picked up the coffee pot with her oven mitt, then rushed across the floor toward the kitchen.

It took her a little longer than I expected to bring back a plate of food. I gobbled it down like a nearly starved to death dog. Every single bite was mana from heaven.

Every person in the place was silent as they watched me eat. Not a one got up to leave. I was eating my last bite when the restaurant door slammed opened with a bang against the wall. I looked up to see Nash rushing toward me.

I didn't get a single word out before he had hold of me, lifting me out of the chair with Lettie in my arms.

"My God in heaven, Ellie. I've been going crazy trying to find you. Where were you? Why did you run away from me?"

"I didn't run away. I told you I had to leave as soon as the roads were clear."

"Yes, but. . ." he started to say more but stopped when he realized how many people were listening and watching us. "Come on. We've got some things to get straightened out."

"No, we don't. I need to talk with Betsy. I hope she'll sell me Maw Wiseman's cabin."

It didn't matter how much I objected. He dragged me out of the restaurant and to his truck before I could pay for my meal. He held onto me with one hand and opened the door with his other hand and tried to shove me in the seat.

"Stop it right now, Nash. You're making a scene. People are watching out the windows."

"I've never been so relieved in my life, or as mad as I am right now."

"Then get over it. I have the right to go and come as I please. If you don't stop your ranting, I'll get in my car and never return again."

The way I said that must have gotten through to him.

"I'm sorry, Ellie. I'm just so relieved to see you. I went to pieces when I thought I'd never see you again. Why did you leave the way you did?"

"I overheard your mother and you talking. I'll not be forced to marry any man. I lived through that once. I won't go there ever again."

"Forced to marry me? I'd never force you to do a thing such as that regardless of how much I love you."

"Like I believe that," I said, referring to him saying he loved me.

Suddenly, his anger faded, and he looked puzzled. "You were forced to marry your dead husband?"

Before I could answer, Betsy came rushing out the door. Her face was flushed. She was gripping her oven mitt.

"Nash, you stop manhandling her right this minute. She and I have some talking to do."

"I'm not manhandling her. I'm not even touching her. She and I have more talking to do than you can ever imagine."

"Phooey," she said. "I'm not letting you bully her. I'll take my shoe to you if you don't get hold of yourself."

Nash grinned. "I've already gotten hold of myself. We're talking to each other like reasonable adults."

Betsy turned toward me. "Perhaps you should get in his truck and let him drive you up the mountain to Mommy's cabin. You can talk there without all these people hearing what you're saying if that's what you want to do. But don't let him force you."

"What do you say?" Nash asked me.

"I'm not getting in your truck. If you want to talk, you can get in my car and hold Lettie while I drive up that road."

"Okay," he said. "I'll agree to that." He reached for Lettie, and I reluctantly allowed him to take her from my arms as we got into my Honda.

"How I've missed this little thing," he said in a low tone of voice. "I feared I'd never get to hold her again."

So that was it. He wanted my baby.

He saw my expression and sensed what I was thinking.

"Of course, I want to be a daddy to this sweet baby. I want to be a husband to you even worse. I hadn't realized how much I loved you until I came back to the house and found you gone. For months, I'd imagined getting down on my knees and asking you to be my wife. I hoped you'd say yes. You seemed more content after Lettie was born."

"I don't want a husband. Life is easier without one."

"You really believe that?" he asked in surprise.

"You already admitted Jolie was the only one you'd ever love."

"That's true until I spent those long winter months with you. You made my life worthwhile. You brought life back to me. I discovered love has a way of creeping up on you whether you want it or not." He held up a hand. "Don't dare take that the wrong way. I love you, want to love you in the worst sort of way. I'm not entirely sure, but I think you have some love for me too."

"Your mother is trying to save face," I said.

He laughed right out loud. "Mom's always trying to save face. I told you once that she's a seer. She told me the first time she set eyes on you that you and I were intended to get married and have a house full of children."

"Giving birth is painful," I told him.

"Finding you gone was equally as painful."

"Did you scream?"

"About every two minutes. Sometimes I'd even go out to the barn and scream out loud. I've slept in your bed every night since you've been gone. Your scent still lingers there."

Chapter 30

Regardless of how much Nash begged, I refused to marry him. I needed more time. As the old saying goes, once bitten twice shy. And I was shy enough for it to be an obsession.

Betsy agreed to rent me Maw Wiseman's cabin until I could get my *head on straight,* her words not mine. I thought I already had my head on straight.

Nash climbed up the back of the mountain to the cabin every evening as the gloaming set it. That was the time when my loneliness took hold – and perhaps his did too.

"Ellie," he said one evening. "Can you trust me enough to tell me the truth of why you won't marry me? Surely you trust me by now."

"I don't like to talk about myself."

"Tell me about your husband."

"I never had one," I suddenly blurted out.

His eyes widened in surprise.

"I thought we were married but found out later that he already had a wife."

"Shit," he said.

"Worse than that. It was pure hell."

"He's not dead?"

"He's dead alright. Rotting in an unmarked grave."

"What happened?"

"My baby's father killed him."

Those words really did surprise him. "Your baby's father?"

"He was married to another woman. A rich woman."

"Why did he kill him?"

"He was beating me. He wanted my paychecks."

"Did the baby's father go to jail?"

"No. An ex-cop along with my only friend covered up his death."

"And your baby's father?"

"Is living unhappily ever after."

Nash had to set down on the edge of the porch. He stared out over the valley down below, deep in thought.

"What else haven't you told me?"

"A lot?"

"Might as well tell me all of it."

"You're right, maybe then you'll understand why I can't marry you."

I started talking telling him about the day my brother was killed and how we all sank into a kind of depression. How my mother thought I was marrying a preacher who would be kind to me.

"How did your parents get killed?" Nash wanted to know.

"They didn't get killed. I did."

"What? You need to explain that one."

I told him about my baby brother and my parents' rejection of me. How I was afraid of my baby being taken away from me by her rich father. So, I ran away.

"And that's how you ended up here.

"Yes, but that's not who I really am, exactly," I added.

He shook his head. "What now?" he asked.

I told him about the car wreck and leaving my driver's license behind. I never told him about any of the money I had. That was my and Lettie's safety net.

"So, you're not really Mary Ellen Tracy?"

"My real name is Ellie Goins."

"That's the name Mom put on Lettie's birth certificate."

"A birth-certificate?" I'd never seen or signed a birth-certificate.

"Mom filled out one when Lettie was born."

"And who did she put down as her father?" I demanded.

"Me," he said.

"Are you kidding me?"

"No. I didn't know it either until I found it right after you left."

"I didn't sign it," I told him as my anger built.

"She forged your signature."

"She can't do that. It's illegal."

"Illegal like being an accomplish to a murder or taking a dead woman's name?"

"It's my word against yours," I told him.

"Even more reason for you to marry me. A husband can't be made to testify against his wife."

"You would testify against me?"

"No. I'd cut my own tongue out first. Maybe that would be enough to prove how much I love you."

"You love me after all I've told you?"

"Honey, what you told me is mostly old news."

"What do you mean by that?"

"When you disappeared, I tried to find out about a young woman by the name of Ellie Goins. I may be a hillbilly hick, but I do know my way around."

"And?" I questioned, surprised at what he'd admitted to.

"I found out about your parents and brothers. I also found your marriage license in the courthouse in Cleveland. I followed your trail to a place called Good Eats two days after you left here. I asked a redheaded woman about a girl named Ellie who used to work with her. She was willing to tell me everything she knew, and I suspected a bit more. And that's where I lost your trail. I have to admit you filled in a lot of blank spaces. I now understand why you're in hiding and running away from even me."

"I see," I told him. Thinking I would probably have to run again, and this time find a way for him not to trace me down. I was glad I still had most all the money.

"Okay," he finally said. "After our true confessions, will you marry me?"

"Are you serious?"

He laughed. "What more hoops do I have to go through to prove how much I love you?"

I thought about an appropriate answer. "Kiss me," I said. And he did.

Chapter 31

~~Epilogue~~

Surprising how fast time passes. It seems like yesterday that I was a scared little girl trying to run away from everything and everyone who had hurt me.

I'm ashamed to admit I never did find out who Mary Tracy was or what and why she had been driving so fast that fateful night. I still thank her for giving Mr. Grason a reason to never look for me, not that he ever would. It was one thing to have sex with an unhappy young girl, and another thing to leave your rich and comfortable life behind, especially when your rich wife had you by the short hairs.

As for Iva Lee, I still think she really was looking out her bedroom window as a girl in a familiar blue Honda drove by her house.

Plus, I was sure she did her own research on a man who suddenly stopped by her restaurant asking questions about a girl he couldn't possibly know. Not to mention that Iva Lee had an ex-cop lover who could help her accomplish anything she set her mind to. Nash's license plate would have been easily traced.

I think that's most likely where Lettie's gift came from on her eighteenth birthday. Lettie's college fund," the note read in a shaky handwriting I kind of recognized as the handwriting of an aged Iva Lee.

It certainly came in handy considering Nash and I had five other children. An even three girls and three boys. Needless to say, Nash always claimed to be Lettie's father. If anybody ever had enough gall to asked how that happened since Lettie was born before we were married, he'd say: *I've been known to make deliveries.*

As for my parents and my little brother. The only time I ever went back to see Mom was when she was at the Cleveland Hospital on her death bed.

"It's me, Mom, Ellie," I said as I took her hand and looked into her cloudy eyes.

"I knew you'd come to take me home," she said. "You were my precious little girl," she whispered. "I always loved you best."

With those words she smiled and eased on into another world. One in which even she could exist in peace.

My Dad had died a few years before Mom without me knowing about his passing.

Little Grant was and still is a stranger to me. Although, I heard he was still living in the house where we were raised, I never went back there again.

Once, I had gone back there to find my roots, but it was Nash who kept me alive and growing.

Nash, the man I went to sleep with every night and woke up with every morning.

As for the little Honda car, it sits behind the barn slowly rusting into the ground. Its tires sunk out of sight in the dirt and manure of years past. Its usable parts robbed for repairs a piece at a time. Still, it lingers on, a fading reminder of my life once upon a time.

~~The End. ~~

www.ingramcontent.com/pod-product-compliance
Lightning Source LLC
Chambersburg PA
CBHW031055260626
47172CB00001B/73